For
Dr Reilly
Love & Light
Joyce

D1566115

BELLE

Rebel In Red Silk

by

Joyce Dunn

Eloquent Books
New York, New York

Eloquent Books
An imprint of AEG Publishing Group
845 Third Avenue, 6th Floor - 6016
New York, NY 10022
www.eloquentbooks.com

ISBN 978-1-934925-35-5   1-934925-35-7

Printed in the United States of America

Book Design: Linda W. Rigsbee

Dedicated to Aunt Belle,
with thanks for showing us the gift of being 'different.'

Table of Contents

Acknowledgments

I'd like to thank everyone at the Writers Literary Agency, and all those at Eloquent Books for their help in getting Belle published. Thanks are also due to my illustrator, Carol Rice, for her talent in portraying the essence of Belle in the cover art.

A great deal of thanks is also due to my immediate and extended family and friends for their encouragement, cheerleading, and helpful critiques during the writing of Belle.

About the Author

Joyce Dunn was raised on a small Nebraska farm, but Omaha has been her home with husband Jim for nearly fifty years, and they are extremely proud of their three sons.

Her career life includes working as a Registered Nurse for twenty years, and being a licensed massage therapist for fifteen years.

Writing has always been her favorite way of expressing herself, even though her official writing career is fairly recent.

Joyce has also written Fate, Chance, or Divine Design, published by Outskirts Press

For more about Joyce, visit www.strinz.com/healing.

Chapter One

1945

We were going to visit my great Aunt Mae, and I wasn't much looking forward to it. The town where she lived was over an hour away. We were taking my great grandma, Aunt Mae's sister, with us. Grandma would spend most of the trip complaining about nearly any subject that came up, scolding my brother and me for any hint of misbehavior or telling my mom about the things grandma thought she should do differently. It wouldn't be any better once we got to Aunt Mae's. We would be required to sit quietly on hard, dining room chairs while the adults visited. Aunt Mae had a nice parlor, but no one was ever allowed to go in there, most certainly not children. It was a museum of sorts with a horsehair stuffed sofa and chairs upholstered in coarse velvet. There were numerous satin pillows with shiny fringe around the edges, all carefully placed on the sofa and chairs. Every square inch of surface was covered with china figurines, vases, and photos in ornate frames. There were even some larger pieces that sat on the floor. One was a statue of a young, black boy, dressed in a red and black fancy uniform, holding one arm up with a ring in his hand. Its purpose had originally been for guests to tie their horses to when visiting. Another was a life-sized, white, porcelain Pekinese dog.

On a previous visit, my brother and I were allowed to walk through this room of hallowed ground, under close adult supervision. Every surface gleamed, and there was not a speck of dust to be seen anywhere. I'm not sure what persuaded Aunt Mae to relax the no entry rules, but we were given to understand it was a one-time thing only.

Aunt Mae's front door opened into her dining room. Sitting at the table was a rail thin woman I'd never seen before. She had raven black hair, shapely black eyebrows, bright red lipstick, and thick pancake makeup. She was wearing red silk lounging pajamas with white polka dots. Her nails were long and also red. A large diamond adorned one finger, and numerous rings were scattered on her other fingers. The final touch was the cigarette in a long black holder. The picture she presented was that of an aging, yet still elegant, movie star in a dramatic role.

None of the women in my mom's family wore any make up to speak of. On special occasions, my mom and her sister would add a little lipstick and face powder. The only time I ever saw grandma or Aunt Mae with make up was when they were in their coffins. Cotton housedresses and full-length aprons that covered their ample bodies, sensible black oxford shoes, long cotton stockings, and hairnets were the daily attire. A slightly classier version of the housedress would be donned for church, weddings, and funerals, along with silk stockings and brightly shined, black, oxford shoes. A hat was required when dressing up, but the hairnet was always in place.

When introductions were made, I learned this was Aunt Belle, a sister of my grandma and Aunt Mae. Her voice was husky and gravelly and has always made me think of Bette Davis. When I see the scene in my mind today, it's as if I'm looking at a black and white photograph with one prominent area of color.

I don't remember anything else about that visit, except it seemed obvious, even to an eight year old, that everyone wished Aunt Belle would just disappear. It was the only time I would ever see her. Her name was rarely mentioned in the family and never when Grandma was around to hear it. One of the primary rules my family lived by was to never say anything negative about anyone in the family. Other people could be criticized or gossiped about, but never a family member. This rule ensured that it would be many years before I learned any more about Belle. The only way my family could deal with someone like Belle, who had so obviously rejected the family's rules, was to pretend she didn't exist.

1900

"Girls stop your dwaddeling and finish up the breakfast dishes. We need to get those weeds out of the garden before it gets too hot. Where's Belle?" Lizzie and Mae had been chattering and taking their time in the kitchen. Working in the garden was one of their least favorite things to do.

At their mother's question about Belle they answered nearly in unison. "I don't know. She never helps when she's supposed to."

Emily found her youngest daughter in Emily and John's bedroom, standing in front of the vanity. She had unbraided her long dark hair and was alternately trying to pile it on top of her head or letting it fall free while turning her head this way and that.

"Rosa Belle! What in heaven's name are you doing? You tie your hair back this minute and come with me to the garden."

When Belle started to protest, Emily picked up a ribbon from the vanity and roughly tied Belle's hair at the nape of her neck, then marched her downstairs.

On the way through the kitchen she spoke sharply to Mae and Lizzie, telling them to hurry up and finish, then follow her to the garden. "And you make sure those dishes are spotless and dried well. And put every single thing away!"

The garden was large, planted with peas, beans, carrots, tomatoes, corn, beets and potatoes. It was necessary to help feed the large family throughout the year. Beside Belle, Lizzie, and Mae, there were two brothers, Ray and David. The boys were expected to help with the animals and work in the field. Gardening was the domain of women. All three girls considered it drudgery, most especially Belle. It began early in the spring when John would plow the area. Then the women took over, raking the hard clods down to pebble size. Peas and potatoes were the first to be planted early in the spring. The rest would wait until the days became warmer. Lizzie and Mae dealt with the tedious drudgery of weeding by complaining about it while trying to finish as quickly as they could, so they could go on to other, more pleasant tasks. Belle rarely joined in with these complaints, remaining quiet, working slowly and methodically, not because she was engrossed in the task or overly concerned about doing the job well. Her silence and slow careful way of working allowed her mind to roam to far away places, dreaming of happier circumstances and conjuring up vivid scenarios of how her life would be once she was old enough to leave all this.

"Belle, if you move any slower, you're gonna have grass growin' on you! Lizzie and Mae have finished two rows, and you're only half way down the first one."

"But Ma, I'm making sure I get all the weeds."

"Don't sass back at me young lady! Just get a move on!"

"Yeah Belle," Lizzie chimed in, "You're making us do most of the work and keeping us out in the sun longer than we need to."

"She never does her share, Ma," whined Mae.

"Girls, you'd do better to spend your energy on those weeds instead of running your mouth. You could both be a little more careful about getting all the weeds. Now, get busy, all three of you!"

When the garden had finally been scoured for weeds, the girls headed for the house to wash the sweat off their faces, the dirt off their hands, and have a glass of lemonade. Then, it was time to bring the wash in off the line, while Emily prepared the noon meal for John and the boys. They had been in the field cutting and raking alfalfa into rows. Even though they washed up at the outside pump before coming to the table, the smell of sweat, dusty clothes, and leather gloves was prominent.

John was eating fast today. "Boys don't tarry with your food. We need to get that fence around the pasture mended. Feels like a storm's comin', and if the cows get spooked, they're liable to go right through the weak spots."

Belle spoke up. "Pa we got the garden all weeded this morning."

Mae quickly added, "But Pa, Belle works so slow, me and Lizzie did most of the work."

"Belle, you need to learn to pick up your pace a bit. There's too much work around here to allow for dwaddeling."

"But Pa I made sure I got every weed in the row!"

"There ain't no reason you can't work fast and good."

"But Pa…"

"Belle, that's enough! There'll be no back talk in this house!"

As soon as John and the boys finished their meal, they were off to the pasture. Maintaining an 80 acre, Nebraska farm left precious little free time. It was hard work and, in many ways a hard life, but it was the only thing John had ever known. He found satisfaction in bringing in a crop at harvest. The times when Mother Nature interfered with this, by way of drought or hail storms, were seen as just one of the trials of life that had to be endured.

The farm was on gently rolling, fertile ground with a small pond in the pasture. John kept about a dozen head of dairy cows that provided milk, meat, and butter for the family, plus a bit of income from selling cream in town. There were also chickens that provided meat, eggs, and feathers for pillows. For reasons that were never examined, the cattle were the responsibility of the men; the women were in charge of the chickens. The only overlap in these duties involved the separating of the cream from the milk. This was Emily's responsibility and, eventually, the girls, when they were deemed old enough to trust with running the machine that did the separating.

The routine of farm life varied little from day to day: up at daybreak to milk the cows, breakfast, the men heading out to the fields, while Emily and the girls cleaned up the kitchen, gathered the eggs, and fed the chickens. The rest of the day was taken up with laundry, cleaning, mending, and baking. There was always a short mid-morning break, when the men came in for sandwiches and a cold drink. Sometimes Emily would pack up this lunch and take it to them in the field to save them time. Then she prepared the noon meal and had the supper ready by 5:00, after which the cows needed to be milked. It was important that the twice daily milking be as close to twelve hours apart as possible to ensure the optimum production of milk. Evenings were spent reading or playing card games. By ten at the latest, everyone was in bed. Their social life consisted of church on Sundays and occasional get-togethers with neighbors.

The local school house was about a mile down the road. Barring dangerous weather such as a blizzard, hailstorm, or heavy rain, the children walked to and from school. During the fall harvest, and again at spring planting time, the boys rarely went to school. John deemed it more important that they stay home to help with the farm work. John had been forced to quit school after eighth grade. His dad needed him to help with their farm and didn't see any benefit in further schooling for a farmer. John always regretted this, but now he felt there was no choice but to do the same with his sons.

The day was hot and sultry, as only an August day in Nebraska can be. Emily and the girls were canning tomatoes. The kitchen felt like a room in hell with the pots of tomatoes simmering on the wood burning stove and pans of boiling water to sterilize the mason jars in which the tomatoes would be stored.

Emily and the girls were nearly as quiet and sullen as the weather. The screen door squeaked and slammed as Belle brought in another pan of tomatoes to be processed. She volunteered for this part of the job knowing it would offer a bit of relief from the steamy kitchen while she washed the freshly picked tomatoes at the outside pump. Emily was aware of Belle's ulterior motive for so quickly volunteering for this part of the job. She could have allowed the girls to take turns with this, but didn't have the energy to listen to any bickering about whose turn it was.

She would never have admitted it, but her youngest child held a special place in her heart. She recognized Belle was cut from a different cloth. Emily had also engaged in flights of fancy, dreaming of far away places, but held no hope that life would be much different for any of her girls than it was for herself. Her independent spirit had been effectively crushed by the daily duties of a farm wife, and John's disapproval of anything remotely resembling independence in a woman.

Emily's mind began to wander back to the days of her youth before John began courting her. She loved to read and devoured nearly every book in the town's small library. Emily was an only child. Her father operated the creamery in their small town of Thayer. Emily's mother, Lily, would occasionally take in mending to supplement their meager income, but greatly resented having to do this. She was raised as an only child and was coddled and spoiled by her parents. The assumption was that she would marry someone who could support her in comfort and continue to spoil her. When Gus arrived in town to become the manager of the hardware store, both Lily and her parents fell under the spell of his charm. He was respectful of his customers and would often entertain them with funny stories. Lily's dad saw Gus as having a good head for business, so when he began showing an interest in Lily, there were no objections from either of her parents. When Gus had money, he would spend it as if there was a never ending supply. He lavished gifts on Lily, and his charming manner prevented both Lily and her parents from questioning the wisdom of his spending habits. His generous spirit led him to extend more credit to some of the hardware customers than was practical. As a result, he was fired from his job a few months after he and Lily were married. After a series of short lived jobs, the creamery came up for sale. This seemed like a golden opportunity to Gus, and because of his charming manner and generous spirit, he was able to convince Lily's dad to help him with the purchase of this business.

Lily was not happy when John became interested in Emily. A farm wife was not what she envisioned for her daughter. Emily loved the country and liked the quiet, no- nonsense-way John went about his life. Her dad's never ending charm often irritated her, especially during the times when money was tight. At these times he seemed to need to pour it on thick. Largely because Lily couldn't see any other immediate prospects for Emily, she and Gus gave their permission when John asked for her hand in marriage.

As Emily filled the last jar with tomatoes, she shook herself out of her reverie. There was just enough time to prepare the noon meal for the men. Because the kitchen was so hot and steamy, dinner was eaten at a table under a shade tree in the yard.

"Mother, we sure need rain," John addressed Emily, "but this weather feels like we may get a lot more than that." It was late in the season for a tornado, but in Nebraska anything was possible. Hail was the bigger worry. The corn was doing well, but a bad hail storm at this point would severely damage the crop.

"At least I got twelve quarts of tomatoes put up this morning." Emily commented.

When the men returned to the field, the girls begged their mom to allow them to go to the pond to cool off a bit before tackling the dishes. Emily was dog tired herself, so she gave permission. "But don't tarry too long. There is still a pile of work to be done."

As the girls hurried toward the pond, Emily indulged herself and went to her room to lie down for a while. This was unusual behavior for her, but lately it had been a struggle just to get through her days. At times, she wondered how she would manage when the girls returned to school in a few weeks, then would quickly console herself that she would probably feel better once the weather cooled off.

"Let's take our clothes off and get really wet and cool!"

"Belle! What is the matter with you?" Mae shouted. "You know what Pa would do to us if he caught us doing that?"

"Oh, he's way off in the other field. That's not a worry. Come on!"

"Belle, you're on your way to hell for sure with all your crazy ideas" added Lizzie. "That is not how young ladies act."

"Well, some young ladies do! In the South Sea Islands. I read about it. Besides, why would God give us a nice cool pond on such a hot day, if He didn't want us to enjoy it?"

Belle started to take her dress off, and Lizzie and Mae both chimed in. "We'll tell if you do that! And we'll tell what you said about God, too!"

Belle pouted but stopped undressing. She knew her sisters would tattle on her. They were just never willing to take any chances or have any fun. She was well aware that her punishment from both Ma and Pa would not be pleasant. The girls settled for taking off shoes and stockings, hiking up their skirts, and cooling their feet. Belle loved the way the mud squished up between her toes, while Mae and Lizzie complained about it. Belle picked up a small stone and attempted to skip it across the water. She wasn't successful in skipping it, but managed to splash a bit of water on Mae and Lizzie who loudly complained.

She picked up a couple more small stones saying, "See that knot on that tree over there? Bet I can hit it." With that she took careful aim and let it fly. There was a resounding smack, and a small piece of bark fell away from the knot. "Let's see you two try that!"

"Why in the world would we want to do something like that? Honestly, Belle, I don't know what gets into you!" exclaimed Mae.

"You just never want to try anything new," snapped Belle.

"I think we'd best be getting back," said Lizzie. They cleaned and dried their feet as best they could in the grass and headed back to the house.

Mae and Lizzie started to clean the kitchen as soon as they returned, while Belle went to the pump to splash cold water on her face and dampen the hair at her temples, then she stopped to gaze at the cumulous clouds drifting overhead. She wished she could be sitting on one of those puffy clouds. From there, she could survey the entire world and decide where she wanted to land. It would be somewhere beautiful and a little exotic. She would wear fine, beautiful clothes, and be admired by all.

"Belle, we'll be late for school if we don't leave now. If you aren't ready, me and Mae will go on without you."

"You just want to go to school because you're sweet on that Charles Grubaugh."

"Am not! All he cares about is farming. But he is good lookin isn't he?"

"Well of course he's interested in farming. After all he is an only son," added Mae.

"I'll just be glad when this year is over and I don't have to go to school any more," said Lizzie. "I can read and do my numbers, so why do I need to waste my time on school when I could be helping Ma here? Maybe you haven't cared enough to notice, but she's been feeling poorly lately."

"Oh, she's fine," replied Belle. "She's just getting old and slowing down some. You fuss too much Lizzie."

"Girls stop that bickering and get yourselves off to school now! And don't tarry coming home this afternoon. I want some help getting pies ready for the church social on Sunday."

When the girls were finally out the door, Emily sat down heavily at the kitchen table and indulged in one last cup of coffee. She would like to allow Lizzie to quit school now, so she would have a little more help during the day, but if she suggested it to John, he would see it as giving in to a child's whim, something he had no patience with. She didn't want to admit to him how tired she felt all the time. In only a little over five months, Lizzie would be finished with eighth grade. Mae had only one more year, and two years after that Belle would also have completed eighth grade. She heaved a sigh, pushing herself up from the table. The boys were already finished with their schooling. She glanced out the window and watched David put the harness on the team of horses and hitch them to the wagon. They would spend most of the day in the field picking corn by hand. David seemed to have farming in his blood, while Ray preferred tinkering with the machinery to actively doing any farm work. Since David was the oldest and would some day take over the farm, she was happy for him that it seemed to be something he loved. She worried about how Ray would make his way in the world, but he was a bright boy and not lazy, so she guessed something would work out for him.

John and the boys worked with a steady rhythm, harvesting the corn. Pull the ear off the stalk, strip the husk using the hook on the special gloves they wore, and toss it into the wagon. Then repeat it again and again and again. It was mindless work and offered a rare opportunity for conversation between the three men.

"Pa, I think the wagon needs some grease in the wheel bearings," commented Ray.

"Seems to me it's workin' just fine," replied John.

"It could do better and will last longer with a little attention."

"There's more pressing things to put our time into. Right now, the priority is getting this corn harvested before the snow starts."

"I heard someone is making a machine you can pull through the field, and it picks and husks the corn, then dumps it into the wagon for you. Won't that be something!"

"Maybe, but it will probably cost a king's ransom. What are ya gonna do when it breaks down? All that money sittin' there, corn waiting to be picked, while someone tries to figure out how to get the blamed thing workin' again. This way may be slower, but you know what you've got to work with and how long it's gonna take to finish the harvest."

"Ray, you spend too much time dreamin' about new fangled notions that probably ain't never gonna happen," commented David.

"Oh, they'll happen David. Sooner or later, they will happen, and I'm gonna find a way to be the guy who tends to those machines when they need attention or fixin."

"Dreamin's fine, Ray, so long as you don't let yourself get carried away with fanciful ideas," said John "You need to keep your feet on the ground and your head outta the clouds, if you hope to get anywhere in this world."

There were only twelve children in the small country school where grades one through eight were taught. A few of the girls might continue on to high school in the nearby town of Utica, but that was the exception rather than the rule. Belle often thought she would like to go on to high school. She loved to read and saw high school as an adventure, something that could help her find a way off the farm. Lizzie was in eighth grade this year, and Mae was only one year behind her. This meant that Belle would be attending her last two years here on her own. Maybe, she could get the teacher, Miss Keller, to help her find a way to attend high school.

The girls arrived at the school house early enough to have time to visit with the others in the school yard before it was time to begin class.

One of the older boys, Charles, spoke to Lizzie when they arrived. "You goin' to the church social on Sunday, Lizzie?"

"Ma's planning on it. We're supposed to help make pies when we get home today," she replied.

"Well, I'll be sure to get a piece of your apple pie. Nobody does apple pie better than you and your ma."

"Why Charles, that sounds to me like you're sweet on Lizzie," teased Belle. Charles' face reddened, as he mumbled something and hurried to join the rest of the boys.

"Belle, you got no call to be embarresin' me like that! You just got no manners at all!"

"Oh, pshaw, Lizzie. I was just havin' a bit of fun with you two."

Miss Keller came to the door with the bell in her hand, signaling it was time to begin the day's lessons.

Miss Jean Keller started teaching at the country school shortly after she graduated from high school and passed her teaching license exam. That was three years ago. She became a teacher because she enjoyed working with children. In spite of the challenges, she still did. In some ways, it was disappointing because few of her students continued their education after completing eighth grade. Miss Keller was raised on a nearby farm and understood the reasoning of the parents who chose not to have their children continue with school. She didn't agree with it, but she understood it. She did her best to make school a pleasant experience for them, and hoped she could instill in them a love of learning that would keep them learning new things and exploring new ideas in whatever way they could find after their formal schooling ended. She saw each child as a unique individual with varying interests and abilities. She also knew how harsh farm life could be, especially if the family was large. One of the ways she had of making each child feel special was to have a small celebration for them on their birthdays. She would bring a cake to school and make a "Happy Birthday" banner with the child's name on it and hang it over the blackboard. For those whose birthdays fell outside the school year, she would have their "party" either during the first or last week of school or near the Christmas break, whichever time was closest to their birthday.

Of the three Mericale girls, Belle was her favorite. She was never shy about asking questions or offering her opinion. Of course, there were times when Belle got carried away with her opinions, and Miss Keller needed to reprimand her. There were times she agreed with what Belle said, if not the blunt manner in which she said it. She tried to instill in Belle the social rules of behavior without preventing her from seeking out and examining new ideas.

"Belle, put that book down, and come help me with these potatoes."

"In a minute Ma, soon as I finish this paragraph."

"Belle! I mean now! You can read after the work is done, not before."

Belle knew from her ma's tone of voice that she better not push it any further. They finished digging the last of the potatoes a few days earlier and stored them on the porch to allow any clinging dirt to dry. Today that dirt needed to be brushed off and the potatoes examined for signs of spoiling. These would be kept in a box on the porch to be used first. The rest needed to be placed in baskets and carried to the root cellar. Lizzie and Mae were put to work finishing the laundry and hanging it on the line.

Belle began singing "The Old Gray Mare" to help relieve the boredom of sorting the potatoes. After only a few minutes of this, Emily snapped, "Belle, will you please stop that singing. I have a headache, and that's not helping any."

Belle and Emily continued to work in silence, until two baskets had been filled.

"Belle, help me get these baskets to the cellar. We'll finish sorting the rest later."

When the two bushel baskets had been taken to the root cellar, Emily told Belle she was going to lie down for a few minutes.

Lizzie and Mae came in from the clothesline just then. All three girls looked at each other with puzzled expressions. This was not like their Ma at all. Lizzie spoke first. "I think Ma has been feeling poorly lately. Maybe we should say something to Pa." Mae and Belle quickly recovered. Belle's opinion was they shouldn't bother their father with a worry that might be nothing. Mae agreed. "You know how he gets when he's worried about something. Let's just try to do a bit more for Ma and wait and see."

Lizzie didn't entirely agree, but she didn't want to have to put up with her Pa's short temper, especially if the worry was for nothing.

John's parents died some years earlier. His sister lived in Omaha with her husband. The only other relatives close by were Emily's parents. Thanksgiving was usually spent with their near-by neighbors who had no family close either, and unless the weather prevented it, John would take the buggy into town to bring Emily's parents out for the day. The meal was a joint affair, and was held at John and Emily's home since their house was a little larger. Emily fixed the turkey, potatoes, and a vegetable dish. Her neighbor, Martha, brought dessert, salad, and bread.

"Do you think we're gonna get snow tomorrow?" Emily asked John.

"Now Mother, you always worry yourself into a state the day before Thanksgiving. The weather's gonna be fine."

"Well, I just hate to think of you and the folks on a five mile ride in bad weather, or Martha and Ed not able to make it over with the little ones."

Thanksgiving Day dawned bright and crisp. It was cold, but there was no wind. John left right after the milking was done, leaving the boys to finish the rest of the chores. Emily was up with him before daybreak, getting the fire in the stove just right so the turkey could cook slowly and not get too dry.

Breakfast was a hurried, piecemeal affair, which caused a bit of grumbling from Ray and David, even though they knew the rest of the day would make up for it. The morning was a flurry of activity for Emily and the girls. It was important to Emily that everything be ready before her guests arrived.

At 11:30, John pulled in with Gus and Lily. Hello's had barely been said and the coats placed on Emily's bed, before Martha and Ed arrived with their two young daughters.

When the meal was over, Emily, Martha, and the girls cleared the table and washed dishes, while the men retired to the living room to visit. After the women were finished in the kitchen, the girls went to their bedroom to play with paper dolls while the adults gathered at the table for a few games of hearts. After an hour everyone decided they now had room for pie. Soon it was time for John to take Gus and Lily back to town so he could be home not too long after dark.

Emily sat in the one easy chair in the now quiet house. The boys were at the barn, taking care of the evening chores, and the girls, thankfully, were still playing quietly in their room. It had been a good day, but Emily was bone tired. "I must be getting old," she thought. "I wish I had more energy." She knew there were still things that needed doing in the kitchen, but she just couldn't make herself get up to do them.

The winter had been harsh, starting in January with frequent snow and sub zero temperatures. Mother Nature seemed to make up for this a bit by producing a glorious, early spring. The pond was full from all the snow melt, and by the end of April everything was lush and green.

"Only four more weeks, and I'll be done with school!"

"But Lizzie how are you gonna manage to see Charles then?" asked Belle.

"Oh, we'll manage," replied Lizzie. "He doesn't live all that far away, and we'll see each other every Sunday at church. I think you're just jealous cause you don't have anyone interested in you."

"No one around here I'd want to have interested in me!" snapped Belle.

The summer went by quickly, as always. Now, it was October and the harvest of corn was going well. The crystal blue skies and crisp air made you want to stop, momentarily, and allow the changing season to wrap its' arms around you.

John, David, and Ray were finishing the last field of corn. Ray had been quiet the past couple of days with very little of his running banter.

"You been awful quiet Ray," commented John. "Somethin' botherin' you?"

Ray was quiet for a couple of minutes, then sighed, and began to speak.

"Well Pa, I've been tryin' to find a way to tell you something. Remember a couple weeks ago when Ed's brother was visiting and came to church? He and I got to talking over coffee after the service. He owns a feed store and livery in Seward and needs to hire another man. It would also involve maintaining the wagons and other equipment. The pay's good, Pa, and I can live with them until I get some money saved up for a room of my own. This is something I really want to do. You know farmin's not in my blood, and I'd be makin' good enough money so's I could send some home from time to time."

"So farmin's not good enough for you?"

"It's not that, Pa. I just don't think I'm cut out for it like David is. He'll take over this farm, someday, which is only right. But I don't want to wind up share croppin' or working as a hired hand on someone else' farm".

"Are you askin' my permission then?"

"What I'd like is your good wishes, Pa. I'm nineteen and it's time I got out on my own."

"Seems like you've pretty well made up your mind. I guess you're at an age where you need to decide what to do with your life, so I won't stand in the way."

It wasn't exactly what Ray would have liked to hear from his father, but it was the best John could do. John was never one to indulge in what he saw as wishful thinking. He often worried that Ray spent too much time doing just that. He would like to have Ray stay on and help with the farm until such time as he could find a place of his own, but he recognized that Ray would never really be satisfied with farm life. A man's heart had to be in it if he was to make a go of farming.

Emily wasn't happy about Ray leaving, but she did understand it was something he needed to do. It brought home the fact to her that her children were rapidly becoming adults. David was courting a girl from town, and Lizzie seemed to be spending a lot of time with Charles. At least, it seemed that Mae and Belle would be around for a while longer, and of course, David would always be involved with their farm.

Chapter Two

Belle was now in eighth grade. Mae finished school almost two years ago. Also, Belle was trying her best to get permission to continue with high school, but John was adamant that it wasn't necessary and was not going to happen. Miss Keller tried to persuade John that it would be good for Belle, but John was a man of firm opinions that were not easily changed. Belle inherited much of her dad's stubbornness and was determined to leave the farm as quickly as she could. She even had a plan. Her folks always spent one day at the County Fair at the end of August. Belle was pretty sure she could get them to allow her to go off with some of her friends once they got to the fair. Then, she would do her best to charm one of the young men running the booths to let her join up with him when the group passed by her farm on the way to the next town. She did not have dreams of living the carnival life, but it would get her off the farm and to more towns, where she was sure other opportunities would present themselves.

The summer seemed to last forever for Belle this year. She did her best not to do anything that would give her folks reason to complain and tried to wait patiently for County Fair time. She talked with her friends at church about how much more fun they could have if they explored the fair on their own. Their biggest concern was getting all the families to attend the fair on the same day. One of the girls came up with the idea they suggest to their parents that all three families go on the same day and share their noon picnic. It was agreed the other two girls would be the ones to approach the parents since everyone knew Belle's suggestions to her parents were often met with skepticism and questions about her ulterior motives. This proved to be a wise decision. All three sets of adults thought it sounded like a fine idea.

The day for the fair trip dawned bright and sunny. Belle managed to slip some extra clothes in an old pillow case and hide them under a bush near the road in preparation for her escape. She hadn't said a word to her friends about her plans, knowing they wouldn't approve or understand and would tell their parents.

Belle could hardly contain her excitement on the way to the fair. When they arrived, they found the other two families had gotten there first and staked out the area for the picnic. While greetings were exchanged all around, Belle joined her two friends, Jane and Mary, and moved apart from the others.

"Do you think we'll be allowed to go off by ourselves?" asked Jane.

"Mary, why don't you be the one to ask first," suggested Belle. "You never get into any trouble so I'll bet your folks will say, 'yes'."

In a few minutes John suggested the men check out the cattle barn while the women look through the baked goods and quilt entries.

"Pa, Jane, and Belle, and me would rather go explore the Midway. Can we please?"

"Well, I don't know if that's such a good idea. We're all going there after lunch so I think you can wait."

"Pa we're old enough now to spend some time by ourselves and looking at pies and quilts is boring. This way we can check out what's on the Midway before we all get there."

"Yeah, I'd really like to do that," chimed in Jane. "Can't we please?"

Mary's mom spoke up and said she thought that would be OK, so long as they are back at the picnic site in an hour. "I think the girls can be trusted to spend some time by themselves, don't you Emily?"

"I expect they can," replied Emily.

"Well, I don't know," said John. "I'm not sure that's such a good idea."

"John, the girls are growing up. I think, maybe, we could allow them a little freedom," added Mary's mother.

"Well, so long as they don't have any money with them and are back here in an hour I guess we could try it, but you keep your distance from those men running the games of chance you hear?"

"Oh, we will Pa," replied Belle. The men headed off to the barn while the women made their way to the pavilion where the baked goods and quilts were on display.

"I hope the judging is all done" remarked Emily. "I always enjoy seeing who gets the blue ribbons. Lizzie and Mae, are you going to the Midway with the girls?"

"I can wait til later," replied Lizzie,"I like to look at the quilts."

"I'll come along, too," said Mae. "I want to see whose pie got a blue ribbon. I still think you should have entered one Ma."

"No, I'd rather just bake things for my family to enjoy and not have to worry about getting it perfect."

The girls headed toward the Midway area, trying their best to remain lady-like, while they were still in view of the adults, then broke out into giggles, once they were out of sight.

"Oh, this is gonna be so much fun," said Jane.

"Yeah, nobody watching our every move," added Belle.

The first part of the Midway they came to was the rides.

"I love the carousel," said Jane. "I could ride it all day."

"I want to go on the Ferris wheel, but Pa's never let me. He thinks it's too dangerous," chimed in Belle.

"Oh, I don't think I'd like that. It just looks too scary to be up so high."

"Oh Mary, you'd love it. Just think how far you could see," said Belle.

After stopping to discuss the pros and cons of the various rides, they came to the games of chance and freak shows. A good looking young man was behind the counter where a china doll or stuffed animal could be won by throwing a ball and knocking over padded figures.

"I wish I had a dime," said Belle. "I know I could win something." They stood and watched while a few young men tried their hand at winning something for their girls. No one was successful.

"They are doing it all wrong," Belle said this loudly enough for the young man tending the booth to hear.

"Well, little lady, how about you come try, if you think you can do better?"

Mary and Jane ducked their heads and started to back away, but not Belle.

"Well, I would if I had a dime. I'd win something, too!"

"You sound awfully sure of yourself," he smiled.

"You've never seen me throw a ball," flirted Belle. " I know what I can do!"

By now the young man was caught up in flirting with Belle.

"My name's Tad. What's yours?"

"I'm Belle. I know what I'm talking about!"

"Is that right? Well, tell you what. You come on up here, and I'll let you have three tries on the house. I gotta see someone who is as good as you say you are."

"Belle! You know what your pa said!"

"Oh, Jane, where's the harm? I'm not spending any money." With that she stepped up to the counter and collected three balls from Tad.

"Now, you gotta stay behind that line there," he reminded her.

"Belle took careful aim and let the first ball fly. It tipped one of the figures, but didn't knock it over. Belle took aim with the second ball, and this time, the figure did fall.

"Pretty good," said Tad, "but one ain't enough to win anything. You gotta get at least two."

Belle gave him a look, then concentrated and let the third ball fly, neatly knocking down another figure.

"So what do I win, smart guy?"

"Now, Belle, I can't rightly let you have a prize since you didn't pay for the chance. You come on back later with some money and give it a try again."

"Well, I just might do that," snapped Belle.

Mary and Jane grabbed Belle's arm trying to hurry her away.

"What in the world were you thinking Belle?" said Mary. "You know how much trouble we'd be in if our folks found out about that?"

"Well, are you two gonna tell em?" asked Belle. "Really, what was the harm? Just a little fun."

"Well, I think we should start back to the picnic area," said Jane. "I don't want to get in trouble by being late."

Emily, Martha, and Edna were just starting to set things out for lunch when the girls arrived.

"Oh, good, girls, you're just in time to help," said Martha. "Did you enjoy yourselves?"

"Sure did" piped Belle. "Ma, I really want to ride the Ferris wheel this year. Will you tell Pa I can, please?"

"We'll see, Belle. I'm not sure he will think it's a good idea."

"But Ma, I'm fourteen now and it's safe. No one's ever gotten hurt on it."

Just then the men arrived.

"Hurt on what?" asked John.

"Belle was asking to go on the Ferris wheel this year," replied Emily.

"Is that right? Well, I don't know. Being that high up in the air doesn't seem like such a good idea to me."

"Oh, Pa, please! Just think how far you could see. I bet I could spot the windmill on our farm."

"Let's eat and have a short rest, then we'll see," replied John.

While it wasn't a yes, it also wasn't a firm no, so Belle was hopeful.

Lunch was fried chicken, baked beans, and a wonderful chocolate cake Martha brought. The adults were content to sit around visiting, but the girls soon became restless and asked to go back to the Midway.

"Well, I guess a little walkin' might be a good idea," offered Jane's dad. "You girls pick up the lunch fixins', and then we'll go."

When they arrived at the carousel, Jane and Mary asked to ride it, and were given the coins to buy their tickets. John started to give coins to his three girls, but Belle asked again about the Ferris wheel.

"Pa, I really would rather ride the Ferris wheel. Please! I won't ask for anything else Pa."

John looked toward Mary and Jane who were shaking their heads.

"Jane and Mary don't want to do that."

"They can ride the carousel, while I'm on the Ferris wheel. I'll be fine Pa, really."

John looked to Emily who gave a small nod and reluctantly agreed.

Belle was beside herself with excitement and began hurrying toward the Ferris wheel. It was every bit as wonderful and exciting as she thought it would be. At one point, it stopped while her seat was at the very top. She was looking out over the Midway and spotted Tad. He didn't have any customers at that point and was looking her way. She waved at him and got a wave in return. A plan began to form in her mind. When her ride ended, Jane and Mary were still on the carousel.

"Ma, I need to go use the privy. I'll be right back."

"You be careful now. We'll wait right her for you."

Belle hurried off to head for Tad's booth.

"Well, hello again, little lady."

"My name is Belle," she snapped.

"Excuse me, Belle. Did you come back to win a prize?"

"Nope, I still don't have any money, but I've got a proposition for you. I'd like to work for you. I know what the secret is to knocking those things down, and my aim is good, as you saw. I could pretend to be a customer and win a prize. That way other people watching would think it's really easy, and you'd get more customers."

"Is that right? What makes you think I need more customers?"

"Well, I don't see a lot of people lined up here right now, do you? Listen, I don't have a lot of time before Ma's gonna come lookin' for me. I really need to get away from here. Your troop goes right by our farm when you leave here. I could be waiting by the big oak tree, if you just tell me when you'd be there."

"You trying to get me in trouble with the law little lady?"

"I told you my name is Belle, and you wouldn't get in trouble. I haven't said anything to anyone and I could arrange it so Ma and Pa wouldn't miss me for several hours. No one would have any idea I went with you."

"Well, I just don't know. I'm not sure the boss would approve."

"Tell you what. You tell me when you'll be leaving here, and I'll be waiting by the big oak tree. If you decide I can come with you, you can stop."

"You are a determined little thing aren't you?"

"I just know what I want," replied Belle.

"Well, we'll be here one more full day, then we pack up and head out early the next morning."

"OK then, I'll be waiting." With that Belle rushed back to where the others waited.

"You were gone a long time, Belle," said Emily. "You all right?"

"Yeah, it's just that there was a line, and I had to wait a bit."

Jane's dad offered to buy cotton candy for everyone before they started back to the wagons for the trip home.

Tad stared after Belle as she hurried away, admiring the way her dark curls bounced on her back. "I wonder why she's so set on running off?" he thought. "She's probably just tired of farm life." Tad grew up in a small town and remembered how badly he wanted to get away and see more of the world. He continued his silent conversation with himself. "Taking her along is a crazy idea, and Big Joe probably won't go for it at all, but Big Joe does like money, and her idea for bringing in customers has some merit. Maybe I'll run it by Big Joe later tonight after he's had a couple beers. She's awful easy on the eyes and has a lot of spunk." At that point a customer came up to his stand and Tad began his line of chatter, putting Belle in the back of his mind.

That night after the Midway closed down, Tad made his way over to Big Joe's wagon where several of the men were sitting around a small campfire enjoying a beer.

"So, how'd everyone do today?" asked Big Joe and listened while the men gave reports that varied from "pretty fair" to "coulda been better," Tad spoke up saying, "I think I've got an idea for increasing the take on my booth. Had this little gal stop by today, and let me tell you she's got a wicked arm. She wants to join up with us and proposed earning her keep by posing as a customer winning a prize so the locals watching will think it's easy to do. Seems like a fair idea to me. What do you think Big Joe?"

"Might be, might be. Think she could knock 'em down often enough to make it worthwhile?"

"Oh, yeah! I'm sure of it. I'm pretty sure she's figured out where the ball needs *to* hit to 'em to knock 'em down, and her aim is dead on."

"So is she comin' back tomorrow?"

"Well no, see that's a bit of a problem. She's wanting to run away from home. Says we go right by her farm when we leave here and could be waiting for us by the road."

"A runaway huh? Not sure that's such a good idea. How old is she?"

"I'm guessin' she's around seventeen. She's sure she could arrange it, so she'd be gone long enough before her folks missed her that they wouldn't think about the carnival."

"So how's she gonna know when we're coming by?"

"Well, I told her when we're leaving, but I didn't promise her anything. She said she'd be waiting though."

"Hmmm." Big Joe finished the last of his beer and stared into the fire for a bit. "Sounds like you've been a bit taken with her Tad."

"Well, I'll have to admit she's easy on the eyes. I do think she'd be an asset to the company though. It's not like she'd be the first runaway you've ever taken on."

Big Joe shot Tad a warning look even though several of the men there knew Tad was referring to himself.

"I suppose we could give it a try, if she doesn't work out she has to leave, wherever we are, and if John Law should come lookin' for her, I'm putting it all on you, understand?"

"Got it, Big Joe. Fair enough."

Belle's mind was spinning during the ride home from the fair. Only one more day! "How can I arrange to be out of the house at least a couple hours without Ma lookin' for me?" she wondered. As they neared the entrance to their farm, she noticed some gooseberry bushes along the side of the road that were heavy with ripe berries. "That's it," she thought. "I'm sure I can get Ma to let me go pick gooseberries."

Belle had a difficult time keeping focused on the various chores the next day. Only one more night here, and she'd be free! Late in the afternoon, she approached Emily, while Mae and Lizzie were busy elsewhere. "Ma, I saw some gooseberry bushes out by the road with lots of berries on them. You think I could go down there early tomorrow morning while it's still cool and pick some? A gooseberry pie would taste so good!"

"Are you sure the berries are ripe?" asked Emily. "It seems just a mite early."

"Well, they looked like it to me, but if I find different, I'll just leave them for a bit longer."

"Your Pa does like gooseberry pie. I guess that would probably be fine."

Belle hardly slept that night anticipating her get away the next day.

As soon as breakfast was over and the kitchen cleaned up, Belle took a basket and headed for the road.

"Just where do you think your going?" asked Lizzie.

Emily spoke up and told her Belle was going to pick some gooseberries and bring back enough for a pie or two, if they were ripe.

"Belle you keep your mind on what you're doing, and don't go off daydreamin', you hear?"

"Yes, Ma, I'll be back before you even know I'm gone."

The bushes were about a quarter mile from the house, and a line of trees shielded the view of the road. Belle made herself walk, not run, until she was out of sight of the house. She gathered the clothes she'd hidden under the bush and hurried to the gooseberry bushes. She quickly began picking berries, always keeping an eye on the road and listening for the sound of wagons. The basket was nearly half full with berries when she saw a large cloud of dust down the road. She ran a short way back toward her house and dropped the basket so it spilled, then quickly hurried back to the road. As the wagons came into sight, she stepped to the side of the road and waved. Tad was riding in the front wagon with Big Joe. He spotted Belle and nudged Big Joe, pointing towards her. Joe halted the wagon, and Belle rushed toward it. Tad helped her up on the wagon.

"Big Joe, this here is Belle, the little gal I told you about who is gonna help me make more money. Belle this is Big Joe. He's the boss of everyone in this outfit."

"Pleased to me you, Big Joe," Belle responded. "Thank you so much for allowing me to join up with you."

"Well, little lady, we have rules here and you'll be expected to abide by them and to do your share of whatever work needs doing. Tad tells me you've a mean arm and a deadly aim, but if that happens not to be true, I can't afford to keep you on, understand?"

"Yes, sir, but you won't be disappointed."

"That remains to be seen, don't it? Tad will explain the rules of the outfit to you. For now, I'm thinking it would be best, if you get back inside the wagon and stay out of sight 'til we get a little further away."

Emily had been busy with the ironing, a job that allowed her mind to wander and daydream, when she glanced at the clock and realized Belle had been gone over three hours.

"Lizzie, Belle is apparently daydreaming and wandering around out there. Will you please go find her and tell her to get back here, right now!"

Lizzie heaved a sigh, and headed out the door. It seemed to her that she was forever being asked to do something for Belle that she should be doing on her own. "I wonder if that girl is ever gonna grow up," she thought. Shortly before she came to the gooseberry bushes, she saw the overturned basket of berries and an area of grass that had been trampled down a bit. She began calling Belle's name but had a funny feeling in the pit of her stomach. After a short time she began hurrying back to the house.

"Ma, I can't find Belle anywhere."

"Oh, that girl! Where in the world has she wandered off to now?"

"Ma, the basket of berries was spilled on the ground a ways away from the bushes."

"Well, she's got to be on the farm, somewhere. She couldn't have just disappeared into thin air. Mae, you come with me and Lizzie. We'll fan out a bit, it won't be a pretty sight when I find her!"

The three of them covered a large area along the road and back towards the pasture, but they found no trace of Belle. It was nearing time for John and David to come in for the noon meal, so the women headed back to the house. John and David were just walking up on the porch when Emily and the girls arrived.

"John, Belle went to pick gooseberries early this morning and hasn't come back. We can't find her anywhere, and the basket of berries was overturned near where she'd been picking them."

"That fool is gonna be one sorry little girl when I find her!" stormed John.

"David, let's get a quick bite to eat, then we'll take the horses, so we can cover more ground faster."

After more than an hour and covering the entire farm, Belle was still missing. By now Emily felt panicky.

"John, what could have happened to her?"

"I'll ride into town and talk to the Sheriff. There was a traveling salesman around these parts, yesterday. Maybe the officer can find out if that stranger is still around and if he knows anything about Belle."

The carnival arrived at their next destination two days later. They were making their way towards their final stop of the season in southern Texas. Belle was having the time of her life. She quickly made friends with everyone, was careful not to ruffle any feathers, and gladly pitched in to help with anything that needed doing.

"Well, little lady, you're about to get your chance to show me if you can earn your keep."

"I promise you won't be sorry, Big Joe."

"Here's what I want you to do. Wander around the carnival a bit, keeping an eye on Tad's booth. When you see there's a good gathering of people nearby, you go over and do your stuff. Once you've won a prize, make a big deal about it, then find a way to disappear. Then be careful not to show yourself again 'til evening when there will be a different crowd. Got it?"

"Yessir, Big Joe. I can do that."

Belle wandered around a while, being careful not to exchange greetings with any of the carnival workers. When a small group of people gathered to watch a young man trying to win a prize at Tad's booth, Belle walked up closer. After the young man had unsuccessfully thrown his three balls, Belle stepped up and rather shyly said she'd like to try.

"Well, step right up here little lady. With one dime and a little luck, you can go home with a beautiful China doll. Belle gave Tad the dime and moved up close to the booth.

"No, no little lady. You gotta stand behind that line. Now go ahead, and give it a whirl. This could be your lucky day. Knock down all three and you get the doll plus a Teddy Bear."

Belle paused, as if she was a little unsure, took aim, then knocked one of the figures over.

"See there! Now, that wasn't so hard was it? You have two balls left."

Belle spent some time taking aim for effect and neatly knocked down the second figure.

"All right! The little lady here has just won this beautiful doll. A large crowd gathered and murmured among themselves.

"Come on little gal, just one more and the Teddy Bear is yours, too."

With that Belle snapped the ball, neatly toppling a third figure.

"Lookie there folks! The little gal just won a China doll and a Teddy Bear. Now if a little gal like this can do it, what's stopping all you strapping young men out there? Here ya go little lady."

Belle squealed with delight, holding up her prizes, and said, "Oh I've got to go show my Pa. He'll be so surprised." With that, she melted away beyond the crowd.

Their little show worked. Tad was kept busy for the next hour taking dimes and offering advice and condolences.

After the carnival closed down that evening, there was a larger than usual crowd gathered around Big Joe's camp. Everyone knew Tad had been busier than usual that day. Some watched Belle's performance.

"Well, little lady, if you can keep on doing what you did today then I'd say Tad knew what he was talking about when he wanted me to take you on."

"I told you she had a mean arm and a dead aim didn't I?" said Tad. "I took in almost $2.00 today."

Belle had never been in a spotlight like this before, and she loved it. She noticed there was some friendly grumbling from some of the others about Tad being the beneficiary of her talent and decided she would try to be especially helpful to the rest of the crew to avoid hard feelings or jealousy.

Chapter Three

Six months had passed since Belle's disappearance. The sheriff questioned the traveling salesman, but since he was still calling on people in the area, it seemed unlikely he had anything to do with her disappearance. John sent word to Ray, and he came home for a few days to help in a wider search. Ray had a soft spot in his heart for his youngest sister and seemed devastated over her disappearance. He'd spent a lot of time with her as a toddler, since Mae and Lizzie weren't old enough to be of help. A few days into the search, Emily realized some of Belle's clothes were missing, as well as a hair brush. When she told John he exploded. "That fool girl has run off! Well if we ain't good enough for her then she can just make it on her own wherever she is."

By now, Emily was crying and pleaded with John to keep looking.

"I can't afford to be taking more time away from the farm. There's nothing more to be done, Emily. I'll let the sheriff know, but that's all I can do."

Emily seemed to disappear into herself with Belle gone. She had little to say to anyone. Mae and Lizzie would often find her standing on the porch gazing toward the road. John forbade anyone to speak of Belle. Lizzie and Mae found themselves needing to take on more of the responsibilities of running the house with only minimal direction from Emily.

"Mae, what are we gonna do about Ma?" asked Lizzie. "I'm worried about her."

"I am too. I tried talking to Pa about it one day and he shushed me, saying there was nothing wrong with Ma, and you and me were old enough to do more around the house anyway."

"Mae, Charles wants me to marry him."

"Well, Lizzie, I guess I'm not all that surprised."

"I told him maybe we needed to wait a bit 'til Ma is feeling better, and I'm not sure what Pa's reaction will be."

"Yeah, sometimes, it's hard to know what he's thinking. He might think you need to stay home a while longer to help with the work. Where do you think you'd live if you got married?"

"Well, Charles' pa has been feelin poorly and says he wants Charles to be taking over the farm. Charles has already talked to his folks about it. We could live upstairs for a while and then build our own small house on the farm, too, but that would put a heavier burden on you, Mae."

"Yeah, it would do that. Maybe, you two could wait just a bit longer to see how Ma's doing, and if she doesn't perk up, well, you two need to get on with your life. I'll manage."

"That's probably the best plan. I just don't want to wait too long and risk havin' him change his mind."

That night, at supper, David spoke up. "Ma, Pa, I got something I want to talk to you about. You know I've been seeing a lot of Ann Granger, and, well, we'd like to get married. I haven't talked to her pa, yet. I wanted to talk to you two, first. Do you think we could live here, at least for a while, if we was to get married? We could use the spare room upstairs, and Ann could be a big help to Ma and the girls. You like Ann, don't you, Ma?"

Emily was a little slow to respond, then said, "Well, yes. I like Ann fine," and then was silent.

"Pa, what's your thoughts?" asked David.

"Well, son, I guess I shoulda seen this comin'. Guess maybe I shoulda been payin' more attention. You say stay here for a little while. What's your long range plan?"

"Well, Pa, Old Man Miller has forty acres he wants to sell. I figure I could rotate it between alfalfa and wheat and bring in some money selling the hay and wheat. It's close enough by so it would be practical to keep up what I've been doing here, too. Then as soon as we could, I'd like to build a small house on that land. I'm pretty sure I could get the bank to loan me the money for the land."

"Well, I've got a little put by that I'd be willing to contribute to help you get started. Sounds like you've been thinking about this for a while. What do you think, Mother?"

"Why that sounds fine."

Mae and Lizzie had been glancing at each other during this conversation. Lizzie gave Mae a quizzical look and Mae nodded her head slightly.

"Uh Ma, Pa, I've got something I wanted to tell you too," said Lizzie. "Charles wants me to marry him."

"Is that right?" John interjected, before she could go on.

"Yes, Pa. See we've been talkin' about it, and he's talked to his folks and they would be willing to have us live with them, and Charles and me thought we should wait a bit before he talked to you cause I know Ma's been needin some extra help, and I didn't want to leave it all to Mae, but if Ann's gonna be here then that would be different." All this had been said in a rush with Lizzie barely taking time to breathe. There was a short silence before Lizzie added, "So can I tell Charles he can speak to you, Pa?"

"Well, Mother, what do you think?" he asked Emily.

"Well, I'm not sure," she replied.

"Charles seems like a level headed boy, and his pa's got a good piece of land there," said John.

"Well,…yes,…." replied Emily.

"Well, Lizzie, it sounds like there ain't any big objections here, so you can tell Charles he can come speak to me."

"Oh, Pa! Thank you."

Mae spoke up saying, "Looks like we're gonna be having two weddings."

David spoke up saying, "Me and Ann thought we'd like to get married in April. The farm work's fairly light up 'til then, and if we wait much longer, it's gonna be hard to find the time for a celebration."

"Maybe, you and Ann and Charles and Lizzie could have a double wedding. Wouldn't that be fun!" said Mae.

"Well, that might be an idea. I'd have to see how Ann feels about it. What do you think, Lizzie?" David asked.

"That might be kind of fun. Don't you think so Ma?"

Emily's voice was sad, as she said, "Two of my children getting married and leaving at the same time."

"Well, no, Ma, David's not leaving. Him and Ann will be living here, and I won't be that far away."

"Emily, I think this might be the best idea, if Ann has no objections," commented John. "Unless Lizzie and Charles wanted to wait 'til next fall. Otherwise time's gonna get a little tight."

"Oh, I think it would be much nicer to have a double wedding," said Lizzie.

"Well, then, that's settled, unless Ann doesn't like the idea. If it's OK with her you four can decide on the date."

"I'll talk to her tomorrow, Pa. We probably don't want to wait too long to set the date, if this is what we're gonna do."

"Ma, I'll need a new dress to get married in. When can we go look for fabric?"

"I don't know. I can't think just now. I have a headache and am going to go lie down for a bit."

David and Ann, Charles and Lizzie were married in a double ceremony in mid- April. Everything went smoothly, in spite of the difficulties with the wedding preparations. Emily seemed to pull even farther into herself and couldn't be counted on for any help with either the planning or the preparations. Ann's mother had been very helpful, even taking Mae and Lizzie to town to get the fabric for the new dresses. John managed to ignore or discount any expression of concern about their mother by Lizzie and Mae.

Everyone used the winter break time to make needed repairs and touch up the painted decorations on their booths. It was a relaxed time and gave Belle the opportunity to get to know everyone better. Belle's friendly nature and accepting attitude allowed her to be treated as one of the "family." Stella, the bearded lady, was especially taken with Belle and cajoled Big Joe into providing some funds for additional clothes for Belle.

Belle enjoyed the relaxed pace and loved not having to deal with bitter cold weather and deep snow. She was ready for the excitement of travel when spring arrived, though. During the early months of the season, they were engaged at special festivals. Later in the summer, the county fairs would begin. At a local festival in Oklahoma, the carnival was set up in a the city park. In the early afternoon, there was entertainment at the park bandstand; later in the evening there would also be dancing. Since the Midway was deserted during the afternoon entertainment, Belle listened to the musicians and watched the vaudeville acts. She liked the country western music the band played. When the band took a break, the guitar player came over and stood beside Belle.

"So, did you like our music?" he asked.

"I like it a lot."

"Well, you should come back tonight for some of the dancing. There's just nothing like dancing to country western."

"I'm not sure I can get away, and I've really never done any dancing."

"Heck, it's easy. I can show you how."

"Won't you be busy playing?"

"Nope, we only play in the afternoon. There's another band coming in for the dance. My name's Bill. What's yours?"

"I'm Belle."

"You with the carnival then?"

"Yes."

"So, what do you do?"

"Oh, odds and ends. Just kinda help out wherever I'm needed. What do you do, when you're not playing a guitar?"

"I work with the blacksmith, but music's my real love, and I hope to make it my only job someday. Been savin' my money to head down to Tennessee. That's the place to be, if you want to get anywhere in the country music business. I figure by next summer I'll have enough saved so I can leave."

"That sounds pretty exciting. What does your family think of that?"

"Well, my mama died a few years ago, and daddy, well, he don't much care one way or the other. So you gonna let me teach you some dancing tonight, Belle?"

"I'll see. If I can get away, I'll come. Where will I find you?"

"Right here beside the bandstand. I'll be lookin' for you."

The Midway was nearly deserted by 9 p.m., the dancing being the bigger attraction. Belle decided to slip away to the dance. She hadn't told anyone where she was going, figuring it was none of their business and not wanting to take a chance that someone would object. As she approached the bandstand, Bill came up behind her.

"So, you were able to get away huh," he asked.

"Yeah, things had gotten pretty quiet."

"You ready for a dance?"

"I told you I don't know how."

"There's nothing to it. All you have to do is let your feet follow along with what I'm doing. Come on."

With that, Bill grabbed her arm and led her up on the dance floor. Bill was a good dancer and knew how to lead his partner so they moved almost as one. In a short time, Belle forgot that she had never danced before and followed his lead with few missteps. They kept dancing through three songs before taking a break to catch their breath.

"Now, I'm not sure you were telling the truth about not knowing how to dance. You were great!"

Belle was laughing and insisted this was the first time she'd ever danced. "You just make it seem so easy," she said.

"Well, it is. You just let your feet and body follow the music. It's the next best thing to actually making music."

Just then Tad appeared. "Belle, what are you doing? Everyone's wondering where you were," he said.

Tad and Bill were a study in contrasts. Bill had dark wavy hair, with brown eyes that twinkled, and a tall slender body. Tad was tall, also, but more muscular. His blonde hair fell across his forehead in a constant state of slight disarray, and his eyes were pale blue.

"I was just having a bit of fun dancing, since there was nothing going on at the Midway," Belle replied.

"Well, you're wanted back at camp. It's time to start shutting down and packing up. Come on, now."

Tad watched Bill during this conversation and spoke rather sharply.

"You could ask me a little nicer, you know," said Belle.

"It's your job. I shouldn't have to tell you that. Now, tell this hick goodbye, and get a move on."

"His name is Bill. He plays guitar in one of the bands. I'll come in a few minutes."

"You'll come right now, if you know what's good for you."

Bill stood quietly up to this point, but now took a step forward saying, "There's no need to get nasty. We were just doing a little dancing. You got no call to be treating a lady like that."

"Is that right? Well, this is none of your business, so I suggest you just walk away. Unless you want me to help you out."

Belle moved between the two young men saying, "Tad that's enough! I'm coming. Bill, thanks for the dancing, but I need to get back now." With that she began walking back toward the Midway. Tad and Bill continued to glare at each other for a few minutes until Belle turned and shouted, "Tad, I thought you said there was work to be done!"

The summer passed quickly for Belle. Her mind frequently returned to the good looking guitar player in Oklahoma. Dancing with him that night had seemed a bit like something from a fairy tale. She wondered if she would ever get to see him again. She liked everyone connected with the carnival, but felt restless and wanted to move on to something better. During their stay at the winter camp, she learned the carnival would return to the town in Oklahoma where she danced with Bill. She did a lot of daydreaming about him, wondering if he was going to get to Nashville this year, as he hoped. "It would be great if I could go with him," she thought, then panicked that he might have already left.

The carnival arrived at the Oklahoma town in early June. Belle was kept busy helping to get everything set up, but her mind was on getting to the bandstand to see if Bill was playing again this year. Things slowed down at the carnival by mid-afternoon, allowing Belle time to slip away. The music sounded familiar, as she neared the bandstand. Then she saw Bill playing with his group. She made her way up close to the bandstand, and was able to catch Bill's eye, giving him a huge smile, and a wave. As soon as the band took a break, Bill hurried over to Belle. "Hello, Belle. You're back."

"Sure am. Your music sounds great."

"Well thanks. So where all have you been this past year?" he asked.

"Oh, all over I guess. Always on the move, you know. Except for the winter months, of course. We set up camp near Corpus Christi in Texas, then. So how's your plans for Nashville coming?"

"I'm going! Finally, tomorrow in fact."

"Oh, that's so great. Wish I could be going with you. Nashville sounds like an exciting town." Just as Belle's thoughts often involved Bill the past year, he often dreamed of Belle and the dance they had shared. Partly on impulse, partly because he wasn't looking forward to making the trip to Nashville alone, he said, "Well, then, I think you should come with me. We'd make a great team. You don't have a permanent tie to the carnival do you?"

"Well, no, not really," she replied.

"OK, then. It's settled. You're coming with me."

For just a moment Belle had no ready reply, something that didn't often happen with her. She quickly recovered. "Oh, would I ever love to, but I don't have any money to help with the travel expenses. I just work for room and board for Big Joe."

"Who's Big Joe?" Bill asked.

"He owns the carnival."

"Well, that sounds like all the more reason you should come with me. I can manage the travel expenses, and I'm sure you could find a job once we get to Nashville, so's you could have your own money. Doesn't that sound better than workin' for room and board? Heck, that's close to being a slave."

"I never thought of it that way, but I guess you're right." She paused briefly then said, "OK, I'll come with you."

"Great! Now how are we gonna manage getting you away from the carnival?"

"We'll be packing up tonight and leaving around daybreak tomorrow. I could probably slip away late tonight after everyone is asleep. Where would I find you?"

"How about you come to the water tower. It's not far from my house. I could wait near the carnival, but somebody might see me and think I was up to no good. I sure wouldn't want any trouble, just before I'm set to leave. Just before *we're* set to leave."

"It might be midnight or later before I can get there," Belle cautioned.

"Not a problem. I'll be there before midnight and wait for you. This is gonna be great."

"I'd better be getting back. I won't come to the dance tonight. No need to give anyone cause to wonder if I'm up to something," said Belle.

"Well, I'll miss dancing with you, but then I guess we'll have lots of opportunities to dance once we get to Nashville. See you later tonight, Belle."

With that, Belle hurried back to the carnival. The Midway was getting busy again, so she began wandering around, waiting for the right moment to go into her act.

She hadn't been entirely truthful with Bill about not having any money. It was true she didn't get a salary from Big Joe, but Tad would often give her a small tip when the take had been extra good. She'd been able to save a few dollars in the past year.

It was nearing 11:00 p.m. before all the preparations for leaving in the morning had been completed. Belle shared sleeping quarters with Stella and knew she was a sound sleeper, so there would be no problem slipping out and getting away. She managed to tuck her things away while everyone was busy getting everything ready to leave in the morning. By midnight, Stella was snoring loudly. Belle waited a while longer to be sure no one else was still up in the camp. She left a note for Stella thanking her for all her help, telling her she was tired of carnival life and was taking an opportunity to move on to something better. The full moon allowed her to easily make her way to the water tower. The night was soft and warm with crickets serenading her on the way. Bill saw her coming before she saw him and called softly to her.

"Over here, Belle. Gosh, I'm glad you're coming with me."

"Me too, Bill. I can't wait to see Nashville and watch you playing on a stage there."

When they reached Bill's house, he told her she could have his bed and he would take the couch.

"My dad's a sound sleeper and likes to sleep late in the morning, so he may not even be up before we leave."

There was a distinct odor of beer in the house, and snoring could be heard coming from the back bedroom.

"Sleep well, Belle. We've got a long day ahead of us tomorrow. The train leaves at 7:00 a.m. I'll get you up in plenty of time."

"I'm so excited that I'm not sure I'll be able to sleep much," she replied.

In spite of her excitement, Belle dropped off to sleep quickly, sleeping soundly until Bill shook her arm gently at 5:30. They had a quick breakfast of bread and butter plus a hard boiled egg, then set off for the train station. Bill bought two tickets and soon they were on their way.

The train ride to Nashville lasted two long days. They were both felt weary and gritty when they arrived at midday. A traveling musician had given Bill the name and address of a rooming house, telling him the rates were reasonable. They found their way to it with little difficulty, stopping only once to ask directions from a street vendor.

When Bill enquired about rooms, he was told there was only one available.

"We can't rent that to you two unless you're married. This here is a respectable establishment."

"Well sir, you see, that's what we're here for, to get married."

"Sorry, but unless you're already married, I can't let you have the room."

"But we're meeting with the preacher later today."

"You come back here after you do and show me the piece of paper. If the room's still available then, you can have it."

"How about you rent the room to me now, and we'll come back to move in after we're married?"

"Well, I reckon that would probably work, but you gotta pay for the room now, and there won't be no refund if you can't show me the marriage license."

"Fair enough. What's the rate for a week?"

"$5.00."

Bill paid the $5.00, then asked if they could leave their bags with him. He wasn't willing to take a chance with his guitar though and took it along when they left.

As soon as they were a short distance down the street, Bill stopped and turned to Belle. She had not uttered a word since the bizarre conversation at the rooming house.

"Belle, I know this seems a little crazy, but I just didn't know what else to do. My buddy told me rooms could be hard to come by here and a bit pricy. I just couldn't take a chance on not being able to find something I could afford. You understand don't you?"

"Well, marriage wasn't exactly something I'd planned on," she replied slowly. "And I'd kind of planned on having a nice wedding when the time did come."

"I know, Belle, but we've gotten along great these past few days haven't we? And we don't have to actually, um you know, be man and wife 'til you're ready. And if you decide later on that being married to me isn't such a bad idea, well, then I'll give you a really nice wedding celebration. Whaddya say?"

"Seems like I don't have a lot of choice. If I say no, you're out the $5.00 you paid for the room. And I'm dog tired and rotten dirty, so let's just find a preacher so we can go back to the room."

"Ah, thank you, Belle. I really am sorry, but I just didn't know what else to do. We passed a church a couple blocks back on our way here. Let's head for there."

The church was a small, white frame building with the standard steeple. A sign in front told them it was The Lamb of God Baptist church. The day was warm and muggy, and when they stepped through the front door, the air inside felt even heavier. It took a minute for their eyes to adjust to the dim light.

Belle spoke softly, "I don't think there's anyone here, Bill."

Bill took a deep breath, cleared his throat, and said, "Is there anyone here?" The sound of his voice seemed to echo through the empty space, but in a moment a door opened to one side of the pulpit and a short, balding gentleman in a dark suit walked through.

"What can I do for you Brother and Sister?" he asked.

"Well sir, uh, Reverend, we'd like to get married," Bill replied. "My name's Bill Dawson and this here's Belle Mericle."

"So, you're here to find out when the church is available?"

"Well, uh, no Reverend. We'd kinda like to get married today."

"Is that right? And just why did you pick this church?"

Bill started to reply, but Belle interrupted saying, "Reverend we've just arrived in Nashville. My Bill here got an offer to come to Nashville to work at the Grand Ole Opry, maybe even get to play his guitar, but we had to leave Oklahoma in a hurry 'cause they said they couldn't hold the job for him very long. We didn't have time to get married before we left, but I promised my ma we'd get married soon as we got to Nashville. That's why we're in this state of disrepair."

"Sister Belle, marriage is a serious thing. You sure this ain't just a spur of the moment thing with you two?"

"Oh, no, Reverend. We've been in love for some time. Our folks gave their blessing, but we were waiting 'til Bill could get a better job to support us. Then this offer came up real sudden, and we just had to get here in a hurry."

"Well, there's also the matter of witnesses. We need two, and my fee is $3.00 Can you pay that?"

"Yes, sir, I can," Bill quickly replied. "Do you maybe have someone in the office that could stand as our witnesses?"

"This here's a small church, son. I don't have any office staff." The minister paused a bit, then said, "Let me go next door to ask my wife and see if our neighbor, Sister Walker, might be able to help out."

"Oh, thank you, Reverend! We'd be so grateful," added Belle.

"You two wait right here. I'll be back shortly."

"You're pretty quick on your feet with your thinking," Bill said to Belle once the minister was gone. "And pretty convincing too."

"Well, I'm tired, hungry, and dirty, and I just want to get back to the room to rest a bit and clean up. I don't want to have to traipse all over Nashville trying to find somebody to marry us," she replied rather snappishly.

Belle's obvious short temper surprised Bill, and he wisely refrained from saying any more. In a few minutes, the minister returned with two ladies.

"Well, Brother Dawson, Sister Mericle, I believe we're about to have a wedding. This is my wife, Sister Jackson, and this is our good friend and neighbor, Sister Miller. Now, you two come over here, and stand by the altar.

"Brother Bill, do you take Sister Belle to be your wife, to love, honor, and cherish til death do you part? If so say, 'I do'."

"I do."

"Sister Belle, do you take Brother Bill to be your husband, to love, honor, and obey 'til death do you part? If so, say, 'I do'."

"I do."

"Then in the name of the Father, the Son, and the Holy Ghost, I pronounce you man and wife. You may kiss the bride."

There was the slightest hesitation before Bill shyly kissed Belle on the lips.

"Congratulations, Mr. and Mrs. Dawson. Now, if you'll give me my fee, I'll write up the marriage paper for you. You'll have to take it to the courthouse on Monday to register it, so's it's all nice and legal, but you are rightfully married now."

Bill paid him the $3.00 and waited while the marriage certificate was filled out. When Reverend Jackson handed it to Bill, Belle spoke up saying, "Thank you Reverend Jackson. We'll never forget your kindness."

"Well, you two just go on and have a good life now. And come back tomorrow for Sunday services. I'll introduce you to our congregation."

"Thank you, Reverend, we surely will," said Bill.

Bill put the marriage certificate in his pocket, and they began walking back to the rooming house. Both were quiet, lost in their own thoughts about what had just happened. When they reached the rooming house, the manager looked a bit surprised to see them.

"Y'all made it back I see. So are you two hitched now?"

Bill handed him the marriage certificate.

"I know the Reverend Jackson," said the manager. "Guess you two are legitimate, now. Here's your room key. It's the first room at the top of the stairs. There's a pitcher of water and a basin in the room. The pitcher is filled every morning, but if y'all want more than that, it's up to you to get it. The pump's just outside the back door there, along with the privy. The bed clothes get washed once a week on Mondays, and we don't allow no drinkin' or smokin' in the rooms. Any questions?"

"No, sir. That sounds just fine. We'll just take our bags now and get settled in."

The room held one bed, one chair, plus a dresser with the wash basin and pitcher of water. There was one towel, one washcloth, and a bar of soap.

"Bill, I really need to wash up a bit. Will you go sit in the lobby for a bit while I do that?"

"Sure, Belle. How long do you think you'll need?" asked Bill.

"Oh, I reckon about twenty minutes should do it."

"Well, I'll see you in twenty minutes then."

When Bill reached the lobby, the manager looked up from the newspaper he was reading and raised an eyebrow.

"The missus wants to freshen up a bit, and she's still a little shy," explained Bill.

The manager only nodded and returned to his reading.

When Bill returned to the room, he suggested Belle lie down with her back to him while he cleaned up. "Then we'll both just rest a bit before we go out to find something to eat."

Belle dozed off, almost immediately. It seemed she'd only just closed her eyes when Bill gently shook her saying, "Belle, I think we should go find some supper before it gets any later. They found a hotel with a dining room a short walk away. During the meal, Bill suggested they do some walking and exploring tomorrow, then set out to find work for both of them on Monday.

When they returned to the room, the fact that there was only one bed hit them both at the same time. They stood silent for a moment. Bill recovered first and said, "Belle, you take the bed. I can sleep just fine on the floor." Belle looked around for a moment, then said, "But that doesn't seem fair. You paid for the room."

"Now, Belle, there's no way I'm gonna let a lady sleep on the floor. I told you we don't have to really be man and wife 'less you want to."

"Well, I am still really tired," she replied.

"OK then, that's settled. I'll turn my back while you get into bed."

Belle slept soundly, not hearing the tossing and turning Bill did throughout the night. When morning came, she noticed his eyes looked heavy, and he had a bit of a haggard look. They spoke little, both being careful to keep their backs turned while dressing.

When they entered the lobby, the manager greeted them with a sly mile, saying "Mornin' Mr. and Mrs. Dawson. I expect you'll be wanting to find someplace for breakfast?"

"That does sound good," replied Bill.

"Well, there's a street vendor a couple blocks over that sells some darn good coffee and pastries."

"That sound OK to you Belle?" Bill asked.

"It sounds really great," she replied.

After they enjoyed some hot, black coffee and a large pastry, they wandered around the town for a couple hours. It was a soft, June morning with a gentle breeze. The temperature was comfortably warm. The streets were mostly quiet, other than the occasional street vendor and the sound of church bells.

"I think this is gonna be a good move, Belle. It just feels right."

"It certainly is peaceful and pretty here," she replied.

By late morning, they began making their way back to the rooming house.

"Bill, would you play your guitar for me this afternoon?" asked Belle.

"Be more than happy to. It's been too long since I've played anyway."

When they returned to the room, Bill picked up his guitar and sat on the chair, while Belle propped herself up on the bed. Bill had only played a couple of songs when there was a soft knock on their door. As Bill opened the door, he was greeted by a white haired gentleman dressed in a suit.

"Pardon me sir, but I couldn't help but hear your playing and singing. You sound right good. I was wonderin' if you'd consider coming down to the lobby to play. I think there's some others here who would surely enjoy listening to your music."

"Well, I guess I could do that for a little while, if it's OK with my wife, Belle," he replied, looking towards her.

"I think that sounds like a fine idea Bill."

"That's very kind of you and I know it will be much appreciated by the others. My name is Edward Douglas."

"Pleased to meet you, sir. I'm Bill Dawson and this is my wife, Belle."

There were a half dozen others waiting in the lobby. Introductions were made, and Bill played several songs.

Everyone seemed to thoroughly enjoy his music, and when he stopped playing the conversations were lively.

"Where in the world did you learn to play like that?" asked Mrs. Billings.

"Oh, I guess I just kinda picked it up here and there," Bill replied. "My daddy had a guitar and I started playing on it when I was almost too little to hold the dang thing. Guess it's just in my blood."

"You're not from around here are you?" asked another gentleman.

"No sir, I'm from Oklahoma."

"So, just what brings you to Nashville?"

"Why my music, of course. I'm hopin' to find work playing with a group and eventually go on the road."

"That right? And what have ya'all been doin' to make a livin' up til now?"

"Well, I worked in a blacksmith shop, but music's the only thing I've ever really wanted to do."

"Well, I certainly wish you luck son. It can be a hard business to get into."

By now, it was nearing evening, and people began taking their leave to go find someplace to eat. As Belle and Bill began walking toward the stairs another well-dressed gentleman who sat quietly during the little concert approached Bill saying, "Son, my name is George Forsythe. I certainly enjoyed your music. I'd be honored if you and your wife would be my guests for dinner at the hotel tonight."

"Well, sir, thank you very much, but that's really not necessary." replied Bill.

"Well, maybe not strictly necessary, but I would surely enjoy the company, and I know a few people in the music business. Might be we could find some common ground."

"That's very kind of you, Mr. Forsythe," said Belle. "We'd be honored to join you for dinner."

"Well good. It's settled then. Let's plan on meeting in the lobby of the Carter Hotel over on Magnolia Street. Is 6:00 OK with you?"

"That will be just fine Mr. Forsythe," said Belle. "We will see you shortly."

George Forsythe's comment about knowing a few people in the music business turned out to be an understatement. He owned a business that booked musical acts into various clubs in the area. While the three of them enjoyed a delicious meal in the quiet dining room of the hotel, he told Bill how impressed he was with his music. "I don't think you will have any problem finding steady work," he said, then added, "Bill your playing is exceptional, but solo acts generally aren't in as much demand as groups. I've got a couple other boys who have great promise too and I believe the three of you just might be a good fit. What do you think?"

"Well, Mr. Forsythe, that sounds like a real possibility. Guess I'm just a bit dazzled with all this happenin' so fast. We only just arrived here yesterday."

"Seems to me like maybe the gods are smiling on you, Bill. Why, if you hadn't chosen that particular rooming house, our paths might never have crossed. Of if I hadn't decided to stop in there this afternoon for a chat with my friend, Clark. He's the manager of the house you know."

Things moved quickly after that meeting. The two other musicians were a good fit with Bill. One played banjo and a harmonica, the other a bass guitar. Very soon, they were able to stay busy playing at various clubs.

Belle found work as a waitress in a small café. She enjoyed the interaction with her customers and soon came to know many of them by name.

Belle soon convinced Bill he need not sleep on the floor, telling him there was no reason they couldn't remain just friends and still share the same bed. She managed to hang a curtain of sorts in one corner of the room to provide each of them a bit of privacy when dressing.

After a few months, Bill suggested they could afford to find more comfortable living quarters. It didn't take them long to locate a small house for rent that they could afford. Belle found she enjoyed playing the part of a housewife. They continued to share a bed, keeping their relationship on a friendship basis.

One night after supper, Belle said, "Bill, I've been thinking. You and me get along really good, and I care a lot about you. I was wonderin' if you might still be interested in us having a real marriage?"

Bill was silent for a moment, then said, "Belle, there's just not much I would rather have. I've been havin' a hard time keeping my hands off you, but I really wanted to keep the promise I made when we got married. I haven't forgotten the rest of my promise either, about giving you a real nice wedding celebration. Maybe George could arrange for us to use the dining room at the Carter Hotel. I'll talk to him tomorrow, and you go out and buy yourself a real pretty dress."

With that, he got up, took her in his arms, and gave her a long kiss. Belle had a dreamy look when the kiss ended. Bill softly said, "Hello, Mrs. Dawson. I do believe it's time we go to bed."

Bill spoke to George the next day, explaining that he and Belle had not been able to have a real wedding, and he now wanted to make it up to her by having a nice celebration. George was generally all business. Only a very few people glimpsed his softer side. He was very fond of both Bill and Belle and immediately began talking about plans for the celebration. "Bill I know you've been doin' well for yourself with your music, but I'd be honored if you'd allow me to give you this celebration as a wedding gift."

"George, that's very generous of you, but it's too much."

"No such thing, my boy. It will be my pleasure. Consider it done."

"George, I just don't know how to thank you," said Bill.

"No need. None at all. Now, let's see when we can get space at the hotel."

Belle went shopping for a dress, as Bill suggested. She wasn't exactly sure what she was looking for, but walking past a small shop, she spotted a dress in the window that took her breath away. It was white taffeta with a low cut scoop neckline. The skirt was full, ending in a large ruffle. The sleeves were full and made of the sheerest chiffon. Woven through the bodice and trailing down the skirt were tiny, pale blue ribbons. She stood gazing at it for the longest time, then reluctantly moved on. She was sure it cost much more than she could afford. Two hours later, she was back in front of the store. Every other dress she'd seen that day seemed dowdy compared to that one. She took a deep breath and stepped through the door.

"Good afternoon," said a woman who looked about fifty. "What can I do for you today?"

Belle took a breath and told her how she and her husband had not been able to afford a real wedding when they got married. Things were better for them now. He was working steady at his music, and they decided to have a small celebration. "I'm looking for a nice dress and just couldn't take my eyes off the one in the window. Is it terribly expensive?" she asked. The price made Belle's heart sink. "Oh, I was afraid of that. I really don't think I can afford to spend that much"

"Well, I'm sure I can find a very nice dress for you that doesn't cost quite so much. My name is Flora Downing."

"Pleased to meet you Mrs. Downing. I'm Belle Dawson."

"Oh, please, call me Flora. Everyone does."

Belle and Flora looked at several other dresses. Belle tried on a couple, but her eyes kept returning to the window. While trying on the dresses, Belle had kept up a lively conversation with Flora, telling her about Bill and his music, and talking about her job at the café. Flora noticed how Belle kept looking at the dress in the window and sighing when trying on the other dresses.

After thinking about it for a short time, she said to Belle, "Dear I can see your heart lies with the white dress, and you'll be disappointed with anything else you might find. I'll let you in on a secret. That dress was made to order for a young woman who was to be married, but circumstances I won't go into prevented the wedding, and I didn't have the heart to make her take the dress and pay for it. Some people know its' history and are reluctant to buy it because of that, but if the story doesn't bother you, I'll be happy to sell it to you for a price you can afford."

"Oh, Flora! I don't know what to say. That is so kind of you. I do dearly love the dress, and I'm not superstitious. How much will you want for it?"

Flora named a price that Belle could meet. Flora wrapped the dress well, and Belle rushed home on feet that seemed to float over the sidewalks.

Bill was there when she got home. As soon as she came in the door, Bill said, "Belle, I've got some great news. We've got space at the Carter Hotel a week from Monday. George insists on paying for the party. Says he considers it our wedding gift. Whaddya think of that?" Noticing the large package she was carrying, he asked, "Did you find a nice dress?"

"You stay right here, and don't come to the bedroom. I'll be right out, and you can tell me if I found a nice dress." Without waiting for him to answer she rushed into the bedroom, quickly changed into her new dress, fluffed her hair, and walked back out to the kitchen. Bill had his back to her when she entered the room. She struck a pose and said, "Well?"

Bill turned and stared for a moment, then slowly said, "Lord amighty, Belle. You are a real vision. That is the most beautiful thing I've ever seen. No, you are the most beautiful thing I've ever seen."

Belle twirled around, the blue ribbons on the skirt gently flaring out. "I know it looks really expensive Bill, but it wasn't." Then she quickly told him the story.

"Well, I'd say that dress was just waiting for you, then," he replied. "Now, I really can't wait for the party, so's I can show you off." Belle suddenly remembered she was barefoot. "Oh, Bill, I think I'm gonna need some shoes for this dress."

"Well, then we'll find you some shoes."

Belle asked her neighbor, Jane Billings, where to go to find shoes that weren't too expensive. She explained about the party and the dress and invited Jane and her husband, Dan, to come. Jane looked at Belle's feet and asked what size shoe she wore.

"I think a six, but to be honest, it's been a long time since I bought shoes."

"Well, that's what size I wear," replied Jane. "I have a pair I've hardly worn. I'd be happy to lend them to you, if you like. Would you like to try them on?"

"Jane, what a nice offer. Are you sure you wouldn't mind?"

"Not a bit. Let's go take a look." The shoes fit fine, and Belle accepted the offer. "Would you like to see the dress?" she asked. Jane was suitably impressed with the dress. She recognized it and knew the story, but said nothing to Belle, assuming she didn't know.

The party was a big success. Forty people attended: musician friends and acquaintances, a few of Belle's customers, and a few people from the rooming house. Most of the musicians brought their instruments, playing solo or in impromptu groups. Nearly everyone took advantage of the music and danced, none more than Belle. She quickly discovered that even though Jane's shoes seemed to fit, they were not comfortable to dance in. So she did what seemed the only logical thing to her and took them off, dancing in her stocking feet. This brought raised eyebrows from some of the ladies and grins from the men. Belle was aware of this and could not have cared less. She was having the time of her life.

The party wound down by midnight. Many of the guests needed to be at work in the morning, as did Belle.

Chapter Four

After the wedding celebration party, Belle decided to write home to let them know she was married and things were fine with her. She addressed it to her mother. A couple weeks later she had a reply.

> Belle,
>
> We all had figured you was dead by now, so your letter was a bit of a shock. Ma passed a few months ago. You know she had been feelin' poorly for a while and after you disappeared, she just kind of withered away. David is married to Ann Granger and they are living here. Ray is living in Seward, working at a livery. Lizzie married Charles, and they are living with his folks. Pa won't allow no one to speak of you. If he had seen your letter before me, we still wouldn't know you was alive. If you write again send it to Lizzie Grubaugh. I'm glad to hear you are married.
>
> Your sister,
> Mae

Belle sat staring at the letter for a long time. Her mind was a jumble of thoughts tumbling over each other so fast she couldn't hold one long enough to fully consider it. The mail had come shortly after noon, and when Bill came home, she was still sitting at the table holding the letter.

He walked in the door saying, "Hello darlin', what's for supper?" then saw there didn't seem to be any cooking going on. "Belle, what's the matter? Are you all right?"

Belle seemed surprised to see him standing there, then slowly replied, "I had a letter from my sister today," and held the letter out to him. After he read it, he came and put his arms around her saying, "Belle, I'm really sorry." Belle only nodded, saying nothing. "Come on, let's go to the café for a bite to eat. Then we can talk about what you want to do."

Belle remained quiet throughout the meal, while Bill chatted about his day and how the rehearsing for a couple of new songs was going. When they finished eating and Belle still seemed quiet, Bill asked, "Belle, would you like to go visit your family?"

"I don't know Bill. It sounds like they really don't want to see me, and you can't just leave the band high and dry that long."

"Well, no, I couldn't, I guess. That's no reason you couldn't go. I'm sure your boss would give you the time off when he hears about your mama. I'm sure things will be fine once they see you."

"You really think so? I'm not so sure."

"Well, Mae did write back to you didn't she? I think it would be a good thing for you to go visit."

"Well, maybe. I just can't think right now."

"You sleep on it tonight, and things will look better in the morning."

It took Bill a couple days of encouraging her to go before she reluctantly agreed. She wrote to Ray, who agreed to pick her up at the train in Seward and take her to the farm.

She was weary when she arrived after two and-a-half days of traveling by train. Ray seemed genuinely pleased to see her.

"Gosh, Belle, it's good to see you. How was your trip?"

"Long. I'm a little worn down," she replied.

"Would you like to stop at my place to wash up a bit before we go to the farm?"

"That sounds good. Thanks."

Once they were on the road, Ray said, "Mae tells me you're married. Tell me about him."

Belle gave him a glowing report about Bill, his music, their friends, and her job at the café.

"Where did you meet him? Is he the one you ran away with?" asked Ray.

"No, I left with the carnival, then met Bill at one of the stops in Oklahoma."

"The carnival! Why in the world would you do that?"

"Oh, Ray, I just had to get away from the farm and that was the only way I could think of at the time. You left the farm, too, so you should understand."

"Well, yeah, I guess I do sort of, but the carnival Belle! You could have been in danger."

"Oh, Ray, they were good people, really. Just a little different. I never planned on staying with the carnival, permanently. Anyway, it worked out fine, so let's just leave it. Ray, do you think Pa is gonna want to see me?"

Ray paused a moment, then said, "Well, we haven't told him you are coming. He took your leaving pretty hard, and you know how single minded he can be. It'll be a bit of a shock, but I'm sure he'll come around."

"What about Lizzie?" she asked.

"Well, that's hard to say. She was always close to Ma you know, and she took her passin' pretty hard. I think she blames you some for that."

"But Ray, Ma was feelin' poorly a lot of the time even before I left."

"I know, Belle. You know our Lizzie's got a fair piece of Pa's hard side to her. Maybe, she's softened a bit, now that she's married and has a babe on the way."

"Lizzie's with child? Nobody told me that."

"Well, she is. She's about five months gone, now."

It was late June, and the weather was about as perfect as you could want. There was a soft breeze carrying the scent of new mown hay. A few puffy clouds decorated the sky, groups of birds seemed to welcome her with soft twittering each time they passed a grove of trees. They were both quiet for the remainder of the trip, each lost in their own thoughts.

When they reached the farm, they found that John and David were in the house just finishing their noon meal.

"Hello, everyone. Look who I found," said Ray. "Our Belle is married now, livin' in Nashville, and wanted to come home for a short visit."

All this was met with silence for a few moments. Ann broke the silence, saying "Hello Belle. It's good to see you."

At that, John stood up quickly saying, "You think you can just waltz back in here like nuthin's happened after what you put us all through? No you can not! You're not welcome here."

David said, "Now Pa," but John interrupted.

"That's enough David. It's time we got back to that hay," and stomped out of the house.

Mae spoke up, "I'm sorry Belle. You know how Pa can be. It's good to see you."

David said, "Belle, I better go catch up with Pa."

After David was out the door, Belle said, "Well, I guess I didn't expect anyone would be thrilled to see me. I just didn't think it would be quite this bad. Ray, maybe we better head back to Seward."

"Oh, now, come on Belle," said Mae, "Pa's gone. You can sit for a spell. Are you two hungry?"

"Well, I wouldn't turn down some food," replied Ray. "Come on, Belle, we can stay long enough to have a bite to eat."

Belle agreed, reluctantly, and Ann and Mae quickly got a couple more plates out. The conversation was a bit strained for awhile, but they did manage to get caught up on each of their lives. Belle asked Mae, "Where is Ma buried?" then asked Ray if they might swing by the cemetery.

"Sure thing, Belle, and it's close to Lizzie's place, so we could stop and see her too."

"Well, I guess I can take one more tongue lashing today. We just won't stay long."

They went to the cemetery first. Belle stood quietly by her mother's grave for a long time, then sighed, and said to Ray, "Well, let's get the rest of this visit over and then head back to Seward. Maybe, I can catch a train yet today."

When they arrived at the Grubaugh farm, Lizzie was at the clothesline, bringing the laundry in. She looked up when Ray and Belle pulled into the yard, but kept working.

"Hello, Lizzie, look who's here," Ray shouted. By now, her basket was full and she began walking towards the house.

"Well, if it isn't the world traveler," she said.

"Hello, Lizzie. How are you?" asked Belle

"Why are you here Belle?"

"Mae told me Ma died, and my Bill thought I should come home for a visit,"

"Did he? So, why didn't he come with you, or did you run away from him, too?"

"Lizzie, you know I never liked farm life. I had a chance to leave, and I took it."

"Well, that's just grand. Would be a sorry day if the great Belle had to put up with anything she didn't like. Never mind what other people have to do."

Belle's eyes narrowed, and she replied, "Lizzie, that's not fair!"

"Now, you listen to me, Belle. You broke Ma's heart when you up and disappeared, and it shortened her life, so don't whine to me about what's fair."

"Ray, let's go. I knew this was a bad idea."

"That's a good idea, Ray. Take your baby sister back to wherever she came from."

"Lizzie, don't be that way," Ray pleaded.

"I'm busy. Some of us have work to do that won't get done if we don't do it." With that Lizzie turned and walked in the house.

Belle was already in the wagon and spoke sharply to Ray, "Let's get going Ray so I can catch a train." Ray slowly walked to the wagon.

Once they were out on the road he said, "I'm really sorry, Belle."

"Don't be. Wasn't your doin'. Let's just forget it and get back to Seward."

It was nearing eight in the evening when they arrived in Seward. Ray was hungry, but Belle insisted on going to the train station first to see when she could get a train back to Nashville. There was nothing scheduled until mid-morning the next day. They went to a small café and had a quick supper. When they finished, Belle said, "Just take me back to the train station. I can sleep on a bench 'til the train comes."

"Don't be stupid, Belle! You're coming back to my place. You take my bed, and I'll sleep on the floor. I'm not havin' you sleep on a bench at the station."

"Ray, you have to work in the morning."

"And you have a long trip ahead of you. You're coming back to my place, and that's the end of it. I've had about all the arguing I can take for one day!"

Ray's place was a small, two room affair, the bed in the living area and a small kitchen. Little more was said between the two, as they prepared for sleep. Ray woke Belle early the next morning, saying he'd take her to the station before he went to work. They had a quick breakfast of coffee, bread, and cheese then left for the station.

"Ray, I'm sorry I was so crabby last night. Thank you for all you've done for me."

"Happy to do it, Belle. I'm just sorry things didn't go better, but I think Pa and Lizzie will come 'round after a little more time has passed."

"Yeah, well, we'll see. Will you write and tell me when Lizzie's baby arrives?"

"Course I will, Belle. You take care of yourself now. And next time, bring your Bill with you."

"Sure Ray. Bye now, and thanks again for everything."

"You're welcome. Take care."

Belle wired Bill telling him when her train was due in Nashville. She arrived at 10 p.m. on a Friday night. Bill was not waiting for her, but a very good looking man approached her saying, "Excuse me ma'am, but are you Mrs. Belle Dawson?"

"I am, and who might be asking?" she replied.

"Pardon me, ma'am. My name is Kenneth Sawyer. I'm an associate of Mr. George Forsythe. Bill had an important engagement tonight, and he asked me to meet you and escort you home. I hope I didn't give you any cause for alarm?"

Belle had lived in Nashville long enough that her somewhat harsh Midwestern Twang was slowly being replaced with the softer speech of the South, and she replied, "Why not at all, sir. You just surprised me a little. It's very kind of you to offer your service."

"Not at all, the pleasure is all mine. Please allow me to carry your bag." Offering his arm to her, he said, "My motor car is this way."

"You have a horseless carriage?" she asked.

"Well, yes, you could say that. Although the more correct term is motorcar. Here we are."

Parked just outside the station was a shiny black Benz Velo.

"My goodness. I've heard of these but have never been this close to one! It's quite impressive."

"Why, thank you. Allow me to help you in, and we'll be on our way. I understand your mother passed recently. Please accept my condolences."

"Thank you. Yes, she had been ill for some time. Do you know where I live?"

"Yes, George and I visited with Bill only a couple of days ago. George has big plans for Bill, but I'll let him tell you about that."

"Really! Well, now you've made me quite curious."

"Oh, it's only good news, I assure you. Your Bill is a very talented young man. Ah, here we are."

"Thank you so much, Mr. Sawyer. I hope we'll meet again when I'm not so travel weary."

Oh, I'm sure we will, and please call me Ken. Everyone does."

"Well, then, Ken, thank you once again, and good night."

Bill didn't get home until the wee hours of the morning. Belle was worn out, physically and emotionally, from her trip and didn't wake even when he got into bed with her. She awoke before him the next morning, and the smell of perking coffee woke him. He stumbled into the kitchen, red eyed, and with the odor of old booze on him.

"Belle, how was your trip? I'm surprised you came back so soon."

"There was absolutely no reason to stay longer. It was about as bad as I'd guessed it would be. You're a sorry lookin' sight. Guess you must have had a good time last night."

"It was a great show, Belle. Tell me about your trip."

"I don't want to talk about it. Tell me about the show."

"Belle, what happened?"

"I said I'm not gonna speak of it right now. So, what time did you get home?"

"It was late, 'bout 3, I guess. The show went really well, then George, Ken and me, and the boys got to talking. Belle, they want us to go on the road. Well, actually on the river. There's a fancy river boat, and they want us to go on it, playing for the entertainment in the evenings. We'd be gone two weeks at a time, but the money's really good, Belle."

"So are you gonna do it?" she asked.

"Well, yeah. See we leave a week from Friday."

"So, I'm supposed to just up and quit my job?"

"No, Belle, see, it would just be me and the boys. Belle, you know I'd hate being away from you that long, but this is a great chance.

There are important people who travel on that boat, and this could lead to something even better. George said he'd keep an eye on you while we're gone. You know, help out with anything you might need."

"Well, it sounds like you've made your decision, then."

"Belle, I just didn't think it would be smart to pass up this opportunity. I came to Nashville to make a real career of my music and I'm sure this is gonna be a big help in that. Please, don't be mad. I won't always be gone this much."

"Well, I hope not. I didn't get married so I could be alone half the time with some man old enough to be my father lookin' out for me."

Nothing more was said between the two of them about Bill's new endeavor over the next week. A few days before Bill left on the riverboat, he met her at the door when she came home from her job at the café. He was dressed in the fancy new outfit he'd bought to wear while performing on the riverboat.

"Belle, I have a surprise planned. Put on your best dress, we're going out for a fancy dinner. But that's not the surprise. You have to wait 'til dinner for that."

"You want me to wear my wedding dress?"

"Yep, that's the one! This is gonna be special. Now, come on, get dressed."

"Oh, all right, but why do I have to wait for my surprise?"

"Just 'cuz. Now come on, get ready."

Bill took her to a very nice restaurant and arranged to have a table in a quiet corner. After a very nice meal, he insisted they indulge in one of the desserts the restaurant was famous for. When they finished that special dish and were having coffee, Belle asked, "So was this dessert the big surprise?"

"Nope. This is the surprise," he said, as he handed her a small box. Inside was a diamond ring. It was made up of several small diamonds set in a rosette pattern and was the most beautiful thing she had ever seen. For a few moments, she quietly stared at it, while Bill sat beaming across the table.

"Do you like it, Belle? I always felt bad that you didn't have a wedding ring."

"Oh, Bill. It is just, amazing"

"Try it on, see if it fits," he urged. She did, and it fit perfectly. She sat, quietly, holding her hand out, turning it slightly so the candlelight produced flashes from the diamonds.

"Bill, I can't believe this."

"Well, honey, this is just a taste of what I'll be able to do for you when my music really takes off. When I'm gone you just look at that ring and remember that us being apart some is what allowed me to get it for you, and that I'll always come home to you."

"Ah, Bill, you've always been so good to me. I'm gonna miss you."

"And I'll miss you every minute I'm gone."

The two weeks Bill was gone passed slowly for Belle. Early evenings were the worst. The longer shadows of late afternoon, the sounds of children being called in from play for supper, the faint smell of cooking on the breeze, all combined to produce a feeling of melancholy. The weekend seemed to last forever. She didn't feel she could go over for a visit with her neighbor and intrude on their family time. She tried going for a long walk, but all she could see were couples strolling together or families playing in the parks. She returned home feeling lonelier than ever.

Bill arrived home late in the evening on the second Friday. She had baked his favorite cake for him and ran to meet him, when he opened the door.

"Oh, Bill, it's good to have you back. I've baked a chocolate cake for you." Bill gave her a long hug, and said, "Gosh, thanks, but I don't want any right now. I'm just tired and glad to be home."

"Well, maybe later, then. Sit down and tell me all about it."

"Oh, there's not a lot to tell. We'd play in the grand ballroom every evening, starting shortly after they began serving the meal. Sometimes people would get up and dance after they finished eating, but mostly they were just busy visiting and didn't pay much attention to us. Makes it hard to keep any enthusiasm going."

"Well, what did you do during the day?" she asked.

"Tried to sleep mostly. Our rooms were back next to the engine room, and it was really noisy."

"Can't you ask for different rooms next time?"

"No, Belle, they keep those for the paying customers. We're just the hired help."

"Well, what does everyone do during the day?"

"Belle, I'm really beat and just don't feel up to talking about it. I'm gonna go wash up a bit and hit the sack."

After waiting two weeks to have some company in the evening, Belle was disappointed and a bit put out. She didn't make an issue of it, figuring a good night's sleep would take care of it. Things were better in the morning and for the next week. Then it was time for Bill to leave again. Before he left he asked George if he could stop by to see Belle a time or two while he was gone, telling him she got pretty lonely in the evenings and on the weekend.

A few days after Bill left, Ken Sawyer stopped by to see Belle. "Good evening Belle. I hope I'm not intruding. I happened to be near your house and decided to stop in to say hello and see if there is anything you need."

"Why, hello, Ken. How nice to see you. No, you're not intruding at all. Would you like to come in for a cup of coffee?"

"Why, thank you, yes."

"What brings you to my neighborhood?" she asked.

"Well, to be honest, I wasn't actually in the neighborhood, but I had some business nearby and decided to stop by to say hello."

They sat and chatted easily about inconsequential things for a while, then Ken pulled out his pocket watch and said, "I'm afraid I'm taking up too much of your time."

"Not at all. I'm pleased to have someone to visit with. The evenings can be rather long with Bill gone."

"Belle, I hope I'm not being too forward, but would you like to have dinner with me this evening? Eating alone is not all that pleasant."

"Why thank you Ken, that would be very nice."

"Wonderful! Where would you like to go?"

"Oh, I'll leave that up to you. Bill and I don't go out that much."

"Very well. I know a place where the chef turns Southern cooking into an art form."

Ken had not exaggerated about the food. He'd taken the liberty of ordering for her: golden fried chicken, black eyed peas, sweet potato pie, and biscuits so light it seemed like you were holding a warm cloud in your hand. Belle didn't remember ever enjoying herself so much. Ken entertained her with stories of his travels in Europe; he described the Berlin Cathedral in wonderful detail, the impressive Brandenburg Gate, the opera houses of Vienna, and the home of Marie Antoinette, the Shoenbrun Palace. He was a gifted conversationalist and didn't monopolize the conversation. He encouraged her to tell him about her life. Belle was not above a little exaggeration, making her life on the farm sound like something out of a storybook, and had him laughing over stories of her time with the carnival.

During Bill's next two weeks of being on the river boat, George Forsythe stopped by one Sunday afternoon for a short visit with Belle. Her neighbor, Jane, invited Belle to join their family for a picnic near the river on Saturday. All this made these two weeks much easier than the first time Bill was gone. Because he was only in town for a week between his excursions on the riverboat, George was not booking any engagements for them. One evening after his second tour on the riverboat, Bill suggested they have dinner at the Carter Hotel. It was an especially warm evening, and both he and Belle were perspiring heavily by the time they neared the hotel. A few doors away from the hotel was a gift shop. When they reached it, Bill suddenly told Belle to wait for him a moment and hurried inside the shop, not giving her time to protest or ask for an explanation. When he returned in a few minutes, he handed her a tissue paper wrapped package.

"What's this?" asked Belle.

"It's a present for you. Go ahead, open it."

Inside was an elegant ivory and silk ladies' fan, painted with delicate blue forget-me-nots.

"What's the occasion, Bill?"

"Because it's such a warm evening, and a fine lady like you should have something like this to cool herself with."

"Oh, Bill, it's so elegant! I'm sure you spent too much money on it."

"No such thing. You're worth it, and I can afford it. Now let's go have dinner, and you can impress all the ladies there with your beautiful fan."

Ken and George each continued to stop to visit with Belle at least once, during the times Bill was gone. When Bill arrived home from his fourth tour he seemed especially tired and looked a bit haggard. He remained a bit short tempered during the week he was home. He tried explaining it away, saying he just wasn't sleeping well on the boat. Belle wasn't entirely convinced this was the reason, and spoke to George about it the next time he stopped by.

George reassured her that Bill probably just had an off week. "It happens with musicians you know, Belle. I'm sure he'll be fine when he gets back this time."

Bill was not only fine the next time, but also brought Belle a beautiful shawl.

"Bill, you are spending too much money on me," she protested.

"No such thing, Belle. I have a confession. I've been making some extra money playing cards in our free time."

"Oh, Bill. I don't think that's a good idea. What if you lose?"

"Now, Belle, don't worry. I know how to handle myself. If I stay up late playing cards after the band is done, I don't have so much trouble sleeping through all the engine noise." What he didn't tell her about was the several shots of whiskey he had during the card games. With enough whiskey in him, he found he could sleep through almost anything.

Belle continued to occasionally have dinner with Ken and delighted in listening to his stories. When she asked him what kind of business he was in, he'd explained he "bought and sold things." "That's why I sometimes go to Europe, to bring back things that can't be found here."

"Like what?" she asked.

"Oh, elegant furniture, or china. Sometimes a few special pieces of jewelry I'm able to pick up at an estate sale."

It was two days before Bill was due back from his sixth tour on the riverboat when she heard Ken's motorcar pull up. When she went to the door, both Ken and George were there.

"Why, George, Ken, how nice to see you both. Come in, please, and I'll put some coffee on."

Neither man said anything as they stepped through the door. Belle started toward the stove saying, "To what do I owe the pleasure of having both of you here?" When she got no immediate response, she turned and noticed they were both looking solemn and uncomfortable.

"Belle," George began. "I'm afraid we have some very hard news for you."

The tone of his voice, the look on both their faces sent a chill down her spine. "What is it?" she asked.

"Belle, there was an incident on the boat and Bill . . . . "

"What happened?" she interrupted, panic beginning to set in.

"Belle, I'm so sorry. Bill was shot. I'm afraid he's gone."

There was a moment of silence before she said, "What do you mean he's gone? How could he have been shot? Where is he? I want to go see him now." Her voice had risen in volume with each question.

George reached out to take her hand saying. "Belle, I'm so sorry. Bill is dead. He was shot by a gambler."

"No, he's not, he's not! You take me to him right now," and she began to cry.

George put his arm around her while she continued to cry and kept saying, "He's not, he's not! I want to see him."

Ken spoke up saying, "Belle honey, you need to calm down." He pulled a flask from his coat pocket and poured a small amount of brandy in a glass, saying, "Drink this Belle. It will help."

She choked on it a bit, but did begin to calm down some.

"Please, George, where is he? Please take me to him."

The boat had returned early due to the shooting, and Bill had already been taken to the morgue. George helped her make the funeral arrangements, and when she continued to insist on knowing what had happened, he explained that Bill had been doing a lot of gambling and drinking. He lost badly one night and, in desperation tried to palm a card. Because he was more than a little drunk and had no experience at cheating, he was called on it by the professional gambler sitting at the game. Harsh words ensued, ending with the gambler shooting Bill through the heart.

Chapter Five

In the few weeks following Bill's funeral, Belle moved through her days in a fog. She still couldn't fully grasp that he was really gone, and would, sometimes, find herself thinking, "Only two more days and he'll be home from the riverboat." Her job at the café helped, but she soon discovered her wages would not cover her expenses. She thought briefly about selling her wedding ring, but couldn't bring herself to part with it. George and Ken continued to stop by frequently to see how she was getting along. During one of George's visits, she confided her money problems to him, asking if he could help her find a better paying job. He told her he would look into it, then insisted she take some money from him to help tide her over.

A few days later Ken stopped by. "Belle, George told me you are needing to find another job. I have a proposal for you. I feel my business might benefit from a woman's touch. I've watched and listened to you and can see you have a good eye for quality and good taste. I'd like to have you accompany me on my buying trips. I'm also considering expanding a bit by bringing back special fabrics, and I believe your help there would be invaluable. I could pay you a salary that I believe would meet your living expenses, plus a commission on the items we sell, providing some additional income for you. What do you think?"

Belle was silent for a moment, then said, "It's a bit overwhelming. I'm not sure what to say."

"Simple, just say yes. It would be a good deal for both of us."

"You really think I'd be that helpful? I've never been around really nice things. My ideas might not be so good."

"Belle, I've known women who have been wealthy all their lives and many of them equate good taste with a high price tag. Good taste isn't something you learn by being rich. It's something you either have or you don't, and you have it."

"You really think so?"

"I most certainly do. Please, accept this offer."

"Well, I doubt I could find a better one. If I accept, you must promise that if my 'good taste' doesn't live up to your expectations, you'll tell me and terminate my employment."

"Very well, you have that promise. One I know I won't be required to keep. I'm leaving for Europe in three weeks and I want you to accompany me. In the meantime, I'd like you to become familiar with my warehouse and some of my customers. You will need some different clothes for Europe and for the times that you will meet my customers, so I want to introduce you to Madame DuPree. She can accompany you on a shopping trip to offer suggestions about what you will need. The purchases will be billed to me and listed as operating expenses for my bookkeeping. You are not to be concerned with price, only with what you will need and what suits you best. Agreed?"

Belle's head was reeling a bit at all this, but she managed to maintain some composure and replied, "Agreed."

"Wonderful! Now, Sunday, I'll come pick you up at 2 o'clock to go meet Madame DuPree. The two of you can set a time for the shopping trip. I'd like to plan on you coming to the warehouse later next week, so you can become familiar with the type of things I acquire before we leave for Europe. Now, is there anything I can help you with before then?"

"No, Ken, I'm fine, thank you. I really should be getting to the café now. I'll need to tell my boss when I'll be leaving."

"Very well, until Sunday then."

Madame DuPree was a very elegant lady in her sixties. Belle was initially a little intimidated by her and the large, lovely home she had. Madame DuPree had the ability to put nearly anyone at ease though, and Belle soon relaxed and visited easily with her. They agreed on a time for the shopping, and Belle was informed that Madame DuPree would pick her up. At the designated time, a beautiful horse drawn carriage pulled up in front of Belle's house, and a gentleman in a uniform came to the door to escort Belle to the carriage.

"Good afternoon, Belle. Are you ready for some serious shopping?"

"Yes, Ma'am, I believe I am. This is a lovely carriage."

"Thank you. Some of my friends are telling me I should get a motor car, but I'm just not comfortable with that idea. I hope you don't mind."

"Not at all. Ken's is the only motor car I've ever been around. They are rather noisy aren't they?"

"Indeed. The noise makes it very difficult to have a conversation while traveling."

When the shopping was finished, Belle was returned to her home and had her many parcels carried into the house. She felt a little overwhelmed. The afternoon of shopping produced six dresses, three pair of shoes, two hats, two handbags, the necessary undergarments, plus luggage for the trip to Europe.

The next week-and-a half was a whirlwind of activity. Ken guided her through his warehouse, taking time to give a bit of history on some of the pieces, talking about his customers and the types of items each preferred or specialized in. He also filled her in on what he had paid for some of the pieces and what he expected to sell them for to his retail customers, adding that from time to time he was able to sell directly to a customer, which increased his profit margin even more. The prices made Belle's head spin. She didn't indicate that to Ken, but she was intrigued with the prospect of meeting people who were able to buy these items.

They boarded a train for Charlotte two days before the ship was scheduled to sail, giving them a night in Charlotte to rest from the train ride. Ken was well known at the hotel where they stayed, and the service was excellent. They had an early supper and retired to their separate rooms.

After bidding Ken good night and closing the door, Belle looked around her room and shook her head. "I just feel like I've fallen into some kind of fairy tale," she thought. "I can't believe I'm really going to Europe." Things moved so quickly in the past three weeks that there hadn't been time for all this to fully soak in. Ken had told her they might be gone as long as two months. Suddenly she remembered she never wrote to Ray to tell him that Bill had died. "I really need to write to him to let him know I won't be able to answer any letter from him for a while." Ken had explained that if she needed anything she could pull the bell cord in her room and someone from the hotel staff would get whatever she needed. She did so now to request some stationery, pen, and ink.

Dear Ray,

I have so much to tell you. I'm not sure how to start. Two months ago my Bill died. He was working as a musician on a riverboat and was shot by a gambler. I found I was not able to support myself on the salary from the café and asked Bill's manager if he could help me find another job. Another associate of his has his own business. He buys fine things from all over the world and re-sells them. He asked me to work for him, helping him choose items. Tomorrow morning, we sail for England and will travel to some other countries in Europe, as well. We might be gone two months. I still miss Bill but can't believe my good luck in finding this opportunity. I'll write again when we are back in Nashville.

> *Belle*

Ray read Belle's letter, then read it again. Belle was a widow and on her way to Europe? It was only a few days ago that he'd written to tell her Lizzie had the baby, a healthy boy. He guessed she hadn't gotten it before she wrote this letter. He didn't like the idea of her going off to Europe with some man but couldn't think of anything he could do about it now. In two days, he'd be going back home for the christening of Lizzie's baby. He wasn't sure if he should tell them about Belle's letter or not. Belle was still a very sore subject, especially with Lizzie and John. He kept hoping they would get over it, but so far, that hadn't happened. "Still they ought to know about this," he thought.

The day of the christening was chilly but sunny and pleasant. Ray waited until they returned from church and had dinner before he gave everyone the news from Belle's letter. There was a moment of silence before John spoke up in a tense voice.

"Ray, there was no need to bring that kind of news to a happy occasion like today. Belle removed herself from this family, and I see no reason why anyone here needs to be bothered with talking about her. You'd do well to remember that and not bring her name up in this house again. Is that clear?"

"Pa, she is your daughter. I thought you'd want to know."

"No sir! She is not my daughter. You forgetting her running off killed your mother? Now, this discussion is over, you hear?" John's voice had risen, and he slammed his hand down on the table with his last words. "Now, Ann, I think I'd like some of the apple pie I've been smellin' all morning."

The conversation was strained while dessert was served, and everyone seemed relieved when it came time to clear the table and the men retired to the living room. While the dishes were being washed Lizzie spoke up saying, "Leave it to that girl to cause problems, even when she ain't here."

"Now, Lizzie. You better not let Pa hear you sayin' anything about her," cautioned Mae. "Did I hear the baby crying?"

"He's probably getting hungry," replied Lizzie and headed off to the bedroom to nurse him.

As Ray was leaving, Mae managed to pull him to the side, and quietly say "Ray, you just got to remember not to bring up Belle when Pa or Lizzie is around. You can pass on news to me in letters if you like. I just can't help worrying about what's gonna become of her."

"I know, Mae, but I'm sure she'll be fine. She has been so far, in spite of all she's done."

Belle not only was fine, she was having a wonderful time. The ocean crossing was a smooth one. Belle spent a good deal of time standing on deck, looking over the railing at the never ending movement of the ocean. She found it very relaxing, and in some way, a bit mystical. Then there had been the glamorous evenings: splendid dinners with many foods she had never heard of, sharing dinner at the Captain's table one evening, the music, and dancing after dinner. The ballroom was on the second deck, and large enough to accommodate all 400 passengers. The floor was made of oak, set in a parquet pattern, and the room was lit by several crystal chandeliers. There was a large stage at one end of the room for the orchestra. Tables, covered with floor length white linen cloths, were arranged around the perimeter of the room, the chairs had padded seats covered in wine colored velvet.

Ken was a good dancer, but not as good as Bill had been. Bill had been able to lead Belle so effortlessly, it felt as if they were moving as one. With Ken, she had to concentrate a bit more to follow his lead. Her memory of dancing with Bill brought on a little sadness, but because of the festive air of the ballroom, and the several men besides Ken who wished to dance with her, she didn't have time to dwell on the sadness.

They had been in London a week now and acquired a number of beautiful items: a Chippendale dining set, exquisite porcelain pieces, and some fine English woolen fabric. Ken also allowed plenty of time for sightseeing. Buckingham Palace was a bit of a disappointment to Belle. The size of it, the grounds, and the palace guards were impressive, but the building itself lacked any sense of grace in its lines. Hesitantly, she voiced this to Ken, and he agreed. "The English often seem to place more emphasis on function rather than form," he said. Then he took her to Westminster Abbey to point out an exception to this. It was magnificent.

"My goodness, Ken, I can't begin to think how long it must have taken to build this." Even though Belle had rejected her farming heritage, much of the practical mind of a farmer stayed with her. The idea of someone designing a building of this magnitude and building it was more than she could comprehend.

"I don't know the exact number, but it took some years to complete," replied Ken.

Ken also took her to the church where Shakespeare was entombed. Miss Keller had referred to Shakespeare a few times, but Belle admitted to Ken she had never read any of his work. Ken bought a copy of *The Taming of the Shrew* and presented it to her, asking her to let him know how she liked it. The sightseeing he was doing with Belle was more than entertainment. He had been impressed with Belle's intelligence and poise from his first meeting with her, but knew she would need to have her education expanded, if she was going to fit comfortably into his world. He kept his relationship with her strictly on a business and friendship basis, so far, but he had plans to expand it to much more than that. Her combination of innocence, practicality, and inquisitiveness intrigued him, and he felt he would be hard pressed to find a more suitable, not to mention enchanting, woman for a wife.

The next day, they departed for Bath, one of the old Roman strongholds in England. "There is a merchant in Bath I've dealt with before. Often, he has an antiquity or two that will bring a good price in the States. I've also been told there is a small estate between here and there that is being auctioned for payment of debts. Have you heard of Stonehenge?" She confessed she had not. "Then I have a lovely surprise for you, as the estate in near Stonehenge."

They had been on the road for about four hours. It was a cool day with a light breeze. The countryside consisted of gently rolling hills with only a few groves of trees scattered here and there, mostly near small villages.

"Look to your right, Belle," suggested Ken. There in the middle of an otherwise barren plain stood a circle of giant stones. "That, Belle, is Stonehenge."

"But what is it?" she asked.

"No one knows for sure. The circle of stones date back beyond recorded history. Some say it was an area of Pagan worship." They stopped a short distance away from the circle. "Would you like to stretch your legs a bit and have a closer look?"

"I would indeed," she replied.

As they approached the circle, Ken continued, "One of the mysteries of this place is where the stones came from, since there is no place within a few hundred miles that has this kind of stone."

They reached the circle and walked through the center of it. They walked about in silence for a few minutes, then Ken asked, "Well, what do you think?"

Belle began feeling a little strange, shortly after walking into the center of the circle. She couldn't quite define it, though it was not an unpleasant feeling. As a result, her response came rather slowly.

"Ken, this really is a wonder isn't it? I almost feel as if I'm in a great cathedral."

"Yes, it can have that effect on you," he replied.

Slowly, they walked the circumference of the circle. Belle continued to be quiet and thoughtful and found she was unwilling to speak of her strange feelings to Ken. When they completed the circle, Ken suggested they continue on their way.

"The estate we are visiting is nearby. The auction isn't until tomorrow but a mutual acquaintance arranged for me to have this private showing, and if the price is agreeable, he is free to sell me anything I might choose." Belle turned to look back at the standing stones, as they continued on their way.

Ken found several pieces at the estate he wanted. A price was agreed upon, and arrangements were made to ship them to New York City.

"Why are you shipping them to New York City?" Belle asked.

"Oh, didn't I tell you? We'll be going there before we return to Nashville. I have a small warehouse there, and these are the things that will sell well in that area.

Ken acquired a few more things in Bath. From there, they made their way to the coast and boarded a ship that would take them across the channel to Waterford, Ireland. There they visited a factory that produced some very fine crystal.

Belle fell in love with the crystal. The president of the company took them on a tour of the factory, and in the showroom he demonstrated to Belle how you could tell crystal from ordinary glass by gently tapping it with the nail side of your finger, producing a lovely soft chime.

The next day, they boarded a ship bound for New York City. The second night out, Ken went to Belle's cabin to escort her to dinner. When she opened the door, Ken asked if he could come in for a moment. As he stepped inside, he handed her a small box wrapped in silver with a wine colored ribbon. "I have a small gift for you," was all he said.

"Oh Ken, how sweet. What is the occasion?"

"No special occasion, I just wanted to give you a little something extra to show my appreciation for all your help. Go ahead, open it."

Inside was a crystal vase from the Waterford company. A small rose was etched into its side.

"Oh, Ken, this is lovely. Thank you so much."

"I saw how much you admired the crystal, and your full name is Rosa Belle, isn't it?"

"Yes, it is. I don't remember telling you that."

"It came out one evening, when you were telling me stories of your life on the farm. It stayed with me, because Rosa Belle translates into 'beautiful rose'. I thought it was quite appropriate."

"That's very sweet of you to say so, Ken. I think I'll need to hand-carry this with me all the way home to be sure it doesn't get broken."

"You could do that, I suppose, but it might be more practical to use the heavy packing box I kept for it. Shall we go to dinner, now?"

Over the next few days, Ken and Belle spent nearly all their time in each other's company. It was their fifth day out, and Ken and Belle were standing at the rail watching the ocean, when Ken said, "Belle, unless you object, I've arranged for us to have a private evening meal in my quarters tonight. We've only two more days before we arrive in New York, and I'd like to spend an evening just with you. Is that agreeable?"

"Why, yes, that will be fine."

"Wonderful! I need to go let the steward know it's confirmed. I'll see you at seven in my quarters."

Belle continued to stand and watch the ocean, wondering what prompted Ken to arrange a private dinner for the two of them. Because she enjoyed his company so much and because he'd never been anything but a gentleman with her, she didn't give it a great deal of thought.

They finished the meal and were enjoying a second glass of wine that evening, when Belle said, "Ken, this has been such a lovely evening. I've really enjoyed visiting with you without the distraction of all the other passengers. Thank you for arranging this."

"It's been my pleasure. I have to confess I did have a bit of an ulterior motive. You have been a delightful companion on this trip and I greatly appreciate the opinions you've offered concerning the items I've acquired. I find I've fallen in love with you."

Belle sat stunned for a moment, and Ken hurried on. "I know you loved Bill and it's been only a short time since his death, but I believe time is an arbitrary thing and shouldn't be allowed to interfere with following your heart's desire. What I'm saying Belle, is that I want you to be my wife."

"Ken, I, well, I really don't know what to say. I know that sounds phony but it's true. I had no idea you felt we were anything more than friends and business associates."

"I understand. You've enchanted me from the moment we met. What could be a better basis for marriage than to have a good friend and business associate for my wife with the added bonus of loving her, of course? Do you think you could learn to love me in time?"

Belle was still a bit flustered and briefly fell back into her Nebraska speech pattern. "Well, I reckon I could. I've enjoyed this time with you, as much as you say you have."

"Do you think you could give me an answer tonight? I would so like to be able to announce our engagement while we are dining at the Captain's table tomorrow. I know I'm probably moving too fast, but I would love to be able to introduce you to people as my fiancée. Tell you what, let's take a stroll around the deck, get a little fresh air, and give you a little time to process all this."

"That sounds like a very good idea," she replied.

They walked quietly for a time. It was a beautiful moonlit evening and since nearly everyone else was in the main ballroom at dinner, they had the deck to themselves.

Belle was grateful for the quiet. It felt like her brain had deserted her. Either her thoughts were jumbled and bouncing so fast she couldn't follow them, or everything froze up and she couldn't think at all. Finally she said, "Ken, I really can't give you an answer tonight. Let me sleep on it, and I promise I'll give you an answer at breakfast tomorrow."

"Fair enough" he replied. Would you like to have another glass of wine?"

"No, I really think I need to go back to my room. I hope you're not upset?"

"No, it would take more than that for me to be upset with you."

As they arrived at the door to Belle's cabin, Ken leaned forward and gave her a gentle kiss on the mouth. "Good night, sweet Belle. I look forward to breakfast."

Belle sat in her cabin for a long time, staring at nothing, trying to organize her thoughts. Finally she got up to undress and get ready for bed. As she did she began talking out loud to herself.

"What in the world am I going to do? Ken is a wonderful man, but Bill has only been gone a little more than three months. If I say no to him, will he decide he doesn't want to keep me on as an employee? If that should happen, what could I do? Maybe he would be willing to wait a while for an answer. Oh, no, I promised him I'd give him an answer in the morning. Why did I do that? Of course this isn't the first time I've made a fast decision. I agreed to go to Nashville with Bill when I barely knew him. Ken can give me the kinds of things I've always dreamed of. I do love helping him find beautiful things to sell. I would really hate it if I couldn't continue to do that. Maybe we could have a long engagement. Surely he wouldn't object to that would he? I wonder what Ray would think of this? 'Course I know what the rest of the family would say! Well, who cares what they think. I think Bill would understand. I still love him, would that be fair to Ken? Bill's gone, how long do I need to put my life on hold because he's gone? What was it Ken said—"Time is an arbitrary thing." Can I really afford to say no to Ken and risk being completely on my own again? Oh pshaw! I can't think any more tonight. I'm going to sleep."

Belle's sleep that night was restless and full of dreams, the kind that hover almost within reach of your memory when you wake. By the time she was dressed, she had decided what she was going to tell Ken. He said he would escort her to breakfast, so she sat calmly waiting for his knock. When she opened the door, Ken greeted her with a tenuous smile saying "Good morning Belle. Are you ready?"

"I believe I am. Shall we go?" Ken offered his arm saying, "So are you going to be technical and make me wait until breakfast has been served for my answer?"

Belle couldn't resist teasing a bit and replied, "Well, I did say I'd give you an answer at breakfast, didn't I?" Ken sighed and said, "Indeed you did."

"I'm teasing, Ken. You can have your answer now. I would be honored to be your wife."

"Oh, Belle!" Ken swept her up in an embrace saying, "You've made me a very happy man. I promise you won't regret it."

They spent the entire day together, and when they parted to dress for dinner, Ken asked her to wear the blue velvet gown that evening, adding, "It does such wonderful things to your eyes, you know. I'll be by about 6:30."

"Why so early?" she asked. "Dinner isn't until 7:30."

"I know, but I have another small surprise for you."

She laughed and said, "You know you make me a little crazy."

"Ah, but 'a little crazy' only adds to your charm."

Ken was back promptly at 6:30. As he stepped into her cabin he said, "I won't keep you in suspense any longer. Here is your surprise," and handed her a small box. Inside was a pair of sapphire earrings.

"Oh Ken, these are so beautiful"

"Put them on. They will be perfect with your dress."

After she did, Ken said, "I do have one more surprise for you. I planned to give it to you last night, but that didn't go exactly as I'd hoped, so now you have two tonight." With that he took her left hand, removed her wedding ring and slipped a large diamond ring in its place, then handed the wedding ring to her. "Belle, I don't expect you to stop wearing Bill's ring. We can have it sized to fit another finger, but it would be a bit awkward to have a wedding ring from one man and an engagement ring from another on the same finger don't you think?"

"Yes, I imagine it would," she said slowly. "Ken, you really do overwhelm me at times."

"I know. I just have never had much patience for waiting when I know what I want. Do you like the ring? Because if you don't, we can return it, and you can pick out something you like better."

"Oh, no, Ken. It's wonderful! I can't imagine finding one I would like any better."

"Well, then, shall we go to dinner so we can share our good news with everyone?"

The dining hall was not quite as large as the ballroom, the floor covered with wine carpeting. The tables were draped with white linen, the wine colored linen napkins matched the carpet, and the velvet covered chair seats. The Captain's table was larger than the other tables, seating twelve. Tonight Ken and Belle were seated at this table.

As dessert was served that evening, Ken asked the Captain if he might intrude on the meal for a moment to make an announcement. "I want to share my good news with you. My good friend and valuable business assistant, Belle, has agreed to become my wife."

This was met with applause and a flurry of congratulations and good wishes. A few minutes later the Captain excused himself from the table and walked to the orchestra. Soft chamber music had been playing during the meal, but in a few minutes, there was a drum roll, and the Captain stepped on the stage.

"Ladies and Gentlemen, I have a happy announcement to make. I've just been informed by Mr. Ken Sawyer that Miss Belle Dawson has agreed to become his wife." When the applause died down, he continued, "Ken, Belle, would you two do the honor of starting the first dance of the evening?" With that, the orchestra began playing "The Blue Danube Waltz," and Ken led Belle onto the dance floor. They danced through two songs before returning to the table. Throughout the rest of the evening there was a steady stream of people stopping by the table to wish them well, along with several gentlemen asking for the pleasure of a dance with Belle. It was long past midnight before Ken and Belle returned to their cabins. As they stopped at Belle's cabin, Ken said, "Belle, I can't begin to tell you how happy you've made me today. We only have one more full day before we arrive in New York and I have a somewhat outlandish suggestion for you. Let's have the Captain marry us tomorrow."

"Get married tomorrow? Here?" she replied.

"Yes, I know it feels rushed, but the week we spend in New York is going to be a little hectic and this way we can at least have time together at night. I think a shipboard wedding would be rather romantic, don't you? I know it's not quite the same as having a big wedding back in Nashville, but we can have a grand wedding celebration party there after we return. Please say, 'Yes', Belle."

Belle looked at him for a few minutes, not saying anything. Finally, she sighed and said "I don't suppose you would be willing to wait until morning for an answer would you?" He smiled and said, "Not really."

"What if I say 'No?'"

"Well, I guess I would just have to live with that wouldn't I? Please don't, Belle. I promise you won't regret it."

She paused another minute or two, then sighed and said, "All right, Ken. I'm just too tired and overwhelmed to argue with you. If the Captain is agreeable, I'll marry you tomorrow."

"Ah, Belle, thank you. This will make a lovely memory, the first of many great memories we'll make together. I promise. You sleep as late as you like tomorrow, and I'll see you in the dining room whenever you are ready. Good night, my darling."

"Good night Ken. Until tomorrow." Belle was too tired to even begin processing the events of the past twenty four hours and fell asleep almost as soon as she lay down.

Ken was so sure he could talk Belle into this that he'd already made arrangements with the Captain. They would have the ceremony in the afternoon and use the dinner hour as a reception. It was tradition for the last evening meal on board to be an extra elegant affair. Ken played up the romantic aspect of a shipboard wedding to both the Captain and Belle, though his true motive was of a more practical nature. Because of his standing in the community in Nashville, it was expected that he would have a large, formal wedding. Ken had no family, or at least none he cared to acknowledge. Belle's family was far away and not on the best of terms with her from what Bill had told him, and Belle didn't have any female friends in Nashville that would have been appropriate to use for her attendants. None of these things would be an issue at a wedding reception held sometime after the actual marriage.

Belle looked and felt a bit dazed when she met him for a late breakfast the next morning.

"Good morning Belle. I hope you slept well?"

"I did, although I had the strangest dream. I dreamed we were going to be married aboard ship today." For just a moment Ken wasn't sure how to respond. Then he noticed Belle was smiling.

"Well, then, I think we should make that dream come true don't you? I had a similar dream and have already spoken to the Captain. He suggested 4:00 p.m. for the ceremony."

"Oh Ken, this is all moving so fast I can hardly collect my thoughts."

"I know Belle, but you won't regret it, I promise."

"Well, since you seem to have everything under control, what do you suggest I wear?" she asked.

"I think your ivory-satin gown would be perfect."

After they had eaten and strolled around the deck a while, Belle told him she thought she should return to her cabin to rest.

"That's probably a good idea. When it's time, I'll come get you."

When Ken arrived at her door that afternoon, he handed her a small box. "My wedding gift for you," was all he said. Inside was a delicate sapphire necklace to match the earrings he'd given her.

"Oh, Ken," was all she could think of to say.

"Let me help you put it on." When he had, he stepped back, shook his head and said, "It's perfect with that dress. You are truly a vision."

The dress had a high neckline with a smooth bodice, a perfect frame for the necklace. Tucked inside the bodice on a satin ribbon was her wedding ring from Bill. She couldn't wear it on her hand until it had been resized, but she wasn't willing to just put it away.

Word of the wedding quickly spread to all the passengers, and most of them were in attendance for it. The Captain wore his dress uniform and the couple that Ken and Belle had often dined with was asked to stand up with the couple as their witnesses. The ceremony itself was brief. The time between the wedding and the evening meal was taken up with the passengers coming to the newly weds to offer their congratulations and best wishes.

As everyone began moving towards the ballroom for an evening of dancing, the Captain pulled Ken aside, and informed him that he'd arranged for a separate table for Ken and Belle, plus the couple who had acted as their witness'.

Generous amounts of champagne and other fine wines were consumed throughout the evening. It was nearly 2 a.m. before Ken and Belle retired to Ken's cabin. Because Belle wasn't accustomed to drinking as much as she had, she wasn't feeling very well. Ken helped her out of her dress and into bed. By the time he undressed, she was sound asleep. Ken had also indulged too heavily in the wine and was content to just fall asleep with his arm around Belle.

The sound of the ship's whistle announcing their approach to New York harbor awoke them the next morning. "Good morning, Mrs. Sawyer. We need to get dressed so we can go on deck to watch the Statue of Liberty welcome us home."

Belle was still a bit groggy and had a massive headache. She had brought the clothing she planned to wear today to Ken's room the day before and slowly began dressing. "I have a terrible headache, Ken."

"Take this. It will help," he said as he handed her a glass of water with a packet of aspirin powder dissolved in it. "Then we'll get some coffee."

They arrived on deck, just as they were entering New York harbor. In spite of not feeling well, Belle was duly impressed with the sight of the Statue of Liberty.

By the time they arrived at their suite in the Waldorf Hotel, Belle was feeling a little better. "Belle honey, I really have to meet with the manager of my warehouse to see if everything arrived. You stay here and rest and we'll have dinner here at the hotel tonight. If you need anything before I return the hotel, the staff can get it for you."

Belle was still in a mild state of shock over the events of the past 48 hours and offered no objection to this.

She spent the day taking a relaxing bath, washing her hair, resting, and sorting through her thoughts. "My life has gone from boring and tedious to a rapid series of one adventure after another," she thought. "The carnival was fun, and my life with Bill was wonderful. I wonder what Ma would think if she could see me now?"

This reminded her of how supportive Bill had been when she'd gotten the news about her Ma's death. "Ah Bill, I still miss you," she said out loud. Bill's ring was still on the ribbon around her neck. She held it with her right hand. Then held up her left hand. "I'm only eighteen and have been married twice," she thought, then she shook her head, and glanced at the clock, realizing Ken would return soon, began to dress for dinner.

Ken appeared shortly after she had finished dressing. "Hello, darling. Did you have a relaxing day?"

"I did. Was your day successful?" she asked.

"I'm starving. Let's go to the dining room, and I'll tell you about it over dinner," was his reply.

As they ate, Ken explained there were some problems, and he would need to spend most of the next day with his manager again.

"Oh, no. What happened, Ken?"

"Well, several things, actually. It seems someone broke into the ware-house while we were in Europe, and some things are missing, so I'll need to meet with the police to see what they have discovered about the rob-bery. Also, some of the pieces we bought haven't arrived, and I'll need to do some follow up on that. I'm really sorry, Belle, but I did warn you that our time in New York would be a little hectic. Why don't you use tomorrow to do some shopping for yourself? The hotel concierge can rec-ommend some nice places to shop and arrange transportation for you. Buy as many clothes as you like and anything else that takes your fancy."

"Well, I suppose I could use a few extra dresses," she said, trying to hide her disappointment over spending another day alone.

"Very good. Maybe we can take in some entertainment tomorrow evening. I'll ask the concierge if he can recommend anything. How does that sound?"

"That would be nice," she replied.

As soon as they returned to the room Ken swept her up in an embrace and a long passionate kiss. "Now Mrs. Sawyer, shall we truly begin our marriage?" he said, as he began unfastening the buttons on her dress.

Ken's lovemaking was more aggressive than Bill's, and she found herself feeling vaguely disappointed as he rolled over and immediately fell asleep.

The rest of the week in New York was a repeat of the first day. Belle asked to go with Ken to the warehouse, but she was told, "It's not that different from the one in Nashville, and I really don't have time to show you around properly."

Belle discovered she enjoyed shopping, and after being reassured by Ken that money was not an issue, she spent two more days buying items of clothing, including some very nice lingerie. She also found a jeweler who was able to resize Bill's ring and have it ready before they left New York. As they boarded the train for Nashville, Ken noticed she was wearing it on her right hand, but decided not to say anything about it.

George met them at the train station in Nashville with Ken's motorcar and a hired wagon to transport their luggage.

"Welcome home, Ken. Belle, you are looking lovelier than ever."

"Thank you for saying so, but as travel weary as I am, I find it a little difficult to believe."

"Nevertheless, it's true. Now, if you'll point out which pieces of luggage are yours, I'll see to it they are delivered to your house, first."

"Well ,George," said Ken, "that won't be necessary. You see, you are now speaking with Mrs. Ken Sawyer."

George was momentarily taken aback, but he managed to recover quickly after looking from Ken to Belle and seeing her smile broadly. "Well, well, I must say, it isn't often someone can surprise me like this. Congratulations to you both. Did the wedding take place in Europe?"

Belle spoke first, saying, "No, we were married on board the ship by the Captain on our last night out. Ken can be quite impatient and quite convincing, when he puts his mind to it. And it was rather romantic."

"Yes, I'm sure it was," replied George. "Well, let's get you two home then."

Belle had never been to Ken's home and was a bit surprised when they pulled into the drive of a very large estate. It was typical of many of the homes of wealthy Southerners, tall pillars supported the roof over the large verandah which ran the entire width of the house. It was surrounded by large trees with a carriage house in back.

"Well, Mrs. Sawyer, we're home. What do you think?" asked Ken.

"It's beautiful! I had no idea you had such a large home."

They were met at the door by a Negro woman. "Welcome home, Mister Ken," she said.

"Thank you, Dora. I have a surprise for you. This is my wife, Belle. Belle, this is Dora. She does a wonderful job of taking care of the house for me."

"Well, Lord amighty, Miss Belle, but you sho is beautiful. Welcome."

"Thank you Dora," was all that Belle was able to reply.

"Dora, I'm going to show Belle the house and grounds. Will you see that our things are taken to the master bedroom and unpacked?"

"Yessir, Mr. Ken, right away."

Ken took Belle on a tour of the large two-story home. He also introduced her to Selma, another Negro woman, who was in charge of the kitchen and Joshua, a Negro man responsible for maintaining the grounds.

That night after dinner, Belle told Ken she was unsure about how she should deal with Dora, Selma, and Joshua. Ken replied, "Oh, you'll do fine, Belle. You just need to supervise them and give some direction, kind of like your mama did with you and your sisters. They have all been with me for a few years, so it isn't like you'll need to train them."

Three months after Ray received the letter from Belle telling him she was leaving for Europe another letter arrived from Nashville. This one was on fancy stationery with a printed return address that read:

Mrs. Kenneth Sawyer
26 Cypress Avenue
Nashville, Tennessee

Inside was a letter from Belle.

> Dear Ray,
>
> It seems every time I write to you I'm telling you of a major change in my life. Ken and I are married. The wedding took place on-board ship just before we arrived in New York City. I know this seems too fast, but Ken is a wonderful man, even if a bit difficult to say "no" to. He loves me and treats me like some kind of royalty. And I think I'm beginning to fall in love with him. I know Bill would understand and be happy for me. I hope you can do the same.
>
> Please, give Lizzie my congratulations on her son, even if she

doesn't want to hear from me. I wanted to send a gift, but I wasn't sure what she would want, so I'm enclosing some money for you to pass on to her.

I think of all of you often, and want to assure you I'm very happy. Please write and fill me in on news from the family.

Belle

Ray read the letter a second time. There was a $20.00 bill tucked in the letter.

"Well, I'll be!" thought Ray. "Our Belle sure doesn't let any grass grow under her."

He wasn't sure what to do about the money. Belle was still a forbidden topic with both Lizzie and John. He hoped he could convince Lizzie to take the money. With another child on the way he was sure she could use it. He would be going out to the farm in a couple of weeks for Easter, and he would give it to her then. "I think I'll write to Mae and fill her in before then," he thought, so he wrote a short note to Mae, filling her in on the news from Belle's letter, then wrote a longer reply to Belle.

Dear Belle,

Well, you certainly are full of surprises! It does seem like you are moving awfully fast, but since you tell me you're happy, I'll go with that. I'll be going to the farm in a couple of weeks for Easter and will give the money to Lizzie then. Lizzie is expecting another child, and Ann and David are expecting a baby this fall. Mae met a young man from David City when he was here visiting some friends. She spent some time with him while he was here and they have been exchanging letters. She indicated to me it may be getting serious, so we may be having another wedding before too long. I don't have a steady girl, but am happy working at the livery. We had a fella come through town a while back with one of those new motor cars, and he let me examine it. It surely is a wonder what they are doing with machines these days.

Pa and David are kept busy with running the farm, and the extra forty acres David was able to buy from Old Man Miller. He and

Ann plan to build their own house on that land as soon as they can manage it.

Congratulations on your marriage. I would love to see you, but just don't see how I could manage that long a trip now. Write again, and fill me in on your life.

Ray

Easter was late this year and coincided with Lizzie and David's wedding anniversaries. The women outdid themselves with a large meal of ham, sweet potatoes, mashed potatoes, gravy, green beans, two salads, two kinds of pie, and a large decorated cake in honor of the anniversaries. By mid-afternoon everyone was feeling a bit miserable from eating so much.

Ray spoke up saying, "I think I need to walk off some of this meal. David, Charles, Pa, you want to come too?"

"You boys go ahead," said John. "I believe I'll just sit for a spell."

While they were walking Ray filled David and Charles in on the letter from Belle and gave Charles the $20.00. "I didn't want to bring it up around Pa and Lizzie and cause hard feelings again, but I thought you and Lizzie should have it."

Charles seemed a little embarrassed, but said ,"Well, I can't deny this will come in handy. Maybe, I just won't say anything to Lizzie. I don't like getting her riled up, especially now with another baby comin'."

David spoke up asking if Mae knew anything about all this. "Yeah, I wrote her a note filling her in as soon as I got the letter from Belle. I thought she should know, too."

Belle's life had been something of a fairy tale the first two years of her marriage to Ken. She was involved with his business, cataloguing items, and doing his bookkeeping and once accompanied him on a trip to Chicago to personally deliver some items to one of his better customers.

That slowly began to change about three years ago. Ken would often be gone for a few days to call on customers who lived some distance from Nashville. There was always some reason why he couldn't take Belle with him. The reasons he gave didn't make much sense to her, and she began to wonder if the real reason involved another woman.

Then he began finding reasons why she didn't need to help with the business, finally telling her he no longer thought it appropriate to have his wife helping in the business. "It just sends the wrong message Belle. I'd like you to get more involved with Nashville society and do more entertaining. That's also important for my business you know."

For the next year, Belle put all her energy into becoming more involved with Nashville's finest families. She hosted numerous dinner parties plus a grand Christmas ball. The time she and Ken were able to spend together became less frequent, and their conversation more superficial. After a year-and-a-half of this, Belle was completely bored with society life and dissatisfied with her marriage. Her attempts to talk about this to Ken were not well received. Either he needed to rush off to a meeting of one kind or another or told her she was just being affected by the weather and would feel differently in a few days.

She began turning down invitations to many of the afternoon teas held by the wives of men with high standing in the community. She also turned down some dinner invitations without consulting Ken. The extra time this gave her was used to visit the library, reading newspapers from other major cities and checking out books to read at home. For several months, Ken did not seem to notice the decline in their social life.

One day Ken came home in a foul mood. "I had lunch with Councilman Lacy today and found myself in an embarrassing position. He said he hoped you were feeling better and was sorry we had to miss their dinner party last week. What is going on, Belle?"

"I just didn't feel like spending another evening engaging in social gossip and meaningless conversation, so I declined the invitation saying I did not feel well."

"Obviously, you didn't think it was important enough to consult me first? Did you even bother to think how this would make me look?"

"If I tried to talk to you about it, you would insist we go and talk me into it, like you always do. It never occurred to me that I might be damaging your fine reputation."

"Belle, how can you be so dense? Many of these people are customers of mine, and it's the wives who initiate the purchases they make. If they take a dislike to you, it damn well will reflect on me and on my business!"

"Well, how in the world did you ever manage to get your business going without me I wonder?" Belle snapped.

"Don't get sassy with me, Belle. My business has nearly doubled since we got married. Did you think that was just coincidence, or did you even notice?"

"Well, since you've seen fit to have someone else take care of the cataloguing and bookkeeping, how would I have known that?"

"You are impossible! I want you to plan on a dinner party here Saturday week. I'll give you a list of who to invite, and you will not turn down any further invitations, is that clear?"

By now, Belle was so angry that she barely trusted herself to speak, but she managed to say in a terse voice, "Perfectly," then turned and left the room.

Ken slept in one of the guest rooms that night and for the next several nights. Their only conversations consisted of brief exchanges about the details of the dinner party.

The night before the party Ken came back to their bedroom. "I'm sorry I've been a little short tempered, Belle, but these social contacts are very important to me. I'm sure no lasting damage has been done, but we do need to stay closely involved with the Nashville society. You understand that don't you sweetheart?"

Belle sighed and said, "I suppose I do."

"That's my girl. Now, let's go to bed. You'll have a busy day tomorrow supervising everything for the party."

Ken made love to her that night, but for Belle, it felt as if he was simply going through the motions.

For the next few months, their routine returned to what it had been before Belle's minor revolt. The endless rounds of dinner parties, teas and luncheons bored her to tears. To deal with this she began drinking more when they were out. On several occasions the amount of alcohol in her body led to her expressing some opinions in a blunt manner. Ken's attempts to chastise her for this made her angry, and as often happened with Belle when she was angry, she became more defiant. She began blatantly flirting with some of the men at the parties, which did not sit well with their wives.

She would also frequently address one of the Negros, who served the food, by name, asking about their family, or their opinion of the weather. The first time this happened, Ken explained to her that it was not something that was done in Southern society. After the third similar incident, Ken exploded, saying, "Belle, this has got to stop! You have become an object of gossip. It's bad enough that I find you helping Selma in the kitchen, or working alongside Dora, but I will not tolerate this kind of behavior in public. Do you understand?"

"Excuse me, are you telling me you won't tolerate my being friendly to anyone you don't approve of?"

"It's not a matter of who I approve of, Belle. The nigras are here to serve us. Treating them as equals is just not done. They recognize we are their superiors, and it only confuses them when you try to engage them in social conversation."

"That is the most ridiculous thing I've ever heard!"

"Belle, you've lived in Nashville long enough that it should be obvious to you that being friendly with our nigras just isn't done."

"Well, explain something to me, then. Just who was it that decided we are superior to them?"

"Oh, for God's sake, Belle. Even a small child can see that's just the way it is. I will not have my wife disgracing me by continuing this kind of behavior. I'm going to the club. I expect you to have pulled yourself together by morning." With that he stomped out of the house.

The next morning at breakfast Ken asked, "Have you calmed down?"

"I'm calm."

"Well, I'm happy to hear it. I'm sorry I was so blunt with you, but you just didn't seem to understand what I was trying to tell you."

"Oh, I think I understood perfectly," she said, then added, "Selma dear, could I have a little more coffee? How is that new grandbaby of yours?"

Selma quickly poured the coffee, mumbled a short response about her grandchild, and quickly went back to the kitchen.

It was mid-afternoon on a Monday when Ken unexpectedly came home.

"You're home early today. What prompted this?" Belle asked.

"Sit down, Belle, I need to talk to you" he replied.

"Well, this sounds serious. Am I to get another lecture on the proper behavior of a good Southern wife?" Belle was still angry over the tongue lashing Ken had given her after a party they attended Friday night, and the fact that he moved into the guest room again.

"No lecture, Belle. Simply this. I can no longer tolerate your behavior and attitude. I'm divorcing you. I've already spoken to my lawyer. The reason for the divorce will be listed as infidelity on your part. I've arranged to have him bring the papers here for you to sign this evening. You may keep your wardrobe and the jewels I've given you over the years. In addition, I'll buy you a train ticket to anywhere you want to go and give you $100.00. This way we can avoid the hassle and embarrassment of going to court."

"And what if I don't sign the papers?" she asked.

"The divorce will still be granted, I assure you. I have people who will testify to your infidelity. The difference will be that you will leave here with nothing but the clothes on your back. My lawyer will be here at five, so you have until then to decide. If you agree to this I will expect you to be on a train to somewhere, no later than Saturday."

With that Ken left the room and walked into his study.

Belle sat stunned for a few moments, and then she got up and slowly walked to her room. Once she was in the bedroom, she began pacing the floor and talking to herself.

"Infidelity! When he's the one who takes off for days at a time! I've never believed those trips were strictly business. He should have just kept me on as an employee, it would be so much easier to just fire me. Of course he couldn't do that and mar his proper image. Heavens no! The only acceptable thing to do was to have a wife as his social secretary. I'm so sick of all the phoniness I could puke! Well, fine. I'll sign the damned papers."

With that she sat down and began to consider where she should go. It didn't take her long to decide on New York City. She loved the atmosphere of the city and was sure she could find some employment there.

"A hundred dollars!" she thought. "That won't last me very long."

Then she remembered Ken usually kept some money in a dresser drawer, for emergencies, as he'd once explained. "Well, this is definitely an emergency." She went to the drawer and found the money still there. He had apparently forgotten about it when he'd moved into the guest room two nights ago. She counted it and found there was $200.00. She tucked it into her bodice, then went to find Dora to ask her to have her luggage brought to her room, saying only that she was going to take a trip. After that she went to Ken's study to tell him she would sign the papers and would like to leave for New York City as soon as possible.

Chapter Six

It was a cold, windy, late March day when Belle arrived in New York City. She brought one small trunk and one piece of luggage that she could carry. A porter offered assistance with the trunk and helped her find transportation. She had no idea where to go, so she asked the cabbie to take her to an inexpensive hotel. Because of how she was dressed, he took her to a moderately priced hotel rather than one that would have been less expensive, but bordered on being slum lodging.

She paid for a week's stay, hoping that would give her enough time to get her bearings, find employment, and more permanent lodging. She decided to tell people she was recently widowed and use Dawson as her last name. Bill's ring was on her right hand, Ken's on her left. She kept her other jewels in a small pouch that she wore under her clothing.

Her hotel was on the lower East side, a very different part of New York City than she had known during her visit to the city with Ken. Her first few days were spent reading newspapers and doing a lot of walking to get familiar with this part of the city. During one of her walks, she stopped in a small bakery that also sold coffee. She was the only customer. When she commented on how good the coffee and pastry was, Mrs. O'Brian took it as an opportunity for some conversation.

"I'm glad you're liking it. Things get a little slow here this time of day. What brings you in this way, if I might be so bold as to ask?"

"I've just recently arrived here, and am trying to get familiar with the neighborhood," Belle responded.

"And just what brings a fine Southern lady like yourself to these parts?"

"My husband recently died, and I just couldn't face staying in Nashville with the reminders of him all around me."

"Ah, I'm sorry to be hearin' that. So where do you be stayin' now?"

When Belle told her the name of the hotel, she said, "Well, sure and that's a fair walk from here. So what are your plans if ya don't mind me askin?"

"I need to find some kind of employment as soon as I can, and I'd like to find a small flat to rent."

"And just what kind of employment will you be wantin'?"

"I'm not sure. I've done bookkeeping for an import/export business. I also waited tables before I was married."

"Dear me, where are my manners!" she exclaimed. "My name is Mrs. O'Brian, but please call me Iris."

"It's nice to meet you Iris. I'm Belle Dawson."

"I don't like bein' the bearer of bad news, but I'm thinking opportunities for finding work in this neighborhood are pretty thin. Most places are small family businesses, like ours, and can't afford to be takin' on help. My boy, Tommy, works at a nice hotel uptown. I'll ask him tonight if he has any ideas for a job in that area. Maybe, you could stop back in a day or two to see what he says."

"That's very kind of you, Iris. I'd be grateful for any help."

"So when did your husband die, if ya don't mind me askin?"

"It was a few months ago."

"You've no family in Nashville?"

"No, I was raised in Nebraska, and my Bill was from Oklahoma. We met when he was in Nebraska visiting some relatives."

"And just how did you wind up in Nashville then?"

"My Bill was a musician and thought he needed to be in Nashville to make a real go of his music. He was right, too. He was doing very well."

"And, you've no babes?"

"No, we hadn't been married all that long."

"Ah, well, you're young. There's still time."

By now, it was late afternoon. Iris noticed the time and said to Belle, "You should be thinkin' about gettin' back to your hotel soon. It's not a good idea for a lady to be walkin' alone after dark in this neighborhood."

"Yes, that's probably a good idea. I've enjoyed visiting with you. If it's all right, I'll stop back tomorrow to see if your son has any suggestions for me."

Belle returned the next afternoon and was warmly greeted by Iris. "Good day to ya, Miss Belle. Would you like a cup of coffee?"

"That would be nice. Thank you, Iris"

Iris brought a cup of coffee and a pastry to the table. "Oh I don't need the pastry Iris."

"Oh, go on with you. It's on the house. I may have some good news for you."

"Really? Well tell me. I could use some good news."

"Well, my boy, Tommy is the doorman at the Conaught Hotel uptown. He suggested you come to the hotel tomorrow morning. Now, he's not allowed to chat with people on the street, so he says you should go in to the desk and ask for someone you know isn't there. Then, when you come out you can ask him for directions to a dress shop, and he can tell you of a few places that you can check out for a job. How does that sound?"

"It sounds very encouraging, Iris. Thank you, so much."

"Twasn't nuthin. I'll give you directions for getting there on the trolley. It's much too far to be walkin'."

Belle sat and visited with Iris for awhile, until another customer came in, then she bid her good day and began walking back to her hotel. She learned that Iris and her husband Dan had come from Ireland nearly twenty years ago, shortly after getting married, and now they had three boys.

The next day was sunny and mild. Belle hoped it was a good omen. She nodded to Tommy, as he held the door for her, went to the desk, and asked what room Mr. John Mericle was in. After checking the registration book the clerk informed her they had no one registered by that name. "Oh dear. I wonder if he missed his train. My father always seems to manage to be late for his appointments."

"Would you like to leave a note for him?" the clerk asked.

"Yes, that's a good idea. Thank you." Belle wrote a few nonsense lines on the paper given to her, tucked it into the envelope, and gave it to the clerk, saying she would check back later. As she left the hotel she turned to Tommy and said, "Excuse me, but could you direct me to a small dress shop that I've been told is nearby?" Tommy directed her to a shop a few blocks away and added there were a couple of others she might want to check out, telling her where they were.

She visited three women's clothing shops. At the first two, she was told they didn't need any more help. The third one was on fifth Avenue, a shop called Rose Fashions. She crossed her fingers and walked in. A silver haired lady greeted her. "Good morning, madam. How may I help you?"

"Good morning to you. I'm new in town and looking for employment. I was told you might be hiring," Belle replied.

"Indeed, who told you this?"

"The doorman at the Conaught Hotel."

"Ah, Tommy. How do you know Tommy?"

"Well, I don't really. I met his mother, and when I told her I was looking for a job, she suggested Tommy might have some leads for me."

"As a matter of fact, I have been considering hiring someone to help. I find my stamina isn't what it used to be. Do you have any experience?"

"Not in women's clothing sales. I do have experience meeting the public and have some experience with bookkeeping and inventory. I worked for an import/export business for a while."

"Really. Where was this?"

"In Nashville."

"And how does your husband feel about having a working wife?"

"I'm recently widowed. I came to New York to remove myself from all the reminders of our life there."

"Ah, I'm sorry to hear that. His estate is not adequate to support you, then?"

"No, my Bill was a musician. His career was becoming quite successful, but he hadn't been at it long enough to accumulate any real savings."

"I hope I haven't offended you with all these questions, but if I'm to have someone working for me, I need to know something about them. I can see your taste in clothing is quite good. How would you feel about spending today in the shop, so I can see how you relate to my customers?"

"I'd be happy to do that ma'am"

"Very well then. My name is Rose Downey. And you are?"

"I'm Belle Dawson."

"Very good. Well then, let me acquaint you with my shop and merchandise. I expect it won't be too much longer before I have a customer or two. I'd like you to just observe while I wait on the first customer, then you can try your hand with the next one."

During the course of the day, Belle waited on several customers and sold two dresses. As Mrs. Downey was beginning to close for the day, she said to Belle, "Well my dear. You did very well today. If you still think you'd like to work here, the job is yours."

"Oh, thank you, Mrs. Downey! I enjoyed myself today and would love to work here."

"I suspect it will be beneficial for both of us. When there are no customers present, please call me Rose." She then told Belle what the salary would be, asking if that was acceptable. Belle readily agreed, even though she wasn't sure just how much it would cost to find a flat."

"Where do you live now?" asked Rose. Belle told her the address of the hotel, adding that she was hoping to be able to find a small flat.

"Well, that's a fair way to travel every day. I'll ask around about something to rent that would be a bit closer for you. You be careful going home, and I'll see you here at 9:00 tomorrow morning."

Belle walked back to the Conaught Hotel, hoping Tommy was still on duty, so she could thank him. He was just leaving for the day when she walked up. "Hello Tommy. We didn't get officially introduced. I'm Belle Dawson."

"Happy to meet you Mrs. Dawson. I guess you're already knowin' my name. Have you spent the whole day lookin' for work then?"

"No, Tommy, thanks to you, I've been hired at the Rose Fashion shop. Thank you so much for your help."

"The pleasure was mine. I believe we'll be taking the same trolley home. Would you like to walk with me?"

"That would be lovely," she replied. During the ride, Tommy suggested she come home with him for supper to celebrate, adding that he would walk her home from there later.

"Oh, Tommy, that's a nice offer, but I couldn't impose on your mother like that."

"Nonsense. Me mum's a great cook and loves havin' company. She'll be wantin to hear your good news. Now, no more arguin'. You'll be having supper with the O'Brian's tonight."

The O'Brian clan was a lively bunch. Tommy was 19, Patrick 16, and Ian 12. Iris was indeed a great cook. It was a simple meal of Irish stew and soda bread, but Belle didn't think she'd ever had anything that tasted better. Dan was a quiet man, and it was obvious he ruled his family with a gentle, yet firm hand. When the boys good natured horseplay began to get out of hand, a quiet word and a look was all it took to settle things down. When the meal was over, Belle insisted on helping with the kitchen cleanup, then she began saying her goodbyes. Tommy spoke up saying, "Mum, I told Mrs. Dawson I'd walk her home."

"A good idea, son. Belle, have a good day tomorrow, and come back to see us again."

"That I will. Thank you for a lovely evening and for your help in finding me a job."

During her first few weeks at Rose Fashions, Belle discovered that Mrs. Downey had a sizeable number of repeat customers, most of whom were women in their forties or older. Belle soon came to know many of them by name and developed a rapport with them in spite of their age difference. Rose had been helpful in locating a flat that Belle could afford which was half way between the shop and the hotel where Belle had initially stayed.

Now and then, the customers would bring their daughters with them. The fashions Rose carried were considered a little to "matronly" to appeal to the younger women. Belle asked Rose if she ever considered expanding her merchandise to include fashions more appealing to young women.

"It has crossed my mind now and then" Rose admitted. "I tend to be a creature of habit and stay with what is working rather than venture into new territory. Why do you ask?"

"I've noticed some of your regular customers bring their daughters in with them from time to time. I think it might be easy to gain some new customers by carrying items that would appeal to the younger women. Maybe, you could add a small display of costume jewelry."

"Well, you may be right. Let me think about it," Rose said. A month later she approached Belle as they were closing. "I've been thinking about your suggestion to add a line for younger women. I do think it's a good idea. As I mentioned before, I'm a creature of habit, but I do recognize that has some drawbacks. If I do this, I'd like to rely on your judgment in choosing what to add to our inventory. How do you feel about that?"

"Well, I'm honored that you would ask me Rose. Yes, I'd be happy to help with that."

"It would be more than helping, Belle. What I had in mind was giving you a budget to work with and turning the buying over to you."

"Really! Well, now I really am honored."

"Can you stay late tomorrow, so we can discuss this further?"

"Of course, I'd be happy to."

A few months after the new line was added, a young woman came into the shop, accompanied by a young man. Their resemblance was quite striking, and when Belle commented on this, she was informed they were twins. The young woman then said, "We enjoy doing things together, and I value his opinion about the clothing I choose."

Her brother added, "We don't always agree about the fashions she chooses, and when we don't, hers is the opinion that rules."

"Well, I think that's as it should be," replied Belle. "A woman must feel good about what she wears, or it won't look good on her, and of course, she is the only one who can say if she feels good about it."

"Thank you! I've tried to explain that to Johnny, but you said it very well."

"Ah, what can a mere man begin to understand about the inner life of a woman," he joked. She purchased two dresses, a necklace, and a pair of earrings that day. After they left the shop, Rose came up to Belle, smiling. "I knew I was doing the right thing when I hired you, Belle. That was the son and daughter of John Honeywell, the vice president of the New York State Bank."

Belle maintained her contact with the O'Brians, occasionally having a Saturday evening meal with them. They were a close family, and Belle enjoyed the playful joking the family engaged in. Iris liked having another female around to visit with. She lost two daughters in infancy and treated Belle as a combination daughter/friend. The O'Brian's were Catholic, and their faith was a big part of their lives. The fact that Belle was raised in the Methodist Church never seemed to be an issue with them. Belle often heard comments about "The Irish" or "Them damned Micks" from people on the trolley, and sometimes from her customers. The concept of prejudice never came up during her childhood, largely because there was no other group of people in their community that could have been perceived as being different or foreign. Her first exposure to prejudice occurred in Nashville where Negroes were treated as slightly backward children at best, or sub-human at worst. These attitudes saddened and angered her. She took people at face value, always assuming the best unless their behavior proved otherwise. The idea of someone being considered "less than" because of their race was a concept she just couldn't grasp. There was a time or two when she attempted to counter the comments she heard from her customers, but Rose quickly told her she needed to keep her views to herself while at work. This was not an easy task for Belle, who had never been one to keep her opinions to herself or temper them to suit others. Even though Belle had difficulty keeping her opinions to herself, she was not above altering the truth a bit to serve her purpose. In response to questions from Rose about her family, she told the truth about being raised on a farm, and her brothers, sisters, and her mother dying. She also painted a picture of financial hardship, indicating she left home to help ease that burden. Of course she did not reveal anything of the circumstances of her leaving, or the fact that her father and one sister would not allow anyone to speak of her and never wanted to see her again. She hadn't written to Ray since leaving Nashville. She just wasn't ready to reveal this new chapter in her life to him and risk losing his good will, too. She did frequently think of her family and wonder if the day would come when she could see them again without all the animosity they displayed on her last visit. Those thoughts would bring on some melancholy, followed by thoughts of Bill and regrets that their life together had been so brief. Most of the time, she pushed these thoughts aside and held onto the fantasy that she had told Rose.

Johnny and Julia Honeywell became regulars at Rose Fashions, and Johnny soon began a mild flirtation with Belle. After a few weeks, he stopped in late one afternoon, unaccompanied by Julia. "Mrs. Dawson, I find myself with a free evening and would be pleased if you would join me for dinner." Belle thanked him but declined, saying she had other plans. "Well, perhaps, another time then?"

"Yes, perhaps," she answered.

As they were closing, Rose asked Belle why she hadn't accepted his offer. "Well, I wasn't sure it was a good idea."

"And why not may I ask?"

"Because of who he is and because I'm not sure I'm ready to begin socializing with a man."

"Well, if he asks you again, I think you should say,' yes.' It is only a dinner, after all, and you need to get out with people your own age."

A week later, Johnny was back, alone again, late in the afternoon. Rose saw him approaching the shop and said to Belle, "Now, if he asks you again, say 'yes'."

He did, and Belle reluctantly agreed. In spite of her doubts, she had a very enjoyable evening. Thanks to Rose, Johnny was aware Belle was a widow. Rose was fond of Belle and told a few of her favorite customers of Belle's plight.

During the evening, he said to Belle, "I understand your late husband was a musician. There is a small club I know of that features some nice musical groups and has a great dance floor. Would you like to go with me next Saturday?"

Belle hesitated only a moment before saying yes.

When the evening was over, Johnny insisted on accompanying her in a cab back to her flat. "I'll pick you up here at 8:00 next Saturday. Thank you for a lovely evening."

"I enjoyed myself, too," she replied. "I'll look forward to Saturday."

During the following week, Belle found she really was looking forward to an evening of music and dancing. Rose was a bit of a gossip and enjoyed following the lives of some of her customers and their friends. She told Belle that Julia and Johnny's mother died giving birth to them. They were the only children and were denied nothing by their father.

"Oh, but I've been told they aren't nearly as spoiled as they might be under the circumstances. Everyone tells me they are nothing but a credit to their father." Rose said.

The musical group at the club was a Dixieland band. This brought back memories of Nashville, some painful, some pleasant. "I thought you might enjoy some Dixieland, since you lived in Nashville for a time," Johnny said. "Was this the kind of music your husband played?"

"No, his was Country Western, but we did enjoy listening to Dixieland. It's just hard not to feel good around this music, isn't it?"

Johnny was nearly as good a dancer as Bill had been. It was after midnight when they both agreed they should bring the evening to an end. When they reached her flat, Belle said, "Johnny, thank you for a lovely evening. I haven't enjoyed myself so much for a long time."

"Believe me, the pleasure was mine. May I call on you again?" he asked.

"I'd like that. Good night, Johnny."

"Good night, Belle."

Over the next few months, Johnny took Belle to other clubs, out to dinner, and once to see a Broadway play. Her striking good looks, dark hair, and brilliant blue eyes were what first attracted him to her. As they spent more time together, he found her opinions and views on various subjects a refreshing change from the conventional and superficial conversations he was accustomed to from the young women in his circle of friends and acquaintances. Belle appreciated the fact that he conversed with her as if he thought what she said had value. It reminded her of Bill, and to some degree, the early months of her time with Ken. After one particularly enjoyable evening together, Johnny became more serious than usual and said, "Belle, I think I'm falling in love with you. My family has a tradition of having Sunday brunch for our family and a few close friends. I'd like for you to join us next Sunday."

Belle was silent for a moment, then she said, "Are you sure that's a good idea? I've loved spending time with you, but I'm really not sure I would fit in with your family and friends."

"Don't be silly, Belle. They would love you. Your beauty alone will dazzle them, and by the time they get over that, they will have come to enjoy being with you as much as I do. Well, maybe, almost as much anyway," he joked.

"I don't know, Johnny. I'm not sure I'm ready for that."

"Fine, I won't pressure you, but please give it some thought. I'd really like to introduce you to my father."

Over the next few days, Belle was distracted at work. Rose asked her if anything was wrong. Belle denied anything was wrong, saying she'd just been feeling a little off lately and thought maybe she was coming down with a cold. "Well, you take care of yourself now. Why don't you take off a little early today and go home to get some extra rest?"

"Thank you, Rose. Maybe I will do just that."

Belle was reluctant to tell Rose about Johnny wanting her to meet his father, knowing that she did love to gossip. When she left the shop, she took a trolley to visit Iris. There were no customers in the bakery, as Belle hoped.

"Belle, what brings you here at this time of day?" asked Iris.

"Rose told me to go home a little early today to get some extra rest."

"Have ya not been feelin well then?"

"I feel fine. I just have a problem that I'm not sure how to handle and wanted to talk to you about it."

"Well, have a seat, then. I was just about to close up anyway. I'll put the sign in the door and get us some coffee." When she'd poured the coffee and sat down, she said, "Now what is it that's troubling you dear?"

"I've been seeing this man. I met him when he came in the shop with his twin sister. I enjoy his company a lot, Iris, but now, he wants me to meet his family."

"Well, that sounds like he's getting serious, then. So, what's the problem?"

"It's his family Iris. He is the son of a banker, and I'm not sure I'd fit in or that they would approve of me."

"Ah, well then. And what are your feelin's for this young man?"

"I like him a lot."

"Well then, I think you should agree to meet his family. You're a darlin' girl and no one would mistake you for anything but a lady."

"But Iris, he's from such a different background than me. I had a friend in Nashville who became involved with a man of a higher social standing than she was. At first it was fine, they even planned to marry, but after a while, he started becoming critical of her speech and behavior after they had been with his friends. Eventually, he broke their engagement and her heart. I'm just not sure I want to risk getting into a similar situation."

"On the other hand, do you want to risk losin' him by not giving it a chance? You've said you like him a lot. Does that mean ya don't love him?"

"Oh, Iris, I don't know. Maybe a little. He's so different from my Bill, and we were so happy together."

"And you'll always have those good memories, but ya mus'nt measure every man you meet by your Bill. Ya won't ever find a duplicate ya know, and you're much too young to be thinkin' of not marrying again some day. I think what ya need to be doin', now is either stop seein' him altogether or take a chance, meet his family, and see what happens."

Belle sighed and said, "Well, maybe you're right. I do enjoy spending time with him, and Johnny isn't nearly as pretentious as the man my friend was involved with." Then she smiled and said, "I guess if I was brave enough to come to New York by myself I can take a chance on this, too."

"That's my girl! You'll be fine, however it turns out. I do need to be getting home now. Would ya like to come have supper with us?"

"Thank you, but I think I'd rather go home, put my feet up, and just relax this evening."

"You come back, and tell me how things go then."

"I will Iris. Wish me luck."

"That I do, but you won't be needin' it. You'll be fine."

Belle spent the evening reviewing her conversation with Iris, as well as her own thoughts and feelings.

"Iris is right," she thought. "I won't ever find another Bill, but I sure don't want to find another Ken either. Johnny doesn't seem to be anything like Ken. He has a wonderful sense of humor; he can laugh at himself, as well as make me laugh. He never talks about his job at his father's bank. I've met a few of his friends, when we've been out, and they seem nice, not phony or superficial like most of Ken's were. I've met his sister and I like her. His father can't be all that bad to have raised two kids as nice as Johnny and Julia. OK, I'll tell him I'll come to his Sunday brunch and see what happens."

Johnny insisted on having a cab bring her to their home on Sunday. It was a large, second floor apartment, overlooking Central Park. The gathering turned out to be somewhat larger than Johnny led her to believe. There was Uncle Ed and Aunt Harriet; a brother and sister-in-law of John Sr.; Aunt Emily, a widowed sister of John Sr.; plus a dozen more who were friends of either John Sr. or Julia and Johnny. It was an informal gathering, and the food was served buffet style with small tables set up at various spots. There were two maids who kept the coffee cups and juice glasses replenished and the serving dishes replaced as needed. In a short time, Belle found herself feeing more at ease than she expected. In the next two months Belle and Johnny saw each other at least one evening a week, often more. Belle did not tell Rose how often they saw each other, but she confided her growing feelings toward Johnny to Iris. Johnny was also not revealing his feelings for Belle to any of his friends, but he confided in Julia and enlisted her help in choosing an engagement ring. Because he wanted to surprise everyone with the engagement announcement, they pretended the ring was for Julia's birthday when they purchased it. He planned to give it to Belle on a Saturday evening, have her attend the Sunday brunch, and make the announcement there. Two days before this happened, an article appeared on the society page of the newspaper.

> It's been reported that a certain young banker has been frequently seen in the company of a dark haired, blue- eyed beauty. Could this be something serious or merely a young man's fling?

Rose never missed reading the society page, and when Belle came to work the next morning, she was immediately greeted with, "Well, well. Have you been keeping secrets from me?" When Belle asked what she meant, Rose handed her the article. "Now, please, don't try to tell me this isn't you and Johnny they are referring to," Rose said, smiling broadly.

Belle seemed a bit flustered and replied, "Yes, we have been seeing each other, but I really don't think it's newsworthy."

"Oh, you don't know New York that well, dear. When someone as beautiful as you is seen in the company of one of the city's most eligible bachelors, it's considered newsworthy."

Julia also saw the article and pointed it out to Johnny. His response was to throw the paper down and mutter, "Damned busy bodies." Then added, "Julia please don't show this to dad, yet. I'm going to ask her to marry me tonight and announce it at tomorrow's brunch. I want it to be a surprise for everyone."

"I'm not sure dad will appreciate being kept in the dark, but I'll keep your secret for you," she said.

Johnny took Belle to a small, out-of-the-way, Italian restaurant, hoping to avoid any familiar faces. They were seated at a corner table. Nothing was said about the newspaper article during the meal. When they finished eating, Johnny reached across the table and took Belle's hand, saying, "Belle, a while back I told you I thought I was falling in love with you. Well, that's no longer true. What's true now is that I'm head-over-heels in love with you. Belle, darling, will you marry me?"

With that he set the jeweler's box near Bell and opened it. Belle paused a moment, looking from the ring to his face, and said, "Are you really sure you want to marry a widow who was raised on a farm and now works in a lady's dress shop?"

"The one I want to marry is the most beautiful, charming, intelligent woman I've ever met or ever hope to meet."

"Oh, Johnny, I just…"

"Do you love me Belle?"

"I do, but…"

"Then, I don't see any problem. Please, say 'yes.'"

She paused another moment, gave a nervous laugh, and quietly said, "Yes." Johnny hadn't realized he'd been holding his breath, but as soon as she said yes, he gave a long sigh, leaned across the table to kiss her, and then placed the ring on her hand. It was a half-karat emerald-cut diamond with two small sapphires on either side. "I hope you like it. The sapphires are to match your eyes."

"It's beautiful. I do love you Johnny. Please don't ever break my heart."

"Belle, what a silly thing to say! I'd rather cut my own heart out than hurt you in any way. Let's have one more glass of wine, before I take you home. I'm picking you up tomorrow for our Sunday brunch. We'll give everyone our good news there. Deal?"

"Deal," she replied, smiling.

Johnny timed their arrival at the brunch, so they would be the last to arrive. As soon as they walked in, Johnny said, "Good morning, everyone. I'm sorry we're a little late, but I have an announcement to make and wanted to be sure everyone was here when I did. Belle just agreed to be my wife."

Belle was feeling a little uncomfortable and blushing slightly. Julia led the congratulation, and everyone began talking at once.

When the conversation quieted down, John Sr. spoke up saying, "Well this is quite a surprise, but then Johnny has always loved pulling off a surprise. This is one of your more impressive ones, son. Congratulations to you both. Now, I'm sure everyone is hungry, so let's eat."

When the meal was over, the ladies all had to see the ring and exclaim over it. The men were gathered around Johnny, joking and congratulating him.

During a lull in the conversation. Aunt Emily spoke up saying. "Johnny you know you are going to break a lot of hopeful hearts, when this news gets out."

"Oh, I doubt that, Aunt Emily. It's more likely it will be the young men of the city who will be disappointed."

As they were leaving, John Sr. said to Belle, "You must come have dinner with us one evening soon, so we can get to know you better."

"Thank you, I'd like that."

"Will this Thursday evening fit into your schedule?"

"I'm sure it will."

"Wonderful. We'll plan on seeing you here at seven Thursday."

When Belle arrived at the shop Monday morning, she found Rose was not yet there. This was unusual, as Rose was always there first to open up. Belle did have a key, so she went in and began getting ready for the day, thinking perhaps Rose might have overslept. After thirty minutes, she began to get worried. When another half hour passed with no sign of Rose, she began feeling a little panicky. Just then, the policeman who patrolled their street walked by, glanced in the window, and tipped his hat to Belle.

She hurried to the door to speak with him. "Officer Brady, may I speak to you a moment. Rose was not at the shop when I arrived this morning and still hasn't come in. I'm worried."

"Hmm. That is very unusual for her. Tell you what, I'll go by her flat just to make sure everything is OK. I'm sure it's just a matter of some unavoidable delay."

"Thank you. I really would appreciate it." An hour later Officer Brady was back, looking very serious. "Mrs. Dawson, I'm afraid it's bad news. Mrs. Downey apparently died in her sleep last night."

Belle stood quite still for what seemed like several minutes, then said, "Are you sure? She was fine Saturday. I know she's been a little tired lately but, is she's really gone?"

"Yes, ma'am. I had the doctor come in which is why it took me so long to get back to you. Do you know if she has any family?"

"I've never heard her speak of anyone. I'm not sure what I should do. Maybe, her accountant at the bank would know if there is anyone."

"I think, perhaps, you should close the shop and go to the bank to talk to him."

"That's probably a good idea. I just can't believe she's gone."

Rose's accountant, Mr. Adams, did not have any information, but he told Belle he referred Rose to a lawyer next door, when she told him she would like to have a will drawn up.

Belle went next door to speak to the lawyer, Mr. Hardesty. She introduced herself, adding that she was an employee of Mrs. Downey.

"Oh, yes, she's spoken of you. She thinks very highly of you, you know." At this, Belle's eyes began to brim with tears.

"Mrs. Dawson, what is it? Are you all right?"

"No, I've come to ask for your help. Rose died in her sleep last night. I don't know if she has any family, and her accountant referred me to you. Is there anyone you can notify?"

"Oh, no, I'm so sorry to hear that. No, I'm afraid that Mrs. Downey didn't have any family members living. She did leave detailed instructions with me as to what she wanted done in the event of her death. I'll begin making arrangements, if that's agreeable with you?"

"What? Oh, yes, that will be fine. This is just too much. My mind has gone blank."

"Understandable. Why don't you sit down for a few moments, and let me get you a cup of tea."

"Thank you, yes that might help." After she had a sip of tea, she said, "Will you let me know about the funeral? I think I should put a notice in the shop window. I'm sure some of her customers might want to attend. Oh! What should I do about the shop after the funeral?"

"I suggest you open again next week. Life does go on you know."

"But how can I do that? It's Rose's shop."

"Well, not exactly."

"What do you mean?"

"Oh, dear. Does this mean Mrs. Downey didn't tell you?"

"Tell me what?"

"Well, Mrs. Dawson, as I mentioned earlier, Mrs. Downey thought very highly of you. Two months ago, she came to me to draw up a will. In it, she stated that upon her death, the Rose Fashion shop and all Mrs. Downey's assets were to go to you."

The next few days left Belle feeling like she had been dropped into a foreign country and didn't understand the language or the customs. Mr. Hardesty efficiently took over the funeral arrangements for Rose. Word of Rose's death quickly spread among her customers. At the small church that she had designated for her funeral the alter was blanketed with flowers, and many people came to the funeral.

When the funeral was over, Mr. Hardesty came up to Belle to ask if it would be possible for her to meet with him the next day to discuss the details of Rose's will. Her initial reaction to his informing her that she was the sole beneficiary of Rose's estate was to insist there had been some mistake. Mr. Hardesty assured her there was no mistake and suggested they could discuss it further after the funeral, when some of the shock subsided. She didn't feel at all ready for this meeting yet, but he was insistent that it was something that shouldn't be delayed. When she arrived at his office, she found Mr. Adams was also present.

"I've taken the liberty of asking Mr. Adams to join us, since he has been overseeing Mrs. Downey's finances for many years. I hope you don't mind," said Mr. Hardesty.

"No, of course not," she replied. The meeting revealed that in addition to the shop, Rose accumulated $25,000 in savings. Papers needed to be signed to transfer everything into Belle's name. Mr. Adams briefly explained how he kept track of the income and expenses and encouraged her to consider investing some of the savings in stocks.

"I'm afraid I could never convince Mrs. Downey to do that. She preferred just keeping it in a savings account."

When the meeting ended, Belle went to the shop to place a sign in the window, stating it would be open again on Monday. Then she walked home, still feeling dazed, and sat gazing out the window. Her thoughts were jumbled and chaotic.

The one clear thought that kept surfacing was "I can't believe my life has turned upside down again!"

Her reverie was interrupted by a knock on the door. It was Johnny. "Belle, honey, how are you?" he asked, embracing her.

"Oh, Johnny, I don't know. I'm fine. It's just that this week has seemed unreal."

"I know honey. It will just take some time. You need to take it easy and rest for a few days."

"Mr. Adams wants me to open the shop Monday."

"Who is Mr. Adams?"

"He was Rose's accountant."

"Well, I'm sure he will begin looking for a buyer for the shop. Hopefully, he will find one soon, and you won't need to go there any more."

"But Johnny, I need to work."

"You really don't, you know. You wouldn't have continued to work there after we were married anyway. I can take care of your expenses until then."

"But Johnny, you don't understand. The shop is mine now."

"What do you mean?"

"Rose left the shop to me in her will. I had a meeting with her lawyer and accountant this afternoon."

"You're the owner of Rose Fashions?"

"Apparently."

"Well, I'll be! Did you know this was going to happen?"

"No! Rose never said a thing. I still can't believe it myself."

"Well, let's go have dinner and celebrate.

"No, Johnny, I'm just worn out from this past week, and it just doesn't feel like something I want to celebrate. It will be so strange to be at the shop without Rose. Tonight, I just want to take a hot bath, not think of anything, and sleep for about ten hours."

"OK, darling, I understand. Will you come to brunch on Sunday?"

"I don't think so. I think I just need to spend the weekend relaxing and getting my bearings."

"Well, everyone will be disappointed, but I'll explain that you are just worn out. Dad wanted me to ask if we could reschedule our dinner for next Friday."

"That should be fine. Thank you for understanding."

"I have a busy week coming up, too, but I'll have Julia stop by the shop to see how you are, and I'll pick you up Friday evening."

The next week went by quickly for Belle. Even though Rose had been getting Belle involved in more aspects of the shop than just doing the buying for the younger crowd and waiting on customers, she discovered there was much more to learn. She had another meeting with Mr. Adams and found she was able to absorb the information he had for her. He again suggested investing in the stock market, but she declined, saying she wanted to wait a bit, until she was more at ease with her new responsibilities.

The dinner on Friday evening, consisted of John Sr., Julia, and Aunt Emily. Aunt Emily had a number of questions for Belle about her family and Bill's career as a musician. Belle told the same story that she told to Rose and Iris. John Sr. added, "These recent changes in your life must be quite a challenge for you, I imagine."

"Yes, it has been a bit overwhelming. I've enjoyed the time I spent at Rose Fashions and feel confident I can continue to offer the same quality service that Rose did."

"Oh, I'm sure you can," added Julia.

Aunt Emily asked what their plans were for the wedding. Johnny spoke up saying, "We haven't really discussed any details or a date. I'd kind of thought a late fall or Christmas wedding would be nice. Would you agree, Belle?"

"I really haven't been able to give it any thought at all yet, but that might be nice."

For the next two weeks, Belle put in long days at the shop, staying after hours to check the inventory and gather the receipts to take to the bank every morning before opening. She had another meeting with Mr. Adams and was beginning to feel more confident about her role as a business owner. Several evenings were spent writing thank you notes to everyone who sent flowers for the funeral. Because of this, she had only been able to spend two evenings with Johnny, plus another Sunday brunch.

Near the end of the third week, Johnny told her he had some bad news. "I'm going to be gone for a month. Dad wants me to go to a bank in Boston and spend time with their manager. I can't say I'm looking forward to it, but I suppose it's something I should do, if I'm to make a career in banking. I just wish you could go with me, but I suppose that wouldn't be very practical, even if you weren't the owner of Rose Fashions. We need to set a date for the wedding, so we can see each other more than a day or two every week."

"I'll miss you too, Johnny, but I'll bet the time will go fast for both of us."

"I certainly hope so. I'm leaving Saturday, so let's plan on a nice dinner Friday evening."

On Monday, as she was closing the shop, John Sr. came in the door.

"Mr. Honeywell, what a nice surprise. What brings you here?" Belle said.

"I'll make this brief and to the point, Belle. I hired an investigator to look into your past. I'm not happy with the information he's given me, though I can't say I was all that surprised."

"You did what? Why?"

"Surely, you understand I couldn't allow my son to bring someone into our family that we knew nothing about. It seems there were a number of things you neglected to tell us. My investigator found no record of your marriage to the musician you tell about. He did find a record of a marriage and a divorce to another man. Now, it seems you've also been able to coerce Mrs. Downy into making you her sole heir. I will not allow Johnny to bring someone of your questionable character into our family. I haven't revealed any of this to him. Johnny can be quite stubborn at times, and you have managed to effectively bewitch him. So to avoid any scene, this is what will happen. You are to arrange for the immediate sale of the shop and leave town with no forwarding information. I expect you to be gone before he returns from Boston. If you can't find a buyer in that amount of time, I'll pay you a fair price for it and have my broker find a suitable buyer."

"You can't possibly be serious!"

"Oh, but I assure you, I am. Let me also assure you I can make life extremely unpleasant for you if you don't agree to all this. That includes not saying anything about this to either Johnny or Julia. Unless you need to have me purchase the shop, I don't expect to ever see or hear from you again. Good day."

Belle stood staring at his retreating back until he was out of sight and for several minutes after. Then the anger set in. "Who the hell does he think he is? He can't possibly do that. Johnny wouldn't stand for it. I'm going to go talk to him, right now. Oh! I can't, he's in Boston. John must have had this planned before he sent him to Boston. I'm going to go see Iris. I'll explode if I don't talk to someone about this."

She arrived at the bakery just as Iris was leaving for the day. "Belle, how nice to see you" was all Iris got out before Belle said,

"Iris, may I please come home with you for a while? I need to talk to someone, and, I'm so mad if I don't, I don't know what I might do!"

"Belle, darling, of course you're welcome to come. Whatever has happened?" It was only a short walk to the O'Brian home.

Belle began speaking in a rush, telling her about John Sr.'s visit to the shop, ending with, "What is the matter with him Iris? I can't talk to Johnny. He's in Boston. Maybe, I should close the shop for a few days and go see him."

By now, they were inside Iris's home. "Belle, darlin', sit down. Let me get you a cup of tea. You need to calm down."

"How can I calm down? He's trying to ruin my life!"

"Now, listen to me, Belle. You're not thinkin' clear. Mr. Honeywell is a powerful man, and I'm believin' he'll do just what he says. You need to think about that."

"But Iris, this isn't right!"

"Ah, well, now who went and told ya things are always right in this world? Men like Mr. Honeywell have always done as they please, and the likes of us canna' do a thing about it."

"But Iris, Johnny wants to marry me!"

"I know, I know, but ya gotta know Johnny probably can't afford to be defyin' his da on somethin' like this."

By now Belle's rage was subsiding, and she began crying. "Iris, what am I going to do? Where will I go?"

"Can ya not go home to your family?"

"No Iris, I can't. There were some problems between pa and me that I haven't told you about. And besides, farm life just isn't for me."

"Well, it doesn't mean you'd need to stay there forever. It's been a long time since you've been home. I'm sure your da has been missin' you."

"No, Iris, my pa is a very stubborn man. I tried going home once after ma, died and it was terrible."

"Well, then, help me with supper. I'm sure we can think of somethin'."

After they had eaten, Iris said, "I've been thinkin' Belle. I have a cousin in Chicago. That might be a place for you to start over. I could write to her, and I know she'd be glad to help in any way she could."

"Chicago? Well, maybe. I'm just too tired to think any more tonight. I'm going home to sleep on it."

Chapter Seven

Belle spent two days feeling sorry for herself, wondering why her life always seemed to fall apart just when things were going well, and asking herself what was wrong with her. She was puzzled as to why Mr. Honeywell said there was no record of her marriage to Bill, then remembered that they never went to the courthouse to register, as the minister suggested. Two days was all she could take of feeling helpless, so she pulled herself together and took Iris' suggestion to go to Chicago. She asked Mr. Adams to recommend a bank in Chicago, then had him make out a check to that bank, keeping enough cash out of her funds for travel expenses. She gave him a vague reason for leaving and asked him not to give out information to anyone about where she went.

She arrived in Chicago on a hot, windy, mid-July day. Johnny's ring was on her left hand, Bill's on her right. Her other jewels were in the pouch she wore under her clothing. She asked the porter at the train station if he could recommend a hotel near the bank Mr. Adams referred her to. Early the next morning, she went to the bank and opened an account. Mr. Adams reminded her the bank would want verification of who she was, so she took the marriage certificate from her marriage to Bill with her. After that, she took a cab to the address of Iris' cousin.

Belle's hotel was in a nice neighborhood, near the lake. The second floor apartment the Hegarty's lived in was in a much poorer part of the city. There were numerous pubs, and the cab passed several churches. When Belle introduced herself, Peg Hagerty greeted her warmly.

"Come in, come in. Iris wrote to tell me you'd be stoppin' by. Would ya like a cup of tea?"

"That would be nice, thank you." Peg had carrot red hair and gray eyes that sparkled with life. She and Belle chatted easily. Belle told her she wasn't sure of her plans but had come into a bit of money and was considering buying some kind of small business. When Peg asked her what she was thinking of, Belle replied, "Well, I worked in a lady's dress shop in New York. When the owner died suddenly, I discovered she had willed the shop and all her assets to me. It was a complete surprise. I suppose I could do that here, but I'm not sure I want to go back to waiting on ladies who have little else to do but spend their husband's money on fancy clothes."

"Have ya done any other kind of work then?" asked Peg.

"Well, I worked in a small café when I lived in Nashville, and I enjoyed that."

"Maybe you could open your own café?"

"Oh, I don't know. I'm not much of a cook."

"Well, now, ya wouldn't have to be doin' the cookin' yourself, ya know. You could hire someone for that, and you could take care of the customers."

Belle spent the next two days touring the city, on foot and by cab, reading newspapers and contemplating the course her life had taken to that point. She began to see that the difficult times all happened when she was involved with those in the upper levels of society. Her thoughts again went back to Bill and how happy they were.

The O'Brian's had been helpful and completely accepting of her. Peg seemed to have the same character as Iris. She came to a decision, and on the third day went back to see Peg. Once again, she was greeted warmly and invited into the kitchen. After Peg poured them each a cup of tea, Belle said, "Peg, I've been thinking about our last conversation. I've decided I really don't want to put myself in a position of dealing with those in high society again. The idea of running a small café appeals to me. I thought perhaps you would have some suggestions as to what part of the city I could consider and, maybe, have some idea about someone I could hire as a cook."

"Saint's alive, Belle! I was talkin' to my Danny about you, and he said "Wouldn't it be something if she decided to do that here in our neighborhood. God knows we could use one."

"Really! You think there's a need for a café here?" asked Belle.

"Oh, I do. Granted, there's not a great deal of extra money floatin' around these streets, but I think havin' a place to gather now and then that wasn't a pub would go over well. Of course, the fare would need to be simple and not overpriced, but I think you could make a go of it."

"So, do you know if there is any space available near here?"

"I can't think of one right now, but I'll bet you could find one. I could ask Father Donnely. He'd be likely to know if there was something in his parish."

"I'd be grateful if you could ask him. Are there any other neighborhoods you could suggest in case that doesn't work out?"

"Well, none that I'm real familiar with. There's a German neighborhood aways from here that might be a possibility."

Belle asked for directions to that neighborhood, and Peg said she could talk to Father Donnely, yet today. Belle left and walked around the neighborhood a bit, then found a cab to take her to the German neighborhood. She spent an hour or so walking that neighborhood and noted that many of the conversations she overheard were in the German language. When she returned to Peg's the next afternoon, she found Peg brimming with excitement.

"Belle, wait 'til ya hear this! Father Donnely said there is a small store front that is empty, and it's only a few doors away from a rooming house. You'd have some ready made customers nearby. Would you like to see it? It's about a twenty minute walk from here."

"Yes, I would. Can you come with me?"

"I can and I shall."

During the walk they met a number of people who knew Peg. Because of this, the twenty minutes became more like forty-five, since Peg introduced Belle to everyone and told them she might be opening a small café nearby. Nearly everyone indicated they thought that would be a fine thing. The store was small and would probably be able to seat no more than thirty people. There were paned windows facing the street that could be opened to let air in. By the time they began walking back to Peg's, Belle was beginning to feel some excitement.

"It seems perfect, Peg. Who would I talk to about the price, and do you think I should put a notice in the paper that I'm looking for a cook?"

"Well, ya could do that, if ya like, but, I'm a pretty fair cook, and me kids are old enough now that I don't need to be to home the whole day. I'd be happy to help, if that would interest you."

Things moved very quickly after that. In only one month Belle found a small apartment for herself, and opened the Irish Rose Café.

She chose the name in honor of the woman who made all this possible. A small shelf was put up in a prominent place on the wall, to display the Waterford crystal vase with the etched rose.

It didn't take long for word to spread that the food was good, the prices fair, and that lingering over a cuppa, visiting with friends, was not discouraged. Belle soon came to know most of her customers by name. It reminded her of when she was with Bill, and worked in the café in Nashville, a pleasant memory, that brought some sadness again over the loss of Bill.

She and Peg became good friends, and Belle was often invited to share a Sunday meal with Peg's family. Peg and Dan had four children: Daniel, sixteen; Eileen, fourteen; Sean, thirteen; and Mary, eleven.

The Irish Rose was open from 11:00 a.m. until 8:00 p.m., Monday through Saturday. During the first few weeks, Peg left at 4:00, to go home, fix a quick meal for her family, then return to the café about an hour later, leaving Eileen in charge of serving the meal, cleaning up, and supervising her younger brothers and sister. It wasn't long before Dan lost patience with this schedule. He and Peg argued about this. "I did'na bargain for a part time wife," he shouted one night.

Belle soon became aware of the tension between them, and approached Peg about it. "Peg, your help has been a lifesaver for me, but I can see the long hours are taking a heavy toll on you and your family. I think I should find someone who can come in around 3:00 or 4:00, to help with the evening customers. You need to be home with your family."

"I can'na deny it's been causin' a wee bit of trouble to home," she replied.

"Do you think Kate O'Grady might be interested in doing that?"

"That she might." said Peg. "She's only seventeen though, and might not be wantin' to be givin' up that many of her evenings. You might talk to the widow Kelly about it too." Neither Mrs. Kelly, nor Kate wanted to work six evenings every week, so Belle hired them both, leaving them to decide which days they would work.

One evening, a group of young men came into the café for their evening meal. They were a lively bunch, joking and flirting with Belle as she took their orders. One of them said to Belle, "You look awfully familiar to me. What's your name?"

Belle smiled and replied, "That's an old line, you know. My name's Belle."

"Oh, my gosh!" he replied. "It wasn't no line. You're Belle Mericle, aren't you? Remember me? Kenny Miller."

"Kenny! I don't believe this. You're a long way from home."

"Yep, sure am. Bein' a farmer wasn't for me, so I up and took off for Chicago. Turns out, I didn't get all that far away from farmin' after all. I'm workin' at the stockyards. Still, livin' in the city is more to my likin' than livin' on a farm. So what got you to Chicago, Belle?"

"Oh, it's a long story, and right now I have customers to take care of."

"Well, sure, I wouldn't want to get you fired. What time are you done workin'? Maybe we could go someplace and do some catchin' up."

"I don't think so, Kenny. It's nearly 10:00 before I get things finished up here. You won't get me fired though, I own the café."

"No kiddin'! Well, I'll be! Your sign says you're closed on Sunday's. How about we get together then?"

"That would be nice." He asked for her address, saying he could come by at 2:00 Sunday afternoon.

As she did the final clean up for the evening, her thoughts returned to the conversation with Kenny. "I can't believe someone from home walked into my café" she thought. "I wonder how long he's been in Chicago, and if he can tell me anything about what's happening with my family? I just couldn't write to Ray after I left Nashville. I suppose I should. Maybe, I won't tell him about New York and Johnny. I'll just tell him things didn't work out with Ken, and that I have my own business. Ray was always on my side, but he'll tell Mae anything I tell him, and I don't want to think about all the gossip and nasty remarks that will cause." As she walked into her apartment, she shook herself mentally, and said out loud, "I can't believe I'm twenty-eight, and worrying about what my family thinks of me!"

Kenny was at her door at 2:00 Sunday afternoon. "Hello, again, Belle. You ready for some re-hashing of the 'good old days'?" he said, then laughed.

"Is that why you left? Because things were so good?" she asked, smiling.

"Yeah, right. You up for a walk? There's a park a ways from here. I thought we could sit under a shade tree, have a beer or two, and catch up on what we've been doin' since leavin' Nebraska. I even brought the beer," he said, holding up a sack he was carrying.

"That suits me fine. It will be a nice change from my usual Sunday routine. I'll just get a blanket for us to sit on."

It was a warm, windy, August day. The park was about a twenty minute walk from Belle's place. It was nearly 3:00 before they arrived, since they stopped briefly, several times, along the way, to exchange greetings with some of Belle's friends.

They found a comfortable spot under a large maple tree. "Whew! This shade feels good," said Kenny, as they sat down. "You ready for a beer? It might be a little warm, but it's wet."

Belle wasn't sure a warm beer sounded good, and was surprised to find it was more refreshing than she had imagined it would be.

"So, how did you wind up in Chicago?" Ken asked.

"Oh, it's a long story. You go first, how long have you been here?" she replied.

"Almost four years now. Your turn. You caused quite a stir when you up and disappeared. Where did you go? No one's ever really talked about it."

"No, I don't suppose they have," she laughed. "I ran away with the carnival."

"You're kidding! What in the world made you do that?"

"I was determined to get off the farm, and that seemed like a good idea at the time."

"Was it? You ever regret doin' that?"

"No, not really. I've been able to go places and do things I'd only dreamed about. You ever go back home?"

"I've been back a couple times, for a visit. I was home just last month. By the way, I'm sorry about your brother."

"What do you mean?"

Kenny looked surprised, and said, "You mean you don't know?"

"Know what?"

"Ray joined the army when we declared war. His ship was torpedoed, and he was lost at sea. Never even got to Europe, to see any action."

Belle turned quite pale, and said, in a small voice, "What?"

"Belle, I'm so sorry. I figured you knew. Didn't anyone write to you?"

Tears were welling in her eyes, and she simply shook her head.

"Take a drink of beer, you're white as a sheet."

She took a swallow, choking slightly.

"Take your time. Just take a couple of deep breaths," he said.

They sat quietly for a few minutes, then, she asked "When did it happen?"

"A couple months ago. Ray signed up as soon as we declared war, and got shipped out as soon as he finished basic training. I can't believe no one wrote to you. Maybe the letter got lost."

"Oh, I doubt it, Kenny. My family has pretty much written me off. All except Ray. I hadn't written to him for some time, so he didn't know I was in Chicago. I was thinking yesterday, that I should write to him. I can't believe he's gone."

"I hear they had a nice memorial service for him. It's a shame you couldn't have gone."

"To tell the truth, I don't think I'd have been welcome, Kenny. Last time I was home, my Pa told me I didn't have any business being there, and Lizzie didn't even want to talk to me."

"Ah, Belle, I'm sorry. That must have been pretty tough to take."

"I guess it was, but not all that surprising. Pa and Lizzie don't forgive easily, and they both blame me for Ma's dying."

"I'm sure that's not true."

"Oh, it's true that they blame me. I just hope they are wrong about me having anything to do with Ma dying. Can we go back now, Kenny. I don't feel much like doing any more visiting."

"Sure thing. I'm sorry I had to be the bearer of such bad news."

They were quiet on the walk back to her apartment. When they arrived, Kenny said, "Are you gonna' be alright? Is there anything I can do for you?"

"Thank you, Kenny. I'll be fine."

"Well, OK, then. I'd like to come back to see you next Sunday, if that OK?"

"Sure, that will be fine," she replied.

As the door closed behind Kenny, she sat down, allowing the tears she'd been holding back to flow. When the tears finally stopped, thoughts began to surface. The kinds of thoughts that she had never allowed to fully form.

"Bill and Ray were the only two men who were ever kind to me, the only ones who really seemed to care about me. And Ma was always good to me. Now, they are all gone. I wonder if it's possible for someone to be cursed. Except for Bill and Ray, I've never had anyone I felt close to, anyone I could talk to without being told I was wrong. Other people have friends like that. What's wrong with me?" She spent much of the evening sitting in the dark, feeling miserable, and sorry for herself. Her sleep that night was restless, and filled with dreams. When she woke in the morning, she felt there might have been some kind of message for her in the dreams, but wasn't able to clearly recall any of them.

When Peg arrived at the café that morning, she noticed Belle was pale and had dark circles under her eyes. "Belle, are you alright?"

"I'm fine, Peg. I just had trouble sleeping last night, for some reason." She had decided last night that she wasn't going to tell anyone at the café about Ray. It would lead to questions about her family, and she didn't want to go into all that with them.

During the rest of that week, Belle managed to present her usual cheerful manner to her customers and staff. Once she was back at her apartment, it was a different story. She continued to mentally replay her life, trying to see what she could have done differently. Other than deep regret for not keeping in touch with Ray, she could not see anything she should have done differently. Bill and Ray began to be the focus of most of her thoughts. "I wish I could talk to them. They could help me" was one thought that surfaced the most often.

One night, while reading the newspaper, she noticed a small ad.

Have you lost someone you love to death? Would you like to speak with them again? Come learn how you can do so. Sunday, August 14, 4:00 p.m., at 3746 Thomas Avenue. Donations accepted.

This was only a little over a week away. "I wonder if this is a hoax of some kind." she thought. She laid the paper aside, but a short while later, tore the ad out and placed it on her bedside table. She told herself she probably wouldn't go, but wanted the information, in case she changed her mind.

Kenny came to the café Friday evening, without his friends this time. "Hi, Belle, I wanted to check to see if it's still OK for me to come over Sunday?"

"That will be fine, Kenny. Is 2:00 OK?"

"Sure is, I'll see you then."

Peg overheard this conversation and, after Kenny left, said to Belle, "I'm that glad to see you're to be steppin' out with that young man. You're needin' a bit of fun in your life. You've been lookin' a wee bit down lately."

"Oh, we're not 'steppin' out', Peg. He's a friend from my home town. We're just catching up on news from back home."

"Well, ya just never know what might happen with an old friend. You're much too young to be leadin' such a solitary life, ya know."

Belle smiled, and walked across the room to wait on some customers who had just arrived.

Belle found herself looking forward to Sunday, and was pleased when Kenny arrived a little early.

"Would you like to go back to the park again?" he asked.

"I hoped you might suggest that," she said. "This time, I've got the beer for us, and I made some sandwiches."

"Well, all right! Let me carry that basket."

The day was warmer than the previous Sunday had been. The wind, that was nearly a daily occurrence in Chicago, saved them from being completely miserable with the heat.

"Sometimes, I find the wind a bit tiring here," commented Belle, "but it does feel good today, sitting here in the shade."

"Know what you mean. I guess we should be used to it though, 'cause Nebraska can be pretty windy too," replied Kenny. "So, how are you doing, Belle?" he asked.

"Oh, I'm fine, I think. I just keep wishing I had kept in touch with Ray. Have you ever lost someone you cared about Kenny?" she asked.

"Not really, except, maybe, my grandma. I was in seventh grade when she passed. She used to tell some good stories."

"Really, what kind?"

"Oh, lots of things. Some of them were so outlandish, I kinda had to wonder how much she made up. My dad always said a story wasn't worth tellin' if it wasn't good, and if it wasn't, Grandma would make it good."

They both laughed, and Belle asked, "Do you remember any of them?"

"A few, I guess. One time, she told us about seeing a ghost."

"Really?"

"Yep, said it was her brother, who had died as a young man."

"So, what did she say about it?"

"Well, she claimed she had just gone to bed one night, when she heard someone call her name. Said she sat up, and there was her brother, standing at the end of the bed. Claimed he said to her 'You need to take care of things,' but when she asked him, what things, he just disappeared."

"I can see why you'd remember that story. Do you think it was true?"

"Oh, who knows? Maybe, maybe not. Could be she'd been asleep, had a dream, and thought it was real."

"Be nice if it was true, don't you think?"

"Oh, I don't know. I think something like that would scare the bejesus outta me," he laughed.

"I saw an ad in the paper the other day about a meeting. It said you could learn how to talk to people who have passed on."

"You're not thinkin' of goin', are you?"

"Oh, I'm not sure, probably not. But, I keep thinking, if that was possible, I could talk to Ray again, or maybe my Bill."

"Sounds to me like you are thinkin' of goin'. You be careful, if you do. Could be a bunch of charlatans just wanting to get money outta you."

"Yeah, you're probably right."

They spent the rest of the afternoon talking about the people back in Nebraska. She learned that Lizzie now had three children, and that

Mae was married, and living in David City. Her brother, David, and Ann had two boys, and were still living on the farm with John.

"You think you'll ever go back home again?" asked Kenny.

"Oh, I don't know, maybe. Ray always said he thought Pa and Lizzie would get over being so angry after some time had passed. So, how come you're not married by now Kenny?"

"Well I'm not really sure marriage is for me, I guess. Besides, I've just been havin' too much fun on my own."

"Is that right? What kinds of things do you do for fun?"

"Well, I probably wouldn't tell anyone else from back home this, but I like to do a bit of honky tonkin'. There's a few places here where you can dance all night, and just generally have a good time. You ever do any dancin'?"

"Bill and I used to dance a lot. He was really good."

"Well, you should come with me some night. Would do you good."

"I'd like that, but I'm at the café six nights, and by the time we close, I'm bushed."

"You need to find another girl to come in and take over for you some of the time. Life's too short to do nuthin' but work six days a week."

"You sure you're Kenny Miller from Nebraska? That doesn't sound like anyone I grew up around," she laughed.

"Yeah, I guess, maybe you and me was cut from a different cloth."

"I guess we were. We should probably be heading back. It will be getting dark before too long."

As they were saying good night, Kenny said, "You do some thinking about what I said about getting more help so's you and me can go honky tonkin' now and then."

Belle laughed, and promised she would consider it.

As she was getting ready for bed, she noticed the newspaper ad again. "I'm going to go," she thought. "Maybe it is a hoax, but I want to go see for myself."

There were seven women at the meeting, plus the presenter, who introduced herself as Margaret Oswald. She began by talking about the soul, or spirit being an entity that survives the death of the physical body, citing examples of those who had been contacted by someone in their lives who had died. "Generally, it seems, these contacts take place when there is some message the departed wants to relay to those still on the earth plane. They don't appreciate those who want only to engage in a parlor game, asking trivial questions, such as whether or not to buy a particular dress. How many of your are here today out of simple curiosity, as opposed to feeling a need to have contact with someone you loved?" No one raised their hand. "I'm happy to see that," she said. Belle raised her hand. "Yes, you have a question?"

"Yes, you said a spirit will only appear if they have a message for someone here. What about someone here wanting to tell them something?"

"That can, and does happen. However, it usually happens only if the spirit also has a message to pass on. I assume you have something you would like to say to a departed loved one?"

"Yes, but I would also like some advice from them."

"The advice you seek, does it involve something significant in your life, a personal matter, perhaps?"

"It does."

"Does anyone else have any questions?" When there was no response, she continued. "Very well, then. Shall we get started?"

The chairs were arranged in a circle, window shades were drawn to darken the room, and several candles were lit. Margaret explained that a spirit would usually speak through her, but could also appear in a physical manifestation, such as a cloud of vapor, an object moving, and, in rare cases, as they had looked while still alive. She then asked them to join hands, breathe deeply, relax, and focus their thoughts on the person they wished to contact. After a few moments, Margaret began speaking, but in a very deep, husky voice, quite different from her earlier speech.

"Anna, I will always love you, but it's time for you to love another."

The woman named Anna gave a small gasp and began to quietly weep.

There was another period of quiet before Margaret again began speaking. This time, she addressed Belle.

"Belle, you still wear my ring. You must remember you are different." After a very short silence, another voice came from Margaret.

"He's right, Belle. You must remember you are different. That's why you left home."

For a moment, Belle had difficulty breathing, then took a breath, and touched the ring Bill had given her. She had put the ring Johnny gave her away with her other jewelry some time ago, but continued to wear Bill's. There were messages for two of the other women present before the session ended, but she had been unable to focus on anything but the voices that had been directed to her.

Margaret gave a big sigh, and slowly said, "I believe our session is finished for today. I hope it was of some help to you. I am never aware of what transpires in these sessions, and would ask that each of you keep whatever you heard directed to another in strict confidence." She got up and began to raise the shades in the room. "If you found today's session to be of value to you, there is a bowl on the table where you may leave a donation. The amount is up to you. I hold these sessions once a month. The next one will be September 20th. I am also available for a limited number of individual session, if that is something that interests you."

Most of the women seemed a bit overwhelmed by what they had just observed, and there was little conversation among them as they began to leave. Margaret's home was in a neighborhood of large Victorian homes, with wide streets and large shade trees. Because it was several miles from Belle's apartment, she had taken a taxi, asking the driver to return for her at 6:30 p.m. It was now only 6:00, and Belle asked Margaret if she would mind if she waited on the porch for her taxi.

"Of course you may. Would you like a glass of lemonade? It's such a lovely evening, I'll join you while you wait." She went inside to get the lemonade and sat down in a chair near Belle when she returned.

"I hope you found today's session helpful?"

"Yes, it was, I think."

"Sometimes, the messages we are given seem too brief to be fully understood. In time, the meaning usually becomes clearer."

Belle was absently fingering Bill's ring. Margaret noticed, and asked, "Does your ring have special significance for you?"

"Yes, it was my wedding ring from Bill."

"And yet, you are wearing it on your right hand."

"I married another man after Bill died, but couldn't bring myself to put his ring away, so I moved it to my right hand. The second marriage didn't work out very well."

"Ah, I'm sorry to hear that. I do sense that you and Bill had a very special connection."

"Yes, we did. Oh, here's my cab now. Thank you for the lemonade."

"You're welcome. I hope I'll see you again."

Belle spent the evening lost in her thoughts, finding she had difficulty following any one thought through to any kind of conclusion. As she drifted off to sleep, she kept hearing the voices from the afternoon, repeating, over and over, 'You're different.'

Belle made it known that she would like to hire someone to fill in some evenings, waiting on customers. With so many men gone to war, there was no shortage of women who needed work. Within a short time, she hired a young woman named Susan to come in three days a week from 4:00 p.m. until closing. Susan proved to be very good with customers, as well as reliable. It didn't take Belle long to feel comfortable leaving the café, giving Susan the responsibility of closing up for the day.

Her thoughts often returned to the elusive message of 'you're different' that she was convinced had come from Bill and Ray, but exactly what it meant continued to elude her.

She began spending an evening every week or two with Kenny, going to clubs, dancing, and having a few drinks. It seemed most of the people at the clubs also smoked cigarettes, and it wasn't long before Belle decided to try it too. She found she enjoyed smoking, and would often have a cigarette to relax after coming home from the café.

Because of her striking appearance; black hair, blue eyes, ivory skin, and petite figure, she had a steady stream of men, young, and not-so-young, asking her to dance. The fact that Kenny danced with a number of different women sent a clear message that Belle was not considered "his girl."

One evening while dancing with a man she had danced with several other times, he said to her, "You're not like the other women here."

"Really! Why would you say that?" she asked.

"Because you're different—in a good way, but just different."

Belle had drunk several beers that evening, and flippantly replied, "You're not the first person to tell me that."

"Well, then, it must be true, huh?" he replied. My name's George, but my friends call me Spats, 'cause I like to wear 'em on my shoes."

In her previous encounters with George, Belle had noticed his fine clothing, and the shiny black shoes with white spats he always wore. "Well, I think I like the name George better, so that's what I'll call you. My name's Belle," she replied.

"That's a lovely name, but it doesn't sound very Irish to me."

"And why should it?" she asked.

"Well, with your looks, you gotta be Irish."

"Not that I know of. I was born Belle Mericle."

"Well, I'm bettin' there was some Irish somewhere in your family."

At that point the band took a break, and Belle said, "Thank you for the dance, George."

"Oh, it's my pleasure. I hope we can do it again when the music starts."

"Not tonight, I need to be getting home."

"So early?"

"It's not that early for a working girl, George."

"So where do you work? I'll bet they could do without you for one day."

"Not really, it's my own business."

"No kiddin'! See, I told you, you was different. What kind of business?"

"I have a small café."

"Well, I have to eat, so I'll come by to check it out. Where is it?"

Belle told him, then found Kenny and they headed for home.

"I'm really glad to see you having such a good time, Belle," Kenny said on the way home. "By the way, do you know who that was you were dancing with?"

"No, only that he said his name was George."

"George Donovan, also known as Spats, 'cause of his shoes. He's on the Mayor's staff, an assistant of some kind, as I understand it."

George, "Spats" Donovan came into the Irish Rose a few days later for lunch. "Hi, Belle, I told you I'd stop by, and here I am. What's good to eat?"

"Hello, George, we have a pretty simple menu here, but today's special is Irish Stew. It's hard to beat."

"Sounds good, that's what I'll have then. So, how long have you had the café?"

"Almost a year and a half now," she replied.

"Well, good for you! Runnin' your own business is hard work."

"Sometimes, but I enjoy it."

"You goin' dancin' Friday night?"

"I thought I would."

"Well, how's about you let me pick you up? Ridin' in my Ford will be a lot more fun than ridin' the trolley."

Belle laughed and said, "I suppose it would."

"So, is that a yes?"

"That's a yes."

"Great, how about I pick you up at seven and we get some dinner before we go dancin'?"

"I don't think so, George. I need to spend some time on paper work."

"Well, OK, if you're sure. Will you give me a rain check on dinner?"

"Sure, why not."

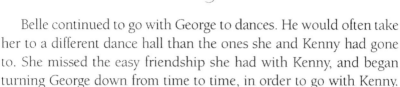

Belle continued to go with George to dances. He would often take her to a different dance hall than the ones she and Kenny had gone to. She missed the easy friendship she had with Kenny, and began turning George down from time to time, in order to go with Kenny. When George realized this, he started spending more of his evenings at the place where he knew Kenny and Belle would be.

One evening, he approached Kenny when Belle wasn't around and said, "Listen, it looks to me like you're tryin' to move in on my girl, and I don't like it."

"George, Belle and I are friends from back home. There's no movin' in goin' on here."

"Yeah, well, that ain't the way it looks to me. She's been sayin' no to me driving her to the dance a lot, and then I find out she's goin' with you. She's a classy dame, and deserves more than a hick from Nebraska, you hear?"

"You're right, George, she is classy. Why don't you ask her what she deserves?"

George grabbed Kenny's arm, saying, "Now, listen you—-"

At that point, Belle came up to them and said, "What's going on with you two?"

Kenny spoke first, "George thinks I'm tryin' to push him outta the picture with you."

"George! What is the matter with you? Kenny and I have been friends since we were kids."

At this point, Kenny said, "I'll see you in a little bit, Belle," and moved off.

"Look, Belle, it just don't seem right that you go out with me a bunch of times and then decide you want to ride the trolley with him instead."

"George, I enjoy spending time with you, but I am not your property. If you ever treat Kenny like that again, you won't be seeing any more of me. Is that clear?"

"Ah, now, Belle, don't get all huffy."

"Then, don't act like you own me."

"I'm sorry, Belle. I just thought it looked like you was ditchin' me. Can I take you to dinner one night soon to make up for it?"

"Sure, George, dinner will be fine."

"OK, then, how about Thursday? I'll pick you up at seven."

"That will be fine."

"Can I take you home tonight?"

"I don't think so. I came with Kenny, so I'll go home with him."

On the trolley ride home, Kenny asked, "What the hell was that all about with George?"

"He was apparently under the impression he could dictate my activities. I set him straight."

"I thought you liked him."

"I do, Kenny, but I'm not ever gonna put myself in a position to be told what I can and can't do by a man. I had my fill of that in Nashville."

"So, Bill was pretty bossy, huh?"

"No, not Bill, after Bill died, I got married again."

"Well, I'll be! You're full of surprises, ain't you? So, Dawson wasn't Bill's name?"

"Yes, it was. The marriage to Ken was a mistake, so when I left Nashville, I went back to using Bill's name."

"When you talk about Bill, it sounds like you're still in love with him. So, why did you get married again?"

"Oh, it's hard to explain. After Bill died, I couldn't support myself working as a waitress. Ken had his own import-export business and offered me a job. Then he and I went on a European buying trip. He kind of overwhelmed me, and talked me into having the ship's Captain marry us just before we returned home."

"Good God! You've been to Europe?"

"Yes, England and Ireland."

"Well, I'll be. You really are somethin' else."

"Sometimes I don't even believe everything that's happened to me since I left the farm," she laughed.

"So, has it been worth it?"

"It's been worth getting off the farm. I just wish things could be a little more normal sometimes."

"Well, ya know, you're not exactly a normal kind of person, Belle."

"I wonder why that is?"

"Who knows, just the way you were made, I guess. It's not really a bad thing, ya know. If you and me was normal, we'd still be back on a farm in Nebraska."

"Yeah, I suppose you're right."

"The trolley arrived at Belle's stop and Kenny said, "Goodnight Belle. See you at the dance next Friday?"

"I don't know. I may take a week off and just stay home."

"Well, see ya later then."

"Goodnight Kenny."

As she walked to her apartment her thoughts were on the conversation she'd just had with Kenny, and those thoughts led her back to the session with the spiritualist when she had been told 'you're different'. She had not returned after that first session. Now she began to wonder if it would be possible to get an answer to what that statement meant. She wasn't comfortable with the idea of being 'different' and not 'normal'." Maybe I'll see if I can get a session with Margaret on Friday. I'd really like some answers", she thought, even though she wouldn't have been able to state exactly what questions she wanted answers to.

While having dinner with George Thursday evening, he asked if he could take her dancing the next night.

"Not this week, George. I have something else I have to do."

"You goin' out with Kenny again?"

"George, I told you, Kenny and I are not 'going out'. But, no, I'm not going dancing this week."

"So, what are ya doin' then?"

"It's personal business George."

"You in any kind of trouble? 'Cause I could probably help take care of it for you."

"No, George, I'm not in trouble."

"Well, if you ever need anything, you just tell me. My job with the Mayor's office lets me be able to take care of things other people can't. And you know, I'd like nuthin' better than to be able to take care of you."

"George, if I ever need your help, I'll ask for it. But, I don't want to be taken care of by anyone."

"Well, why not? I thought that's what every woman wants."

"Not this woman. It puts you in a position of feeling inferior."

"That's nuts! It just means someone cares about you."

"Well, I see a big difference between being cared for and being cared about."

"You do have some weird ideas. Guess I was right when I told you that you were different."

"I guess you were."

Belle's appointment with Margaret was at 5:00 p.m. Friday. Margaret greeted her warmly.

"Belle, how nice to see you again. How are you?"

"Oh, I'm fine, just a little confused. Which is why I wanted to see you again."

"Well, come sit down, and tell me how I can help."

"When I was here before, my brother and my husband spoke through you. They both said the same thing to me."

"And what was that?"

"They told me I needed to remember I'm different. I'm not sure what that means or what I'm supposed to do about it. I was hoping you could contact them again to get some clarification for me."

"Well, first Belle, you need to understand that it isn't me who's contacting them. I'm simply the vehicle they use to communicate. I can try to help you contact your brother and husband, but I can't promise anything."

"I understand. How much do you charge for an individual session?"

"I don't charge for my service. Any donation you would like to make is up to you. Would you like to get started?"

"I would."

"Fine, let me darken the room a bit, then I want you to close your eyes, breathe deeply, and relax. Picture your brother and husband... what are their names?"

"Ray, and Bill."

"OK, picture Ray and Bill in your mind as clearly as you can. Then tell them you would like more information regarding the previous message they gave you."

It seemed to Belle that they sat in silence for a long time, with nothing happening. She was finding it hard to feel relaxed. She felt herself give a long sigh, her eyes began filling with tears, and said to herself, "Oh Ray, Bill, I really wanted to hear from you."

With that, Margaret stirred in her chair a bit, and began speaking in a voice that sounded very much like Bill. "Belle, you are fine. You need to enjoy being different."

There was a short pause, and another voice said, "That's right Belle. Different is your charm and your gift. Enjoy it."

There were a few more moments of silence before Margaret began to stir and open her eyes. She looked at Belle for a moment, and said, "Well, were we successful?"

"Yes, though I'm still not sure I really understand what they are telling me."

"If you like, I'd be happy to discuss it with you. Sometimes we are so emotionally caught up, that the obvious eludes us."

"Well, it sounds kind of silly. Their first message was 'you're different.' This time, all they said was that I need to enjoy being different, that it's my charm and my gift."

"OK, so you sound like you are not comfortable being different."

"No, not really. It has brought me a lot of criticism."

"Yes, I imagine it has. People do seem to have problems with things they perceive as not being normal, and 'normal' is usually defined as being like they are."

Belle laughed, and said, "A friend of mine recently said if he and I were normal, we'd still be on a farm in Nebraska."

"Exactly, you've chosen a different path. That makes you different. It's probably because you are basically different that you chose that path."

"That path has led me into some things that were not very pleasant."

"Ah, but how many of them were pleasant? How many of them were things you may have dreamed about when you were still on the farm? Try this. When someone tells you they think you are different, see it as a compliment. You don't need to feel superior, just enjoy being who you are."

"It sounds very simple."

"And it is, but sometimes, things that are quite simple may not be all that easy. Just keep reminding yourself that, for you, being different is a good thing."

Belle smiled and agreed to keep that in mind. "Thank you Margaret, you have been very helpful."

Belle spent the rest of the weekend doing small chores around her apartment, and took a long, leisurely walk on Sunday afternoon. Once again, she found herself reviewing all the events of her life. "I was raised by 'normal,' conventional people, generally everyone I grew up with was considered 'normal.' I wonder why I've always been so different?" Her thoughts continued to tumble around her head, and eventually settled on, "OK, so fine, I'm different. I have no idea why, and really, can't picture myself being anything other than what I am. So, I'll take Bill and Ray and Margaret's advice and just enjoy being different. Margaret is right, it hasn't all been unpleasant." When she reached this point, she suddenly felt lighter, and more content.

Over the next several months, Belle kept busy with the café, spending some of her Sunday's with Peg's family, and going dancing, either with Kenny or George. The 18th Amendment had produced some increase of business at the Irish Rose. With the pubs closed, it filled a need for a gathering place for some of the working men. Of course, prohibition did not eliminate alcoholic beverages. Belle was aware that the coffee she served was often fortified once it was delivered to the table.

Peg approached her about this. "Belle, I'm thinkin' you're askin' for trouble, allowin' the boys to bring in their little bottles."

"Peg, the law only says I can't sell or manufacture an alcoholic beverage, so I'm not breaking any law."

"Well, maybe that's true, I'm just hopin' it doesn't lead to trouble."

"So long as they behave themselves while they are in here, and buy food and coffee from me, I see no reason for me to put my nose in any of the rest of their business."

"Some of the wives are none too happy with their men continuing to drink. They asked me to talk to you about them drinkin' on the sly here."

"Tell them I understand, but it's not my place to be telling my customers what they should or shouldn't do. Not unless they start causing trouble in here, and so far, they haven't."

George continued to come to the café for a meal now and then. Belle began to notice that George was spending a good deal of his time with the customers who liked to add their own mix to the coffee. When she became aware that money was changing hands between him and some of her customers, she spoke to him about it.

"George, I can't have you doing business out of the Irish Rose."

"What do you mean?"

"Come on, George! I'm not blind or stupid. What they add to their coffee is their business, but I'm not going to allow them to be buying the stuff out of my café."

"You turnin' into one of them temperance women, Belle?"

"George, you know damn well I'm not! I'm a business woman looking after my own interests. You are not to make any more transactions in my café, is that clear?"

"OK, OK, don't get your dander up. There's plenty of other places to do my business."

"And, so long as you use those other places, what you do is no concern of mine. Are we clear?"

"Loud and clear," he replied.

George continued to stop in to the café on a somewhat regular basis, sometimes for a meal, sometimes just to sit and chat over coffee with some of the other customers. Belle made it a point to observe his interactions with her customers, but saw no evidence that money was changing hands. George would often leave with one or two of the men, and she noticed their conversations would continue for a short time while standing on the sidewalk. She was sure this involved the buying and selling of bootleg liquor, but since he was off her property, she kept her word, and didn't interfere.

After some months of this, Peg approached Belle one morning before any customers had arrived. "Belle, I'm sure you know George has been sellin' booze to some of the men who come in here."

"Yes, but so long as he keeps his business outside, I don't see any reason to get involved."

"I know, I know. I just thought you might want to mention to him there's been some guys hangin' around the neighborhood. Dan thinks they might be revenuers, lookin' to catch him doin' business."

"Well, I imagine he's aware of it, but I'll pass it along. Thanks, Peg."

When Belle mentioned this to George, he assured her there was no problem. He was part of a small group that had developed a very lucrative business bringing wine and liquor in from Canada. In addition, one of the men owned a small place in the country, not far from Chigago, where they produced their own beer. Their business had done so well, thanks in part to a few bribes to local law enforcement, that they began to be a bit complacent about maintaining vigilance. As a result, George and one of the other men were arrested a month after Belle's warning to him. Because of George's involvement in Chicago's political machine, and the fact that the agents had not been able to find any real evidence, George and his friend only spent two nights in jail before being released.

Chapter Eight

Belle continued to go dancing with either George or Kenny, and a few times with a couple other men she had met at the dances. George had grudgingly accepted Belle's explanation that Kenny was only a friend from home, even though he wasn't all that happy about it. He was playing poker with some of his buddies on a Saturday night, when one of them said to him, "So, Spats, how's come your lady friend is steppin' out on ya?"

"She's not steppin' out. Kenny's just a friend from her home town."

"Yeah, well, I know Kenny, and the guy I saw her with the other night wasn't Kenny."

"You're lyin'," George said.

"Spats, if I was you, I'd be careful about callin' your friends liars. Maybe you should ask your fine Belle about it."

"We playin' poker, or just gossipin' like a bunch of old hens?" George replied in an angry voice.

The next afternoon George was at Belle's door, knocking loudly.

"George, what brings you here?" Belle asked.

"Me and you need to have a talk."

"What about?" she asked.

"I been hearin' talk that you're steppin' out on me, and I ain't talkin' about Kenny either. So what's the deal?"

"Well, first of all, George, I'm not steppin' out on you, because I've never considered us to be an exclusive item. But, yes, I have gone dancing with some other men now and then."

"Well, Jesus, Belle! No self respectin' lady goes out with more than one guy. What do you think people are gonna be sayin' about you? Or me, for that matter."

"Now, you listen to me George. I got over worrying about what busy bodies think of me a long time ago. If that's a problem for you, then I guess you'll just need to find someone that's willing to be told what she should and shouldn't do by a man. That's not who I am. I'll be happy to continue to go dancing with you, so long as we're clear who's in charge of me. Otherwise, I guess you'll just need to move on, and no hard feelings on my part."

"God, you're a difficult woman, Belle!"

"I've been told that before."

"I just bet you have! I don't think I can do that, Belle. My friends wouldn't understand. They'd just think I was bein' a patsy."

"I'm sorry to hear that, but I meant what I said about no hard feelings."

"Well, OK. So long Belle. I'll be seein' you around, I guess."

"I'm sure you will. Bye, George"

After George left, Belle gave an exasperated sigh, thinking, "I will just never understand men! If a guy is seeing more than one woman, or even if he's married and having an affair, no one says much about it, or at most, they just shake their head a bit. But let a woman do the same thing and she's branded as a fallen woman. But what I really don't understand is that women let them get by with it!"

The following Saturday Kenny arrived in the car he had recently purchased, to take Belle to the dance. During the ride to the speakeasy, Belle told him about the conversations with George. "I just don't get it, Kenny. Why do men think they have to be the only man in a woman's life?"

Kenny laughed, and replied, "It beats me Belle. Just the way most men are wired I guess. Me, I figure if I can play the field, why shouldn't they. But, like we've talked about before, you and me are cut from a different cloth."

Belle sighed, and said, "I suppose you're right. Don't you ever find it frustrating, that others think there's something wrong with you?"

"No, not really, but then I think men are cut a little more slack about being a little different. I wouldn't worry too much about it if I was you. Just keep doin' what seems right to you. It's part of your charm, you know."

"You're a good friend Kenny. I'm glad we ran into each other. What are the odds of that, in a city this size?"

"Just meant to be, I guess. Here we are, let's go have some fun."

During the evening, Belle spent some time with one of the other men she'd gone dancing with a few times. His name was Jim Edwards, and he owned a small insurance agency. He was a little older than Belle, in his early forties. His wife had died a little over two years earlier, and he had no children. Besides being a great dancer, he enjoyed reading as much as Belle did. Belle had gone to dinner with him a few times, and had thoroughly enjoyed discussing the books they had read. Belle was sitting with him during one of the breaks the band took when he said, "Belle, have you heard about the plans for building a new library?" he asked.

"I did read something about that. Aren't they having some trouble getting the city to commit to spending the money for it?"

"That they are. There is a group of supporters who are trying to raise some private funds. The city fathers have indicated if enough private funds could be raised to pay for half of it, the city would OK the rest. There is a fund raising dinner/dance being held in three weeks. Would you like to go with me?"

"I might. What do the tickets cost?"

"That's not an issue. I've already bought two tickets. You would be my guest."

"In that case, I accept. It sounds like a fun evening, and I'd be happy to contribute some money to get the library built."

"Wonderful! It's going to be formal, so wear your prettiest dress."

She told Kenny about it on the way home that night. "So, hob nubbin with high society, huh?" was his response.

"No, it just sounded like a nice evening, and for a good cause. I haven't had an occasion to get really dressed up for a long time, and I do enjoy that."

In the next week, she went shopping and found a pale blue, silk dress, with a band of dark blue and clear crystal beads around the dropped waistline. A dark blue shawl and pearl gray pumps completed the outfit. She then took her sapphire necklace and earrings out of her safe deposit box, and after thinking about it for a few minutes, also took the diamond and sapphire ring Johnny had given her.

When Jim arrived to pick her up on the night of the dinner, he took one look at her and said "Wow! You are a sight to behold. I think you will make me the envy of every man there tonight."

Belle laughed, and said, "Thank you Jim, but I think you are exaggerating."

The dinner was held in the grand ballroom of one of Chicago's more luxurious hotels. Belle and Jim arrived shortly before dinner was to be served, and most of the three hundred other guests were already present. Heads did turn, as Jim led Belle through the crowd to their table. The tables were round and seated eight. The other six were already at their table when Jim and Belle arrived. Introductions were made. There was another insurance agent, the editor of a neighborhood newspaper, the owner of a small bookstore, and their wives.

The table setting was elegant. White linen table cloth and napkins, fine china edged with a gold rim, heavy sterling silver knives, forks, and spoons, crystal water and wine glasses, a bowl of red and white roses, and large crystal decanters of water and wine. Even though prohibition was in effect, it was often loosely enforced, especially at gatherings such as this one.

A series of short speeches followed the meal, extolling all the advantages of the new library. An artist's rendering of the proposed library was displayed, and pledge slips were passed out to all the guests. This was immediately followed by the president of the Chicago Times newspaper standing up to announce a pledge of $5,000.00. When the applause died down, the chairman of the library committee thanked the president of the Times, including thanks to all attending for their support, and invited all to enjoy dancing for the remainder of the evening.

Jim led Belle onto the dance floor. "Are you enjoying yourself?" he asked.

"Very much so. It's not very often that I'm able to discuss books that I've read."

"I have a friend whose wife belongs to a book club. I could introduce you, if that's something you would be interested in."

"Thank you, I'd like that."

As they returned to the table, the editor of the neighborhood newspaper asked Belle to dance.

"I understand you own a small café," he said to her. "How did that happen, if I may be so bold as to ask?"

"Well, the short version is, I inherited some money, but still needed to support myself. I've always enjoyed working with people, and the rest, as they say is history."

"I'll have to come check it out sometime."

"Please do. The fare is simple, but I have a very good cook."

As the song ended, and they began to walk back to their table, a gentleman approached and said, "Pardon me, but could I have the next dance, Belle?"

As Belle turned to look at him, her smile froze, and she became quite pale. The editor didn't notice, and said, "Go right ahead, Belle. I'll see you back at the table later."

As the music began, Johnny took her left hand, placed it on his shoulder, then taking her right hand in the dance position said, "Surprised to see me, Belle?"

"Johnny, what are you doing in Chicago?"

"I live here."

"You live here?"

"You used to be better at conversation than this, Belle. I guess you thought you were done with me after you ran away. Bit of a shock seeing me, I suppose."

"I, I didn't run away."

"Really? What would you call it, then?"

By now Belle was regaining some of her composure. "Why don't you ask your father. I'm sure he could explain it to you."

"What is that supposed to mean? Why would he know why you left?"

"Because he's the reason I left. He hired an investigator to look into my past, and didn't like what he was told. Right after he sent you to Boston, he told me I was to sell the dress shop, and leave town without talking to either you or Julia, and that if I didn't, he would make life very difficult for me. I was going to go to Boston to tell you, but my friend said you were in no position to defy your father, and that he was powerful enough to make good on his threat to make my life miserable."

"You're making this up."

"I'm not. I loved you, Johnny, but it didn't seem I had any choice."

The music ended, and she said, "I really need to get back to my table."

"Will you dance with me again later?" he asked.

"I don't know."

"Belle, we need to talk more about this."

"Maybe, ask me later. Thank you for the dance," she said as they reached her table.

Jim turned to her as she sat down, and said, "How do you know Johnny Honeywell?"

"He's a friend from New York," she replied.

"So you've lived in New York then?"

"I did for a short time, several years ago."

Belle did her best to stay focused on the conversations at her table, with minimal success. "Johnny is here in Chicago. I don't believe this!" she thought. She quickly drank her wine, and asked for another. After a short time, she excused herself to visit the powder room. As she returned to the ballroom, Johnny approached her. "Dance with me Belle. I need to talk to you."

She hesitated only a moment before saying, "All right, let's dance, and you talk."

"Were you telling the truth, about my father?"

"I was."

"It doesn't sound like you put up much of a fight for me."

"Oh, for God's sake, Johnny! Are you going to tell me your father would not have kept his word about making my life miserable? He could easily have ruined my business, and spread who knows what kind of stories that would have made me an outcast in your society."

"I would have stood up for you."

"You would have defied your father, and risked losing his financial support, maybe even your job at the bank? I doubt it."

"You don't think very much of me, do you?"

"Johnny, I thought the world of you, I loved you. But, I grew up with a very different lifestyle than you, and I've seen what happens when someone of your father's social standing wants someone like me out of their world. I don't mind fighting for what I want, but I'm smart enough to know when I don't have a snowball's chance in hell of winning."

"You've changed, Belle."

"Six years will do that, I guess. So, what are you doing in Chicago?"

"I'm working in a bank, of course. After you disappeared with no explanation, I decided I needed a change of scenery. What do you do in Chicago?"

"I own a café."

"So, you are still a business woman. And are you married?"

"No, I'm happily single. What about you?"

"I'm single too. I see you kept my ring. I'd like to see you again Belle."

The wine was making Belle speak more flippantly than she felt, and she answered by giving him the name and address of the Irish Rose, telling him to come by for lunch anytime.

A week later, Johnny walked into the Irish Rose at lunch time, and sat down at one of the tables. Belle walked over saying, "Hello Johnny. I see you found my place. What would you like for lunch?"

"What do you recommend?"

"Today's special is a hot roast beef sandwich, but anything on the menu is good."

"The special sounds fine. And a cup of coffee."

Belle delivered his sandwich and coffee, and went to wait on several other customers who had just arrived. When he'd finished his meal, Belle came to clear the table, and asked, "So, what do you think?"

"The food is very good, as promised. And the café has a nice homey feel to it."

"I'm glad you approve. Is there anything else I can get you?"

"Yes, some of your time. I really need to talk to you Belle."

She hesitated a moment or two, then said, "This really isn't the time or place. I could meet you Sunday afternoon."

"Where would you like to meet?"

"There is a park about a mile from here. I could meet you there, by the fish pond. Is that OK?"

"That sounds fine. Tell me how to get to the park."

She gave him directions, and he left, saying he needed to get back to the bank.

In his dark suit, crisp white shirt, and tie, Johnny had stood out from the other customers, most of whom were working men in overalls or jeans. One of her regular customers said, "Seems like The Rose is attracting some higher class customers, Belle. You gonna go and get all fancy on us now?"

"No, Frankie, I'm not. He is a friend from when I lived in New York."

Peg had also been very aware of Johnny, and the interaction between him and Belle. Later in the day, she said to Belle, "So, your friend seemed like maybe you'd been a wee bit more than just friends."

"You don't miss much, do you Peg? Yes, we were a little more than friends."

"And, now?"

"And, now, I don't know. It's a long story, Peg."

"Well, we don't have any customers right now, and I don't need to get home right away. I'm a fair listener, ya know."

"That you are Peg, and a good friend. Johnny and I were engaged, but he's the reason I came to Chicago."

"Had a fallen out did ya then?"

"No, it was his father. He's a big shot banker, and didn't like the idea of his son marrying a nobody from Nebraska. He told me I had to leave town without telling Johnny, or he would make my life miserable. I had no doubt that he would do just that, so I sold the dress shop I owned, and here I am. I ran into Johnny the other night at the library fundraiser I went to."

"So, what happens now?"

"I don't know, but I agreed to meet him Sunday afternoon. Now that his father is several hundred miles away, I guess the least I can do is give him an explanation."

"So, do ya still have feelins' for him?"

"I don't know, Peg. I loved him once, now, I just don't know."

"Well, thanks for fillin' me in. I'll be waitin' to hear how your meeting turns out on Sunday."

Belle awoke early Sunday morning, after a restless night of sleep.

She was restless and nervous about meeting Johnny, both looking forward to it and dreading it. She tried to keep busy with routine household tasks, but the morning hours seemed to drag on endlessly. By noon, she couldn't stand it any longer, and began walking to the park. Mother Nature seemed to have gone out of her way to produce perfect weather on this late May day. Even though she walked slowly, she arrived at the park a little after 1:00.

She strolled around the park some, before heading for the fish pond, where they had agreed to meet. Even though it was only 1:30, she found Johnny was already there, waiting.

"Hello Belle. I see you're a little early too."

"Yes, I guess I am."

"Shall we find someplace to sit down?"

"Sure. I brought a blanket to sit on. There's a big maple tree over there that might be nice to sit under."

"Thank you for coming today, Belle. It didn't seem like you were pleased about seeing me at the dinner the other night."

"I was just shocked over seeing you here," she said. "I thought I had you tucked safely away in my past."

"And, is that where you would prefer I stay, in your past?"

"I don't know how to answer that, Johnny. There are a lot of things I need to tell you before we can continue with this conversation. It may take a little time, so please, just listen."

She then proceeded to give him the full story of her life, including the part about running away with the carnival in order to get off the farm, and her subsequent estrangement from her family. When she'd finished, she gave a big sigh, and said, "So, now you know why your father didn't want me to marry you. I don't know if I ever would have told you all that, or not, but now, it seemed the only way to really explain why I left without leaving any word as to where I'd gone."

"Well! I knew you were an unusual woman when I fell in love with you, I just had no idea how unusual."

"Yes, well, you can see why your father didn't consider me suitable daughter-in-law material. Actually, he was probably right, I'm not sure I would have ever really fit in your world."

"No, I don't think that's true, Belle. I just wish my dad had kept out of it. I've never really gotten over you. I've done some dating, of course, but I find I'm always comparing them to you, and no one ever measures up. I really want you back in my life, Belle."

"Oh, Johnny, do you really think that's a good idea? What about your family?"

"My dad died a year ago. It's just me and Julia now."

"Even so. You made a comment the other night that I'd changed, and you were right. You are still a wealthy banker, and I'm living in a poorer part of town, serving meals to the Irish working class. I like what I'm doing, and I like the people in my neighborhood. That's not really a picture of a typical banker's wife, now is it?"

"None of that matters to me, Belle."

"But, I'll bet it would matter to your friends and business associates, and that would affect you."

"Belle, I want to keep seeing you. Please say yes. We'll deal with whatever we have to when it comes up."

"Ah, Johnny. I think your father was right when he told me you can be stubborn about what you want. All right, I'll agree to have dinner with you, or go dancing, now and then. Let's just leave it at that for now."

"Fair enough. May I buy you dinner tonight? I have a car, so we can go wherever you would like."

Belle laughed, and said, "Fine, you can buy me dinner tonight, and since you are driving, I'll leave it up to you as to where we go."

Over the next several months, Belle continued to see Johnny about once a week, but also made it a point to go dancing with Kenny or Jim Edwards from time to time. She tried to maintain some emotional distance from Johnny, with only minimal success.

One night over dinner, Johnny said to her, "Belle, I've never stopped loving you, and I think you love me too. Am I wrong?"

Belle was silent for a few minutes, then said, "No, you're not wrong."

"Then marry me, Belle. Let's not waste any more of our lives being apart."

"Johnny, it just wouldn't work. Our worlds are too far apart."

"It will work, Belle! We can make it work."

"I won't give up the café, Johnny. I tried being a proper society wife once, and it was a disaster."

"But I'm not him Belle. I don't want to change you. I just want you with me. You can keep the café, just hire some more help, so you don't have to spend so many hours there."

"And just how many hours a week will you be willing to let me spend there?"

"Belle, I'm not going to dictate your life. I just want to spend as much time with you as I can. You can decide how much time that is."

"You know, if any other man said that to me, I'd call him a liar."

"I'm not lying, Belle."

"No, somehow I don't think you are."

"So, will you marry me?"

Belle sighed, and said, "I will, I just hope I'm not making a mistake."

"You're not, Belle, I promise. So, can we set a date? What kind of wedding would you like? Let's go shopping for a ring tomorrow."

"Slow down Johnny. You've already given me a ring, remember?"

"Yes, but I think it would be good to get a different one now, a symbol of a fresh start. This time, I'd like to have you pick it out."

Belle laughed, and agreed that might be a good idea, then added, "I don't want a big wedding. I'd like to have some of my friends from the café there, and I'm sure you have some people you'd like to have. Mixing those two groups at a big wedding just wouldn't be practical. May is only a couple months away. We could have a small ceremony in the park where we talked last year, and a picnic meal for the reception. That way, I don't think anyone would feel too out of place. How does that sound?"

He smiled, and said, "It sounds just like you. I like it."

A week later they did go shopping for a ring. Johnny told her, several times, in fact, that she was to pick a ring she liked, regardless of the size or the price. "Dad left Julia and me a nice inheritance, and the stock market has been very good to us, so please, get exactly what you want."

Belle found a rather large ring, more like a cocktail ring than an engagement ring. The rosette pattern of the diamonds reminded her of the ring Bill had given her. She took Johnny's suggestion, and had the first ring he'd given her re-sized, to wear on her index finger.

Three weeks before the wedding, Johnny asked her about her family. "Would you like to have them here for the wedding?"

"I really don't think they would come," she replied.

"It's been a long time. Do you really think they are still that upset with you?"

"Oh, I think it's a good possibility. I'd rather not have our wedding spoiled by finding out they are still not over it."

"In that case, I have another suggestion. Our bank is opening a branch in Lincoln, Nebraska. I've been asked to go there the first week in June to check on things. Lincoln isn't all that far from your home town, is it?"

"No, I suppose not. Maybe an hour."

"We could take the train to Lincoln, and I'm sure one of the bank officers could find a car for me that we could use for a few days, when I've finished with the bank business. What do you think?"

"Oh, Johnny, I don't know. I'm not sure I'm ready for another welcome like the one I got the last time I was home."

"But, you don't know that would happen. Families are important, Belle. I think you owe it to yourself to go see them again."

"Let me think about it, Johnny.'

"OK, but don't take too long. I'll need to get our tickets, and make hotel reservations."

Over the next few days, Belle bounced between feeling Johnny was right about taking her back to Nebraska, and feeling she was right about the welcome she would get from her family. She decided to talk to Kenny about it. She explained Johnny's plan, then said, "I just don't know. It would be nice to see Mae, Lizzie, and David again, and meet their children. But, I'm really not ready for another rejection, like the one I had the last time I went home."

"That's been a long time ago, Belle. Your pa's gone now, Ray's gone, and I'm bettin' the worst that could happen would be that everyone might be a little uncomfortable at first, but they'd be glad to know you're OK."

"You really think so, Kenny?"

"I do. You know, Mae's married and livin' in David City, Lizzie is a widow and workin' at a telephone office in the little town of Tamora. David is still farmin' your pa's place. It wouldn't be that hard to see all of them. You're a grown woman now, and even if the worst happens, at least you'd know you gave it a fair shot. And you wouldn't be alone this time, you'd have Johnny with you."

"You're probably right, Kenny. Oh, what the heck. I might as well give it a try. It will be nice to get away with Johnny for a while too. You're coming to the wedding, aren't you?"

"Wouldn't miss it."

The wedding took place as planned. Belle and Johnny were not involved with any church, so they had a justice of the peace marry them. Julia had come for the wedding, and seemed genuinely pleased that Johnny and Belle had found each other again. She was married to a long time friend of Johnny's, who acted as best man. Belle had chosen Peg for her matron of honor.

Belle had chosen a simple dress of sky blue crepe de chine, with a skirt that billowed softly in the gentle breeze. She carried a simple bouquet of daisies and white peonies, and wore a simple gold necklace with a small pendant in the shape of a bell, that had been Johnny's wedding gift to her.

It was late evening before the guests began taking their leave. As the last of the guests said their goodbyes, Johnny turned to Belle, saying, "Well, Mrs. Honeywell, are you ready to go home?"

"I believe I am."

Chapter Nine

Peg had agreed to take charge of the Irish Rose while they were gone, and Belle had found another woman to help wait on customers.

"Peg, thank you so much for doing this for me. I'm not exactly sure how long we'll be gone. Johnny doesn't know how much time he will need to spend at the bank, and of course, I have no idea how the visits with my family will go."

"Oh, I'm sure everything will be all you're hopin' for. You just have a good time, an don't ya be worryin' about anything here. The Rose will be just fine 'til you get back."

They boarded the train for Lincoln one week after the wedding. Everything seemed to be going smoothly at the new bank, so they spent only two days in Lincoln. Belle had used the time while Johnny was at the bank to find some gifts for her family. Trying to decide what to get proved to be a challenge. She finally settled on a pretty scarf for Lizzie, Mae, and Ann, and some leather gloves for David and Mae's husband, Orville. Because she knew nothing about the children, she bought several pounds of chocolates and other sweets. The bank manager had persuaded a car dealer to loan Johnny a Ford model A for the trip, promising him a lower interest rate on his next loan.

They left Lincoln early the next morning, planning to stop first in Tamora to se Lizzie, then on to David's farm near Thayer, and finish their round of visits in David City, where Mae lived.

Having only lived in New York City or Chicago, Johnny was amazed at the amount of open space as they drove west from Lincoln. "It feels like you can see forever out here," he said.

"Yes, it does. Sometimes I miss that," Belle replied.

It was one of those June days in Nebraska that made you wish it could be June all year. A warm, not hot, sunny day, with a light breeze, and a crystal blue sky decorated with a few puffy clouds. It took them about two hours to reach Tamora. The town was tiny, even by Nebraska standards, with a population of 300. As Johnny parked the car in front of the telephone office, Belle took a deep breath and said, "Well, I guess this is it. Wish me luck."

"It will be fine, Belle. I'll be with you. Just take my hand if you feel nervous."

A small bell tinkled as they opened the door. Lizzie was sitting at a bank of telephone cables, with her back to the door. She had a headphone on, and was speaking to a caller. "Just a moment and I'll connect you," she said, picking up a cable and plugging it into an outlet. Then she turned, and said, "May I help you?"

"Lizzie, it's me, Belle. How are you?"

There was a brief silence, before Lizzie said, "Oh, lawse, Belle! We all figured you must be dead."

"Nope, not dead. This is my husband, Johnny Honeywell. Johnny, this is my oldest sister, Lizzie."

"How do you do, Lizzie, I'm happy to meet you."

"I do just fine, thank you. How in the world did you find me, Belle?"

"You remember Kenny Miller? He's living in Chicago, same as me. I ran into him a while back, and he told me you were working here."

Just then, there was some shouting outside, and four children came running through the door. "Ma, you should see the car that's out front," said a boy who looked to be about twelve years old.

"Yeah, Ma, come look," said a girl near his age.

"Kids, where are your manners? Can't you see I have visitors?"

With that, all four became quiet and a little wide eyed.

"Are these your children Lizzie?" asked Belle.

"This is Jesse, and this is Vera. They are mine. Charles and Sis are my grandchildren. My oldest daughter, Greta died and their pa ran off, so I'm keeping them. Kids, say hello to your Aunt Belle."

This was met with a series of shy 'hello's'.

"Oh, I almost forgot," said Belle. "I have something for you. I'll go get it from the car." She returned in a moment with a large basket, full of chocolates, cookies and other candy. The scarf was wrapped in tissue paper, and she handed this to Lizzie.

"I wasn't sure what you might like, but I figured everyone likes sweets. Please, help yourselves," she said to the children.

Lizzie spoke up, saying, "You can each have one. I don't want you spoiling your lunch."

"Here, let me help you open the packages. You tell me which ones you'd like." said Johnny. After they each made their choice, he asked, "Would you like to come out to see the car? Maybe I could take you for a ride around the block, if that's all right with you Lizzie."

"Well, I don't know—"

"Oh, please Ma, we'll be good," said Jesse.

"It's perfectly safe. I'll just take them around the block."

"Well, I suppose, but you kids behave yourself, you hear?"

"Oh, we will, we will. Thanks Ma."

Johnny gave Belle a wink as he led the kids outside.

As the door shut, Belle turned back to Lizzie and said, "I heard that Charles had died. I'm so sorry. What happened?"

"Don't really know. He just got real sick and died two days later."

"And your daughter?"

"She died when she went under the knife for some kind of liver problem."

"Oh, Lizzie, I'm so sorry. Is there anything I can do to help?"

"No, Miss High and Mighty, we're doing just fine."

"Lizzie, don't be that way. I was hoping we could mend some fences from the past."

"Some things just ain't meant to be mended, I guess. You just rest easy when you get back to your fancy life in Chicago, cause we do just fine on our own."

At this point Johnny pulled up, and the kids tumbled out of the car. "Thank you Mr. Honeywell. That was super," said Charles. "I can't wait 'til I'm old enough for a car." As they came back in the office, Charles and Jesse started telling Lizzie how great the car was.

"That's nice boys. I'm glad you had a good time. Now, tell your Aunt Belle and Uncle Johnny goodbye. They are busy people, and have things to do."

All four began speaking at once, saying goodbye, and thanking Belle for the candy.

"You're welcome. I'm glad you like it."

"Will you come see us again?" asked the girl they called Sis.

"We'll see, Chicago is kind of a long ways away. Let's go Johnny, Lizzie has to keep her attention on the switchboard."

After they were in the car, Johnny looked at Belle and asked, "Are you OK?"

Belle was near tears, and simply shook her head.

"What happened?" he asked.

"Just the same thing that always happens with Lizzie. She wants nothing to do with me."

"I'm sorry, honey. What is the problem between you two?"

"She blames me for Ma's death."

"I'm sure that's not true."

"It probably isn't true that I'm responsible, but no one will ever convince her of that. Do you think we could find a place to stay in Seward tonight? I'm really not up to any more family today."

"I'm sure we can. I saw a hotel when we came through town."

They checked into the hotel, had supper, walked around the square for a while, and retired early.

Belle woke early the next morning, feeling refreshed and a little more optimistic about seeing David. They had a light breakfast of pastry and coffee at the bakery, and began the drive to her childhood farm. There were two young boys playing in the yard when they arrived. The boys stopped what they were doing, and stared at the shiny, black and pale green Ford. Belle and Johnny got out of the car, and Belle said to the boys, "Hello there. Is your Ma or Pa at home?"

Just then, Ann came out on the porch, with a small girl clinging to her skirts. "Good morning, What can I do for you?" she said.

"Hello Ann, it's Belle, remember me?"

"Belle! Well for lord's sake, come in. You'll have to excuse the mess, I've been baking bread. Please, come in the living room, and have a seat. I'll tell the boys to go fetch David. He's in a nearby field, mending fence."

She went back to the porch, and said to the boys, "Tommy, Eddie, run out to the field and tell your Pa his sister is here."

She returned to the living room, and asked if they would like a cup of coffee.

"If you have some ready, that would be nice," replied Belle. "Ann, this is my husband, Johnny."

"It's very nice to meet you. I'll just be a minute getting the coffee."

"Can I help?" offered Belle.

"Oh, heavens, no. It's no trouble."

When the coffee had been served, Ann said, "This is quite a surprise. We all kind of figured you might be dead, after all these years with no word from you."

"Yes, well, after my last visit, it didn't seem like anyone was too interested in hearing from me."

"I know. I'm sorry about that. I felt bad for you, but you know how your pa could be."

Just then David walked in. "Well, I'll be!" he said. "We didn't think we were ever gonna see you again. Tommy, Eddie, come in here and say hello to your Aunt Belle."

The boys said a shy hello, and Johnny reached out to shake their hands, saying, "It's nice to meet you boys. May I ask how old you are?"

Tommy spoke first, saying, "I'm seven and Eddie is six."

The little girl had left Ann's side and gone to her Pa. David picked her up saying, "And this is Rose. She's a big girl of three already, aren't you?" Her response to this was to bury her face in his shoulder. David laughed, and said, "She's kind of shy. So, what brings you out this way after all this time?"

"Johnny had business in Lincoln, and thought since it was so close, I should come with him to see my family."

"Well, I'm really glad you did. You'll stay for dinner, won't you? We've got a lot of catchin' up to do."

"Well, I'm not sure. We don't want to impose, and keep you from what you were doing," said Belle.

"Oh, don't be silly. It's no bother at all," said Ann.

"None at all," agreed David. "That fence can wait a bit longer. So, have you seen Lizzie or Mae yet?"

"We stopped in Tamora yesterday. It didn't go very well."

"Yeah, I suppose it didn't. Lizzie's a lot like Pa, not much on changing her mind."

"Oh, I nearly forgot. I've brought something for all of you. Johnny, would you get tht basket from the car, the one with the red ribbon."

"Sure thing, be right back. Boys, would you like to come out and have a close look at the car?"

"You bet!" said Tommy, and he and Eddie hurried to follow Johnny outside.

It was a few minutes before Johnny and the boys returned. Ann asked Belle if she had any children.

"No, Johnny and I are newly married."

"Oh, I thought you were married when you were here last."

"I was, but he died before we could start a family."

"I'm sorry to hear that."

Johnny and the boys returned with the basket, and Belle handed out the gifts. "I hope the gloves fit, David. I wasn't sure of the size."

"They fit just fine. Mighty nice. Thank you, Belle."

"This scarf is so lovely. Thank you," said Ann. "You kids can each have one piece of candy or one cookie. We'll be eating dinner soon."

Belle helped Ann with the meal preparation, while the men visited and kept an eye on the children. The conversation was lively during the meal. When they learned that Belle was planning to drive to David City, David suggested they call Mae, to let her know they would be coming.

Belle insisted on helping Ann clear up after the meal before they left. She gave her address to Ann, with promises to keep in touch.

"Well, that was a nice change from yesterday," Johnny said, as they drove away. "Two down, one to go."

They arrived at Mae's house shortly before 4:00 p.m. Mae had been haunting the front window in anticipation, and rushed out when she saw them drive up. Belle had barely gotten out of the car, when Mae grabbed both her hands, saying, "Well, lordy, lordy! I don't believe this. Belle, it's good to see you."

"It's good to see you too, Mae."

Johnny had come around the car to stand beside Belle. "Mae, this is my husband, Johnny. Johnny, my sister, Mae."

"It's good to meet you. Well, come in, come in, don't just stand there. You look good, Belle. I guess life is treating you OK then?"

"Mostly it is, yes. You have a nice home, Mae."

"Thank you. My daughter, Ellen, will be home from school soon, and Orville should be here not long after. He's on the police force here in town. David tells me you went to see Lizzie."

"We did, yesterday. It seems like she has a lot to handle, all on her own. I offered to help, and she blew up at me."

"I'm not surprised. That woman wrote the book on stubborn. Me and Orville have offered to help too, but she won't have none of it. She could have sent Charles and Sis to live with Frank's sister in Oregon after Greta died and he took off. I tried to talk her into doing that, but she wouldn't have none of it. For a while she supported them all by washing dishes in a café in Thayer. Then this job at the phone company came up, so things are a little easier for her now. Not easy, mind you, but a little better. Enough about Lizzie, I want to hear all about you."

Ellen came in the door at that point, introductions were made, and a few minutes later, Orville arrived. After a short conversation, Belle remembered the gifts she had brought, and went to the car to get them. Belle was pleased to see the gloves she'd bought for Orville did fit. Mae exclaimed over the scarf, saying, "Lordy, Belle, this is so nice, I'm not sure when I'll ever have an occasion to wear it. Thank you."

They visited for a short time, with Belle giving a thumbnail sketch of her life, leaving out certain details. Then she looked at the clock, and said, "We really should be going, before it gets dark."

"Why, you'll do no such thing! I've got a nice supper going, and we have a perfectly good spare room. You can stay here tonight, and be on your way in the morning."

"Mae, that's really nice of you to offer. Are you sure we won't be imposing?"

"Not at all, we have lots of catchin' up to do."

They ate at the dining room table. Mae walked Belle through her parlor, showing off her prized collection of china figurines, and souvenirs she'd brought back from their vacations, but then returned to the dining room table for more conversation before they retired.

In the morning Mae served a breakfast of pancakes, bacon, and eggs. Goodbyes were said, along with promises to keep in touch.

Mae and Orville sad down for one last cup of coffee after Belle and Johnny had left.

"I hope that girl has finally settled down," said Mae. "Johnny seems like a respectable, successful man, don't you think so Orville?"

With rare exceptions, Orville was a man of few words. This was no exception, and he responded with a simple "Yup."

"I wonder what she's really been up to all these years. It seemed to me there were some holes in her story, between the time her first husband died, and getting married to Johnny. Didn't you think so?" asked Mae.

"Could be, I guess. Well, I better get to work now."

As Belle and Johnny drove out of town, he asked, "So, are you glad I talked you into this trip?"

"I am. It was good to visit with David and Mae. I guess Lizzie will just never change. Once she makes up her mind to something, that's pretty much it. And she's made up her mind that I'm to blame for our Ma dying."

Chapter Ten

Their lives became quite busy as soon as they returned to Chicago. Johnny's apartment was a little small for the two of them and he wanted to buy a house. With his schedule at the bank, and hers at the café, finding time when they could both look at houses was a bit of a challenge. It took them nearly six months to find a house they could agree on. It was a modest Victorian style home, on a tree lined street a mile from Lake Michigan. Belle wasn't entirely happy with the house, because of the distance from her café. After several arguments about it, they came to a compromise. Belle would agree to the house, if he would agree to her learning to drive and getting a car. Belle continued to work at the café five days a week, leaving early two of those days in order to spend the evening with Johnny.

Eight months after moving in, Johnny began pushing for them to begin doing some entertaining.

"We've been settled in here for a while now, Belle. You're happy with the furnishings, aren't you? Let's start with a small dinner party for some of my associates at the bank. We can hire a cook, and someone to serve the meal. It's important that we develop a circle of friends."

Belle agreed, even though she had some reservations about how well she would be accepted by his business associates and their wives.

The dinner party was a success. Johnny had invited two of the men he worked with at the bank, along with the real estate broker who had helped them find their house. Conversation during the meal was pleasant, touching on some current events, and a theatre that had recently opened.

As the last of the guests departed, Johnny turned to Belle and said, "Now, that wasn't so bad, was it?"

She laughed, and agreed that it had been a pleasant evening.

"See, I told you there was nothing to worry about. We'll have to do this more often."

A few weeks later they received an invitation for dinner with one of the couples that had been at the dinner party they had given. When they arrived, Belle discovered it was a larger gathering than she had expected. As their coats were taken from them, Belle leaned toward

Johnny, and quietly said, "Did you know there were going to be so many people here?"

"I didn't want to say anything to you, because I knew you would worry about it. It will be fine," he replied.

There were ten couples present. Wine and hors d'oeuvres were served by maids in black and white uniforms. When it came time for dinner, Belle and Johnny found themselves seated next to the president of the bank.

"Mr. Harrison, I don't believe you've met my wife, Belle. Belle this is our bank president, Mr. Harrison."

"It's good to meet you, Mr. Harrison."

"Oh, please, call me Edwin. And this is my wife, Dora. Dora, this is Johnny and Belle Honeywell. Johnny has become a valued member of our staff."

"Hello Johnny, Belle. I understand you are newly married."

"Yes, we were married last spring," replied Belle.

"Oh, yes, I remember. We had a previous engagement, and were unable to attend your wedding," replied Dora. "So, how did you two meet?" she asked.

"Oh, it's a long story. We met when Johnny was still in New York City."

"Are you from New York?"

"No, my family is in Nebraska."

"Really! You are a long way from home. I imagine you miss your family."

"I do, but we were able to visit them shortly after we got married, when Johnny went to Lincoln to see how the new bank was faring."

"Do you like to read?" asked Dora.

"Oh, yes, I've always enjoyed books."

"I belong to a little book club. We'd love to have you join us. We meet the second Wednesday of the month."

"Thank you for asking, but I don't think that will be possible. I work on Wednesday evenings."

"Really, where do you work?"

"I own a small café."

Edwin spoke up, saying, "A business woman. I'm impressed. You hadn't mentioned this Johnny."

"Didn't I? I suppose the opportunity never presented itself," he replied.

"Where is this café?" asked Dora.

Belle gave her the address, and Dora replied, "Goodness, that must be a bit of a challenge."

"Why do you say that?"

"Well, it is in an Irish neighborhood, isn't it? They are a little… different, aren't they?"

"Well, I guess I am too. Maybe that's why I have a number of good friends there," replied Belle.

Their conversation was interrupted at this point when the host stood and said, "Thank you all for being here tonight. We're delighted to have you as guests in our home. I thought we might be more comfortable having our coffee in the parlor."

The parlor was a good sized room, with numerous comfortable chairs, a sofa and love seat, and easily accommodated the guests. The coffee was served in delicate china cups.

As so often happens at social gatherings, the men tended to clump together to talk business and sports, while the conversation among the women revolved around children, and shopping. These topics held little interest for Belle, and she found herself smiling, and nodding, while feeling a little bored and out of place.

After a short time, one of the younger wives came to sit beside Belle.

"I'm Ann Morrison. I'm sure you've met so many new people tonight, you're having trouble remembering names. My husband, Don, works with Johnny. I heard you telling Dora that you own a café. That must be quite a challenge. I can't imagine doing something like that. Do you plan to continue that, now that you're married?"

All this was said as if she were under a time limit to get it all out.

Belle smiled, and replied, "It can be a challenge sometimes, but I enjoy it, and plan to continue with it."

"Well, you just remember you have a very good looking husband at home. There are any number of women who would love to be in your shoes, so don't leave him alone too much," she said, ending with a giggle.

Shortly after this, the guests began taking their leave. On the drive home Johnny asked Belle,

"Did you enjoy yourself?"

"It was fine."

"Well, you were the best looking woman there, you know. I like showing you off. Maybe we could have another party before too long."

"Johnny, it's only been a few weeks since we had the dinner party. I think we can wait a while."

"I suppose you're right. We'll probably be getting more invitations now. I like taking you places."

"You know what I'd like to do? Go dancing. We haven't done that since we got married."

"No, I guess we haven't. OK then, we'll go dancing some night."

A few weeks went by with nothing further being said about dancing. Belle was working extra hours at the café while she tried to find a replacement for the girl who had been filling in on the days Belle went home early. Johnny had been gone several nights during that time also, due to some after hours meetings to discuss possible changes in some of the bank's policies. One morning, while they were having breakfast, Johnny handed Belle an invitation that had come in the mail the day before. It was for a dinner dance that was being held to raise money for one of the several causes Dora supported. This one was for some new equipment at one of the city's hospitals.

"This will be a formal affair Belle, so go buy yourself a new dress."

"Johnny, Peg and Dan are having a party to celebrate their twenty fifth anniversary that night. I told her we'd be there. I told you about that last week."

"Did you? I guess it slipped my mind. We really can't afford to turn down this invitation, Belle. I'm sure Peg will understand."

"Whether she understands or not isn't the point. I promised her we'd be there."

"I'm sorry, Belle. It can't be helped. We'll send them a nice gift."

"Or, we could send our regrets to Dora, along with a nice donation."

"Belle, you don't seem to understand how that would reflect on me at the bank. It wouldn't set right that we were turning down this invitation to go to some Irish anniversary party."

"Are you telling me I have no choice?"

"I guess I am. I'm sorry Belle, but this is important."

With that she stood up, and said, "I have to get to work," and left the room.

Johnny got up to follow her, saying, "Belle, don't be mad. I'm sure Peg will understand."

Belle was at the front door. She turned and said, "She might, I don't," and walked out, letting the door slam behind her. She also slammed the car door, and began talking to herself.

"Son of a bitch! I'm supposed to break a promise to a friend just so he can look good for his boss! Well, I'm just not going to do it. I'll go to Peg's party by myself. I'm sure he'll have no trouble telling a lie to explain why I'm not with him." She gave a short, loud yell, pounding the steering wheel, and continued, "I can't believe he's doing this. What is the matter with him!"

She arrived at the café earlier than she needed to, got the coffee started, and began cleaning tables and counters that needed no cleaning. Peg arrived a short time later.

"Well, aren't you the early bird today?" Peg said.

"I needed to get out of the house."

"Ah, so the honeymoon is over, huh?"

"It would seem so."

"You want to talk about it?"

Belle gave an exasperated sigh, and said, "We got an invitation to a fancy dinner dance to raise money for the hospital. I told him we couldn't go because it's on the same day as you and Dan's party. But he seems to think his business associates are more important than friendships. Well, I'm not going Peg. I'll come to your party by myself."

"Now Belle, calm down. I don't think that's a good idea."

"Well, why not? We got your invitation first, and I told you we'd be there. I told him too, but it seems it just 'slipped his mind.'"

"Well, that's a man for ya. You might as well get used to it. Sometimes we have to do things we'd rather not, just to be keepin' the peace."

"But, Peg, you and Dan are my good friends. This just isn't right!"

"Well, maybe it isn't, but people like bank presidents sometimes have different rules. This is important to Johnny, and I don't think you should be fightin' him on this. We'll miss you at the party, but because we are good friends, we understand."

"Oh, Peg, I'd much rather be at your party."

"I know. Some things just can'na be helped. Now, I'd best be getting' on with some cookin' Why don't ya have a cup of coffee, and calm down a bit. Oh, I almost forgot. I've got some good news. My Danny is courtin' a nice girl, and she needs a job. I told her to come by this mornin' and talk to you. I think she'd probably be very good. Her name is Anna."

At 10:30 a young woman walked in the door. Peg was in the kitchen, and Belle was behind the counter. Belle looked up when the door opened, and said, "Good morning. Are you Anna?"

"Yes, Ma'am."

"Let's go sit at the table over there in the corner. Would you like a cup of coffee?"

"No, thank you, Ma'am."

Belle smiled and said, "Please call me Belle. Ma'am makes me feel like a very old woman. Peg tells me you'd like to be a waitress."

"Yes Ma…yes, I would. I need a job."

As the two of them talked about the job, and the times Belle needed extra help, Anna began to relax, and talk easily. Belle learned that Anna's father had been sick for awhile, and unable to work. After the details of the job had been discussed, Belle asked, "How soon can you start?"

"Any time you say," replied Anna.

"Could you come back at 3:00 today?"

"Yes. Does this mean I have the job?"

"It does. Let me show you around, so you'll know where things are when you start this afternoon."

"Thank you. I promise you won't be sorry."

"I'm sure I won't."

The lunch hour was busy, giving Belle little time to think about her morning with Johnny, and the conversation with Peg. By 2:00 things had become quiet, and she told Peg she would be leaving after Anna arrived.

"That's a good idea. It will give you time to make a nice dinner for Johnny, to make up for your fight this mornin'. I think you'll be glad you hired Anna. She's a hard worker and a level headed girl."

Anna arrived at 2:30, wearing a pretty gingham dress, with her long blonde hair neatly tied at the nape of her neck. Belle and Peg reviewed a few more things with her, and Belle left for home.

Belle had dinner waiting for Johnny when he came home. "Well, this is a surprise," he said. "I thought you'd be working late again."

"Peg found a girl to work some afternoons and evenings for me, and she was able to start today."

"Well, that is good news. Maybe I'll get to see a little more of you now."

"Johnny, I'm sorry I was so mad this morning. I just really wanted to go to Peg's party."

"I know, and I'm sorry. It's just that I don't want to do anything else to upset Mr. Harrison."

"What do you mean? Is he upset with you?"

"A little. .He didn't realize I had taken some extra time to visit your family when he sent me to Lincoln. I don't think it's a big problem, but I don't want to do anything else to rock the boat right now."

"I'm sorry. I guess I shouldn't have opened my mouth."

"You didn't know. I probably should have said something to you. So, when are you going shopping for a gown for the party?"

"Oh, I don't know. Do you really think I need a new dress?"

"Absolutely. There will be a lot of important people there, and I want you to wear something that really shows off your dazzling beauty."

"Aren't you just the charmer tonight," she laughed.

"I'm serious. Buy something really elegant. I can afford it, and you deserve it."

"You make it sound like you're putting me on display."

Johnny noticed a slight edge to her voice when she said this, and replied, "Now, Belle, you're putting words in my mouth that aren't there. I'm just proud of my wife, and like to have others see what a gorgeous thing she is."

"OK, OK, now stop, before it gets any deeper in here. I'll find myself something elegant to wear."

Mondays were generally a slow day at the café, so Belle asked Anna if she could come in earlier so she could go shopping.

Peg overheard the conversation, and said to Belle, "So, goin' shopping for some fancy duds, are ya?"

Belle sighed, and said, "Yes, Johnny made a big deal about me getting something 'really elegant' so he can 'show me off'."

"You don't sound very excited about it."

"I like pretty things as much as any woman. It's just that the way he put it made it sound like I'm some kind of possession he's showing off."

"Well, you just have a good time finding something you like, and don't be readin' more into his compliments than is there."

Belle spent the afternoon trying on gowns at some of the city's nicer women's shops. She hadn't found anything that she really liked, and was about to give up for the day, when the sales lady produced a red silk ball gown. On the hanger, the dress didn't look to be anything much different than several other gowns she'd tried on. But she liked the brilliant red color, and the feel of the silk, so decided to put it on. Once she had the dress on, it became much more than it had seemed to be when on the hanger. It was sleeveless, with simple lines, and a very plunging neckline. It fit as if it had been made for her, clinging to her slim body in a most attractive way.

The sales lady said "Oh, Mrs. Honeywell, I think this dress was made just for you."

"You don't think the neckline is a little…too much?" asked Belle.

"Oh, no. This is the latest fashion, and you have just the body to wear a dress like this."

"Well, it does feel wonderful. OK, I'll take it."

"Wait, before you take it off, let me show you a necklace that would be perfect with it."

The necklace was ornate, made of jet beads and delicate silver filigree. Belle's creamy complexion and dark hair made a perfect setting for it. When she agreed to the necklace, the saleslady said, "Might I also suggest some black satin pumps, and a black beaded handbag?"

As Belle drove home with the several packages, she began thinking out loud. "I don't believe what I just spent! But, he did say he could afford 'elegant'. If he wants to show me off, this should do it."

She hung the dress in the back of the closet, and put the other items away. When Johnny came home, she told him she'd spent the afternoon shopping, and had found a dress.

"That's great! Can I see it?"

"No, seeing it on the hanger doesn't do it justice, and I want to wait and surprise you on the night of the party."

"Oh, come on, Belle. Put it on for me now."

"Nope, you'll just have to wait. It's only five more days."

"Well, will you at least tell me what color it is?"

"It's red."

"Really! I don't think I've ever seen you wear anything red."

"No, I guess I haven't."

"You're sure you won't show it to me?"

"Positive. A little mystery is supposed to be good for a marriage," she said, then dramatically fluttered her eyes, and laughed.

The party was on Saturday. Belle spent the day doing little jobs around the house. Johnny was busy with some work he'd brought home from the bank. Even though Belle had initially dreaded going to the party, she was now looking forward to it. By mid afternoon she decided to take a bubble bath, and arrange her hair in a French twist. She waited until Johnny was in the bathroom shaving, before she put her dress on, then went to the living room to wait for him. When she heard him coming down the stairs, she got up to stand where he would see her as soon as he came in the room.

He came down the stairs saying, "Belle, will you help me with…" looked up and stopped mid sentence.

"Well?" she said, smiling.

"Good grief!"

"You said you wanted me to get something elegant, didn't you? Do you like it?"

"I, well, that is an amazing dress."

"What was it you wanted me to help with?"

"What? Oh, yes, my cufflinks."

As she walked toward him to take the cufflinks from him, she said, "You haven't said if you like the dress."

"It is amazing, Belle. You are beautiful. Do you think maybe the neckline is a little daring?"

"I'm told it's the latest fashion."

"Really? I'm certain no one will fail to notice you tonight."

"Isn't that what you wanted?"

"It is. I just hadn't pictured anything quite so…dramatic."

She had been attaching the cufflinks during the conversation, and now said,

"You look very handsome in that tuxedo. Shouldn't we be going?"

He looked at his watch, and said, "Yes, I guess it is time."

The dinner dance was held at one of the city's more luxurious hotels. Johnny was the only bank employee, other than the Harrisons, there. Mr. Harrison had gone to college with Johnny's father, and was grooming him for the position of vice president of the bank.

At $200.00 a plate, the guest list was made up of the cream of Chicago society. Mayor Daly was acting as emcee, and the poet, Carl Sandburg, was scheduled to speak.

Johnny and Belle were seated at a table with Edwin and Dora Harrison and the editor of the Chicago Daily News, Henry Smith and his wife, Florence.

The menu consisted of pork medallions, new potatoes in a cream sauce, baby brussel sprouts seasoned with a peppery butter sauce, plus a green salad with raspberry vinaigrette dressing. Sorbet was served immediately following the meal, and just before the dessert of Black Forrest cake.

While the guests were lingering over dessert and coffee, Mayor Daly began speaking. After the usual round of thank you's to all who had participated in planning the evening, and the guests for their support of a worthy cause, he introduced the head of the hospital, Dr. Daniel Adams. Dr. Adams spoke of the advances being made in medicine, and the increasing role technology would play in treating illness and injury. He then gave a description of the X-Ray machine, stressing it's safety, and it's benefits in making an accurate diagnosis.

"I can't begin to tell you how much your generous support tonight will help to make medical care received here in Chicago some of the best in the nation."

This was followed by Carl Sandburg reading from some of his works. After reading for about fifteen minutes, he concluded with, "Ladies and Gentlemen, your presence here tonight is an excellent example of the heart and soul of Chicago. But now, I suspect your ears have been assaulted long enough for one evening. I'm told we have some excellent musicians waiting, and this beautiful dance floor is begging to be used. So, enjoy the rest of your evening."

As the applause died down, and the musicians prepared to begin playing, Belle turned to Henry Smith, and said, "Mr. Sandburg is as good a speaker as he is writer, isn't he? I always read his articles in your paper."

"Yes, he is a talented man, even if a little daring in some of the things he writes. However, that's a good part of the reason I hired him."

The band began their first piece, and Johnny said, "Belle, would you like to dance?"

"I would," she replied.

Henry and Florence Smith followed them to the dance floor, while Mr. and Mrs. Harrison elected to stay at the table.

"Remember the last time we were at a similar gathering?" asked Johnny.

"That I do."

"There won't be another old flame showing up here tonight like I did, will there?"

She laughed and said, "Not a chance."

They danced through two songs before returning to the table. Ted and Jane Miller, friends of the Harrisons, had stopped by the table to visit briefly. Introductions were made, and after a few minutes, Ted asked Belle for a dance. Johnny in turn asked Jane to dance, and the two couples walked back to the dance floor.

"Your wife is a beautiful woman. Where did you ever find her?" asked Jane.

"We met in New York," he replied.

"Really? You must tell me all about it."

"There isn't much to tell. I met her through my sister. Have you lived in Chicago long?"

Jane continued to ask more questions about Belle, and Johnny continued to give vague answers, then change the subject.

Meanwhile, Ted was quizzing Belle.

"So, how did you meet Johnny?" he asked.

"We met in New York when he and his sister came to the dress shop where I was working."

"So, you are in the fashion business?" he said, as his eyes dropped to her plunging neckline.

"No, I was simply working in a ladies dress shop," she replied, beginning to feel a little uncomfortable. "So, do you work at the bank too?"

"Oh no, my family has been friends with the Harrisons for years. My family is in the shipping business. We own several freighters that transport goods across Lake Michigan."

The song ended and Belle thanked him for the dance, saying "I think I need to sit for a while."

"Good idea. Would you like some punch?"

"That sounds good, thank you."

"I have a little something I could add to the punch, if you are interested," he said, patting his pocket.

"Well, sure, why not," she replied.

When they returned to the table, Henry Smith was smoking a cigarette. Belle took a pack from her hand bag, and he quickly leaned forward to light it for her.

"Ted arrived with the punch for Belle just as Johnny and Jane were returning. A few pleasantries were exchanged before Ted and Jane returned to their table. Johnny glanced at Belle's cigarette, and raised his eyebrow slightly, which Belle chose to ignore.

A short time later, another gentleman approached, and asked Belle for a dance, which she accepted.

"Belle certainly seems to be enjoying herself," remarked Mr. Harrison.

"Yes, she does love to dance. We haven't had the opportunity for a while. I guess she's making up for lost time," responded Johnny.

Conversation lagged for a few minutes while they watched Belle dance. As she returned to the table, Ted approached with a tray full of glasses of punch, all of which had been fortified with some vodka from his pocket flask.

"You folks appeared to be in need of some refreshment, so I took the liberty of procuring some for you," he said as he set the tray on the table, with a small flourish.

"Thank you Ted, that was very thoughtful," said Mr. Harrison.

"Happy to help. Now, I need to do the same for my table," he said as he retrieved the tray and walked off.

"Henry, what do you think it will take for the city to get the crime level down in Chicago," asked Johnny.

Before Henry could answer, Dora spoke up, "Something has to be done. All these shootings and violence are a disgrace to the city. The Irish seem to be the ones who are always involved."

"It does seem that way," Henry replied. "But it isn't strictly true. Al Capone seems to be the one behind most of it, and he's not Irish, you know. To answer your question, Johnny, I'm not sure. There are indications that some of our police force are willing to look the other way, in return for cash favors."

"Well, that fits with what I just said. Look at how many Irish we have on the police force. They do seem to be a people who delight in violence," said Dora.

"That's a little harsh, isn't it? Painting an entire population with one brush," said Belle.

"I'm sure that isn't what she meant. Oh, I've always liked this song, let's dance Belle," said Johnny.

Once they were on the dance floor he said, "Belle, please stop and think a minute about what you say to people. Otherwise you can sound a little harsh."

"You thought what I said to Dora was harsh, but not what she said about the Irish?"

"That's not the issue. It just isn't a good idea to ruffle the feathers of someone like Mrs. Harrison."

"Oh, I see. My opinion doesn't count, but hers does?"

"Belle, stop it! This isn't the time or place."

The music ended, and Belle said, "I'm going to the powder room, I'll see you back at the table," and walked away.

When Belle was in the stall in the ladies room, she heard two women who were talking while repairing their make up.

"Did you see that woman in the red dress?"

"You mean the dress that's only half there? She's pretty hard to miss. She has certainly had a lot of different dance partners. I wonder who she is?"

"Someone said her husband works at Mr. Harrison's bank, and, they are sitting at the table with the Harrisons."

"Really? It would seem she needs a little education in how the wife of someone in banking should conduct herself. I can't imagine Mr. Harrison is too pleased about her behavior tonight."

"I don't imagine her husband is either. Why in the world would he allow her to wear something like that?"

Belle was about to deliver a few choice words to these two, but as she came out of the stall, they were at the door, and leaving. She spent a couple of minutes furiously washing her hands, and muttering under her breath, then took a deep breath, and started to return to the table. Two more women came in at that point. She smiled and said, "Good evening."

Their response was to simply nod briefly, and continue walking toward the stalls.

As she walked back to her group, she began to notice people turning their heads to look at her as she passed other tables. By the time she reached her table, she was inwardly fuming again. She lit another cigarette, and took a large swallow of her drink. Johnny was engaged in conversation with Mr. Harrison, and Mrs. Harrison was visiting with Florence. After a few minutes, Belle interrupted Johnny, saying, "Honey, I seem to have developed a massive headache.

Could we please go home now?"

"Are you sure?" he asked.

Dora overheard this, and said, "I'm so sorry Belle. Maybe you need a little fresh air."

"Yes, I do think a change of air might help. I'm sorry to interrupt the evening. Good night everyone."

After they were in the car, Johnny said, "What was that all about? I've never known you to have a headache."

"I'd just had all of 'high society' I could take for one night."

"What is that supposed to mean? I thought we were having a good time."

"Oh yeah, we were! Other than the bigoted remarks about the Irish, and your defense of Dora when she made them, the catty remark about me I overheard in the ladies room, the snubs I got from some of the women, the stares I got from other tables, and your obvious disapproval when I lit a cigarette. Other than all that, it was just a lovely evening."

"Belle, it's time you grew up a little. You can't be criticizing people like Dora Harrison in public, and did you really think if you wore that dress, people wouldn't stare at you or talk about you?"

"Does that mean you don't approve of my dress?"

"It might be fine, if you were an actress on stage, but it was hardly the best choice for this type of occasion."

"So, why didn't you say something before we left home?"

"It was a little late then, wasn't it? You don't have any other dress that would have been appropriate for tonight."

"Is that right? Maybe I should spend some time with Dora, so she can tutor me in how to be a proper lady."

"Maybe you should."

"That will happen about the same time that hell freezes over."

The rest of the trip home was spent in silence. When they reached home, Belle gathered her nightgown from their room, went to the spare bedroom, and locked the door.

"Belle, what are you doing? Come to bed."

"I'm sleeping here tonight. Good night."

"Belle," he shouted, then pounded the door once and stomped off to their bedroom.

When Belle went down to the kitchen in the morning, Johnny was already there, drinking coffee.

"I made some coffee. Are you over your tantrum?"

"Is that what I was doing, having a tantrum?"

"What would you call it?"

"How would I know? If a high society person like yourself says it was a tantrum, I guess this little old farm girl will just have to take your word for it."

Belle, stop it! You're being unfair."

"Am I? I seem to remember you saying you didn't want to change me, you just wanted to be with me."

"I'm not trying to change you. It's just that sometimes you're more outspoken than you need to be."

"So, I need to learn to just be quiet and pretend something is OK, when it isn't?"

Johnny gave a big sigh, and said, "Why do you have to be so obstinate? There's a time and place for everything. It's called manners."

"So, now I have no manners?"

"Belle, what exactly are you so upset about?"

"I thought I told you that last night, but apparently you didn't understand. First of all, I have absolutely no tolerance for bigotry. And Dora's remarks about the Irish were just that, bigoted. Second, you tell me to go buy an elegant dress, one that will get me noticed, and now you tell me it was inappropriate. And, third, I really don't like the condescending attitude of your society friends for anything that is at all different from their world."

Johnny was silent for a couple of minutes, then said, "I don't think there's any point in discussing this further right now. I have to go to the office for a while. I'll see you a little later." With that, he got up and left.

Belle picked up his coffee cup and threw it after him, hitting the door after he'd already gone through it. She stormed about the house for a while, aimlessly moving things from one place to another, ranting and swearing out loud about the idiocy of people in general, and Johnny's refusal to see her side. When she had calmed down some, she picked up the shattered coffee cup, then decided she needed to get out of the house. She drove to a park, and walked for nearly an hour, then sat down in some shade to watch a group of children playing ball. After a while, she decided to drive to Peg and Dan's, to hear about their party.

It was nearly two o'clock when she knocked on their door. Peg opened it, saying

"Belle, what a surprise. Come in. Is Johnny with you?"

"No, he had to go to the office for a while. I wanted to hear all about your party."

"And I want to hear about yours. How was it?"

"Oh, there's not much to tell. Just an evening with a bunch of stuffed shirts. I know yours was a lot more enjoyable, so tell me all about it."

"We did have a good time. I've even got some cake left, would you like a piece?"

"That sounds good," said Belle, realizing she had not eaten anything yet today.

"We did have a good time last night. There were about sixty people there. Dan has a friend who plays the fiddle, so he and a couple of his friends provided the music. We danced 'til almost 2:00, and didn't get home 'til nearly 3:00. We're both a bit worn down today. Ah, but 'twas worth it! So, did everyone like your new dress?"

"I'm not sure 'like' is the right word. It's a new fashion with a pretty low neckline."

"Ah well now, someone has to be the first to wear a new fashion, and who better than you?" Peg said and laughed.

"I suppose. I was a little uncomfortable before the evening was over."

"I'm sorry to be hearin' that. You should never feel bad about you ya are, Belle."

"You're a good friend, Peg. I knew coming here would make me feel better."

They visited a while longer, and Peg showed Belle the gifts they had received at the party. After about an hour, Belle said she really should be getting home.

When she walked in the house, Johnny was standing there, and immediately said, "Where in Heavens name have you been?"

"I went for a drive, and stopped over to see Peg."

"You could have told me you were leaving. I was worried sick. What was so important that you couldn't wait until tomorrow to see Peg?"

"I wanted to get out of the house for a while, and decided I'd go see how Peg and Dan's party was."

"It's nearly 4 o'clock. I've been home since 1:00, and was looking forward to spending a quiet Sunday afternoon with you. I suppose you had to tell her all about our fight too."

"As a matter of fact I didn't. Maybe I should have. You walked out of here saying you'd see me later. I didn't realize I was supposed to wait quietly until you decided you wanted to spend time with me."

"You have a real talent for twisting things around, you know that? Let's just drop it. Would you like to go out for dinner tonight?"

"That's your answer? 'Just drop it'. This morning you said there was 'no point in discussing it further right now.' So, when do you think will be the time to discuss it further?"

"Whenever you can stop acting like one of your rowdy Irish friends, and talk things out in a civilized manner."

"In other words, speak in a soft voice, and talk around the issue without really settling things. That probably isn't ever going to happen. Do you think you could at least tell me why you're so mad about me not being here when you got home?"

Johnny was silent for a couple minutes, then said, "I thought you'd left me again, like you did in New York."

"That's not fair! You know I had no choice."

"I'm not convinced that's true. My father was a reasonable man. I'm sure you could have talked things out."

"Your father was not a reasonable man, and he had no interest in talking to me. I was given an ultimatum and told he never wanted to see me again. I've told you this before."

"I know. You're probably right. I just wish we could have had our life in New York, like we'd planned."

"You're not happy here?"

"Oh, it's all right. It's just not New York."

"I'm sorry, Johnny. Sometimes things change, and we just have to make the best of it."

"You're probably right. So, would you like to go out for dinner?"

"I've got some leftover roast beef in the ice box. Let's just have sandwiches here tonight."

The remainder of the evening was spent doing a few household chores, and reading the Sunday paper. Their conversation was minimal, and limited to comments about some of what they read in the paper.

As they prepared for bed, Johnny said, "I'm sorry you didn't have a good time last night."

"Me too," she replied. "I'm sorry you miss New York."

"Well, who knows, maybe we'll get back there someday. I'm sorry if I seemed critical of you. I do love you, you know."

"I know, and I love you, Johnny."

Johnny took her in his arms, and tenderly made love to her. Both fell asleep feeling happy and content.

Chapter Eleven

For the next few weeks, their lives returned to the usual routine. Then one night when Johnny came home, and before he even had his coat off, said, "Belle, do you think you could arrange a small dinner party on short notice? A friend of mine from New York will be here next week. I thought Friday would be good."

"That's a week from today! That's pretty short notice."

"I know, honey, but I'd really like to do this while he's here."

"We couldn't even get the invitations out in decent time."

"Well, I'm just thinking a small group of people I work with. I could give them the invitations on Monday, and explain the short notice."

"So how many people are you talking about ?"

"Well, Edwin and Dora, of course. Don and Ann Morrison and another couple you haven't met, Stanley and Mary Cooper. He's the vice president of the bank."

"That's a total of nine people! Johnny, I doubt I can find anyone to help with the meal on this short of notice, and I really don't want to try doing it myself, for that group. You know I'm not that good a cook."

"Well, how about this, a cocktail party. You could manage some small refreshments for that. Maybe Peg could help."

"Well, I suppose I could do that. Who is this friend, and what is he coming to Chicago for?"

"His name is Walt Boyer. His family and mine have been friends for years. He called me at work today."

"How did he know where to reach you?"

"Julia gave him my phone number. It will be great to see him again. You should probably order some flowers Monday. There is a new deli I've heard about that is becoming quite popular for it's fine caviar and other delicacies that would be perfect for this. I can check it out on my lunch hour Monday, and see what they have. How does that sound?"

"I guess that will be OK. I'll need to know if you order anything, so I can plan the other things around it."

"Oh, sure, I'll let you know Monday night. You don't mind doing this, do you? I'm really looking forward to seeing Walt again, and introducing him to some people from the bank. Wear something nice, go buy a new dress if you like."

"That didn't work out so well the last time you told me to do that, remember?"

"Ah, Belle, let's not get into that. You know what I mean, a nice cocktail dress."

"I'll sort through my gingham frocks, and find something suitable."

"Belle…"

"OK, I'm sorry. I'll find a nice dress that you will like."

When Belle came home from the café Monday evening, she found Johnny brimming with excitement again.

"Belle, this new deli is fabulous! They can provide everything we need, and deliver it all ready to be served. You won't have to do a thing, but set out the glasses and dishes. We'll make it a serve-yourself buffet. Did you get the flowers ordered?"

"No, I didn't have time. I'll do it tomorrow."

"Well, don't forget. Maybe we should have some candles on the table, too."

"You've got this all planned out, it seems."

"Well, I know you're busy with the café, and I want this to be a nice evening for Walt."

"You never did tell me why he came to Chicago."

"He's in banking, and is in town on some business."

"Is he married?"

"Yes, but his wife wasn't able to come with him. They have two young children."

During the quiet times at the café the next day, Belle said to Peg, "Johnny is so excited about his friend Walt coming to town. I've never seen him quite this way. He has basically made all the arrangements for food, and wants me to get a nice cocktail dress."

"Well, then ya should. He can afford it, so why not? Take off a bit early today, and go shopping."

"Maybe I will."

Belle found a simple black satin chemise dress that she thought

Johnny would approve of. She also bought a long rope of faux pearls, and a pearl encrusted hair comb.

The party was scheduled to begin at 6:30. Johnny came home from the bank early, changed his clothes, then left to pick up Walt. During the short time he was home, there was a steady stream of questions from him regarding the preparations for the party.

"Johnny, calm down. Everything is ready. Go get Walt, and let me get dressed in peace."

"Well, OK, if you're sure. I just want everything to go well."

"It will, now go!"

Johnny and Walt arrived back at the house at 6.00. Belle was in the dining room, making a last minute check of the table, when they arrived.

"Belle, we're back," said Johnny.

As she walked into the living room, Johnny made the introductions.

"Belle, this is my good friend, Walt Boyer. Walt, my wife, Belle."

"How do you do, Walt. It's nice to meet you."

"Hello Belle, the pleasure is all mine. Johnny, you didn't tell me what a beautiful wife you have. Belle, you are a vision of loveliness."

Belle laughed, and thanked him.

"Do you like living in Chicago, Belle?" asked Walt.

"I do."

"It isn't New York, though, is it?"

"No, it has a different personality, but my life has been good here. It's beginning to feel like home."

"Really? You don't miss New York?"

Their conversation was interrupted by the arrival of Ann and Don Morrison. The remainder of the guests arrived within a short time of each other. Johnny poured wine for the ladies, and a highball for the men, then invited them to help themselves for the remainder of the evening.

The party was going well, with everyone mixing nicely. Ann approached Belle, and said, "These refreshments are wonderful. How did you ever manage all this on such short notice?"

"I really can't take credit for it, Johnny found a deli that specializes in this sort of thing, and ordered everything."

"Really? Well, you certainly do have a thoughtful husband."

Walt was standing nearby, and added, "Yes, Johnny is a man of many talents."

At this point, Dora approached Ann, saying, "Ann, I wanted to talk to you about a possible selection for our next book club meeting." The two excused themselves and walked off.

After the two women walked away, Walt said to Belle, "You look very lovely this evening Belle. I'm sure you've been told before that you have the most amazing blue eyes."

"Well, thank you. They really aren't something I can take credit for, though, are they?"

"Maybe not, but Someone knew what He was doing when He added your creamy complexion and dark hair. It's an incredible combination." As he was saying this, his fingers lightly brushed her temple, and cheeks. "You really should come to New York with Johnny."

Belle took a small step away from him, and said, "If he ever goes back to New York, I'm sure I'll go with him."

"Wonderful! I'll look forward to seeing you there. Who knows, that may happen sooner than you think."

At this point, Edwin and Dora approached Belle, and Dora said, "Belle, thank you for a lovely evening. We really must be going now. Walt, it was very nice to meet you."

Walt took Dora's hand, and with a bit of a flourish, kissed it, saying, "The pleasure was mine."

"Good night, Dora, Edwin. Thank you for coming," added Belle.

As so often happens, the first guests to leave sent a signal, and the others began saying their goodbyes and leaving too.

After everyone had left, Walt said, "Johnny, thank you for arranging this evening. It's always nice to get to know people in a social setting, and of course, meet their wives. Sort of gives you a more complete picture of the man, doesn't it?"

There was a slight hesitation before Johnny replied, "Yes, I suppose you could say that."

"When do you return to New York?" asked Belle.

"I'm taking the train back on Sunday morning. Do you think we could meet for lunch tomorrow, Johnny? I have a few more things I'd like to discuss with you."

"That will be fine. Shall I pick you up?"

"Sure, shall we say 12:30? I probably should be getting back to my hotel. There's some paperwork I need to review. Do you mind driving me back?"

"Of course not, I'd planned on it," replied Johnny.

"Good night, Belle. It's been a real pleasure being in your home."

"Good night, Walt. Have a good trip home."

While Johnny drove Walt back to his hotel, Belle began clearing off the table, and putting things away. When he returned he said, "I think that went very well, don't you?"

"Yes, it was a good party."

"What do you think of Walt?"

"Well, he's—very charming, isn't he?"

Johnny laughed, and said, "He does lay it on a little thick at times, doesn't he? Thank you for being such a wonderful hostess. I'm beat. Let's go to bed, and finish the clean up in the morning."

"That sounds like a good idea. If I do much more tonight, I'll probably spill something on my new dress."

Johnny had consumed several highballs during the evening. He embraced Belle as they got into bed, but was soon snoring softly.

Belle was an early riser, and had all the remnants of the party cleaned up and put away before Johnny came downstairs.

"Johnny, I'm going to the café for a while. I need to check the inventory to see what I need to order on Monday. I probably won't be home before you leave for your lunch with Walt."

"OK, let's plan on eating out tonight. There's a new French restaurant I've heard of that is supposed to be very good."

"That sounds nice. I'll see you later this afternoon," she said, and left to go to the café.

The French café was small, seating only thirty. It was on a quiet side street, not far from Lake Michigan. The tablecloths were a pale mauve color, with dove grey napkins. A pink rose in a crystal bud vase adorned each table. The food proved to be as exquisite as the quiet surroundings.

"This is a wonderful change of pace, Johnny. I'm glad you suggested it," said Belle as they were having a second glass of wine.

"It is a pleasant surprise for Chicago, isn't it? I miss the variety of fine dining places that New York has."

"Ah, but is there anything like The Irish Rose in New York?" Belle joked.

Johnny smiled, and said, "Oh, I'm sure there is, somewhere. Belle, there's something I want to talk to you about."

"This sounds serious," she replied.

"It is, but in a good way. Walt is opening his own bank. Well, with the help of some investors, of course. And he wants me to come to New York to work for him."

"He's opening a brand new bank? That sounds a little risky."

"Not really. The economy is good, the stock market has been very stable, and doing well for some time now. All things considered, it's an opportune time to be doing this."

"I thought you liked your job here," she said.

"Well, I do, it's OK. But this would give me much more opportunity for advancement. Also, if I do this, I'd want to invest some funds in the bank, and that could prove to be a very good thing in the long run."

"I don't know, Johnny. I really like Chicago. It's begun to feel like home to me. And I really wouldn't like to give up The Irish Rose."

"Belle, I know the café has been good for you, but don't you think maybe it's time you outgrew that?"

"Time I outgrew it? What, like some childhood game?"

"Well, yes, a little. It's not the kind of thing the wife of a banker is usually engaged in, now is it? I'd like to see you spend more time in our circle of friends, and not have to work so hard."

"Did it ever occur to you that I enjoy what I'm doing?"

"I know you enjoy the contact with people, but there are other ways to do that."

"Yes, I know. I had some experience with that in Nashville. It was a disaster."

"Belle, don't judge me and my friends by your experience with Ken."

"What happened to 'I don't want to change you?'"

"The other part of that, Belle, was 'I just want to be with you'. Your little café keeps me from being with you as much as I'd like. I really think this is something we should seriously consider."

Belle was silent, and after a moment, Johnny said, "Will you at least come with me to New York to check this out further?"

"That sounds like you've already decided to go."

"I have. I told Walt I'd come for a week, and give him an answer after that."

"So, Walt's business here in Chicago was actually you, is that right?"

"Well, yes."

"And you didn't feel the need to be honest with me about that?"

"No, I didn't, because I thought it was a good possibility that you would react just as you are doing now. I didn't want that to be an issue when you met Walt. Just come with me to New York. After I meet with some of the other investors, and get more information, it's possible I may decide I don't want to do this. Please, at least come with me. Julia would love to see you again."

Belle was again silent for a few minutes, and then said, "You told Walt you would spend a week in New York?"

"Yes."

Belle sighed, and said, "All right. I'll come with you for a week, but I can't promise anything more than that."

"Fair enough, thank you, Belle. This is really important to me."

"So, when are you planning on leaving?"

"A week from today. Walt is arranging a meeting with the other investors."

The next morning, Belle told Peg that she was going to New York City with Johnny for a week.

"Well, good, it's about time ya had a wee vacation I'll be happy to keep things runnin' for ya while you're gone."

"Thank you, Peg. That means a lot."

"Ya don't seem very excited about the trip."

"No, I'm not. Johnny is thinking about moving back to New York, and I really don't want to do that."

"And why is he wantin' to go back?"

"A friend of his is planning to open his own bank, and wants Johnny to work for him. Johnny is also considering investing in the bank. It just feels like he's taking a risk he doesn't need to."

"Well, your Johnny's a smart man. I wouldn't be worryin' about that. Will ya be seein' Iris while you're there?"

"Of course! It will be great to see her again, and have some of her wonderful pastries."

Johnny booked a suite at the Waldorf for them. It was nearly ten p.m. when they checked in. They were both feeling travel weary, but Johnny phoned Walt to let him know they had arrived.

"I've scheduled the meeting with the investors for Wednesday morning. I thought you might like to have a day to rest a little before meeting them. Jenny and I would love to have you and Belle come to the house for dinner tomorrow."

'That sounds fine, Walt. I am a little bushed right now. I'll give you a call in the morning. Goodnight."

Belle and Johnny had a leisurely breakfast in the hotel dining room the next morning. After they returned to their room, Johnny placed a call to Walt. When he was finished, he said to Belle, "Walt wants to meet me for lunch, to discuss some things about the bank. Do you mind?"

"No, I thought I'd drop by the bakery to see Iris."

"Really? Are you sure you should go to that neighborhood by yourself?"

"Johnny, I lived in that neighborhood, remember?"

"I know, but you didn't have much choice then. I just don't like the idea of you being in that part of town by yourself."

"Johnny, I'm not made of glass! I may even run into some other people I know. Now, stop your fussing."

"Well, just be careful. I should be back by 3:00, at the latest. You remember we're having dinner with Walt and his wife tonight?"

"Yes, Johnny, I remember."

Belle left the hotel a short time after Johnny did, and stopped in a nearby book store to browse. She bought two books she wanted to read, then continued by trolley to Iris' bakery. The bell over the door tinkled as she walked in, and Iris looked up.

"Well, Saint's alive! I don't believe what I'm seein'" she said.

"Hello, Iris. It's good to see you again."

"Belle! What are ya doin' in New York?"

"Johnny needed to come for some business, so I decided to join him."

"Ah, yes, Peg wrote to tell me you're a married woman now. I'm happy for ya."

"Thank you. I'm sorry I haven't written to you. I'm not very good at writing letters, and I keep pretty busy with the café."

"Well, come sit down. I'll get us some coffee and pastry, and you can tell me all about your life in Chicago." When she returned with the coffee, she said, "Now, first ya must tell me how ya managed to hook up with Johnny, and how his da is takin' it."

Belle laughed, and said, "I guess I do have a lot to tell you. It doesn't seem possible that eight years have gone by so quickly."

Afternoons were generally quiet at the bakery. Belle and Iris had been talking non-stop, catching up on each other's lives, when Belle noticed the clock on the wall.

"Good grief! It's nearly 3 o'clock. I really need to get back to the hotel, Iris. Johnny thought he would be back from his meeting by 3:00. and he was fussing a little about me coming to this neighborhood by myself."

"Ah, yes, our men do love to think they need to protect us poor helpless women, don't they?" laughed Iris. "It's been wonderful seeing you again. How long will ya be in town?"

"Just a few days. I'm not sure what Johnny's schedule will be, but I'll stop back again, if I can."

"I hope ya can, but if not, you have a safe trip home. Give my love to Peg."

"That I will, 'bye, Iris."

It was nearly 4 o'clock by the time Belle got back to the hotel. Johnny was in the lobby when she walked in.

"Belle, where have you been? Are you all right?"

"I'm fine, Johnny, I just lost track of the time."

"Really, Belle, I wish you'd be a little more considerate. I was worried about you."

"I'm sorry, Iris and I were so busy catching up, and time just flew by."

"I was just about to find a policeman. I couldn't even remember exactly where the bakery is. How could you possibly have that much to talk about with her?"

"Johnny, calm down! Everything is fine. What time is our dinner tonight?"

"It's at 7:00. I'm surprised you even remembered that. Let's go to the room, so we can change."

There were several other people waiting for the elevator, so Belle didn't respond to this last remark, but as soon as they reached their room, she said, "That remark was uncalled for."

"What remark?"

"That you were surprised I remembered we had dinner with Walt planned for this evening."

"Well, I told you I'd be back before 3:00. I couldn't imagine you would spend that much time with Iris, and I didn't know what to think."

"You don't give me a lot of credit, do you?"

"Come on, Belle. Let's not fight. I was just worried. Let's just relax before we need to leave. Do you want to take a bath?"

"No, I don't feel the need to. I think I'll read a little. I stopped at a bookstore before I went to see Iris. How did your lunch with Walt go?"

"Oh, fine. He's found a building that would be suitable for the new bank, and wanted me to see it. We're meeting with some other investors tomorrow. Walt said we should come over about 6:30 tonight."

Walt and Jenny had a large apartment in uptown Manhattan, not far from Central Park. Walt introduced Jenny to Belle and Johnny, as well as his three children.

"These are my children," said Walt. "Andy is 8, Melissa is 5, and Amy is 4. Say hello to Mr. and Mrs. Honeywell."

Andy immediately stepped forward, offering his hand to Johnny, and said, "I'm pleased to meet you, Mr. and Mrs. Honeywell."

The girls were more subdued, standing close to their mother, and said a shy hello.

There was another young woman standing quietly behind the children. Walt said, "Jane, would you take the children to their rooms now. You may read them one story before they go to bed. Understood children?"

All three quickly replied, "Yes, Papa."

Melissa then asked, "Papa, will you come tuck us in?"

"Not tonight, Melissa. Mama and I have guests. I'll see you in the morning. Goodnight."

After Jane had left the room with the children, Walt said, "Jane helps us out with the children sometimes. I keep telling Jenny we should have a full time nanny, but she thinks she wants to be more involved with the children's care, don't you Jenny?"

"Well, they are young for such a short time. I saw very little of my mother when I was young, and don't want to do that to my children."

"Yes, well, Jenny, is dinner nearly ready?" asked Walt.

"I believe it is. Shall we go to the dining room?"

A meal of prime rib, cheese soufflé, fruit salad, and baked Alaska for dessert was served by an older woman.

"Jenny, that was a wonderful meal," said Belle as they were having dessert. "This dessert is amazing."

"Thank you. I enjoy cooking."

"You did this all yourself?" asked Belle.

"Well, most of it. Mrs. Jones helped too."

"Well, you outdid yourself," added Johnny.

"Yes, my Jenny is quite the little homemaker, isn't she? Though sometimes she indulges a little too much in her own cooking, don't you dear?"

Jenny blushed, and said quietly, "Well, I need to be sure everything tastes right."

"Belle, you are looking especially lovely this evening," said Walt. "Has Johnny been telling you all about the new venture?"

"No, he hasn't said a great deal about it yet," replied Belle.

"Waiting to get the full story tomorrow, are you Johnny? I think you'll be impressed with the other investors. You know, Belle, I'm planning on making Johnny Vice President of the bank. What do you think of that?"

Belle hesitated a moment, then said, "That sounds very impressive."

"What time are we meeting tomorrow?" asked Johnny.

"9 o'clock. I want to get an early start, so we'll have plenty of time to discuss everything."

"In that case, I think we should be getting back to the hotel."

"I'll have the doorman hail a cab for you," said Walt.

"Thank you for the wonderful meal, Jenny. It's been a pleasure meeting you and your children," said Belle.

"Well, good night, then. Belle, I hope I'll see you again before you return to Chicago," said Walt, then took her hand and kissed it.

When they were back in the hotel room, Belle said, "Your friend Walt is a little obnoxious with his family, isn't he?"

"Oh, that's just Walt. He's always been a 'take charge' kind of guy."

"Well, if you ever treat me like he treats Jenny, you'll find yourself without a wife."

Julia telephoned the next morning to invite Belle to have lunch with her at the Russian Tea Room. Belle enjoyed Julia's company, but even though she knew Johnny's income from the bank, plus his inheritance, made them financially comfortable, she could never get used to the prices at places like the Russian Tea Room. Her parents had probably never spent in a month, what her and Julia's lunch cost.

The rest of the week went by very quickly. Johnny spent most of each day with Walt, and seemed excited when he filled Belle in on the day's events each evening. Belle spent another afternoon with Julia at a luncheon Julia had arranged with some of her friends. By the time their scheduled departure on Saturday arrived, Belle was more than ready to get back to Chicago.

On the train ride back, Johnny told her that he wanted to accept Walt's offer.

"It's a great opportunity, Belle. I don't think I can afford to pass it up."

"But you've been doing very well at the Chicago bank, and we've made a home in Chicago."

"Chicago isn't home for me, Belle. New York is. I really want to go back."

"And I really don't. So, how are we going to work this out?"

"Belle, I think you are just focusing too much on your bad memories of New York. I know you could be as happy there as you are in Chicago."

"So, my feelings don't really count, is that what you're saying?"

"No, Belle, that isn't what I'm saying. This is a great opportunity for both of us."

"What about the Irish Rose?"

"I'm sure it won't be hard to find a buyer for it. Walt wants me to come back soon, to be involved in all the decisions from the beginning."

"It doesn't sound like you are giving me much choice."

"Well, no, I guess I'm not. I plan to give Mr. Harrison my two week's notice when we get back."

"Two weeks! Johnny, there is no way I can be ready to leave in two weeks."

"I know. I thought maybe you'd be willing to handle the sale of our house, and the café, and join me as soon as you could."

"So much for wanting to spend more time with me," she said.

"Belle, this is only temporary. Things will be better after we get settled in New York, you'll see."

Mr. Harrison was not happy when Johnny told him he was leaving, and asked him to leave immediately, rather than stay for two more weeks.

"I'm sorry you feel that way, Mr. Harrison. I just feel this is an opportunity I can't afford to pass up. I'll finish up some things on my desk, and leave at the end of the day."

"That won't be necessary. I'd prefer that you gather your personal belongings, and leave now. I misjudged you. I thought you had more loyalty. Good day, Johnny."

As he said all of this, he walked to the door, and stood aside, holding it open for Johnny.

When Belle arrived home from the café that evening, Johnny had his bags packed, and setting by the door.

"What is this?" she asked.

Mr. Harrison didn't want me to stay for two more weeks. In fact, he didn't even want me to stay today. This just reinforces to me that I've made the right decision. So, I've decided not to waste any more time here. I'm leaving for New York in the morning. I'm sorry to have to leave you with making all the arrangements for selling the house, but I really think I should get involved with all the planning of the New York bank, as soon as possible."

Belle wasn't sure how to respond to this, so remained quiet.

"Belle, don't be upset. This is going to be a very good move for us, you'll see."

"You've dumped a lot on me in a very short time, and without really consulting me about any of this, so I really don't think you should expect me to be jumping up and down with excitement."

"I know, it will just take some time. The theatre season starts in a couple weeks. Maybe you could arrange a few days off, come to New York, and we'll take in a show or two, and do some shopping for a place to live."

"I'll think about it. Right now, I'm going to read for a while and go to bed. It was hectic at the café today. What time do you leave tomorrow?"

"My train leaves at 7:00 a.m., so I guess I should head for bed before long too."

In the morning, their goodbyes were a little strained. He told he where he would be staying, and promised to call frequently.

For the next few days, Belle was quieter at work than usual. She didn't say anything to anyone about Johnny's plans for them to move to New York. Peg noticed Belle was quiet, and preoccupied, but decided not to say anything, instead just wait until Belle was ready to talk about whatever was bothering her. After a week of minimal communication from Belle, she'd had enough. When the afternoon help came in to relieve both her and Belle, Peg took Belle by the arm, and said, "Let's go for a short walk." Once they were outside, she said, "You've been walkin' around for a week like you were about to bury your best friend. What's up?"

Belle sighed, and said, "I've been trying to make a decision. Johnny has taken a job in New York. I'm supposed to be getting our house and the Irish Rose sold, and go with him. He's been gone a week, and I haven't been able to bring myself to do anything about either one."

"Well, now, no wonder you've been about as silent as a grave."

"Peg, I just don't think I can do it."

"Well, sure an' that's a big order to handle. Could ya' not get someone at the bank to help?"

"No, Peg, that's not it. I just don't think I can go back to New York. Johnny said I could probably find another café there that I could buy, but I don't believe him. I know he'd rather I didn't work at all. I'm just not cut out to be a society lady, spending my days shopping, or going to luncheons and teas with other women who have nothing better to do with their time. Peg, I think I'm going to have to divorce him."

"Well, that sure sounds like you've got yourself between a rock and a hard place. Did ya' not tell him you didn't want to go?"

"I did, several times. He just wouldn't listen, and finally said I had no choice, because he just knew it was the right thing to do!"

"Ah, Belle, I'm sorry. Are ya' sure ya' canna' work things out with him?"

"I think the only working out would be for me to do just what he wants. I just don't think I can do that."

"Sounds to me like you've already made the decision."

"Yeah, I guess I have. I haven't wanted to admit that, and then take the next step."

"When there's a hard thing to do, it's best just to dig in and do it. Putting it off won't make it come easier."

"I know, Peg. Thanks for listening. He wants me to take some time off to go to New York, see a play, and start looking for a place to live.

I guess I'm going to have to go. I can't very well tell him over the phone that I'm not going to move to New York."

"No, that probably wouldn't be a good idea," Peg laughed.

"Can you take over for me for a few days next week?"

"Of course I can."

Belle called Johnny that evening, and told him she could come to New York on the following Tuesday. When he asked how the sale of the house and café was going, she replied that she was working on it.

"Well, hopefully, it won't take long. I miss you. I haven't had time to check out any apartments, but Walt has given me a couple of ideas. I'll make time, so we can look together when you're here."

"I can only stay until Friday. Peg can't take over for me any longer than that."

"I was hoping you could stay at least a week. I'll be so glad when you're out from under the responsibility of the café."

Belle ended the conversation by saying, "My train leaves at 7 a.m., so I'll see you Tuesday afternoon."

"I can't wait. Pack something nice to wear to the theatre. Bye honey."

She was still a little ambivalent about her decision to leave Johnny. "I don't know why he can't be happy staying in Chicago," she thought. "Maybe I should talk about this with someone. Peg is so against divorce because of her faith, I don't think she can be very objective. Kenny always seems to see things pretty clearly." With that, she picked up the phone and called him.

"Hi Kenny, it's Belle."

"Well, hello. What's up?"

"I was wondering if you could come by sometime Sunday. I have something I'd like to get your opinion about."

"Sure thing. What time?"

"How about lunch? I'm not a great cook, but I think I can manage a decent lunch."

"I'm sure you can, noon?"

"That will be fine. See you then."

Kenny arrived shortly before noon, with a six pack of beer. "I thought a warm August day like this called for some beer."

"That's perfect. I decided to take advantage of the end of summer, with burgers, corn on the cob, and sliced tomatoes."

"Wow! I don't think I've had that meal since I left the farm. I'm not much for cookin', and you just don't find this stuff on the menu in any restaurants, do you?"

"Come on out in the kitchen. I'll have it ready in a few minutes."

Kenny opened a beer for each of them, and asked, "Where's Johnny?"

"He's in New York. That's why I wanted to talk to you."

"What's up?"

"Let's eat first. It may take a while. What have you been up to?"

"Oh, pretty much the same old, same old. I haven't seen you at any of the dances for a while."

"I know. I'm overdue for kicking up my heels a bit. Let's eat in the dining room. The kitchen is a little steamy, and there's a nice breeze through the other room."

When they had finished eating, Kenny said, "How about another beer while you tell me what's going on?"

When he returned from the kitchen with the beers, Belle said, "Johnny quit his job, and has moved to New York."

"You're kidding! What brought that on?"

"A friend of his from New York is opening a new bank, and talked Johnny into going to work for him."

"You don't sound very happy about it."

"I'm not. I'm not sure I trust his friend Walt, and I really don't want to move back to New York. But I couldn't talk him out of it. I'm supposed to be selling this house, and the Irish Rose, so I can join him. He's been gone two weeks, and I haven't done anything about selling either one. Kenny, I just don't think I can go to New York, and become another 'society wife'. When I complained about giving up the Irish Rose, Johnny said I could probably find another café to buy in New York. But he doesn't like to have me working, and I know he'll find reasons for me not to do that once I get there. I've just about made up my mind to leave him."

"Just about?"

"He wants me to come to New York for a few days to look for an apartment. So, I told him I'd do that this week. What I really am planning is to go so I can tell him face to face. But, then I think maybe I'm crazy for giving him up, and all the security that goes with being his wife. I just wanted to get your opinion on all of this."

"You want me to tell you what to do?"

"No, not really. But, you're always so level headed, and you know me pretty well. I just need to hear your thoughts on this."

"Hmmm, well, let's start with the easy stuff first. Is Johnny's name on the deed to the Irish Rose?"

"No, I'm the owner."

"Well, that's good. You'd be in no danger of losing it. Then, there's the thing of divorce. The courts don't grant them all that easy, without a good reason, like him being unfaithful to you. You think he has?"

"No."

"Then, he's probably gonna' have to be the one to ask for the divorce, on the grounds that you're deserting him, which means he probably wouldn't have to give you any kind of financial settlement."

"Well, I managed before I married him, and I can do it again."

"OK. Then there's the harder stuff. Do you love him?"

"I do, I think."

"You think? That's usually something that has either a yes or no answer to."

"I know," she said, and sighed. "He's been good to me, but he just wouldn't listen at all to me when I said I didn't want to go to New York, and that Chicago seems like home to me. It's just starting to feel like a replay of when I was married to Ken."

"Well, that doesn't sound good."

"It doesn't feel very good, either. When we first met, it didn't seem like he wanted to change anything about me. Now it feels like he wants me to become like all the rich women he grew up with. I just can't do that, Kenny."

"No, I don't imagine you can. Sounds to me like you've already made up your mind, and don't need my opinion."

"But, it's really helped to talk about it with you. My mind just kept going in endless circles when I tried to think this through on my own."

"Well, I'm glad I could help then. You know you can always call on me for anything you need, don't you?"

"I do, Kenny, and that means a lot."

"You know, you might want to talk to a lawyer before you go to New York. When are you leaving?"

"Tuesday morning."

"Well, I know a guy who is a lawyer, and he seems pretty OK to me. Why don't I call him, and see if he could meet with you tomorrow?"

"Thanks Kenny, that's probably a good idea."

Johnny was waiting when Belle's train arrived, and greeted her warmly with an embrace and a kiss. "It's so good to see you again. How was the train ride?"

"It was fine. It's good to see you too."

"I thought we'd have a quiet dinner tonight, do some apartment hunting tomorrow, and go to the theatre Thursday evening. Julia is hoping the two of you can get together sometime Thursday. I told her it might depend on how successful we are tomorrow."

"A quiet dinner sounds good. I need to freshen up a bit first."

"Of course." He hailed a cab to go to the hotel. When they got to the room, he said, "Why don't you take a nice long bath. We've got plenty of time. Then we can go to dinner. I've found a lovely little French café."

"A bath sounds really good right now."

The café was small and quiet. The waiters wore long aprons in the European style. Johnny ordered a bottle of Bordeaux wine, and after they had ordered, Belle asked, "How are things going with the bank plans?"

"They are moving along nicely. We have four investors, including Walt and myself. It looks like we'll be ready to open in a month. I'll take you there tomorrow to show it to you. I think you'll be impressed with what the designer is doing with the lobby."

Just then their food arrived, and for a few minutes the conversation focused on the meal. After a short time Johnny asked, "What time would you like to start looking at apartments tomorrow?"

Belle hesitated a moment before saying, "Johnny, I need to talk to you."

"What is it, is something wrong?"

"I can't live here Johnny. I've thought about it, a lot. It's about the only thing I have thought of for the past two weeks, and I just can't do it."

"Belle, that makes no sense. Why in the world do you think you can't live here?"

"Because I can't be who I think you want me to be here."

"What is that supposed to mean?"

"Think about it Johnny. You know I grew up in a very different way from you. I've always worked. I like working, I like being the owner of a café. Can you honestly tell me I'd have your full support in finding another café to buy here?"

"Belle, you're with me now. You don't have to work."

"That's not the point. You're not listening to me. Besides, that's not the only thing. I like to dance. I like going to dance halls and dancing with several different men. I'm pretty sure that wouldn't happen here."

"Belle, this is crazy. You don't know what you're talking about. You haven't even given New York a fair try."

"That may be true, but I've seen how your friends and family spend their time, and it's just too much like what I had in Nashville with Ken. I just can't do that. Can't you consider coming back to Chicago?"

"Absolutely not! I've invested too much time and money here with Walt. And I don't want to live in Chicago. You'll just have to find a way to learn to like New York."

"No, Johnny, I don't. I promised myself years ago that I'd never again put myself in a position to be told what I could and couldn't do by a man. It's a promise I intend to keep. You can either find a way to come back to Chicago, or you can divorce me."

Johnny leaned back in his chair, and glared at Belle for a moment, then said, "I see. I suppose one of those brawny Micks that hang around your café is back there waiting to console you, is that it?"

"That was totally uncalled for, and you know it! But, it does point out another big difference between us. You don't like the Irish, and look down your nose at them. I see them as honest, hard working people who would do anything in the world for a friend."

"You don't have any grounds for asking for a divorce."

"I'm aware of that, but you do. You can accuse me of deserting you."

"Well, you've just got this all planned out, don't you?"

"I told you I've done nothing but think about it for the past two weeks."

"You know you won't get a penny from me if I divorce you under those circumstances."

"I assumed as much."

"Then I think this evening is over," he said as he motioned for the waiter to bring the check.

They were silent during the taxi ride back to the hotel. When they arrived, he handed Belle the key to the room, saying, "I'm going to stay at Julia's tonight. Hopefully you can find a train back to Chicago tomorrow. My lawyer will be contacting you there."

When Peg walked into the Irish Rose on Thursday morning, Belle was already there. "Well, this is a surprise. I thought you weren't going to be back 'til Saturday," she said. "Did things not go well for ya' then?"

"I guess they went about as well as they could have. When I convinced him I wasn't moving to New York, he asked me to leave. I did try to get him to leave New York, and come back here, but he's as stubborn about staying there as I am about not living there."

"So, how are ya' doin' now?"

"Believe it or not, I'm relieved." When Peg raised her eyebrows, Belle continued. "I know, I'm a little surprised about that too. I think that trying to be who I am, as well as who he wanted me to be was more of a strain than I realized."

"So, what happens now?"

"He said he'll have his lawyer contact me about a divorce."

"Well, I'm that sorry it had to come to this."

"I know Peg. I'm beginning to think I'm not meant to be married. Thank goodness I hadn't done anything about selling the café. I guess I better think about finding someplace else to live too, as he'll be selling the house now."

Chapter Twelve

"Happy New Year, Belle."

"And to you, Kenny. Let's hope 1932 is better than the last couple of years have been."

"I'll second that. It's been kinda rough for you, hasn't it?"

"You could say that. But, everything is settled now, and it's time to move on with my life."

"All that divorce and estate mess is cleared up, then?"

"It is, finally. You know, it would have been much easier if the divorce had been granted before Johnny died. But because we were still technically married, I was the beneficiary of his estate. Julia wasn't happy about that, and hired a lawyer to contest it. I really didn't want to fight her on it, but my lawyer said that since my name was also on the title to the house, that I should keep that much, at least. I knew Johnny shouldn't have taken that job with Walt, but I couldn't convince him of that. When the crash happened, Walt just up and disappeared, apparently with whatever cash was on hand at the bank, leaving his wife and kids on their own. I never did like that man. And Johnny just couldn't face life without all the wealth he'd grown up with."

"So this house is yours now, huh?"

"It is, but I'm going to sell it. I don't need all this room, and I'd rather live closer to the café."

"So, did you kick up your heels last night?"

"Not really. Peg and Dan had a few friends over for pot luck. I was home not long after midnight. How about you?"

"Yeah, I went dancin'. It was a good crowd."

"That sounds good. It's been too long since I've been to a dance. Now that things have settled down, I'm going to start doing that again."

"Great! How about next Saturday?"

"I'll plan on it. I just made a beef and noodle casserole, and some biscuits for lunch. I hope that's OK."

"Sounds just fine. So, how's the café doing? I know things are a little tight for everyone these days."

"Not as well as it did a few years ago, but I'm managing."

"You still keep in touch with any of your family?"

"I hear from Mae and David from time to time. I tried writing to Lizzie a couple times, but that seems to be a lost cause. She's never written back. Mae says she and Orville are doing OK, but David and Ann are struggling a bit."

"You ever think about going back for a visit?"

"Oh, I don't know. Maybe when things pick up a little at the café."

"Well, when you're ready, give me a holler. We could go together and save some money. I'm pretty sure my old jalopy is still up for a trip like that."

"That sounds like fun."

Belle rode to the dance with Kenny on Saturday. They had an understanding that if either got a better offer during the evening, there was no obligation for them to return in each other's company.

Belle was having a great time. By 10:00 she had danced nearly every dance. She was sitting at a table, having a beer, when someone tapped her on the shoulder, saying, "Well if it ain't the old married lady."

When she turned, Spats was standing there.

"Hello George. I'm not old, and I'm no longer married."

"Ditched the guy, huh?"

"Something like that. It's a long story. How are you, George?"

"Me? Never better. You up for another dance, or did all them other guys wear you out?"

"I'm always ready for another dance."

After they were on the dance floor, she asked, "So what are you up to these days, now that booze is legal again?"

"Bought me a little bar."

"Really? I'm surprised you're here on a Saturday night, instead of minding the store."

"It's a little neighborhood joint, kinda quiet like, and I got me a good man to keep an eye on things when I ain't there. How about you? You still in the food business?"

"Yes, I'm still running the Irish Rose."

"Well, I'll be. So, what happened to your marriage?"

Belle hesitated only briefly before saying, "He died."

"Oh, I'm sorry. But I never thought you two was a good fit anyhow. You're too classy to be hangin' out with some high and mighty, phony banker."

Belle laughed, and at that moment the song ended. "George, I need to go to the powder room. I'll see you later."

"That a promise?"

"It's a promise."

Belle had just returned form the powder room when another gentleman asked her to dance.

When that dance ended, Kenny tapped her on the shoulder, saying, "I've barely danced with you tonight."

"We can fix that right now," she replied.

The band began playing a waltz. "So, it looks like you're having a good time," he said.

"Oh, I am! I'd almost forgotten how much I enjoy this. How about you?"

"Yep, me too. In fact, I've got a sweet little blonde I'd like to take home. You think you can find a ride?"

"Now, Kenny, you know what our deal is. You go right ahead. George is here, and I'm betting he'll want to drive me home, but if not, there's always a taxi."

"OK, if you're sure."

"Kenny, I'm a big girl. I'll be fine."

George approached Belle a short time later for another dance. "So, you gonna let me drive you home tonight, or are you tied up with somebody else?" he asked.

"No, I'm not tied up, and I'd be happy to have you drive me home."

"Well, great!"

She and George left shortly after midnight. When they were in the car, Belle said, "George, its' good to see you again, but I need to get something straight with you. I'm done being involved with any one man exclusively. I'd be happy to see you from time to time, so long as you're OK with me not being 'your girl.'"

"Belle, you are the damndest dame I've ever met. But, I guess if that's the rule, I can live with it. Runnin' the bar don't give me enough time to be holdin' hands with some clingy dame anyhow."

For the next several years Belle's life consisted of working at the café six days a week, spending occasional Sunday's with Peg's family, and dancing several nights a month. She often went with Kenny or George to the dances, but sometimes went by herself. She dated a few of the men she met at the dances, but only so long as they were willing to keep the relationship casual.

One spring day in 1941 she asked Kenny if he was ready for a trip to Nebraska.

"I was wonderin' if you was ever gonna' take me up on that offer," he replied. "Sounds like a good idea. It's been a while since I've been home, and even longer for you."

"I know. The café has kept me busy, and things were a little tight for a few years after the banks crashed."

"And you're just never sure you're ready to face your family again?"

Belle laughed, saying, "You do know me well, don't you Kenny? It shouldn't bother me so much after all this time, especially since David and Mae have kept in touch."

"Some hurts just take a long time to heal, I guess. So, when do you think we should go?"

"Peg can fill in for me anytime, so you tell me what works for you."

"I'll talk to my boss tomorrow.

I've got some vacation time comin', so that shouldn't be a problem."

They left on a cool, rainy day in late May.

"I hope the weather is nicer than this when we get to Nebraska," Belle said.

"Oh, I'll bet it will be. May's usually a pretty good month in Nebraska."

The rain stopped later that day, and the rest of the trip was pleasant, and uneventful. They arrived at Mae's late in the afternoon of the second day. Mae was at the door before Belle could knock.

"Belle! It's good to see you."

"It's good to see you too, Mae. You remember Kenny Miller?"

"Well, my land Kenny. It's been a long time since grade school."

"That it has. Good to see you Mae."

"Well, come on in."

"Oh, I can't stay. My folks are expectin' me for supper, so I'd best be on my way. I'll be back to pick you up Friday morning, Belle. That should get us back in time to rest up a bit before goin' back to work on Monday. "See you Friday morning then. Enjoy your visit."

"Come on in Belle. You want a cup of coffee?"

"That sounds good, thanks, Mae."

"I baked some sugar cookies too. Orville does love his sugar cookies. How are you Belle? You look tired, and thin as rail. Don't you eat your own cookin'?"

Belle laughed, and said, "I'm fine Mae, a little weary from the trip is all. And I don't do the cooking for the café. You know I was never that good in the kitchen."

"Well, you didn't hardly stick around long enough to get some practice, I reckon."

"Somehow I doubt more practice would have changed that," she replied, her tone sharper than she had intended.

"Now, don't get your back up. I didn't mean nuthin' by that. David and Ann are coming for supper tomorrow. Lizzie even said she'd come too. Her kids are all married now, and she's livin' in Seward in a little apartment. I asked Sis and Vera, too, but Sis is expectin' and didn't feel up to it, and Vera says she and Henry can't get away just now. They live about thirty miles away, over by Staplehurst."

"Who is Sis?" Belle asked.

"Oh, that's Greta's daughter, Peggy. But Lizzie started callin' her Sis, and it just kinda stuck."

"What about the boys?"

"Well, Jesse's married, and livin' in Omaha, and of course Charles died a few years back."

"Oh no, I'm sorry to hear that."

"Didn't I write and tell you? I thought I had."

"I'm sure I would have remembered something like that. What happened?"

"Don't really know. He took sick with the flu or something, and two days later he was gone. Sis took it kinda hard."

"I suppose she would have."

"Yeah, and their no good dad didn't even come back for the funeral. Lizzie wasn't even gonna' notify him, but Sis took on so, she finally relented. Didn't surprise nobody but Sis that he didn't come. She just won't hear a bad word about him, even though he's never been much of anything but a no account drunk."

Belle wasn't sure how to respond to all this, and was saved from the need to by the arrival of Ellen.

"Oh, Ellen, honey, you're home," said Mae. "You remember your Aunt Belle? Maybe not, you were just a little girl when she was here last."

"Hello, Aunt Belle. I remember you brought me candy."

Belle laughed, and said, "I'm afraid I didn't do that this time."

Ellen blushed, and quickly said, "Oh, that's all right. I didn't mean to sound like I was asking for something."

"You just forgot your manners there for a minute, didn't you?" said Mae.

"I'm sorry Mamma."

"Oh, heavens," said Belle. "That was a perfectly natural comment. Don't think a thing about it."

"Ellen, you'd best go change your clothes. You don't want to get that nice outfit spoiled."

Ellen ducked her head, and left for her room.

"Ellen works at the bank, and they like to have their people dress nice. Orville should be along soon. I've got a pot roast in the oven for supper."

"Can I help with anything in the kitchen?"

"No need. Maybe you'd like to freshen up a bit, and hang your clothes up before supper. Your room is the last one down the hall."

"Well, if you're sure I can't help. I am a little grimy from the trip."

Mae busied herself in the kitchen, checking on the roast, setting the table, and opening a jar of the peas from her garden that she had canned only last week.

Orville came home during the preparations asking, "What's for supper?"

"I've got a pot roast in the oven. It will be ready soon."

"Good, I'm hungry."

"Belle's here."

"That right? When did she get in?"

"Oh, maybe an hour ago. She's in her room unpacking, and cleaning up from the trip."

Just then, Belle came into the kitchen. "Hello Orville. How are you?"

"A little weary from my day. Hardware store got broken into, and some kid thinks his bike was stolen. I suspect he just lost it, or loaned it to a friend, and doesn't want to tell his folks. And you can't believe the paperwork just those two things involves! The Chief seems to think we should act like the FBI or something."

Ellen came into the room at that point, and Orville said, "Ah, there's my little girl. Did you have a good day honey?"

"It was fine, Daddy."

Mae had been busy carrying serving dishes to the table, and said, "Well, it's ready. Let's eat."

She had cooked a large roast with generous amounts of potatoes, carrots, and onions simmered in the juice from the meat. There was also a large bowl of peas, a gelatin salad with fruit and marshmallows, and dinner rolls.

It seemed to Belle that there was enough to feed twice as many people, but by the end of the meal, there was very little food left.

"Belle, you hardly ate anything," Mae said. "You feelin' all right?"

"I'm fine, and I've had more than enough, thanks. It isn't often I sit down to a large meal like this. Everything was great, Mae."

"Well, you should eat more. You could use a little more meat on your bones," commented Orville. "Got any dessert, Mae?"

"I've got some of your favorite sugar cookies. I'll be makin' some pies for tomorrow night."

"It's easy to see why they are all so heavy," thought Belle. "I think they must eat like this all the time."

Mae, Ellen, and Belle cleared the table, and washed the dishes, while Orville had a cigar, sitting at the table reading the paper. When the women returned to the dining room, he commented, "Sounds like them damn German's are getting pushier every day over there. I'm just glad Roosevelt is smart enough to keep us outta it."

"It sounds like it's getting pretty bad over there," offered Belle. "I've read that there are a lot of people trying to immigrate to America."

"Yeah, mostly Jews.

I think the government's right to keep a lid on it. Them damn Jews is always whining about something. Personally, I don't see no advantage for us to take in boatloads of dumb peasants."

"Now Orville, don't go getting all riled up. It ain't good for your blood pressure. Did you hear the Swanson girl went to live with her aunt in Lincoln? Rumor is she's with child. She was always a little wild, and her folks could have done a better job of keeping an eye on her."

"That's for sure. She was always goin' out dancin' with one boy or another, or goin' to one of them racy picture shows. I know you think we're hard on you, Ellen, but you can see from something like this, that we're only doin' what's best for you."

Ellen quietly replied, "I know Daddy."

"Well, I think we should be heading for bed. Tomorrow's another workin' day. Belle, you don't mind waitin' on the bathroom 'til we're in bed, do you? Since you don't need to get up early," asked Orville.

"That's fine. I think I'll go to my room and read for awhile."

"Well, see you in the morning then, or after work if you're a late sleeper."

"I'm usually not. Goodnight everyone."

Belle was awakened by the sound of soft tapping on the door to the next room, and heard Mae saying, "Ellen, honey, it's time to get up. Breakfast is almost ready."

Belle quickly got dressed. When she got to the kitchen she found Orville drinking coffee, Mae busy whipping up batter for pancakes, and bacon frying on the stove. Ellen arrived just as everything was ready to be served.

"You look nice this morning," Mae said to Ellen. "Now be careful you don't spill anything on you."

Breakfast was over quickly, and Orville and Ellen left for work.

"You want another cup of coffee before we start our day?" Mae asked.

"Sounds good," Belle replied, as she lit a cigarette.

"You smokin' these days I see," said Mae.

"I do. I enjoy it, especially with a cup of coffee after a meal."

"Never tried it myself. Not many women in these parts do. You ever miss Nebraska?"

"Not really. Chicago feels like home now."

"Well, I don't think I'd care for a big city. We go to Lincoln about once a year or so, and that's too big for me. From what I hear, it's nuthin', compared to Chicago."

"Chicago is much larger, but it has some advantages."

"That right? Well, we'd best get to clearin' up the breakfast stuff. I need to work in the garden a while. Orville and Ellen always come home for lunch, then I'll need to do a little cleaning and start supper for tonight."

"Let me do the kitchen clean up," offered Belle.

"No, that's all right. You wouldn't know where things go anyway. You can wash, and I'll dry and put away."

Orville and Ellen drove up shortly after noon. Lunch consisted of roast beef sandwiches, potato salad, canned peaches, and cookies.'

After they left to go back to work, Mae said, "Ellen's been pesterin' us to let her buy a car, and learn to drive, but we're not sure that's a good idea. She's still pretty young. Maybe in a few years."

"How old is she?" asked Belle.

"She turned twenty last winter."

Mae was a whirlwind of activity all afternoon, baking pies, dusting furniture and knick knacks that were already gleaming, and getting the chicken cut up and ready to be fried. Belle's offers to help were always declined for one reason or another.

"You just relax, you're on vacation."

"Maybe I'll go for a short walk, it's such a pretty day."

David, Ann, their daughter Rose, and Lizzie arrived at 5:00. Mae was busy in the kitchen, and Ellen answered the knock on the door. Greetings were exchanged, and Mae called from the kitchen, "I'll be out in a minute, I just gotta get this chicken turned so it don't burn."

After a brief hello to Belle and Ellen, Lizzie moved toward the kitchen saying, "I'll see if Mae needs some help."

"Lizzie, you don't need to be out here, go on in and visit. I'll be there in a minute."

"There's plenty of time for visiting. I figured you could use some help."

Mae stopped what she was doing, looked at Lizzie for a long minute, then shook her head, saying, "All right, then, you can carry the water pitcher to the table. And try to be nice tonight."

Lizzie contributed little to the conversation during the meal.

"How are your boys?" Belle asked David and Ann.

David was like his father, a man of minimal conversation. His only response was "They're doin' fine."

Ann added, "Tommy's got a girl he seems serious about. We like her too, so we may be having a wedding before long. And Eddie takes after Ray, always tinkering with the machinery on the farm."

"Rose, what's your favorite activity?" Belle asked.

"I like gardening."

"Really! She must have gotten that from you, Ann. None of us girls were ever too wild about it."

"But it was necessary to keep food on the table, right Mae?" added Lizzie.

"Yep, still is, which is about the only reason why I have a garden."

"We could get all our stuff from the store, but it don't compare to home grown stuff, does it David?" added Orville.

"No, I guess it doesn't."

"How about you, Belle? I don't suppose you do any gardening?" said Orville.

"Well, since I live in an apartment, there really isn't any place to have a garden. But, no, I probably wouldn't even if I had a place."

"Yeah, most city folk can't be bothered with something like gardening."

Ann spoke up at this point, saying, "We really should be going, David. Rose has school in the morning."

"Thanks for coming tonight," said Belle. "It's been good seeing you again."

"Maybe we should help with the dishes first," added Lizzie.

"Oh, you don't need to do that. Me and Belle can do that. You got a little drive ahead of you yet tonight," said Mae.

"Well, if you're sure," replied Ann.

"Heavens, yes. Don't worry about it."

When Mae and Belle had finished the clean up, Orville reminded everyone it was time for bed. "What time are you leavin' in the morning?" he asked.

"I imagine Kenny will be here by 8:00."

"Well, goodnight then. See you at breakfast."

Belle was awake by 6:00, and was dressed and had her things packed by 7:00, when breakfast was ready. Orville and Ellen were out of the house shortly after 7:30.

"Let me help with the dishes before Kenny gets here," said Belle.

"So, are you and Kenny sweet on each other?" asked Mae.

"No, we're just good friends."

"Well, he comes from good stock. You could do worse."

"And I have. I don't think marriage is for me."

"That right?"

Kenny knocked on the door at this point, and Mae let him in.

"Mornin' Kenny, Would you like a cup of coffee?"

"No, thanks, Ma fixed a big breakfast before I left. You ready to go Belle?"

"I am. Mae, thank you for everything. It was good to see you."

"Don't wait so long to come back next time."

Once they were in the car, and driving away, Belle heaved a big sigh.

"That bad, huh?" said Kenny.

"Oh, I guess not. Just another reminder of how different I am from my family. How was your visit?"

"It was OK. Me and my brothers don't have a lot in common either. Guess we just have to be reminded of that from time to time."

The trip back to Chicago was uneventful. They arrived late Saturday night.

"Sleep well, Belle. I'll talk to you later in the week."

"Thanks for the ride, and the company. See you later," she replied.

Belle arrived at the café early Monday morning, and found Peg already there.

"Welcome back. How was the trip?"

"It was OK."

"Just OK?"

Belle smiled, and said, "Yeah, I just got reminded again of how little I have in common with my family. How did things go here?"

"Well, I do have some news for you. I just wish I did'na need to be givin' it to you."

"What is it?"

"Well, we had a visit from a gentleman last Wednesday. Seems he's bought this building, and feels the need to raise the rent."

"Really! Did he say how much?"

"He did."

"Well?"

Peg named the figure, and Belle shouted "What? That's double what I'm paying now."

"I know, and he does too. Says a good businessman woulda been raisin' it some every year, and he figures this is a fair price. Says it will be due June 1, which is next week."

The following May, Belle was informed by the owner, a Mr. Jones, that he was raising the rent again. It wasn't the drastic increase it had been the year before, but was enough to cause her some concern.

"Peg, I think I'm going to have to raise my prices again. I'm not sure how much longer I can manage, if he keeps raising the rent this much every year."

"He is a greedy old sod. I've heard rumors he's hopin' to drive you out, so he can open a bar here. Just what this neighborhood needs, another pub!"

Some of her customers grumbled about the prices, and even though many of her regulars continued to come in as often as they had, she frequently needed to dip into her savings to meet expenses.

George stopped in for a late lunch one day. "You feelin' OK Belle? You look tired, and you haven't been out dancin' for a while."

"I'm fine, George."

"Well, you don't look like you feel fine."

"Did you want to order something?"

"How about your special. That's always good."

Belle kept busy cleaning tables, refilling salt and pepper shakers, or popping into the kitchen while George was there.

Peg's afternoon replacement came in, and Peg left. George paid his bill and followed Peg out. He caught up with her a short way from the café, saying, "Peg, wait up a minute."

Peg turned, and said, "What is it George?"

"I wanted to ask you about Belle. Is she OK?"

"She's fine, George."

"You sure? She looks tired, and was kinda short with me today. You know what's goin' on? She doesn't have some guy givin' her problems, does she? Cause if so, I'll set him straight!"

"No, George, it's nothin' like that."

"Then what is it?"

"George, if Belle didn't tell you, I'm thinkin' she would'na want me blabbin' either."

"Listen, Peg, you know I'd do just about anything for Belle. You tell me what's wrong, and I promise I won't let her know you told."

Peg sighed, and paused, then said, "Well, all right then, but if she ever finds out I told you, I'll put an Irish curse on you that you'll never get over. The landlord keeps raisin' the rent on her, and it's causin' her some worry."

"So, who is this mope?"

"No, George, I've said all I'm gonna. Now don't be causin' her any more grief with your bullyin' ways."

"Me, bully?"

"Yeah, well, you just remember, you cause her any more grief, and you'll have me to deal with."

"Well, I sure don't want that," he laughed. "I'll be good, I promise. And thanks for fillin' me in."

In the next few weeks, Belle noticed there were several new customers that came in about once a week. George was also stopping in more often, sometimes sharing a table with one of the new faces.

Then December 7, 1941 arrived. Most Americans had followed the war in Europe to some extent, while feeling comfortable, and maybe a little smug, that it wasn't affecting life in America. The destruction at Pearl Harbor now made that illusion impossible.

Within a short time, the numbers of customers at the Irish Rose decreased drastically. Most of the younger men enlisted into one of the armed forces. Then rationing of things like sugar and gasoline began. Belle was now routinely dipping into her savings just to meet monthly expenses.

George came to the café one afternoon, when he was pretty sure things would be quiet.

"Belle, come sit down a minute. I got something I want to talk to you about."

Belle poured two cups of coffee, and joined him at a table.

"Listen, I know things have got to be pretty tough for you here. I've got a proposition for you. I've bought a little bar down close to the docks. How about you come to work for me there? Be kind of a hostess for the joint."

"Oh, George, I don't know. Do you think that's a good idea, opening a new business now?"

"I do. Lot's of our boys will be leavin' on ships and they'll be wanting to fortify themselves a bit before goin' off to war, and there's factories nearby that are already startin' to gear up to make supplies for the war. There's even a small dance floor in the bar, so's they can kick up their heels a bit. I can pay you a decent wage, and maybe take some of them worry lines off your pretty face. Whaddya say?"

"I don't know, George. I need to think about it."

"Well, don't think too long. I'm gonna be ready to open in three weeks. I really think this will be a good deal for both of us, Belle. I can take you down and show you the place on Sunday, if you want. You think you can give me an answer by next week?"

"OK, I'll go look at it, and give you an answer next week, but I'm not making any promises."

"Fair enough. I'll pick you up about 2:00 on Sunday."

The next morning Belle told Peg about George's offer.

"Well, ya know I'm no fan of pubs, but this might be a good thing for you. I don't see things pickin' up here, 'til after the war, anyway, and who knows when that'll be."

"You might be right. I just hate the thought of giving up the Irish Rose. And I feel like I'll be leaving you in a bad spot."

"I know, it's hard givin' up on something you've put your heart in, but sometimes life just don't give us much choice. And ya don't need to be worryin' about me. Dan heard about a factory that will be makin' uniforms for our boys, and they are lookin' to hire more people. That's something I could do."

"Well, I told George I'd go with him Sunday to look at the place. He wants my answer next week".

Sunday was a gray, cold, windy, late March day. Traces of dirty snow and slush lined the streets and sidewalks near the docks. The front of the bar was only twelve feet wide, the window covered with grime.

"I know it don't look like much from the outside," George said, "but I'm havin' a big sign made that says "Spat's Joint," and painting the front white with black trim."

The size was misleading from the outside. Even though it was only twelve feet wide, it extended back at least thirty feet. A walnut and brass bar ran along one side for about fifteen feet. At the back of the room was a twelve foot dance floor, with and old upright piano set to one side, between the bar and the dance floor. Tables and chairs filled the remaining space.

"It still needs some cleanin' up, and the mirror behind the bar has to be replaced. You can see it's got a lot of possibility. Once word gets out, I don't think keepin' the place full will be any problem. Whaddya think?"

"You might be right. It is a nice surprise on the inside. What would my salary be?"

George named a figure that seemed more than fair to her.

"I'll think about it, and let you know in a few days."

"I hope your answer is yes. You'd add some real class to the place, ya know."

"Thanks for showing it to me, but I really should be getting back."

"Aw, I was hopin' we could spend some time together today."

"Not today, George. Some other time, I promise."

When she got back home, she telephoned Kenny. "Hi Kenny, it's Belle."

"Well, howdy stranger. What's up?"

"Are you busy? I've got something I'd like to talk to you about."

"Uh Oh, this sounds serious."

"It kind of is."

"Well, I can be there in a half hour. Will that work?"

"That will be great."

Belle filled Kenny in on her financial problems with the café, and told him about George's offer, then asked, "What's your opinion about this?"

"You askin' me what you should do?"

"I'm asking you what you think."

"Well, it doesn't seem like all that bad an idea. You think you'd like workin' in a bar?"

"I don't know, I might. Peg told me about a uniform factory that's hiring. That might be an option. I just don't see how I can keep running the café without going broke."

"Now, Belle, I really can't see you sitting at a sewing machine all day, can you?"

Belle smiled, and said, "Probably not."

"Well, since it sounds like you know you need to give up the Irish Rose, maybe you should give the bar a try. If it doesn't work, then you can look for something else."

"Thanks, Kenny. You always seem to be able to put things in perspective for me."

"Well, I do what I can," Kenny said, and laughed. "How about we go get a bite to eat, my treat?"

"That sounds good."

Belle slept better that night than she had in a while. The next morning she told Peg of her decision. "Can you stay and help for a couple more weeks?" she asked. "George says it will be about three weeks before the bar is ready to open."

"I think I can probably do that, unless the factory won't wait that long to let me start."

"If that happens, I'll figure something out. I don't want you to lose out on that job because of me. I guess I better let Mr. Jones know he won't be getting any rent from me next month. Maybe he'll buy the tables and chairs from me."

Mr. Jones wasn't unhappy about Belle leaving. He agreed to buy the tables and chairs, though he paid her much less than they were worth.

Peg applied at the uniform factory, and was told they couldn't guarantee her the job if she wasn't able to start right away. As a result, Belle closed the Irish Rose two weeks before George's bar was ready to open. She spent the first few days catching up on odd jobs around her apartment, and writing to Mae and David. David's oldest boy, Tommy, was married, and had a child on the way. Eddie, his youngest son had enlisted in the Navy.

After four days of these activities, Belle was bored to tears, and telephoned George. "George, I've had to close the café earlier than I thought. I have way too much time on my hands, and wondered if there is anything I could do to help you get ready to open?"

"Don't much like bein' a lady of leisure, huh?"

"Not really."

"Well, if you don't mind usin' some elbow grease, the bar could use a good polishin'."

"That sounds fine. What time do you want me to show up?"

"The boys are here by 8:00 in the mornings. How about I pick you up? It's not that far outta my way."

"Thanks, that would be nice."

"OK, I'll see you a little before 8:00 tomorrow."

George's comment about the bar needing polishing was an understatement. There was a thick layer of grime that needed to be washed off. She then spent several hours polishing the walnut wood to a high gloss with linseed oil. After that, she tackled the brass rail, polishing it 'til it glowed. At 4:00 George suggested they stop for the day.

"You want to go out for dinner tonight? You've earned it."

"Oh, not tonight, George. I'm beat and grimy to my core."

"OK, but plan on a nice meal with me Saturday. I ain't takin' 'no' for an answer."

"Well, in that case, the answer is yes," she laughed.

Belle spent several more days scrubbing, polishing, or making lunch runs for the workmen. Everything was finished and ready one day before the scheduled grand opening. George had flyers printed, and hired a young boy to distribute them. There were a respectable number of customers on opening night. A piano player had been hired, and George and Belle managed to get in a few dances, between taking care of their customers.

George was right about the bar being successful. Most nights there were enough customers for him to declare he had made money. Saturdays were especially busy, since the factory workers had Sundays off.

Belle found she enjoyed working in the bar. She liked observing the camaraderie of the men, especially the soldiers. Some were obviously a little anxious about their upcoming departure for overseas, while others were in the gung-ho mood of going off to win the war.

George was also right about Belle being an asset. Even though she was considerably older than the soldiers, she had retained her slim figure, and was comfortable joking with them, and danced with them when she could.

Occasionally a soldier would ask if he could write to her. "Just send it to the bar, addressed to me. I promise I'll write back," was her standard reply.

"Belle, I knew I was doin' the right thing when I asked you to work here. Our soldiers love you, and are spreadin' the word that there's a good lookin' gal they can dance with here. Even the lady friends and wives of the locals think you're OK. You've got a real way with people. You got any regrets about takin' the job?"

"No, George, I admit I had some doubts, but I'm enjoying it."

"Well, great! It's a good deal for everybody, then."

Kenny came in one Friday evening. "Howdy Belle, figured if I was ever gonna see you again, I'd better come down here."

"Hi Kenny. Working six nights a week doesn't leave me time for much of anything else. How are you?"

"Doin' OK. I miss dancin' with you, though."

"I know, me too, but I do get to do a little dancing here with the soldiers, now and then."

"That right? Got time for a dance with an old friend?"

"Sure thing, just give me a few minutes to get caught up on orders." George walked up just then. "Well, if it ain't the Nebraska boy. How's things?"

"Just fine, Spats. This is quite a place you've got here."

Another man at the bar looked up, and said to Kenny, "You from Nebraska?"

"That I am."

"You ain't from one of them German communities are you? I hear there's a lot of 'em in Nebraska."

"No, 'fraid not."

"You sure? You look awful German to me."

"Well, I really didn't have a say in how I look."

George spoke up saying, "Now Ed, I think maybe you've had more 'n your share to drink tonight. How about you go sit at that table, and I'll have Belle bring you a cup of coffee."

"Well, ain't you just the do-gooder? I don't need no damn coffee."

"Then, back off Ed. I don't need no trouble in here."

"You don't want no trouble, then you oughta be keepin' them Krauts out of here."

"OK, Ed, it's time to leave. Kenny's told you he's not German, and you seem bent on gettin' a fight goin', but it ain't gonna be in here."

As he said this, he took Ed by the arm and escorted him to the door. George was a big man, Ed was not, and decided pushing it any further at this time wasn't a good idea.

"Sorry about that Kenny. Ed gets a little rowdy when he gets a load on. Belle, why don't you go have that dance with Kenny now."

When they were on the dance floor, Belle said, "That kind of attitude just makes me see red!"

"Come on, now. That was just his booze talkin'."

"Well, if the thought wasn't there in the first place, it wouldn't be coming out when drinking, now would it?"

"It's over Belle. Let's just dance and forget about it."

The war continued, and the German army continued to advance across Europe. There were very few Japanese Americans in Chicago, but there was a good sized German community in the city. Most of the

German immigrants lived in the same general neighborhood, but many of them worked at various jobs throughout the city: in breweries, factories, even at the newspaper. Many were second generation Germans Americans, their families having left the chaos in Germany around the time of World War I.

With the war dragging on, and more American men and boys being sent overseas, the German Americans became an easy target for those who needed to vent their anger about the war. Many were fired from their jobs, and given vague reasons for being fired. Signs began to appear in the windows of businesses saying, "Germans not welcome here."

There were rumors that some German American men had been taken for questioning by authorities and not allowed to return home.

Belle occasionally had Sunday dinner with Peg and Dan. Peg's children were usually there, making the afternoon somewhat chaotic, now that there were two small grandchildren. Peg's oldest boy was the only one not yet married, and he was serving in the Navy, somewhere in the South Pacific. They generally tried to keep the conversation on things other than the war, but it was difficult.

"We've not heard from our Dan in nearly two months, and I'm worried sick," said Peg one Sunday in November of '43.

"Oh Peg, I'm sorry. Maybe he's just not in a place where they can get mail out."

"I'm hopin' it's something like that. I stop at the church and light a candle for him every day on my way home from work. Dan won't hardly speak of him at all, he's that worried. How are things down at the bar?"

"Slowing down some. There aren't as many boys shipping out as there were in the beginning, so it's mostly the locals. A few of them tend to get a little rowdy, especially on Saturdays when they know they don't have to go back to work."

"Do you still like the job?"

"Oh, it's OK, I guess. Actually, working six nights a week is beginning to make me feel like an old woman."

"I know what ya mean. I was that glad when they decided to close the uniform factory down on Saturday afternoons. Have ya thought of lookin' for something else?"

"I don't know what it would be. I really can't see myself working in a factory."

"Well, I think ya should give it some thought. You're lookin' a bit peaked."

"Maybe I will."

A couple weeks later, another fight broke out at the bar. Ed had been drinking heavily, and decided one of the other men looked German.

"Kraut, why don't you go back home? We don't need your kind here."

"Who you callin' a Kraut? I'm an American citizen, have been for ten years."

"Yeah, well, I'm bettin' you still got relatives over in The Fatherland that are killin' our boys."

"I'm from Sweden, you damn drunk. Now back off!" With that he shoved Ed, and a brawl ensued.

George got the fight stopped, and threw both men out, but not before a couple of chairs had been demolished. Some of the other men grumbled about Ed being thrown out, since the other guy had started the physical part of the fight.

A few days later a rock was thrown through the front window, with a note wrapped around it that read, "Keep the Krauts out, or else!"

Belle was livid when George told her what had happened. "What is the matter with people?! Don't they ever stop to think that they wouldn't be here either if their ancestors hadn't come to America?"

"I know, Belle, but when we're in a war, people get a little carried away."

"Did you call the police?"

"Belle, the cops can't do nuthin' about this. I can't take a chance on what some hot head might do next. I'm gonna put a sign in the window sayin' "No Germans."

"You're not!"

"Belle, these ain't normal times. I gotta do what I can to protect my business."

"Well, I refuse to be part of this. I quit."

"Now, Belle, calm down. You don't really want to do that."

"Oh, but I do!"

"So what are you gonna do for a job, then?"

"This isn't the first time in my life that I've been out of work. I'll find something."

"Well, if you change your mind, you can always come back."

"I don't think that will happen. To be honest, the hours here have been taking a toll on me. I guess maybe this was just the push I needed."

"Well, good luck then. And if you ever need anything, you call me, you hear?"

"Thanks, George. I appreciate that."

Belle called Kenny the next day. "Hey, Kenny, you up for a dance this weekend?"

"I'm always up for a dance. Did you talk Spats into letting you have a night off?"

"Something like that. Actually, I quit."

"No kiddin'! What happened?"

"I'll tell you all about it when I see you."

"OK, then, I'll pick you up about 8:00 Saturday."

"I'll be ready. See you then."

She also called Peg to tell her what she'd done, and filled her in on what had happened. "I can't say I'm sorry to be hearin' that. I told you to think about doin' somethin' different."

"It seems you were right. Guess I just needed a little push."

"So, do ya know what you're gonna' do now?"

"No idea at all. I'll just have to start reading the want ads."

"Well, if we hear about anything, I'll give you a call."

"Thanks Peg. I'm sure something will turn up."

"You still planning on Christmas dinner with us?"

"You bet."

"All right, then. Let me know how the job hunting goes, and we'll see you next week."

Chapter Thirteen

With Christmas only a week and a half away, the ballroom was decorated with lots of garland, tinsel, and some poinsettia plants. In spite of the war, people were doing their best to maintain the festive atmosphere of the Christmas season. The ladies were wearing their finest dresses. Belle was no exception. She had modified the infamous red silk dress so the neckline was not quite so plunging, and shortened it, more in keeping with the fashion of the day.

"Well, don't you just look amazing," Kenny said when he picked her up.

"I was in the mood for a little glamour for a change."

"It suits you. Shall we go?"

When they walked into the ballroom, many heads turned. Kenny said, "Belle, I think you and me should get on the dance floor right away, 'cause I think I may have trouble getting another dance with you tonight."

Belle only laughed.

Kenny was right. There was a steady stream of men asking Belle to dance. During one of the times when the band took a break, a man approached the table where Belle and Kenny were sitting.

"Hello Kenny, ma'am. What's new with you these days?"

"Howdy, Dave. Not much, just puttin' one foot in front of the other. Dave, this is my friend, Belle Mericle. Belle, meet Dave Markham. He owns a little bookstore downtown."

"Hello Dave. You'll have to tell me where your store is. I love to read."

Dave gave her the address, then asked, "So, do you work? Seems most women do these days."

"Not at the moment, but I'm looking for something."

"Is that right? Maybe fate is at work here tonight. I need to hire someone to help at the shop. You ever do any bookkeeping?"

"I did some, years ago, but I've never had any formal training in it."

"Don't let her fool you, Dave. She ran her own business here in Chicago for years."

"Really, what was that?"

"I had a small café."

"So, what happened?"

"The owner of the building sold it, and the new owner kept raising the rent so much, I couldn't manage. Apparently he wanted it for himself, since he opened a bar there after I left."

"Well, how about you come down to the store Monday. I'll show you around, and we can talk more about the job, if you're interested."

"I'd like that. What time should I be there?"

"Let's say 10:00."

"10:00 it is, then."

The band had started playing again, and Dave asked if she would like to dance. When they were on the floor, Dave asked, "So, are you Kenny's girl?"

Belle laughed, and said, "No, I'm nobody's girl. Kenny and I grew up together. We're just good friends."

Belle arrived at Dave's bookstore shortly before 10:00 Monday morning. It was located in a busy district of downtown Chicago. There was a large plate glass window facing East with the words YOUR BOOKSTORE in large letters. Beneath that in smaller lettering was DAVE MARKHAM, OPERATOR. Inside, the floor had dark green carpeting, with a muted maroon pattern. Near the front door was a display of popular magazines. On the opposite wall was a small counter with a cash register. A sign on the wall behind the counter displayed a quote by Cicero, "A room without books is a body without a soul." Books lined the walls, and the rest of the space was taken up with bookcases placed to allow customers to move easily around them.

A small bell tinkled as she walked through the door. Belle only had time to glance around, when Dave came through a door at the back of the room.

"Good morning, Belle. I'm so glad you came. Welcome to my little store."

"Hello Dave. This is very nice. I like the name."

"I wanted something that would suggest a personal touch. I have a very small office at the back of the store where I do my orders and bookkeeping. I've had the store for two years now, but I'm finding that being a one man operation is a little too much. I'm looking for someone who can help with the bookkeeping, as well as take care of customers when I'm busy with inventory and orders. Does that sound like something you would be interested in?"

"It does."

"Let me show you the office. It's pretty small, but I doubt there would ever be a time when we were both using it."

Dave wasn't exaggerating when he said the office was small. It was a 6x8 foot room, with a desk, chair and two file cabinets.

"I use a simple double entry ledger system," he said, and opened one of the ledger books to show her.

"I used a similar system for my café."

"Great, you're familiar with it then." He then led her back into the store, and began walking among the shelves, pointing out the different categories of books.

"You would need to become familiar with the books I carry and where they are located in the store. I'm afraid I can't offer a large salary." He then named an amount, and asked, "Would that be acceptable?"

"Yes, I can manage with that," she replied.

He smiled, and said, "Well, so far, so good. Do you have any questions?"

"No, I don't think so. You've explained it very well."

"So, do you want the job, or do you need to think about it first?"

"No, I don't need to think about it. I've always loved books. It sounds like a great job."

"Wonderful! When can you start?"

"Anytime, really."

"How about today?"

Belle laughed, and said, "Well, sure, why not."

She spent much of the day browsing the bookshelves, becoming familiar with the inventory. Dave also had her enter the receipts from Saturday morning. The store was open from 10:00 a.m. to 6:00 p.m., Monday through Friday, and from 9:00 a.m. to noon on Saturdays.

At one point, while Dave was in the office, preparing an order, a customer came in, asking if they carried any books by Hemmingway. Belle was able to list the ones on hand, and direct the customer to where they were, resulting in a sale. Dave had stopped to listen when he heard the bell over the door ring. After the customer had left, he came out of the office, and said, "You are apparently a fast learner. I'm impressed with how you were able to direct the customer to what he wanted."

The day passed quickly, and almost before she knew it, 6:00 had arrived.

"Well, what do you think after your first day?" Dave asked.

"I think I'm going to really enjoy this job," she replied.

"Wonderful! See you at 10:00 tomorrow then."

When she got home that evening, she called Peg. "Peg, I have a job."

"Well, that was fast work. So, tell me about it."

"It's at a bookstore downtown. I'll be waiting on customers and doing some of the bookkeeping."

"That will be quite a change for you. When do you start?"

"I started this morning. The owner is an acquaintance of Kenny's, and we ran into him at the dance Saturday night. He's been running the place all by himself for a couple of years, and decided he really could use some help."

"I guess it's a good thing you were at the dance, then."

"It was good timing, wasn't it? I really think I'm gong to like this job."

"Well, I'm that happy for ya, and not the least bit sorry to see ya gettin' out of the bar."

"That was OK for a while, but I can't say I'm going to miss it. I'd better let you go. See you on Christmas."

"We're lookin' forward to it."

After she hung up, she called Kenny to give him the news.

"Congratulations. I didn't figure you'd be out of work very long."

"I didn't ask you, how do you know Dave?"

"We sit in on a poker game from time to time, and then I see him at the dances sometimes."

"Is he married?"

"Nope, he usually comes alone to the dances. I think he's kinda shy."

"He seems nice. I think I'm really going to like this job."

"Glad to hear it. It's gotta be better than standing in that bar all night."

Belle laughed, and said, "Yes, it is."

"Did I tell you I'm goin' home for Christmas?"

"No, when do you leave?"

"In a couple of days. Decided to take a few days off, and treat myself to a family Christmas. It'll be nice to see my brothers and their kids again."

"Well, you have a great Christmas, and tell your family 'hi' for me."

"Will do. You goin' to Peg's?"

"Yes."

"Have a good Christmas yourself. I'll call you when I get back. You want to plan on kicking up your heels with me on New Years Eve?"

"That sounds good. I'll look forward to it."

A few days after Christmas, Dave asked Belle if she would like to go to a dance with him on New Years Eve.

"Kenny and I are going to a dance. You're welcome to join us."

"That might be a little awkward, don't you think?"

"No, Dave, I told you, Kenny and I are just friends. There's nothing romantic going on there."

"It's a little hard to believe a woman like you doesn't have a special someone in her life."

"Well, I don't, and what's more, I don't plan to."

"Really? Why is that?"

"I've been down that path, and don't plan to do it again."

"Someone hurt you then? I'm sorry, but that's no reason to give up."

"OK, Dave, I guess maybe I'd better give you the whole picture. I've been married three times. My first husband died, and the next two were big mistakes. I'm just not willing to travel that road again."

"My goodness! That's quite a story."

"Yes, well, now you know why I said you'd be welcome to join me and Kenny at the dance."

"OK, maybe I'll do that."

After two months, Belle felt she had a good working knowledge of the inventory, and was comfortable with the bookkeeping. Dave had a number of regular customers that she soon came to know by name, as well as the type of reading they preferred. She was often able to direct them to a book Dave had recently acquired, resulting in a sale the customer hadn't planned on.

One day Belle asked Dave if he had a mailing list for his customers.

"No," he responded. "Most of my customers pay cash, and I've never kept a list of those who write checks. Why do you ask?"

"I was thinking it might be helpful if you sent out a short newsletter every month or two."

"Yes, well, I'm a bookseller, not a writer."

"Oh, it wouldn't be that hard. Just a short listing of some of the books you have, with a brief description. You could even use the information on the inside of the book cover for that. People sometimes get overwhelmed in a bookstore, with all the choices, unless they have come in for something specific. This way they could browse through some book titles at their leisure, at home."

"Hmm, not a bad idea, if I had a mailing list, which I don't."

"Well, why don't you do one, have a few copies printed and leave them on the counter. You could include information in it that you plan to start mailing them out, and ask them to notify you if they would like to be on the mailing list. And you could have a sign up sheet sitting beside the newsletter on the counter."

"You're just full of ideas, aren't you?" Dave said, and smiled.

"I just think it would add a personal touch to 'Your Bookstore,' and might increase your customer base."

"I'll give it some thought."

The week before Mother's Day was busy at the bookstore. After one especially busy day, Dave said to Belle, "Would you like to go to dinner with me, my treat. You've earned it this week."

"I think we both have. That sounds good."

During dinner, Dave asked Belle if she was sending a Mother's Day gift to her mom.

"My mother died a number of years ago."

"Oh, I'm sorry. Were you close?"

"That's kind of hard to answer. I suppose so. My sister blames me for Ma's death."

"Really, why is that?"

Belle paused and smiled, then said, "Are you ready for another story?"

"If you're ready to tell me, I'm happy to listen."

"I ran away from home when I was fourteen. Ma died a few years later, and Lizzie thinks my leaving was the cause of it."

"Do you think that's true?"

Belle sighed, and said, "Oh, I don't know. Ma hadn't been feeling well for a while before I left."

"Did she go to a doctor?"

Belle smiled, and said, "No. Nebraska farm women generally just tough it out. They either get better or die."

"So, why did you run away?"

"I just wasn't cut out for farm life. And, I never really fit with the rest of my family. Except for my brother, Ray. We were close."

"But you're not now?"

"He died during the first World War."

"Do you often go back home?"

"Seldom. It's generally not a pleasant experience. Lizzie has never got over blaming me."

"Is she your only sister?"

"No, I have one other sister and another brother."

"But, you're not close to them either?"

"Not really. We get along OK when we're together, but our lives and values are worlds apart. Enough about me. Tell me about your family. Where did you grow up?"

"Right here in Chicago. I'm an only child. Maybe that's why I've always liked books so much."

"Are your folks still here in Chicago?"

"No, they have both been gone for a few years. My mother had several miscarriages before she managed to give birth to me, so by the time I came along, my parents were no longer young."

"Do you have any other family here?"

"No, I'm it for the Markham clan," he said, and smiled.

"This has been a nice evening. Thank you, Dave, but I really should be getting home now."

"Yes, it has been a long day, hasn't it? See you tomorrow."

Two weeks later, Belle was directing a customer to a book he had asked about when the bell over the door chimed. She looked up to see an attractive woman come through the door, and with a little shock realized she knew her. She excused herself, and walked over to the woman who had just come in.

"Margaret, how nice to see you again."

Margaret had stopped to leaf through a magazine, and now looked up and said, "Why Belle. What a surprise. Are you shopping for a book too?"

"No, I work here."

Dave came out of the office at that point, and said, "Hello Margaret, it's been a while since you've been here."

"Hello Dave. Yes, it has. I've been busy."

"Belle, this is Margaret Oswald, one of my favorite customers."

"Yes, we know each other," Margaret replied.

"Is that right? I guess it's a small world, sometimes."

"How are you Belle? I've thought of you often. When did you start working for Dave?"

Belle laughed, and said, "I'm fine. I've been working here since shortly after Christmas."

"How do you two know each other?" Dave asked.

Margaret glanced at Belle, but didn't answer.

Belle said, "I saw her professionally, a few times."

Margaret then spoke up, and said, "Dave knows all about my work, Belle."

"Margaret is quite a lady. I hope you found her helpful."

"Yes, I did."

Another customer came in just then, and Dave offered to help.

"You don't have your café any longer?" Margaret asked.

"No, the building was sold, and the new owner kept raising the rent so much, I couldn't manage."

"Are you happy here, or do you miss the café?"

"I love this job. It's probably the best one I've ever had. The café was good, while it lasted, but to tell the truth, the hours were beginning to wear on me."

"Yes, I can see how that would be."

"It's great to see you again, Margaret, but I'm keeping you from your shopping."

"You must stop by sometime. Maybe some Saturday after you finish here, you could stop by."

"I'd like that. I'll give you a call."

A few weeks later, Belle received a phone call from Peg. She was obviously crying, and spoke in a rush.

"Belle, can ya come over. I need to see you, it's our Danny. We got a telegram today."

"Oh Peg, no! I'll be right there."

When Belle arrived, Peg was still crying softly, her face red and eyes puffy. Dan was slumped over on the couch, his head in his hands. The other children were there, standing quietly with tear streaked faces, and seemed at a loss for even a 'hello' to Belle.

"Ah, Peg," Belle said, as she wrapped her arms around her. "I'm so sorry. When did you find out?"

Peg handed her a telegram, saying, "We got it this afternoon."

Belle took the telegram and read, "...*regret to inform you of the apparent death of your son, Daniel. His dog tags were found on the island of Bataan.*"

At this point Dan raised his head, and said, "Not even a body. Just the bloody dog tags."

Belle stayed for a couple of hours, made coffee and sandwiches for everyone, then said her goodbyes, and left to go home.

She didn't sleep well that night. Dan's death stirred up memories of the loss of Bill and Ray. What little sleep she got was filled with dreams of both of them.

When she arrived at the bookstore the next morning, her face told the story of her restless night. Dave took one look at her, and said, "Belle, are you all right?"

"Not entirely. My good friend Peg got a telegram yesterday, saying her boy had died in the war."

"Oh, I'm sorry. We've lost so many of our boys."

"Everyone keeps saying we'll win this war, but it just doesn't seem like there is an end in sight."

"It does seem that way, but there was a story in this morning's paper, saying we'd captured an island in the Philippines. Something called Bataan."

"That's where Peg's son died. The telegram only said they found his dog tags, not his body. Do you think maybe he could have just lost them?"

"I doubt it. I think they are almost considered another part of the body."

A few days later, there was news of the prisoner of war camp located on Bataan, and details of what would become known as The Bataan Death March. The story appeared on the day of the memorial service for Peg's son, and only intensified their grief.

Belle called Peg every day, and went to see her at least once a week. Peg was not eating well, had lost weight, and aged ten years in the few weeks since they had gotten the news of Dan's death. One day she confided to Belle, "I keep havin' nightmares about Danny. I'm just so afraid he's not at rest 'cause he din'na have a decent burial, or have last rites given to him. Our priest says that's not true, but Belle, we've always been told those things are important. How can it be both ways?"

"Ah, Peg, I'm sure your priest is right. I don't believe God would deny him peace just because he died during a war, when those things weren't possible."

"I suppose you're right, but I can'na seem to stop the nightmares."

Peg's pain was on Belle's mind much of the time, and she kept trying to think of some way to ease her pain. She was talking to Dave about it one day, when things were quiet in the shop.

"I just wish I could find some way to set her mind at ease. Her religion is so important to her, and she is just terrified that her boy won't be able to rest in peace because of the way he died. Her priest keeps telling her that isn't so, but even he isn't able to set her mind at rest. Her husband is in so much pain that he has just completely pulled into himself, and is no help to her."

"You know, Margaret might be able to help, if you think Peg would be willing to see her."

"Of course! I can't believe I didn't think of that. She was a big help to me after my brother died in the first war. I don't know if I can get Peg to go see her, but I'll give it a heck of a try."

Belle called Peg that evening. "Peg, let's go out for lunch Saturday. It's been too long since we've done that."

"Ah, I don't know, Belle. I'm thinkin' I won't be very good company."

"Oh, come on, Peg. It will be good for you to get out, and I'd like to spend some time just with you. I don't care if you're good company or not. Please Peg?"

"Well—-all right then, I'll go. Maybe you're right about getting out."

"Great! I'll pick you up about 12:30."

Belle wanted to get Peg out of the house to talk to her about seeing Margaret. She knew if Dan was there, he would have a fit, and Peg would never agree.

When they were half-way through their lunch, Belle said, "Peg, I know someone that I think can help put your mind at rest about Danny. She helped me a lot after my brother died in the first war. She has the ability to allow those who have passed on to speak through her."

Peg's eyes had opened wide, and her brow furrowed.

"I know that sounds really weird, but please, just listen. She isn't always able to do it, and she makes no guarantees. You'd like her; she's a very gentle lady. If she could contact Danny, he could tell you how things are for him now."

"Belle, that sounds like the work of the devil to me."

"No, Peg, it isn't. You don't believe that when we die, there's nothing left, do you?"

"Well, no, not exactly."

"So, don't you think it's worth a try?"

"I don't know Belle. She probably charges a King's Ransom."

"No, Peg, she doesn't. She will take donations, but it's entirely up to you if you want to do that, and how much."

"What if I find out I'm right?"

"Peg, you're having nightmares about it anyway. And, even if you are right, he might be able to tell you how you could help."

"Dan would have a fit, and probably so would our priest."

"Peg, why do you need to tell them? This is for you, to hopefully give you some peace. I'll go with you."

"How do ya know she's not just puttin' on a show for ya?"

"Peg, when I went to see her, it was Ray's voice I heard. Not only Ray, but Bill, my first husband. I can't see how she could have faked that, she had never even met them. Peg, I know you read the Bible. God spoke through the prophets at one time, and Jesus even came back to speak to people. Why couldn't that happen now?"

"Belle, you're awful close to blasphemy."

"Why would God limit Himself to speaking through a man in only one time period? How could this possibly hurt you?"

"Belle, you are a strange friend!"

Belle smiled, and said, "I know. It's just that I hate seeing you in the pain you're in. I could call Margaret to see if she's free this afternoon. Please say yes."

Peg sighed, and said, "Oh, all right then. I'm thinkin' this is a fool's errand, but if it will keep you quiet, I'll give it a try."

"I'll go call her right now. Thank you, Peg."

Belle returned in only a few minutes. "Peg, she's free this afternoon. We can go as soon as we finish eating."

"Ya must promise me you'll never say anything to Dan, and after today, I don't want to be hearin' anymore about this!"

"I promise," Belle said, and smiled.

When Margaret opened the door, she greeted Belle warmly. "Hello Belle, it's good to see you again."

"Hi Margaret, This is my friend, Peg Hagerty. She's a little nervous about being here."

"That's understandable. Most people are the first time they come. Come in, and have a seat." When they were seated, Margaret addressed Peg. "Do you have any questions for me?"

"Well, I don't really know what I'd ask."

"OK, then, just tell me a little about why you're here."

"I'm here because Belle twisted me arm."

Margaret smiled, and Belle laughed.

"And why do you think she did that?"

"Cause she thinks you can help me with the pain I'm havin' over losin' my Danny."

"Sometimes I can. Now, I don't want to know any more about why you're here, so that you can feel confident that anything you hear is valid. Let me just tell you a little bit about how this works."

Margaret went on to explain how she conducted these sessions, then asked, "Does that sound OK to you?"

"Yeah, I guess."

"OK, then. Let's get started." Margaret darkened the room, and lit some candles. After the three of them had been sitting quietly for a few minutes, Margaret began to stir in her chair. She cleared her throat once, and then a voice sounding much like Danny's said,

"Hello Mum."

Peg gasped, and moved uneasily in her chair.

"Don't be afraid, Mum. I'm fine."

Peg sobbed, and said, "Danny."

"I know you've been worried, but it's beautiful here. I'll be waitin' for ya when it's time for you to come."

"Danny, tell me it's really you."

"Remember how you called me Fancy Dan, cause of that hat I liked so much? Bye Mum. Don't you be worryin' about me no more."

Tears were streaming down Peg's face as Margaret sighed deeply, and opened her eyes. She remained silent for a few minutes, then said, "Are you all right, Peg?"

Peg could only nod.

Belle reached over and took Peg's hand. Everyone sat quietly for a few minutes, then Peg said, "How do you do that?"

Margaret replied, "I don't know. I'm never aware of what is said during these sessions. Did what you heard today help?"

"Oh, yes! I heard my Danny. He says he's fine."

"I'm so glad. Would you like some tea?"

"I think maybe I'd like to be goin' home now."

"Of course. It's been a pleasure meeting you. Feel free to come back anytime."

As they rose to leave, Belle handed Margaret some money. Peg noticed, and said, "Oh, I completely forgot the donation."

"Not today, Peg, this is my treat," said Belle.

"But..."

"Not another word. This is my treat," at which point Peg's eyes again filled with tears.

On the drive back to Peg's, Peg said, "I don't know how I can ever thank you."

"No need. I'm just so happy to see you relieved of that pain and worry. You look like the weight of the world has just been taken from you."

"And that's how I feel. Oh, Belle, how am I gonna explain to Dan?"

"Just tell him you had a good dream about Danny that made you feel he is OK."

Chapter Fourteen

Dave and Belle continued to have dinner together occasionally. Their conversations ranged between books, politics, and philosophy. One evening at dinner their talk turned to families, and personalities.

"I've always wondered why I'm so different from everyone else in my family. Even as a young girl, I never felt like I fit in."

"Sometimes, I think people are born in the wrong place, or the wrong time."

Belle's eyes opened wide, and she said, "That would explain a lot, wouldn't it? How do you think that happens?"

"I've no idea. I sometimes think that's what happened to me."

"You weren't happy as a child?"

"I think lonely sums it up. My mother was nearly forty when I was born, and then she was often ill. My dad didn't know how to deal with that, so he would either hover over her, or sort of withdraw to his own private world. Their involvement with me primarily consisted of making sure I was safe. That meant no bicycle, because I might fall and hurt myself, no going to the park with the other neighborhood kids, because it wasn't safe to be out of sight of your parents, and of course, no sports in school. That left books as my only means of escape, or adventure. So, you weren't happy on the farm?"

"No, I remember daydreaming about leaving when I was still pretty young, maybe ten or so."

"What was so bad about it?"

"Oh, just mostly it was boring, I guess. Everything revolved around work that needed to be done. Even my sisters operated like that. They just never wanted to cut loose and have some fun."

"Like what?"

"Oh, like wading in the pond, splashing water, and having the mud squish up between your toes."

Dave laughed, and said, "That does sound like fun. Maybe you and I could do that sometime. So, how did you get away from the farm?"

Belle smiled, and said, "I arranged to sneak off and run away with a carnival."

Dave laughed, and said, "No kidding! How old were you?"

"I was all of fourteen."

"Good grief! You really were cut from a different cloth, weren't you?"

"It would seem so."

"How long did you stay with the carnival, and what did you do?"

Belle told him about Tad, and making a show of winning prizes, then added, "I left after a year and a half."

"Then what?"

"Oh, that's a long story, and it's getting late. We'll have to continue this conversation some other time."

"I'll look forward to it. See you in the morning."

One day in late October Dave said to Belle, "I've been thinking about Thanksgiving, and would like your opinion on an idea I have. You know I live in my parents' house. It's really too large for me, but I've just never been able to get motivated to sell it, and find something else. I thought it might be nice to host a Thanksgiving dinner, and invite your friend Peg, and her family."

"That sounds like a nice idea. They have always been so good about including me at holiday dinners. It would be nice to do something for them."

"We could invite your friend Kenny, too, since he doesn't have any family here. Do you think they would come?"

"I'm sure Kenny would. I'll talk to Peg, and see what she thinks. There might be one little problem, though. I'm not much of a cook."

Dave laughed, and said, "Well I enjoy doing some cooking from time to time. I'm sure between the two of us, we could manage."

Belle went to visit Peg the following Sunday. Peg had continued to be brighter since her session with Margaret, and she now had another grandchild on the way to look forward to. Dan had remained withdrawn, and focused on the fact that Danny had not had a decent burial. Peg had told him she'd had a vivid dream, indicating Danny was OK, but had been unable to convince Dan of that.

"Peg, Dave wants to have a Thanksgiving dinner at his house, and asked me to invite you and your whole family. How does that sound?"

"Ah, I don't know. Thanksgiving is a family holiday, and we don't really know him."

"I know, but you'll like him. He doesn't have any family, Kenny doesn't have any family here, and neither do I—-well except for you. I consider you my family. Dave's got a big house, and it might be nice for you not to have to do all the cooking. I'm always intruding on your family holidays, and I think it would be fun to have a big gathering of family and friends."

"Well, ya just said you consider us family, so there's no intrudin' at all."

"OK, you're right about that. But this way I could do something for all of you for a change. Please think about it."

"I'll talk to Dan and the kids, and see what they think."

"Great! I really hope you'll come. I think it would make a great Thanksgiving."

A few days later, Peg called Belle to tell her everyone had agreed. "The kids think maybe gettin' their Da away from the house for the holiday would be good for him. All he wants to do is mope and stare at Danny's picture."

"That's probably a good idea. I know he'll like Dave, and you both know Kenny."

"There's one condition though. Ya must let us bring some of the food."

"OK, you let me know what you'd like to bring, and we'll work the rest of the meal around that. Dave's fixing a turkey, of course."

Thanksgiving day was crisp and clear. The menu details had been decided on, and Belle went to Dave's early to help with the preparations. The smell of roasting turkey greeted her as she came through the door.

"Happy Thanksgiving, Belle."

"And to you. It smells good in here."

"One thing my mother did well was to cook. She always said the secret to a good turkey was to cook it long, and slow. Let me show you the house."

There was a large dining room, with a parlor adjoining it. On the east wall of the parlor was a glassed in sunroom, with French doors to close it off from the parlor. On the south wall of the parlor was a fireplace.

"I'll start a fire in the fireplace in a few minutes", Dave said.

The kitchen was good sized, with a large window facing east. The kitchen range was gas, and he had one of the new electric refrigerators.

"I have three bedrooms upstairs. We can put everyone's coat there, and if any of the little ones need a nap, they can use one of the beds."

"You have a wonderful home, Dave. I think this is going to be a great day. Now, what would you like me to do to help?"

"Well, I guess you could peel potatoes."

Belle laughed, and said, "I'm sure I can manage that."

"I'll be fixing some dressing, and I think everything else is pretty much covered by Peg and her family."

The day was even better than Belle had hoped. In spite of not knowing each other well, everyone seemed to become comfortable quickly, and conversation flowed easily. The adults played a game of Chinese checkers, while the little ones napped. Around 4:30, everyone started saying their goodbyes.

After everyone had left, Belle said, "I'll help you clean up the kitchen."

"That's not necessary."

"Don't be silly, this was a wonderful idea you had. I think everyone enjoyed themselves. I'll wash; you can dry and put things away."

As they were doing the dishes, Belle said, "I think this was good for Dan. He seemed to pull out of his shell a little."

"I'm glad everyone came today. This is the best Thanksgiving I've ever had, and I really enjoyed your friends."

When the kitchen clean up was finished, Dave asked Belle if she would like a cup of coffee before leaving.

"Thanks, but I think I'd just like to go home, and put my feet up for a while."

"Well, if you're sure. Thanks for all your help."

"You're welcome. I'll see you in the morning."

For the next few weeks Belle and Dave were kept busy with shoppers coming in for Christmas gifts. Belle got caught up in the spirit of the season, and decided to send some books as Christmas gifts to her family. She chose a book about collectibles for Mae, a biography of a police officer for Orville, a book about farm machinery for David, and one on gardening for Ann. She was having difficulty coming up with something for Lizzie, and finally chose a cookbook that included little homilies as fillers.

Two weeks before Christmas Peg called Belle. "Belle, me and Dan have been talking about Christmas. Dan really enjoyed visiting with Dave and Kenny, and said since they didn't have any family here, it would be nice to invite them over for Christmas day. Do you think they would come?"

"What a nice idea, Peg. I'm sure they will."

"It might get kinda cozy here, we don't have the kind of room Dave does."

"I wouldn't worry about that, it's about the company, not the surroundings."

"Shall I call them, or do you want to ask them?"

"I think you should call them. I'll get their numbers for you."

Christmas day at Peg's was a success. Peg's comment about it being 'kinda cozy' was a polite was of saying her home was wall to wall people. It was noisy, and chaotic, but no one seemed to mind. Dave brought a lovely bouquet of red and white carnations for Peg, and a large box of chocolates to be shared by everyone. Kenny arrived with two bottles of wine.

When the day ended, Dave said to Peg and Dan, "This is the most amazing Christmas I've ever had. Thank you so much for inviting me."

Kenny echoed these sentiments, and gave Peg a hug.

Belle stayed to help Peg with the clean up. Dan came to the kitchen briefly, while the dishes were being washed, and said to Belle, "You have some very nice friends. I'm glad they were here today."

"I do have some great friends, and the Hegarty's are at the top of the list," Belle replied.

Mae hosted the Christmas dinner in Nebraska, a much more subdued affair than Belle's Christmas had been. David and Ann were there, along with their daughter, Rose, and son, Tommy and his wife, Amy. Lizzie came alone. She had spent Christmas eve with her children and their families, but today they were celebrating with their in-laws.

During the meal, Mae said, "Well, what do you suppose prompted Belle to send Christmas gifts this year?"

"Oh, who knows," said Lizzie. "She's probably hooked up with another man, and feeling guilty about ignoring us these past years."

"Well, I'm really enjoying the gardening book she sent," commented Ann. "What was yours about?"

"It's a cookbook. Guess she figures my cookin' could use some improvement, she's such a great cook herself."

David elected to change the subject, and said, "We had a letter from Eddie last week. He thinks things are gonna change for the better with the war pretty soon."

"Well, let's hope he's right. Seems like it's gone on forever, and I for one am getting really tired of this rationing." said Orville.

Ann added, "I think the Victory Garden idea was a good one, don't you, Aunt Mae?"

"Oh, I suppose, but it's really not much different than what we've always done. Probably just a way to try to make us feel better about the shortages," replied Mae.

Mae had dropped the no entry to the parlor rule, in honor of Christmas. By 3:00 when the women had finished the clean up from the meal, Orville was snoring in an easy chair. This seemed to be a signal for everyone to begin taking their leave.

Belle and Dave's friendship continued to grow, and deepen. They would frequently have dinner together, and over time, Belle revealed the details of her unconventional life. During one of these conversations, Dave said, "I wish I'd met you much earlier in our lives. I've always been so conventional, it's just plain boring. It would have been nice to have someone like you in my life to show me a different way. I think we would have made a good couple."

"Oh, I don't know, Dave. Given my history, I'd probably have managed to mess that up too."

"Do you have regrets then?"

"I suppose not really. I've been places, and done things no one else in my family would ever have even dreamed of. I guess if I have any regret, it's that my family never seemed to be able to understand me, or just accept who I am."

"That really is too bad, because who you are is pretty amazing."

Belle smiled, and said, "Thank you for saying that. You and Kenny are the only people who just take me as I am without any judgment. Well, and Bill, he was like that too."

"What about Peg?"

"Yes, Peg is a good friend, though I've never felt comfortable telling her all the details of my life, like I've been able to do with you and Kenny. She's pretty accepting, but I think her Catholic upbringing might make it hard for her not to be a bit critical of some of it."

On May 7th, 1945, the German army surrendered unconditionally, and May 8th was officially declared Victory in Europe day. Even though the war with Japan is still raging in the Pacific, VE day was cause for celebration. Flags and banners bloomed on buildings like springtime dandelions on lawns. Finally, there was real hope that the war would soon be over. In June, that hope was reinforced by the capture of Okinawa, and again in July, when the United States, Britain, and China issued an ultimatum to Japan to unconditionally surrender, or face "prompt and utter destruction." This was not an empty threat, and after atomic bombs were dropped on two Japanese cities, Japan agreed to unconditional surrender on August 14.

For many Americans, the relief over the end of the war was tempered by knowledge of this new weapon called the atomic bomb, and by the stories and pictures coming from Europe regarding the German death camps.

Belle, Dave, and Kenny were at a dance in late August, and everything that could be draped in red, white, and blue, was.

"I wonder how long it will take to bring our soldiers home," commented Dave.

"It'll probably take a while," answered Kenny, "Plus, some will be staying in Germany for some time."

"I had a letter from Ann, saying their son, Eddie, had written to say he will be home in October. They plan to have a party for him, and asked me to come."

"You gonna go?" asked Kenny.

"I'm not sure, I might. I just wish Peg's boy could be coming home too."

"There's a lot of people wishing that same kind of thing," said Dave.

"I know. It's just so senseless! All because one group of people decided they were superior to anyone who wasn't in their group. Sometimes I just really don't understand the Human Race."

"And you could drive yourself crazy trying to," said Kenny. "Sometimes you just gotta deal with what comes, and not try to figure out why."

Belle and Margaret had been meeting for lunch about once a month since the day they had become reacquainted in the bookstore. While having lunch a few weeks after the war ended, Belle told Margaret about being asked to go back to Nebraska for the welcome home party for her nephew.

"Are you going?" asked Margaret.

"I'm not sure. I've never really felt like I'm a part of my family. We just seem to be worlds apart, and my sisters have never really approved of me."

"Family dynamics are often a little strange. Well, maybe always," Margaret said, and smiled. "Still, they are a part of who we are, for good or ill, and trying to remain apart from them never really works very well."

"Are you trying to tell me I should go?"

"I'm just saying, I think you should do what you can to maintain a connection. Doing that doesn't mean you have to stop being who you are."

"I always feel I need to monitor everything I say, even the way I dress, when I'm around them."

"It doesn't work very well, though, does it?"

Belle laughed, shook her head, and said, "Not really."

"So, just go, and be you. Forget about trying to win their approval, that may never happen. Just go to acknowledge that you are a part of the family."

"Well, you definitely put a little different perspective on all this. I've been trying to decide if I should go. Everything you just said tells me that I should. Thanks."

"Family things are always hard to sort out on our own. A little objective observation often helps."

Dave also encouraged her to go back for her nephew's party, and assured her he could manage the store just fine without her for a few days.

Belle took a train to David City. Mae had insisted she stay with them. She packed her red dress, her sapphire jewelry, and wore all her rings. At the last minute, she decided to take a black velvet dress with her, "in case the weather gets cold", she thought.

Her train arrived in David City late in the evening. Mae wanted to visit a while after they got to the house, so it was quite late before they went to bed.

She woke briefly the next morning to the sounds and smells of breakfast being prepared, but decided to indulge herself, and rolled over to go back to sleep. When she woke again, it was nearly 11:00. She combed her hair, put her make up on, and walked to the kitchen in her lounging pajamas.

"My lands, I was beginning to wonder if you were ever gonna get up" said Mae.

"I guess yesterday wore me out more than I realized. Do you have any coffee?"

"It's still warm, I think. I'm gonna be fixing lunch soon."

"Some coffee for now will be just fine."

"Lizzie's coming with Sis and her family. They should be here shortly after lunch. You gonna get dressed?"

"No, I think I'll just wait until it's time to dress for the party," she said, and lit a cigarette.

Lizzie arrived shortly before 2:00. Belle was sitting at the table, smoking, when they arrived. There was a momentary hesitation before Lizzie said, "Hello Belle. This is my granddaughter, Peggy, her husband, Andrew, and her children, Julianne, and Danny."

"Hello Peggy," Belle said. "You were about the size of your daughter the last time I saw you."

Just then the phone rang, and Mae answered it, listened for a few minutes, then started screaming. Orville jumped up, shouting, "Mae, what in the world...?"

Mae could only shake her head, and scream, so Orville took the phone from her, listened for a moment, then said "Oh my God! Lizzie and Sis just got here. Do you want us to come over? OK, then, we'll talk to you a little later."

When he hung up, Lizzie said, "What's wrong?"

"Eddie's gone."

"What do you mean? His train was coming in to Lincoln at 8:00 this morning. David and Ann went to pick him up."

"Yeah, well, the train didn't arrive. It took a couple hours before anyone could tell them what happened. Seems there was a train wreck between Omaha and Lincoln. Eddie was killed."

There was a moment of stunned silence, before Lizzie said, "We need to go over there."

"No, David said Tommy and Amy are with them, and Ann is so upset she doesn't want to see anybody right now. David could hardly talk. I think we should leave 'em be 'til morning, then give 'em a call."

Mae had regained some composure, and said, "I better call the Pastor to let him know there won't be no party in the church basement tonight. He can help pass the word."

"Do you know when they will be bringing Eddie home?" asked Lizzie.

"I don't know nuthin' more than what I've told you. We'll just have to wait 'til tomorrow to find out more. God dammit, just a few more hours, and he would have been home."

Everyone sat in silence for a few more minutes, then Andrew said, "I think, maybe we'd best go on home. You call us tomorrow when you know more."

Peggy had remained silent, with only her face revealing painful emotions. Eddie's death had stirred up memories of the loss of her brother, and some years later, her dad. Belle was also re-experiencing her grief over the loss of Bill and Ray, and had remained silent.

After everyone had left, Mae said, "Belle, you should get dressed. We might have people stopping by, once word gets out."

It took two days for Eddies' body to be returned. The funeral was held the next morning. When Belle appeared in her black velvet dress that morning, Mae raised her eyebrows, and said, "That's a bit fancy for a funeral, don't you think?"

"Well, I don't have a lot of choice, do I?"

"You at least gonna wear a hat?"

"No, Mae, I don't have a hat with me. I don't usually wear a hat anyway."

"Figures," said Mae. "Well, get your coat, it's time we should be going."

By the time the funeral was over, and everyone had departed, Belle had a raging headache. When they returned to Mae's, Belle said, "I'm going to lie down for a while. Do you have any aspirin? I have a headache."

"No, never use the stuff myself," said Mae.

"I'll see you a little later then."

Belle wasn't able to sleep, but being alone, away from the constant chatter, helped. She had been aware of some raised eyebrows at the funeral, and those who had spoken to her seemed to be trying to be overly polite, and had kept their conversations brief, and superficial.

Belle ate very little for supper that evening, which prompted Mae to tell her she really needed to learn to eat more. "It just ain't healthy to be as skinny as you are," was her final comment.

Her train left at 8:00 the next morning. Their goodbyes were brief, and she heaved a long sigh of relief once the train was in motion.

The train arrived in Chicago at 10:30 that evening. She had told Dave when she would be returning, but was surprised to find him waiting for her at the station.

"Dave, you didn't need to do this."

"Well, I was pretty sure you'd be worn out, and figured it would be nice to have a ride ready and waiting."

"It is. Thank you."

"So, how was the party?"

"Oh God! There wasn't one. Eddie's train crashed just hours before he was to arrive, and he was killed."

"Good Lord! I'm really sorry."

"Yeah, it was a bit of a nightmare. I am really beat, so I'll fill you in on the details in a day or two."

"Of course. Why don't you sleep in tomorrow, and come in to the shop whenever you're ready."

"Thanks, I just may take you up on that."

Chapter Fifteen

Dave was sympathetic when Belle described to him her feeling of being on the outside, looking in, with her family, and of their barbed comments indicating disapproval of her.

"I'm really sorry you had such a rough week. It's hard for me to imagine treating another family member like that. Maybe because my family consisted only of me and my parents. I've always regretted not having a large family, but I guess a large family comes with it's own set of problems."

"It sure seems like that in my case," she answered.

"Belle, I've been thinking. We all had such a great time last year at Thanksgiving. What do you think about doing it again this year?"

"That sounds really good."

"Will you talk to Peg, and I'll ask Kenny?"

"Sure."

There was a heavy snowfall the week before Thanksgiving, and the temperature rarely rose above freezing in the days leading up to Thanksgiving, allowing most of the snow to remain clean, and white. Thanksgiving day brought crisp blue skies, causing eyes to tear up from the glare of the sun on the snow. By noon, the temperature had climbed into the forties, and icicles began to form along roof lines. The day was every bit as successful as it had been the year before.

During the afternoon, Dave said, "I think we should plan on this being an annual tradition. What do you think?"

Everyone agreed it sounded like a good idea.

Margaret and Belle met for lunch the week after Thanksgiving. It was the first time they had a chance to visit since Margaret had encouraged Belle to go home for Eddie's part.

"So, how was your trip?" she asked.

Belle sighed, and said, "Do you have time for a long lunch?"

Margaret raised her eyebrows, and said, "So, I take it there were some problems?"

Belle nodded, and Margaret continued, "What happened?"

"Well, to start with, there was no party. Eddie's train wrecked a couple of hours before it was due to arrive in Lincoln, and he was killed. My sister Lizzie, and my niece and her family had just arrived when we got word of what had happened. On top of all the chaos of canceling the party, and making funeral arrangements, there were all the usual disapproving comments from Mae."

"Such as?"

"Oh, like telling me I needed to get dressed, making a sarcastic comment about me sleeping late, and criticizing the dress I wore to the funeral. I noticed a few raised eyebrows from people attending the funeral, when they thought I wasn't looking. Even my little great niece just stood, and stared, like I was something from outer space."

"So, I'm guessing it was difficult for you to remember what I said about your family being a part of who you are?"

"You could say that!"

"Well, I may have been wrong. Since we last spoke of your family, I've had conversations with some other people who have never been able to feel close to their family, and another thought occurred to me. I wonder if it's possible that for some people their true family members are not the ones they grew up with, but the people in their life who respect and accept them for who and what they are."

Belle remained silent for a few minutes, and then said, "This could explain a lot."

"I agree."

"You know, Thanksgiving day with Peg and her family, and Dave, and Kenny felt like what a family gathering should be."

"Then, maybe you should consider them your true family, rather than those you grew up with in Nebraska."

"I wonder why that happens, that we don't grow up with our true family."

"I don't know. In any case, I wouldn't put a lot of effort into trying to figure that out. Just enjoy what you have here."

"Well, with people like you, and Kenny, and Dave, and Peg in my life, that's easy to do."

New Year's Eve of 1945 was more jubilant than it had been since before the start of the war, as was New Year's Day, 1946. There seemed to be more parties, and most of them were more elaborate than had been seen in recent years. There was an increase in the sales of formal wear. Dave, Kenny, and Belle made plans to attend a dance that was to be held at one of Chicago's more luxurious hotels. Belle went shopping for a dress, and found a royal blue taffeta gown, with a full skirt that rustled when she moved. She wore her sapphire necklace and earrings, and adorned her hands with all her rings. Belle rode with Dave, and Kenny met them at the hotel. Dave and Kenny wore tuxedos.

"Well, ain't you just a sight for sore eyes," exclaimed Kenny when Belle and Dave walked in.

"Aren't we all?" Belle laughed. "It just feels so good not to have the war hanging over us. I think everyone is ready to do some celebrating."

"There's a great buffet set up on the other side of the room, and I've got a table staked out for us. I don't know about you, but I'm ready for some food."

"Sounds good to me," said Dave. "Show us where the table is, then we can head for the buffet."

The hotel's kitchen had gone all out in preparing the buffet. At the center of the long table there was a champagne fountain. The remainder of the space was filled with cold salmon, paper thin slices of ham, roast beef, caviar, numerous selections of fresh fruit, tiny petit fours, chocolate candies, nuts, crackers, cheese, and several selections of hors d'oeuvres.

It was the era of big bands, and the hotel had hired a popular band of the day. The tables were arranged around a large parquet dance floor, lit with several crystal chandeliers. Nearly everyone attending had come as a couple, so there wasn't the usual amount of mixing that Belle was used to at dances. While filling their plates at the buffet, Kenny spotted a man that he and Dave often played poker with.

"Hi Dick. Happy New Year."

"And to you, Kenny."

Dick was with a woman wearing a champagne colored satin gown that perfectly matched her pale blonde hair. A brilliant emerald green necklace and earrings prevented her from appearing bland.

"Kenny, this is my cousin, Nicole. Nicole, this is a poker buddy of mine, Kenny."

"Nice to meet you, Nicole."

"No date tonight?" asked Dave.

"Well, I had one, but she had the bad luck of falling on some ice a couple days ago, and broke her ankle."

As it turned out, Dick and Nicole's table was next to the one Kenny had picked. As they returned to the tables, Kenny introduced them to Belle and Dave, and in turn was introduced to the couple Dick and Nicole were with. When the plates were empty, Dick suggested they move the two tables together, to make conversation easier. It wasn't long before Kenny asked Nicole for a dance. The band was playing "Moonlight Serenade". Kenny used the slow dance to get some conversation going with Nicole. She was quiet, and seemed shy. He noticed she was wearing a wedding ring, and said, "Your husband isn't here tonight?"

She hesitated briefly, then replied, "No, he didn't come home from the war,"

"Oh, I'm sorry. This must be a little difficult for you."

"It is. Dick insisted I come. He thought it would be good for me to get out."

"Well, I hope he's right, and that you enjoy yourself tonight. You look stunning in that dress, by the way."

Nicole blushed, and replied in a quiet voice, "Thank you."

Later in the evening, Belle and Nicole were in the powder room together.

"Are you enjoying yourself?" asked Belle.

"I am, more than I expected to," replied Nicole. "Are you and Dave a couple?"

"No, I work in his bookstore, and we've become good friends. Kenny introduced me to Dave at a time when I needed a job, and Dave was looking for someone to help in the store. The rest, as they say, is history."

"Where is his bookstore? I love to read," said Nicole.

Belle told her, and said, "You should come in. We have a good selection of books."

"I just may do that."

Belle and Dave were dancing when the clock neared midnight.

The band gave a drum roll at one minute to midnight, then broke into Auld Lang Syne at the stroke of midnight. Dave leaned down, and kissed Belle. To her surprise, she found herself responding, and prolonging the kiss. When the kiss ended, Dave leaned back a bit, and said, "Wow! What a way to start the New Year."

Belle laughed, a little nervously, and agreed.

When all the bells, whistles, and cheering had died down, the band began playing Moonlight Becomes You.

Kenny had been dancing with Nicole at midnight, and had given her a brief kiss, then said, "That was for luck, that 1946 will be a good year for you."

Nicole blushed, and said, "Thanks. I hope it works."

They continued dancing, and Kenny said, "You know, this song could have been written for you."

Nicole only smiled.

Kenny would have liked to say more, and normally would have, but he was finding himself quite taken with Nicole, and knowing that she was recently widowed, didn't want to push her away by moving too fast.

When they returned to their tables, Dave said, "Kenny, I think Belle and I are ready to call it a night."

Nicole addressed Dick, and said she felt like going home too.

As they were all leaving, Belle said to Nicole, "I hope you will come in to the store, I think you'll enjoy it."

As they stepped outside, they found it was snowing, and there was a new accumulation of about two inches on the ground. The snowflakes were large, and there was no wind, giving the city a quiet, peaceful feeling.

Belle was still feeling a little embarrassed over her reaction to Dave's New Year's Eve kiss when she went to work on January 2nd.

"Morning Belle, did you have a good New Year's Day?" Dave asked.

"I did, a lovely, quiet one. I spent the day cleaning out some drawers, and contemplating what 1946 might bring."

"So, do you have any big changes in mind for the coming year?"

"Not really. I'm not big on making New Year's resolutions, but I do like to spend some time reviewing the past, as a way of, hopefully, avoiding repeating my mistakes. How about you? How was your day?"

"It was quiet too. I used the time to catch up on some reading I've been wanting to do."

"Kenny seems rather taken with Nicole."

"Yeah, I noticed that," replied Dave.

A few weeks later, Nicole did come in to the shop.

"Well, hello Nicole," said Belle. "It's nice to see you again."

"Hello Belle. My winter cabin fever is in full force, and I decided I'd better get out of the house before I started climbing the walls."

Belle laughed, and said, "Winter does seem to last forever, doesn't it?"

"At least the sun is out, that always helps."

"That it does. Have you always lived in Chicago?"

"No, I grew up in Iowa."

"Really. What got you to Chicago?"

"I was working in an insurance office in Des Moines. Bob was one of the agents. We fell in love almost from the first time we met. After we were married, Bob got transferred to the Chicago office."

"Do you have children?"

"No, we would have liked to have a family, but it just never happened."

"Oh, I'm sorry."

"It would have been nice to have part of Bob with me, but in some ways, it's easier not to have a child to raise on my own."

"So, what kind of books do you like?"

"Oh, I'll read almost anything, but I guess historical fiction is my favorite. I always feel they give a more complete picture of history than just reading the facts, since it gives a picture of how history affected the people living through it."

"I couldn't agree more. You might want to browse through this section," Belle said, and led her to one of the bookcases.

Nicole found two books, and as she was paying for them, Belle impulsively said,

"Would you like to have lunch with me on Saturday? We close at noon here."

"Why, that sounds nice. Where would you like to go?"

They arranged to meet at a downtown restaurant. While they were having lunch, Nicole asked, "So how long have you known Kenny?"

"All my life. We grew up together in Nebraska, then chanced to meet again in Chicago."

"He's never been married?"

"No, I guess he just never found the right woman. Why do you ask?"

"He called me the other day, and asked if I'd have dinner with him. I told him I needed to think about it."

"Kenny's a very nice person. You should say yes."

"Maybe I will."

Spring finally arrived in Chicago in late April. Dave arrived at the shop one day with a large bunch of daffodils.

"Oh, what a great idea, Dave," said Belle. "Winter has seemed to last forever. Where did you get them?"

"Out of my back yard. My mother planted a large bed of them years ago."

"They are wonderful. I've always loved daffodils."

The next day Dave came in with another bunch of daffodils. "These are for you to take home, and enjoy," he said.

"Well, thank you! I certainly will."

Dave and Belle continued to have dinner together from time to time, and were never at a loss to find things to talk about.

"Did you know Kenny and Nicole have been dating?" asked Belle.

"Yeah, Kenny mentioned it at a poker game a while back. He seems quite smitten with her. You think maybe he's ready to settle down to one woman?"

"I don't know, maybe."

"We should ask them to have dinner with us sometime, maybe on a Saturday night."

"Sounds like a good idea. Why don't you mention it to Kenny?"

The summer went by very quickly, as summers always do. Kenny and Nicole joined Dave and Belle for dinner a few times, and once the four of them went on a picnic by the lake. It was becoming clear that Kenny was seriously considering ending his days as a bachelor. At least it seemed clear to Dave and Belle.

One Saturday morning in September, Dave said to Belle, "The weather is so great right now, how would you like to pack a small lunch tomorrow, and we go for a drive in the country. We can stop and eat when we find someplace that looks inviting."

"Well, aren't you just becoming the spontaneous one?" she replied, with a smile. "That does sound nice."

"Great, I'll pick you up at ten tomorrow."

The day was sunny; the temperature in the mid seventies, and the wind was mild. They were a few miles outside the city, when Dave turned off the highway onto a gravel country road. After driving a few miles, they came to an open grassy area, scattered with a few large trees.

"What do you think about stopping here?" he asked.

"Looks perfect," she replied.

Dave pulled the car off the road, and said, "Let's walk for a while."

"This looks like a pasture," said Belle, "but I don't see any cattle."

They wandered aimlessly for a while, skirting in and out of the shade from the trees. Both seemed content to remain silent, soaking up the peace of the countryside. After a while, Belle said, "I'd forgotten how quiet the country can be. This was a good idea."

They made their way back to the car, and brought their lunch and a blanket to a nearby shade tree.

"Why is it that food tastes so much better outside?" she asked.

"Don't know, but it does, doesn't it?"

After another short silence, he said, "You know, I envy Kenny. He's found someone he really cares about. And it seems to be mutual."

"Yeah, I'm happy for him. He wants to marry Nicole, but is afraid of rushing her too fast, after the loss of her husband."

"Don't you ever wish you had someone like that in your life?" he asked.

"Oh, I suppose so, now and then. But then, I remember how disastrous most of my relationships have been."

"That doesn't mean it would have to be that way again. Belle, that kiss we had on New Year's Eve wasn't really a 'just friends' type kiss, was it?"

"Oh, Dave," Belle sighed. "I don't know what came over me that night."

"Don't you? Or are you just afraid to admit it?"

"Dave, you know I like you a lot. I just don't want to risk ruining our friendship."

"I'd hate that too. I just don't think it would happen. But, if you feel that strongly, I won't push you. Just give it some thought now and then, OK?"

Just then they heard the sounds of cattle, and looked up to see a small herd heading their way.

"I think maybe it's time we were on the other side of the fence." "Probably a good idea," Belle replied, as they gathered up their picnic things.

The Thanksgiving meal at Dave's that year included Nicole. She had insisted on contributing to the meal, and had brought a cranberry salad, and cookies for the children. As soon as the coats had been put away, and the food placed on the table, Kenny pulled a bottle of champagne out of the sack he was carrying.

"Champagne, Kenny?" said Belle.

"Well, this is a special occasion. I have an announcement. Nicole has agreed to marry me."

There was in immediate chorus of congratulations, and hugs. When things quieted down a little, Dave walked to the china cabinet, and said, "I used to think about selling my Mother's crystal. Now I'm glad I didn't." He handed a crystal wine glass to everyone, as Kenny popped the cork. When the champagne had been poured, Dave said, "A toast to Nicole and Kenny. I'm sure I speak for everyone here when I say we couldn't be happier for both of you."

When the champagne had been drunk, Peg asked, "So when is this weddin' gonna happen?"

Nicole and Kenny smiled at each other, and Nicole said, "You tell them, Kenny."

"We decided on the anniversary of the day we met. What better way to end one year, and begin a new life? It's gonna take place right where it all started. The hotel has agreed to let us use a small meeting room for the ceremony. Then they suggested we let them make a big deal about meeting each other at last year's party, and offered to provide a cake, and separate table in the ballroom where the New Year's Eve party is. Now that will be a reception to remember!"

Nicole spoke up then, saying, "Belle, I'd like you to stand up with me. If it hadn't been for you telling me that Kenny was a nice person, I might not have agreed to have dinner with him."

"And, Dave, I'd like you to stand up with me," said Kenny.

With all the excited talk of the wedding, the meal was temporarily forgotten, until Peg's grandson said, "Gran, I'm hungry. When can we eat?"

The afternoon was spent playing cards, and talking about the wedding. Everyone seemed reluctant to bring the day to a close, so the food was brought out again for an early evening meal.

The wedding ceremony was small, and simple. The only guests were Peg and Dan, and Nicole's cousin along with his date. At Kenny's request, Nicole wore the champagne silk gown she'd worn last year. In addition to her green jewelry, she had found a hair comb with emerald green rhinestones. Her bouquet was a small arrangement of cream colored roses, with lots of greenery. Belle had chosen a simple, pale blue silk gown.

The manager of the hotel was waiting near the entrance of the ballroom. When he saw the wedding party approaching, he gave a signal to the orchestra to begin playing "Here Comes The Bride." After a few stanzas had been played, he stepped to the microphone.

"Ladies and Gentlemen, we have a rather special occasion here tonight. One year ago tonight, Kenny and Nicole met right here in this ballroom. A short time ago, they were married in our hotel. So, you can see what special effect our hotel has on our guests." This was met with some laughter. He then said, "Mr. and Mrs. Miller, would you do us the honor of having your first dance here?"

Nicole blushed, and Kenny laughed, as the orchestra began playing "Moonlight Becomes You."

When the dance ended, there was applause from everyone, as the bridal party made their way to their table.

The hotel manager knew that the society reporter for the Chicago Tribune would be there, and was hoping to get some free advertising by playing up the wedding. He even hired a photographer to take pictures of the newlyweds.

The night passed quickly. Many of the other guests stopped by the bridal table to congratulate the newlyweds. A few asked permission from Kenny to dance with the bride.

When midnight arrived, Dave made sure he was with Belle, hoping for a repeat of last years' kiss. He wasn't disappointed, and even though he knew the quantity of champagne consumed might have played a part in her response, he didn't care.

Nicole and Kenny spent the night at the hotel. Dave drove Peg and Dan home, then turned to Belle, and said, "I don't suppose you'd consider spending the night with me?"

Belle was a little drunk and feeling dreamy. She smiled at him, and said, "Oh, I might."

Dave's lovemaking was warm and tender, and Belle responded in kind. He lay awake long after Belle had drifted off to sleep, feeling like he'd just been handed the world.

Belle woke before Dave in the morning, and was initially confused over the unfamiliar surroundings. Then the memory of last night rushed in. She eased out of bed, trying not to wake Dave. His bathrobe was hanging in the bathroom, so she put it on, and went to the kitchen to make coffee. Her thoughts were a jumble while she prepared the coffee.

"Good grief, Belle! What have you done now?" she thought. "I promised myself I wasn't going to do this again. How am I going to get out of this without hurting Dave, or losing his friendship? Dammit, Kenny! This is all your fault. All that wedding romance, not to mention the champagne." Then what she'd just said to herself sunk in, and she shook her head, and gave a small, cynical laugh. "Kenny would roar if he heard me say that," she thought. "God, why do I always have to complicate things by getting involved with a man?"

By now the coffee was ready, so she sat down with a cup, and a cigarette. By the time she'd finished her coffee, she was feeling a little calmer. "Maybe this time will be different, maybe I can manage being more than just friends without losing his friendship," she thought.

Just then, Dave appeared, wearing pajamas. "Happy New Year, Belle."

"Happy New Year to you. I hope you don't mind me wearing your robe. I really didn't want to put my gown on this morning."

"You look lovely in the robe," he smiled. "Brrr, it's cold in here. I'll light the oven to warm the kitchen. Did you sleep well?"

"I did."

"Any regrets?" he asked.

She shook her head, and said, "No regrets. I just hope I haven't taken the first step toward ruining a great friendship."

"Well, since I'm not a very demanding person, and have no intention of trying to push you where you don't want to go, I seriously doubt that will happen."

Chapter Sixteen

For the next year, Dave kept his word about not pushing Belle. They spent more time together, outside of work, going to movies, or dancing, and she occasionally spent the night at his house.

Kenny and Nicole bought a house in August, and had a housewarming party in early September. At their usual Thanksgiving dinner with Dave, Nicole invited everyone to spend Christmas afternoon with them.

Belle was happier than she had been in a long time. She and Dave shopped together for Christmas gifts for their friends. Belle was having difficulty deciding what to give Peg. One day, while looking for a book she wanted to re-read, she came across the crystal rose vase from Ireland. It no longer held any sentimental value for her, so she decided to give it to Peg.

When the gifts were opened Christmas afternoon, Peg was momentarily speechless over the vase.

"Belle, ya shouldn't be given' this away."

"Yes, I should, Peg. It's been tucked away in a closet. You played a big part in The Irish Rose, and since you are Irish, I think it's best that you have it."

"Ah, Belle, I always admired this so. Thank you, I'll treasure it always."

Dave had given Belle a phonograph, and some records by Benny Goodman, and Glenn Miller. "So we don't have to wait to go to a dance, to enjoy dancing," he explained.

Their New Year's Eve was quieter than the past few years had been Some friends of Kenny and Nicole hosted a small party. It was a congenial group, and everyone enjoyed themselves.

Belle's birthday was in February. Dave gave her a large amethyst ring that just happened to fit the third finger on her left hand.

"Belle, I promised you I wouldn't push you where you don't want to go, and I won't. This past year has gone very well, don't you agree?"

"It has, Dave. It's been great."

"Would you consider moving in with me? You spend a lot of time with me, and it seems kind of silly for you to be paying for an apartment, when I have all this room."

"Are you asking me to marry you?"

"Well, that's a standing offer, as I think you know. But moving in with me wouldn't mean we would need to be married."

"Why, Dave, what would the neighbors think?" Belle said with a grin.

Dave laughed, and said, "Like that's ever been a big issue with you!"

"I guess it would simplify our lives some. OK, if you insist, I'll move in with you."

"Wonderful!" he said, as he embraced her. "It's going to be so nice to wake up next to you every morning."

The next time she saw Kenny, he noticed the amethyst ring.

"So, is that an engagement ring?" he asked.

"No, it's just a birthday gift."

"But you have moved in with him, so why not get married. It would be pretty hard to find a better man than Dave."

"Yes, it would, but why mess with success. He's content with the way things are, and with my track record, I'd probably jinx the whole thing if we got married."

Kenny only smiled, and shook his head, then said, "Well, I'm glad you two found each other, anyway."

Peg had voiced similar thoughts when Belle told her she was living with Dave.

In April, Dave said to Belle, "I think we should close the shop in July and take a long vacation."

"Close the shop for a whole month?"

"Sure, July is always a slow month. I've never taken a vacation, and it doesn't sound like you have either."

"No, I guess I haven't. What did you have in mind?"

"Oh, I don't know. I've never been out of Chicago. Maybe we could go someplace where there is a pond we could wade in and squish our toes in the mud."

Belle laughed, and said, "You don't forget much, do you?"

"That just sounded like a lot of fun when you told me about it. Maybe we could start driving, and see where the road takes us."

Belle smiled, and said, "That sounds like fun."

They put a notice in the bookstore's newsletter, and made plans to leave July first.

As they drove out of Chicago, Dave said, "One of the guys I play poker with is from Nebraska. He tells me that the town of Seward has an outstanding fireworks display every 4th of July. Would you like to head that way for the 4th?"

"We could do that, I guess. My brother Ray lived in Seward for a while."

"Did he? Is that near where you grew up?"

"Oh, about twenty miles east of our farm, I guess."

"Didn't you say your brother still farms your dad's place? Would you like to stop to see him?"

"That might be OK. I haven't had much contact with him and Ann since their son died. I guess I could call him from Seward."

"I hope it works out. I'd like to see where you grew up. Maybe we could even squish our toes in the same mud you did as a kid."

Belle laughed, and said "We'll see."

They drove at a leisurely pace, stopping occasionally to stretch their legs, or eat at a small town café. Late in afternoon of the second day, found them in Omaha. They stayed in the downtown Paxton hotel, and drove to Seward the next day. It was early afternoon when they arrived in Seward on July 3rd, and found a room at the East Hill Motel. The desk clerk asked if they were in town for the fireworks. When Dave said yes, the clerk replied, "Well, it's good you got here when you did. We only have one room left. Lots of people come in for the fireworks."

The temperature was in the 90's, and the motel room was stifling. The fan in the room did little more than move the hot air around. They had asked for directions to the park, and the clerk had added, "We've got a really nice new swimming pool there too."

"Belle, you want to check out that swimming pool, to cool off?" Dave asked.

"That sounds like a wonderful idea."

They gathered their swimsuits, and drove to the park.

The clerk hadn't exaggerated when he said it was a nice pool. It was large, and round, with sides that sloped gently towards the deep center of the pool. There was a platform and diving tower in the center of the pool. By 5:30, they were feeling hungry, and after changing in the locker rooms, headed downtown to find a place to eat. After a leisurely meal at a café, they were tired enough to quickly fall asleep in spite of the heat.

They slept late the next morning, and after breakfast found a pay phone and called David. Ann answered the phone.

"Hello Ann, it's Belle."

"Belle! Is everything OK?"

"Oh, yes, my friend and I are taking a little vacation. We're in Seward for the fireworks tonight. Are you and David going to be here?"

"No, he's in the middle of harvesting the wheat, and doesn't get in from the field until nearly sundown."

"Well, I'd like to see both of you. Would it be OK if we drove out tomorrow?"

"David will be in the field all day, but if you were here about noon, he'll be at the house for dinner."

"We'll plan on that then, if you're sure its OK."

"Of course, we'd love to see you, even if it's only for a short time."

"OK, we'll be there shortly before noon tomorrow."

Belle and Dave spent the morning strolling around the town square, stopping to peek into store windows. On impulse, Belle went into the bakery and bought a cake to take to Ann and David. The day was rapidly heating up, so they decide to go for a short swim before the evening's festivities.

The fireworks display was as impressive as they had been led to believe, and both thoroughly enjoyed themselves.

They arrived at the farm about 11:30 the next day. David came in from the field a short time later, and they sat down to a large meal.

"So, you gonna go see Mae while you're here?" asked David

"I don't know. We haven't talked about it. This whole trip was a kind of a spur of the moment thing."

"Might be nice if you did. She's been kinda lost since Orville and Lizzie passed."

"What?"

"You didn't know? I thought Mae would have written to you."

"No, she didn't. When did this happen?"

"Well, Orville passed a little over a year ago, and Lizzie died last fall. She'd had a stroke and was in the hospital for a few weeks before she passed."

After David said his goodbyes, and headed back to the field, Dave said to Ann, "I've never been on a farm before. Would you mind if Belle and I wandered around some?"

"Of course not, though I'm not sure there's much to see."

"Well, for someone who has lived in Chicago all his life, all this open space is a real treat."

Belle spoke up saying, "I'll help Ann with the dishes first."

"Oh, you don't need to do that, you're company."

"Don't be silly, of course I'll help."

When the kitchen had been cleaned, Dave and Belle left to go walking.

"Show me the pond where you used to wade," said Dave.

Belle laughed, and pointed the way. The large oak tree was still standing near the pond, and they sat in the shade for a while. Then Dave said, "Well, come on, get your shoes off, it's time to do some squishing."

Belle laughed, and said, "Are you serious?"

"Serious as a heart attack," he replied, as he was removing his shoes, and rolling up his pant legs. Belle had worn slacks too, and hurried to catch up with him.

"Wow, you're right, this does feel good," he said.

There were a few pebbles at the water's edge. Belle picked one up and said, "There used to be a knot on that tree. I'd throw stones at it, and could hit it nearly every time. That's how I managed to get the job with the carnival." Then she told him about enticing customers to Tad's booth by knocking down the dolls for a prize.

Dave shook his head, and laughed, "You really were something even then, weren't you? I don't see a knot, but see where that big branch forks? Let's see if you can hit that."

Belle gave him a look, and took aim. She missed the fork, but brushed a small branch hanging near it.

"Guess I'm out of practice," she said.

"Still, that was pretty close."

While they were drying their feet, Dave asked, "Would you like to go see Mae?"

"Oh, I don't know. I don't think so. If she didn't even write to tell me about Lizzie, she probably doesn't care if she sees me or not. I think I would like to go to the cemetery, though, if you don't mind."

"Of course not."

When they returned to the house, they told Ann they were going to the cemetery.

"Lizzie's not buried with your ma and pa," Ann said. "She has her own plot with her husband, and children. But, it's near ma and pa's, so I don't think you'll have trouble finding it."

It was a fairly large cemetery, but Belle remembered the general area where her folks were buried. They found her parents' graves in a short time. Belle stood quietly for a few minutes, listening to the murmur of the soft breeze in the trees, and the occasional birdsong. "There just isn't anything quite so peaceful as a country cemetery, is there?" she said.

"I can't imagine what it would be," he replied.

As Belle glanced around, she noticed a woman placing flowers on a nearby grave. Something about her seemed familiar, and after she watched for a minute, realized it was Mae.

"Dave, I think that's my sister, Mae, over there," she said, and began walking towards her.

Mae was kneeling, pulling a few stray weeds away from a headstone, and didn't notice Belle and Dave approaching.

"Hello Mae."

Mae startled, and looked up. Because the sun was in her eyes, she shielded them, and leaned back.

"Belle! Good lord, what are you doing here?"

"My friend, Dave, and I are on vacation. We went to the fireworks in Seward last night, and stopped out to see David and Ann. Mae, this is my friend Dave, Dave, this is my sister, Mae."

"Friend, huh? I figured he was probably another husband," Mae said as she got to her feet.

Belle's eyes hardened momentarily, then she took a deep breath, and said, "Is that Lizzie's grave?"

"It is. I always like to bring her flowers on her birthday. Lord knows it would have been nice to do that for her when she was alive, but she never wanted anyone to do anything for her. That woman was stubborn as a mule. You two are a lot alike, in some ways."

"Mae, why didn't you write and tell me Lizzie had died?"

"Didn't figure it would make much difference one way or the other."

"Ann told me you lost Orville."

"Yeah, he had a heart attack, and was gone in a few minutes."

"I'm sorry. Is there anything you need?"

"Not a thing, I'm doin' just fine." As she stooped to pick up her tools, she said, "Well, I'd best be gettin' home. You two enjoy your vacation," and with that she turned and walked to a nearby car.

As she drove away, Belle sighed, and said, "I guess some things never change."

They stood beside Lizzie's grave for a few minutes. On the same plot were the graves of her husband, a grandson, and three of her children, one an infant, the other two young adults.

"She was always a little hard around the edges, but she did have a hard life. Let's go, Dave."

"I'm sorry Belle. I knew you weren't close, but I guess I didn't realize just how bad it was."

"Except for Ray and David, none of my family could accept that their way of life wasn't the only way. I was close to Ray, but David, well, I'm not sure how he feels. He's always kept his thoughts to himself, and avoided trouble any way he could."

As they reached the car, Dave said, "Well, we've still got a lot of vacation time left. Where would you like to go from here?"

"Do you think we could go to Mt. Rushmore in South Dakota? That sounds like it's really impressive."

"That's a good idea." Dave dug a map out of the glove box, and after looking at it for a few minutes, said, "We can get there in two easy days, then take highway 14 east right back to Chicago."

They drove north and west, stopping in the small town of

Valentine, Nebraska the first night. Dave was awed by all the open space, and the gentle, rolling sand hills.

"They look like a blanket of green velvet has been thrown over them, don't they?" commented Belle. "Can you imagine traveling through country like this in a wagon train?"

"Not really."

It was early afternoon when they reached Rapid City, checked in to a motel, then drove to Mt. Rushmore. It was the peak of vacation season, and the monument area was crowded. They wandered around for a short time, then decided they would come back in the morning, before it was quite so crowded.

Belle bought a small pair of turquoise earrings for Peg, and some "lucky" rabbit's foot key chains for Peg's grandchildren. At noon they headed back to town to find the city swimming pool, and spent the afternoon there. They slept late the next morning, and headed east after breakfast. When they stopped at the edge of town to fill the gas tank, the man at the gas station asked where they were heading.

"Chicago is our final destination," said Dave.

"Well, there ain't a lot of places to fill up between here and Iowa or Minnesota, so anytime you see a gas station, it'd probably be best to stop."

"Thanks, we'll remember that."

They stayed on highway 14 through South Dakota and Minnesota. At Winnona, Minnesota, they turned south and followed the Mississippi down to Dubuque, Iowa before turning east again toward Chicago.

By the time they reached Illinois, two weeks of their vacation were gone, and Dave asked, "If we keep to the same pace we've been doing, we'll be back in Chicago in three or four days. Are you getting travel weary, or would you like to find someplace to stop for a few days before we head on home?"

"I suppose I am about ready to be back home," she replied.

"Getting weary of me?" he asked.

Belle smiled, and said, "Definitely not. This has been wonderful. You're very easy to be with, you know."

"Well, I do what I can," he said with a grin.

Belle was quieter than usual on the last day of their trip. As they neared Chicago, Dave asked, "You sorry our little adventure is over?"

"No, not really."

"You've been awfully quiet today."

"I know, I've had a nagging headache that won't go away."

"I'm sorry. Shall I stop someplace for some aspirin?"

"No, we'll be home soon. I'll be fine."

They returned to Chicago on a Wednesday afternoon. The house was stuffy and hot from being closed for nearly three weeks, so the first thing they did was open every window. There was a nice south breeze, and Belle decided to take full advantage of it by resting on the lounge in the sunroom.

"Maybe I can get rid of this headache," she said.

"Tell you what, I'll go get some groceries while you're resting."

"Dave, can we not tell anyone we're back just yet? It's been so nice spending time just with you, and I'm not quite ready to give that up."

"I can't think of anything I'd like better."

Belle was sleeping when Dave returned. The sky had become dark with clouds, and within a short time it began raining hard. The wind had not abated and was drenching the sunroom with rain. Dave hurried to close the windows, as Belle awoke. Together they shut the other windows in the house where rain was coming in, then mopped up the puddles.

"How are you feeling?" he asked.

"Much better. Between the aspirin and the luxury of falling asleep with the breeze blowing over me, the headache is gone."

"Glad to hear it. Besides the grocery store, I stopped at a deli and got some things for a light dinner for us tonight. You hungry yet?"

"I am. Let's see what you brought."

Over dinner they reminisced about things they had seen and done on their trip.

"So, how do you want to spend the next few days?" she asked.

"Well, to start with I plan to make love to you until the wee hours in our own comfortable bed, then fix you a late breakfast of my famous French toast tomorrow. After that, who knows."

Belle laughed, and said, "That sounds like a good start. I really need a bath first, I think."

"May I join you?" he asked.

Belle laughed, and said, "It might be a little cozy in the tub, but sure, why not."

They made passionate love long into the night to the sound of rain dripping from the eaves outside the window.

During breakfast the next morning, Dave said, "You know, I have only two regrets in life. The first one is big, I regret that I didn't meet you years ago. The second one is a much smaller regret, and that is that I can't shout to the world that you are my wife."

"Ah, Dave, I wish we'd met years ago too. I guess it just wasn't meant to be. As for your second regret, I know I must seem completely unreasonable, and maybe I am, but every man I've married has either died, or turned into something ugly. I'm just not willing to risk that again. Especially with you. You are the best thing that has ever happened to me. I think the only thing that would convince me to marry you, is if you said you'd leave if I didn't."

"Well, I won't do that. I promised you I wouldn't push you where you don't want to go, and I intend to keep that promise.

Belle's eyes filled with tears as she said, "Dave you really are amazing. I do love you, you know."

"I do know that. Don't cry, Belle. Things are too good between us for tears. How about we go dancing tonight?"

Peg's children gathered at her house every Sunday after church for a large meal. Belle called Peg on Friday to let her know they were back in town, and asked if they could come to visit on Sunday.

"Well, of course ya can, but only if ya promise to come for dinner."

Peg's house was crowded with her children and grandchildren. They were a lively crew, and often there was more than one conversation happening simultaneously. That Sunday much of the conversation was directed to Belle and Dave. Everyone wanted to hear details of their trip.

One of the grandchildren wanted to know if they'd seen any wild Indians.

"Well, I don't know about wild," Belle replied, "but we did drive through a reservation in South Dakota."

"What was it like? Do they live in tipis?" asked Peg's oldest grandson.

"No, they live in very small houses that the government built for them."

"Why'd they do that?"

"Because years ago, our government made the Indians leave where they had been living, and move to a place they call a reservation."

"How come?"

"It's kind of a long story. Years ago, when white men started coming to America, some Indians didn't like it, and killed some white men. This made the white people very afraid of the Indians. Also, the Indians lived on good land, and as more white men came to live here, they wanted to live on that land, and farm it. After a while, there were too many white men for the Indians to fight, so they gave up, and agreed to move to places where our government wanted them all to live."

"So, do the Indians farm there?"

"No, the land is not very good, so the Indians are really poor."

"Well, that just don't sound right."

"No, I guess it isn't, is it. But I brought you all a little gift from Mt. Rushmore. These are lucky rabbit's feet, so if you take care of them, you'll always have good luck."

"Wow! This is really a rabbit's foot?"

"It really is. Peg, I got a little something for you too."

"Ah, Belle, ya didna' need to be doin' that."

"Well, if you don't like the earrings, I'll keep them."

Peg laughed and said, "Not a chance. These are wonderful, thank you."

Over the next several months Belle was plagued with recurring headaches. Sometimes they lasted only a couple of hours, sometimes for more than a day. Dave suggested she might need glasses, and convinced her to see an eye doctor.

"Well, the doctor says my eyesight is fine," she told Dave. "He thought it might be sinus pressure, and told me to see my regular doctor."

"So, when do you go see him?"

"I don't have a regular doctor, Dave. I've never been sick a day in my life. It seems kind of silly to go to a doctor just for a headache."

"Belle, it's not just a headache. You've been having a lot of them for quite a while now."

"Oh, I'll be fine. Maybe it's just the change, and they will let up soon."

The headaches didn't let up, but became more frequent, and on some days, more severe. She started using aspirin several times a day, with minimal relief. She seldom complained, though there were some days the headaches were bad enough to keep her home from the bookstore to rest. Dave continued to try to get her to see a doctor, and she continued to resist.

In February, she had several days with no headaches, and asked Dave if they could go dancing to celebrate her birthday.

"That's a wonderful idea. It's been way too long."

They invited Kenny and Nicole to have dinner with them before going to the dance. They had been dancing for over an hour when Belle experienced a severe stabbing pain at the base of her skull, and stumbled and fell while dancing. The pain was so severe that she was having difficulty breathing, and needed help back to the table. After sitting for a few minutes, the pain abated somewhat.

"I just got a sudden headache, and lost my concentration," she explained.

"I'm taking you home right now, and tomorrow you're going to see my doctor, no arguments," said Dave.

"Has this happened before?" asked Kenny.

"No, I've just been having a few headaches."

"She's been having more than a few, and has refused to go see a doctor," added Dave.

"Well, Dave's right," said Nicole. "You need to go home and rest, and see a doctor first thing tomorrow. This seemed like more than just a headache."

Belle was still in a good deal of pain, and wasn't up to arguing about it. She was sure the headache would be gone by morning, and they could just forget about it.

She was wrong, the headache didn't let up much during the night, so she reluctantly agreed to have Dave take her to his doctor.

The news wasn't good. After a full examination, and X-Rays of her head, the doctor informed here that there seemed to be a mass of some kind near the back of her brain.

"Sometimes these things recede a little for a short time, which is probably why you have some days without headaches. But, over time, it will continue to grow. I'm sorry to have to give you this news, but we just don't know how to treat something like this. All I can do is give you some stronger medicine to help with the pain."

"Are you telling me this is going to kill me?" she asked.

"Barring a miracle, I'm afraid that's true."

He handed her a packet with a few pills of codeine, saying, "These will help until you can get your prescription filled. Let me know if they aren't strong enough."

Because Dave was not a spouse, or a relative, he was not in the room when Belle was given this news. She couldn't imagine how she was going to tell him, but also wouldn't consider trying to deceive him, so she said, "Doctor, Dave and I aren't officially married, but for all practical purposes we are. I can't think how to give him this news. Would you please do it for me?"

"Of course, if that's what you want."

Both Dave and Belle were quiet on the drive home, neither knowing what to say, or even how to begin. When they got to the house, Dave said, "You go lie down, I'll take your prescription to the pharmacy. Have you taken one of the pills he gave you?"

"Yes, he had me take one in the office."

"OK, then, I'll be right back."

The codeine was beginning to make her sleepy, so she didn't argue, but went to their bedroom to lie down. Four hours later, she awoke, and was surprised to see how much time had passed when she glanced at the clock. She slowly sat up, and realized her headache was all but gone. She walked downstairs, planning to make some coffee, and was surprised to see Dave sitting in the living room.

"Dave, why aren't you at the store?"

"You're awake. How are you feeling?"

"Pretty good, I was going to make some coffee. Why aren't you at work?"

"Belle, I wasn't going to leave you here alone. I've made some coffee; I'll get you a cup."

When he returned with the coffee, Belle said, "Dave, you can't stay away from the store every time I have a headache."

"No, I don't suppose I can, but I wasn't going to leave you alone today."

"I guess it's a little late in the day to open now."

"If you're OK in the morning, I'll go in."

"If I'm OK in the morning, *we'll* go in, and if I'm not, you need to go anyway."

"Belle, do you think that's a good idea? I think you should take it easy."

"Dave, just because I have this thing in my head, doesn't mean I'm going to stay home and wait to die. The doctor said it was OK to work as long as I feel like it."

"Honey, I just don't want you putting too much strain on yourself."

"Dave, please don't treat me like I'm made of glass. I hate that. I just want to keep things as normal as we can."

"OK, I guess I can understand that. Are you really feeling better since your nap?"

"I am. I guess those pills do a pretty good job."

For the rest of the afternoon and evening, they carried on as they would have on any other day. In the morning Dave asked, "How are you feeling?"

"I feel fine."

"Are you sure you should go to work with me?"

"Dave, please don't do that. Don't start asking me how I'm feeling. I promise if I'm not feeling OK I'll tell you. Otherwise, just assume I'm fine."

"I'm just concerned about you."

"I know, honey, but remember I said I want to keep things as normal as possible? Well, you never used to ask me every day how I was feeling, so don't start doing it now, OK?"

The day at the bookstore went by smoothly. That evening Kenny called to ask how she was, and what the doctor had said.

"I'm feeling fine now, Kenny. The doctor says I have some kind of growth in my brain. But he gave me some pills that work wonders on the pain."

"Well, that don't sound good to me."

"No, it isn't very good Kenny, but please, don't make a big deal out of it, and for heaven's sake, don't start fussing over me."

Kenny laughed, and said, "Well I can see it hasn't changed your independent spirit none. Just promise me you'll tell me if there's anything I can do for you, and I'll promise not to fuss over you."

"Thank you, Kenny, I will."

For the next few days Belle had only one mild headache, and she was able to manage it with only aspirin. On Sunday she woke with a severe headache that made it difficult to move without the pain increasing. She spent much of the day in bed, and used two codeine tablets during the day. The headache had lessened considerably by Monday morning, but she decided to stay home from the shop.

"You'll call me if you need anything?" asked Dave.

"I will. I just think I'll take it easy today, and see if that makes tomorrow better."

That was only partly true. The other reason for staying home was so she could do some serious thinking about her situation. She felt well enough to fix a nice meal for Dave. The smell of roast beef greeted Dave as he walked through the door.

"Something smells good. Your day of rest must have done the trick."

"It did. I feel fine now."

"Great," he said, as he embraced her.

After dinner Belle said, "Dave, I need to talk to you."

"Uh oh, now what?" he asked.

"I've been doing a lot of thinking today. I'm not sure I can explain why, but I'd like to be buried back home with my parents."

"Now, we don't need to talk about that now."

"Yes, we do. Dying is part of life, Dave. It happens to everyone. I've just been given a preview of when it might happen to me, and pretending I haven't won't change anything. Here's the other thing. Dave, I'd like to marry you."

"Ah, Belle, I didn't think I'd ever hear you say that. Why now?"

"Well, partly for practical reasons. I want you to be able to make arrangements for me without any legal hassles. And, I've just been shown in a rather dramatic way that life is too damn short to worry about the possibility of some stupid jinx."

Dave took her in his arms, and said, "You've been busy today, haven't you. Since you've got everything figured out, what day have you chosen for our wedding?"

"Well, since the best part of my life began in the bookstore, I'd like to have a small ceremony there on Sunday, with just Peg and Dan, and Kenny and Nicole."

"Sunday, huh? I gues that will work, I didn't have any other plans."

They both laughed, and Belle said, "Thank you, Dave."

"For what?"

"Just for being who you are, and loving me."

Belle called Peg that evening to tell her she was getting married. "I'd like you to stand up with me, and could you go shopping with me tomorrow for a dress?"

"Well, sure I can, and be happy to, but why the sudden rush?"

"Oh, it's kind of a long story. I'll fill you in tomorrow. Can I pick you up about 9:30?"

"That will be fine. I canna' wait to hear this story," she joked.

While they were in the car, heading for the shopping district, Belle, said, "I promised I'd tell you why I changed my mind about getting married. Will you promise you'll let me tell the whole story before you say anything?"

Peg gave her a puzzled look, and nodded her head.

Belle told her as simply, and quickly as she could about the headaches, and the mass in her brain, "So it seems I probably won't ever be a really old lady, and it's made me realize that worrying about some possible jinx is pretty silly."

"Ah, Belle," Peg said, tears streaming down her cheeks.

"Peg, please don't cry. Death happens to everyone. Mine just might be a little sooner than I expected. But I want to make the most of every day, and keep things as normal as I can."

Peg shook her head, and said, "Belle, I don't know if you're very wise or just plain crazy."

"Maybe a little of both," Belle laughed. "Now, dry your tears, and help me find the perfect outfit for my wedding."

They browsed through several shops, but Belle couldn't find anything that really pleased her. Peg was getting a little weary, and said, "Do ya even know what you're lookin' for?"

"I guess not. That's probably the problem. Let's check this store, and if I don't find anything, I'll go back and get that blue dress we saw."

They had been in the shop only a few minutes when Belle spotted something red hanging at the end of one of the racks. It was a suit in an oriental design, made of heavy silk. It had a mandarin collar, and braided frog closures on the jacket.

"Look at this Peg," she said as she held it up.

"You want red for your wedding?"

"Why not? Red is a color of courage, and strength, and it's a very different style from what I usually wear. I'm going to try it on."

The suit fit as if tailor made for her, and Peg had to admit she looked stunning in it, even though she still had serious doubts about red for a wedding dress.

Dave was suitably impressed when she modeled the outfit for him.

"I thought it was bad luck for the groom to see the bride in her wedding dress before the wedding," he said.

"Well, I've decided it's time to ignore all the superstitions."

Belle felt good the rest of the week, and spent her days at the bookstore with Dave.

They were married by a Justice of the Peace late Sunday afternoon, and the three couples went out for a quiet dinner afterwards.

Kenny bought champagne, and offered a toast.

"To two of my all time favorite people. May they never be parted."

Over the next few months, the headaches became more frequent, and at times, more severe. There were some days when the codeine didn't seem to help, so she called the doctor. He suggested she try doubling the dose, and to call again if that didn't help.

When she began having trouble with blurred vision, she went to see the doctor.

"Belle, the mass is in the region of your brain that has to do with eyesight. You may eventually loose your sight. I'm sorry."

This upset Belle even more than that original diagnosis had. She could not bear the thought of having to be led around, and treated like an invalid. She began using more aspirin, and started saving the codeine. She also called the doctor to tell hem the pain was getting worse, and he prescribed some morphine.

"This will probably knock you out pretty good, so be sure you're home when you take it."

She was having difficulty sleeping because of the pain, and dark circles began to appear under her eyes. One evening she said to Dave, "Dave, I want to be buried in my wedding suit."

Dave only nodded, then slammed his fist into the couch, saying, "God, I hate feeling so helpless! I wish I could do something for you."

"You do a lot just by being here, and loving me," she replied.

She wasn't able to sleep at all that night, due to the pain. In the morning she noticed her vision was more blurred than usual.

Dave offered to stay home from work, but she insisted he go. "I'll call if there is anything I need. There's no point in you sitting around here while I'm in a drugged sleep."

Belle had managed to save a dozen codeine pills, and six morphine tablets. After Dave left, she went to the kitchen and took all the pills, swallowing them with a large glass of brandy for good measure. It was early September. The day was sunny, with a soft south breeze. After washing out the glass and putting the brandy away, she went to the sunroom, and lay down on the lounge.

Dave found her there when he came home that evening. He stood looking at her for a few minutes, watching as the breeze lifted a tendril of her hair now and then. He assumed she was sleeping, and was glad to see she was getting some rest. After a few minutes, he realized she didn't appear to be breathing. His chest felt like it was being crushed, as he walked to her, and took her hand. It was as cool as glass.

Dave rode the train that carried Belle back to Nebraska. Mae had not been enthused about having Belle buried with their parents, but reluctantly agreed. David and Ann were the only others attending the graveside service. Dave gave Mae money, and asked her to arrange for a headstone. "We were married a few months ago, so her name is Markham." Mae only nodded, and said, "You want a lift to the train station?"

Dave had been so caught up in his grief, that he didn't notice that Belle's grave was at the far corner of her family plot, as far away as possible form her parent's graves.

After Mae dropped Dave off, she drove to the monument company, and ordered a small stone. The only inscription was to be Rosa Belle Mericle, with the year of her birth and death.

"So, she never married?" asked the sales person who filled out the order.

"She was married too many times to count, so I think it's only fittin' she be buried with the name she was given when she came into this world."

Afterwords

BALLAD OF ME

For many years I've grown, learned and done.
And seen many things both terrible and fair.
So hard to believe these years have all gone.
So please, pour a cuppa and pull up a chair
and I'll tell you some things of which you may not be aware.
I began as a farm girl near a small town,
where wide was the sky and clear was the air
and sweet was the smell of new plowed spring ground.

When I was but sixteen I met someone
who dared me to put a curl in his hair;
Then spent my time dreaming of a man named Dunn.
And he gave me his name after only one year
of his joking and loving and all around care.
Three sons we now have, all of them grown.
We've watched them and loved them through many a year.
If life gives rewards, then they are my crown.

But I'm more than a mother, I've had lots of fun
becoming a nurse; raising flowers so fair;
I've painted some pictures; belly dancing I've done;
ballroom dancing with hubby; flying planes through the air;
knitted mittens for hands and hats for their hair;
sewn things like pajamas or a beautiful gown
that made me feel wonderful, regal and fair.
And in each of these things, every one, I have found

a way to be me, tackle each with some care.
I'm nearing the end of my many-year saga but I've known
for a while that giving massages year after year
will not be the last way in which I have grown.

–Joyce Dunn

Printed in the United States
135808LV00003B/4/P